READY TO
KILL

Also by Andrew Peterson

First to Kill
Forced to Kill
Option to Kill

READY TO KILL

A Nathan McBride Novel

ANDREW PETERSON

Text copyright © 2014 Andrew Peterson
All rights reserved.

Published by Thomas & Mercer, Seattle

www.apub.com

Amazon, the Amazon logo, and Thomas & Mercer are trademarks of Amazon.com, Inc., or its affiliates.

ISBN-13: 9781477822807
ISBN-10: 1477822801

Cover design by Jason Gurley

Library of Congress Control Number: 2013922354

Printed in the United States of America

To Abedonia Marie Fagan (1954–2009) and Tarsilla Martinez Davidson (1929–2013), the best sister- and mother-in-law a guy could ask for. Both of them now walk in grace with God.

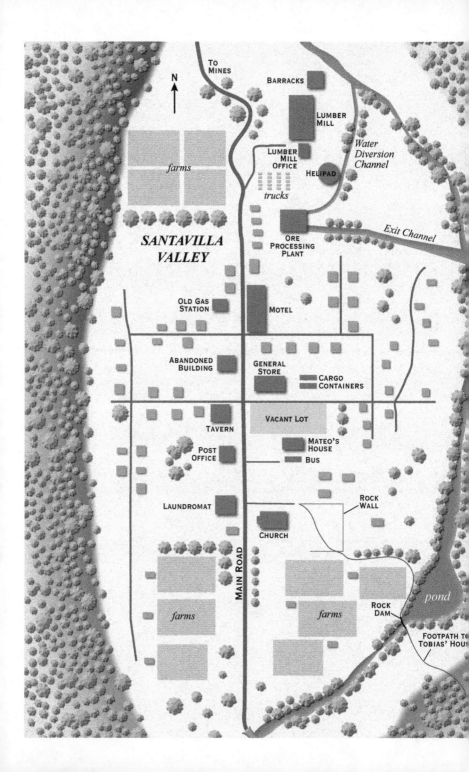

CHAPTER 1

Pastor Tobias awoke to the sound of metal rattling. He was a light sleeper—it didn't take much to rouse him. He pulled the insect netting aside and hurried over to the window. On the road below, a column of four pickup trucks approached the one-lane bridge at the south entrance to the valley, the truck beds clanging over the rutted road and the headlights bouncing. The pickups negotiated the final hairpin turn and began crossing the wooden bridge. Tobias's small home, more like a tin shack, overlooked one of the most remote areas of northern Nicaragua. He looked at his watch—2:00 am. No one should be arriving in the middle of the night.

This wasn't good; he'd seen it before.

Across the valley, lights flicked on as other people heard the caravan of trucks. Most of Santavilla's fifteen hundred residents remained asleep, but that would change soon enough.

Tobias threw on some clothes, grabbed his flashlight, and started down the path. Several hundred feet below, the trucks rolled past his position. Being careful with his footing, he picked up his pace. Although in his midseventies, Tobias kept himself in good physical shape. Still, a misstep on this trail could be fatal—the mountainside angled sharply away, creating a fall he'd never survive. He adjusted the focus on his flashlight to make the beam wider.

The trucks picked up speed, their beds rattling again in sequence as they hit a deep rut. From his current position, Tobias couldn't see the vehicles, but their headlights cast eerie shadows through the trees. To his right, a village elder stepped out of his hut.

"Pastor Tobias, what's happening?"

"I don't know."

"I'll get dressed and come with you."

"Thank you, but please stay here. I'll go see what's going on."

"Are you sure? I don't mind."

"I'm sure. I'll be right back."

Tobias began a medium-paced jog when the terrain became more manageable. Half a minute later, he crossed the creek, using the earthen dam, and cleared the last of the big trees blocking his view.

The trucks had fanned out from the road and formed a semi-circle around Mateo's home, their headlights harshly illuminating the tiny structure. Each pickup produced two men. At this distance, Tobias couldn't see much detail, but two of them wore the trademark white buttoned shirts associated with El Jefe's criminal band. The other four were dressed in green combat uniforms, and they carried assault rifles with large magazines.

"Wait!" he yelled.

The gunmen either didn't hear him or chose to ignore his command. With building anger, Tobias watched one of them kick open the front door. A few seconds later, they dragged Mateo's wife out the door. Mateo staggered out after her, holding a hand to the side of his head. He'd obviously been struck, probably with the butt of a rifle.

Dressed only in a T-shirt and underwear, the woman offered no resistance as they pulled her across the gravel. Mateo yelled something and tried to free his wife from her assailant's grasp, but a different gunman drove the barrel of his rifle into Mateo's stomach. Mateo clutched his midsection, doubled over, and fell to his knees.

Nearly out of breath, Tobias yelled, "Stop this!"

One of the white shirts—who Tobias recognized as El Jefe's chief enforcer—grabbed a bullhorn from the cab of his pickup. A metallic voice echoed across the landscape.

"Residents of Santavilla, let this serve as an example of the price of disloyalty. El Jefe is a generous man and pays you well for your work. Hoarding will not be tolerated."

"Stop!"

Several gunmen turned toward Tobias as he closed the distance. The enforcer issued a hand signal, and they brought their weapons up but didn't fire.

Tobias pointed at the leader with the bullhorn. "What are you doing? This is an outrage! You can't just break into people's homes in the middle of the night."

"It's much worse than that, old man."

One of the uniformed mercenaries grabbed Pastor Tobias by the arm. The flashlight fell from his hand as he felt the iron grip on his biceps. He grimaced from the pain. The thug was purposely hurting him.

The enforcer motioned to several of his men. "Search the house."

Two mercenaries disappeared inside. Tobias listened to the destruction as the men tore the place apart.

"Please," Mateo said, "my wife is very ill and needs pain medicine. I have no extra money. El Jefe pays us pennies, and—"

"Silence! I will hear no more of your insolence."

Mateo tried to get up. "Please, I'll—"

The mercenary who'd struck Mateo in the stomach stepped forward and kicked him in the rib cage. Mateo curled into a fetal position.

"Enough," Tobias yelled.

A high-pitched shriek came from inside the house.

"Leave her alone!" Tobias jerked free and ran toward the door. He didn't make it.

A sharp blow on the back of his head grayed his vision. Fighting to remain conscious, he fell to his hands and knees. One of the mercenaries grabbed his left wrist and began hauling him toward the trucks. Tobias wasn't a small man, and the mercenary had trouble dragging him. A second man joined the effort, and Tobias felt his shoulder strain to the dislocation point. He cried out as the two men yanked him to his feet. The white-shirted enforcer stepped forward and backhanded Tobias across the cheek.

"This is not your business, old man. You cause only pain and suffering with your foolish beliefs. And now you've caused your own."

A wave of nausea took the pastor. He bent over and vomited.

A second, higher-pitched scream emanated from the house as one of the gunmen yanked Mateo's daughter, Antonia, through the door. In her early twenties, she too wore only a T-shirt and underwear. The man shoved the young woman to the ground next to her father.

Mateo managed to uncurl himself and rise to his knees. He wrapped his arms around his daughter, who glared at the gathering of mercenaries with bald defiance.

"Please don't hurt my family," pleaded Mateo.

The gunman who'd pulled Antonia outside handed the enforcer a tiny glass vial with a black cap. It was about an inch long and half an inch in diameter, filled almost to the top with gold flakes that shimmered in the headlights.

Before the enforcer brought the bullhorn up again, he gave Mateo's daughter a long look, then smiled. She quickly averted her eyes.

"Everyone knows the rules. All gold panned on free Sundays must be turned over to El Jefe for cash payment on the same day it is obtained. No hoarding is allowed."

Tobias knew Mateo was guilty. He'd planned to use the gold as currency to buy opium for his sick wife. In many areas of Nicaragua's gold belt, it was regularly substituted for money. Mateo's reason for keeping the gold wasn't to enrich himself, only to ease his wife's suffering.

"El Jefe is not without mercy," the enforcer continued. *"He has decided to spare this man's life, but he must be punished."*

The mercenary on the leader's left removed a pair of tin snips from his thigh pocket.

Pastor Tobias felt a second wave of nausea. "What are you doing? Stop!"

Without a word, the gunman grabbed Mateo by the hair and forced his head to the side. In a fluid motion, the gunman snipped off the upper half of Mateo's ear. A semicircular chunk of bloody cartilage fell to the dirt. Mateo's wife covered her mouth, stifling a scream.

With an expression of disbelief and shock, Mateo looked down at his severed flesh, fell to his knees, and howled. He pressed a hand against the wound.

Tobias tried to free himself and cried out in pain when his shoulder strained again. "You call that mercy?"

"Let him go," the enforcer said.

Despite his injured shoulder, Tobias managed to remove his shirt while rushing over to Mateo's side. Mateo's hand was already covered with blood. Tobias hadn't realized an ear could bleed so much.

"Mateo, let go of your ear. I'm going to apply pressure with my shirt."

"I need the gold to buy my wife's opium. She's very sick . . . I'm not a bad man."

"Bless you, Mateo. You don't deserve this." Tobias folded his shirt into a tight square and pressed it firmly against the wound.

The enforcer asked, "Is there something you'd like me to tell El Jefe?"

With resignation, Mateo looked up. "I'm sorry." He lowered his head again.

"I'm certain your apology will be accepted. I trust this unfortunate . . . misunderstanding won't happen again."

"No, sir, it won't."

"Hold this in place," Tobias told Mateo, then stood and squared off with the enforcer's men and lowered his voice. "You tell your boss he won't get away with mutilating people like this."

"You are dangerously close to pissing me off," said the enforcer. "Perhaps you'd like to experience the tin snips yourself."

Tobias squinted, knowing the threat had teeth. As much as he wanted to lash out, he knew it wouldn't do any good, and he certainly didn't want half his ear cut off. "You will answer to God for this." Tobias returned to Mateo's side and turned the makeshift bandage over.

"Is that so? Then where is your God? Where? Your ignorant beliefs are poisoning the town."

"It is *you* who are poisoning the town," Tobias yelled. "You supply the miners with mercury, but you don't teach them how to handle it safely. Mateo's wife has severe mercury poisoning from working the mills all day. The rivers and streams in this area have fifty times the safe limit. Mateo's wife is nearly deaf from the crushing drums. Rubber gloves and ear protection are cheap, but your greedy boss doesn't supply them. The mill workers are exposed to mercury vapor all day long. Your boss's mining operation is slowly killing everyone in Santavilla. You—"

"Enough! I will not debate this with you. El Jefe gives these people work and protects them. You give them nothing."

"I give them hope, something you'll never have."

The enforcer narrowed his eyes. "Is that a threat?"

"It's not a threat," said Tobias. "Their faith gives them hope, even through savage injustices like this."

The leader waved a hand. "Need I remind you that El Jefe has shown mercy tonight? Things could've been much worse. This discussion is over." The enforcer raised the bullhorn. *"Hoarding gold will not be tolerated. I trust everyone understands the consequences now."*

Tobias told Mateo to keep pressure on his ear and approached the enforcer again. Two mercenaries crossed their rifles, blocking his path.

"I know what Macanas is doing," Tobias whispered.

The enforcer reached for his sidearm but stopped. A twisted smile formed. "Be careful, old man."

Then, as quickly as they'd arrived, the gunmen turned, piled into their trucks, and drove slowly out of town.

Mateo told his wife to go back inside the house.

Tobias averted his eyes while she limped through the door. Clearly, Mateo had been ratted out. There was no way Macanas could've known about Mateo's secret gold stash otherwise. Tobias inwardly flinched at the thought of a snitch living among them. Someone had betrayed Mateo, and he intended to find out who it was. He had his suspicions, but being a man of God and having no proof, he needed to temper his desire to judge.

"Run to my home," he told Antonia. "Get the hydrogen peroxide solution. It's in the small cabinet above the sink. Grab the first-aid kit too. Here, take my flashlight."

Antonia took the flashlight but didn't leave until Mateo said it was okay.

Tobias helped Mateo get to his feet. "I'll stay with you until we get your bleeding under control. The hydrogen peroxide is going to sting, but it should help to prevent an infection."

"Thank you, pastor. You're a kind man."

"If only kindness could protect us. Things are only getting worse here. I'm going to ask for help."

Mateo looked up at him, wide-eyed. "We can't go to the police. No one else cares about us. Who is going to help?"

Tobias looked toward the receding pickups. "Someone I should've asked long ago."

CHAPTER 2

El Jefe's enforcer lived a double life. The residents of Santavilla knew him only by his nickname, Franco, short for *el francotirador*: the sniper. Last night, he'd been the white-shirted man with the bullhorn—Macanas's enforcer—but none of them knew he was also Macanas's feared hit man.

During the briefing this morning, Macanas had been furious about Franco's report of Pastor Tobias's defiance, but even more furious about Tobias's parting comment. Macanas now saw Tobias as more than just a small-town troublemaker. So here Franco was, returning to Santavilla for the second time in as many days. Over the past few months, Tobias had become increasingly critical of Macanas's mining operations. The man had actually tried to start a labor union. The audacity was laughable. A labor union? After a few outspoken miners' houses mysteriously burned to the ground, all talk of forming a labor union had ended. The sad thing was, the townsfolk didn't appreciate what El Jefe gave them. Without his protection, they'd be subject to constant marauding by rival criminal gangs. At least El Jefe paid a fair wage. Other mine owners were far less generous.

Franco kept himself in top physical shape, a necessity in his profession. At age forty-seven, he possessed better stamina than most men half his age. He had some gray invading, but for the most part, his hair remained black, nearly the same color as his eyes. Having never known his parents, he didn't know which side of the equation his super dark irises came from, but he liked the hard look they gave him. At five foot seven, he stood at average height, but that was his only average trait. He spoke three languages and possessed extensive computer skills. In addition to being an expert in both surveillance and countersurveillance, he could make and disarm bombs and reload ammunition. His hand-to-hand combat skills were also finely honed.

The Range Rover hit another deep pothole, and Franco's head nearly hit the side window. He inwardly cursed and remained silent. Walking would be preferable. And faster. Voicing his displeasure to his driver would accomplish nothing. He couldn't remember the last time he'd seen a FOMAV work crew out here grading the road. The Range Rover was an exquisite vehicle, but its state-of-the-art suspension system was no match for this road's ruined surface. He made a mental note to organize a few Saturday work crews and get the worst of these potholes filled. Two or three days ought to do it. Besides, it's not like these people had anything better to do. When they weren't working the mines, most of them sat around smoking marijuana, drinking moonshine, and watching the trees grow.

One kilometer shy of the town, Franco ordered the driver to stop. The two white shirts in front remained silent and didn't turn around. Fear had an undermining effect on the soul. Both of them knew they could be in Franco's crosshairs one day. It didn't take a major screwup to fall out of Macanas's favor. The boss wasn't unfair to his men, but these two clowns already owned two strikes and needed to be on their best behavior.

Wearing a woodland combat uniform, Franco exited the SUV, donned his backpack, and slung his Remington 700 over his shoulder. There were much more modern sniper rifles available with all kinds of bells and whistles, but he knew this weapon inside and out. He'd recently read an article in a gun magazine about an expensive optical system that could track a target after its laser acquired it. He didn't begrudge leaps in technology; he just preferred the old-fashioned way. There was no substitute for hand-eye coordination and the skill of nailing a wind correction.

Franco slipped into the thick undergrowth lining the road and waited for the SUV to continue on its way. Before beginning his ascent of the steep mountainside, he held perfectly still for several minutes, listening for anything other than the sounds of the forest.

He looked at his watch and logged the time at 1650 hours. His ride would return at exactly 1900 hours. He preferred shooting in the early morning or late afternoon because he liked the sun low and behind him.

In another five hundred meters, he'd intersect an ancient trail. Local folklore said the trail dated back to the Mayans, but Franco didn't put much weight on native legends. From there, he'd head north toward his shooting position overlooking Santavilla. He had plenty of time—the church meeting didn't adjourn for another hour—so he felt no need to hurry.

Franco didn't know why he felt so comfortable in the jungle, only that he always had. As a child, he'd sneaked out of the orphanage and explored this damp and mysterious world more times than he could remember, and it had never ceased to amaze him. Perhaps it was the rule of opposites. These mountains were teeming with life, something he lacked in his soul. He had no illusions about who he was—Macanas's chief of security—and he never second-guessed his role as an enforcer.

Keeping his senses on high alert, Franco continued his hike up the mountain. He stopped every hundred meters or so and inhaled deeply, smelling for tobacco or marijuana.

Even though it was early in November at the end of the rainy season, the leading edge of a thunderstorm loomed on the western horizon. He thought it unlikely anyone would be up here, but he didn't rule it out. Assumption led to mistakes, and mistakes weren't tolerated. A happy boss was a generous boss, and he intended to keep the money flowing.

Ten minutes later, Franco found the trail and followed it north. Making his way through the foliage, he sensed countless forest creatures tracking his progress—mostly birds and primates. Jaguars lived in these mountains, but they didn't concern him. Snakes were a different matter, and there were many poisonous varieties up here.

He followed the trail for another klick as it gradually dropped in elevation. In several areas, he had to make detours around fallen branches. Thirty meters short of his shooting position, he stopped and removed his backpack. Within seconds, he turned himself into a shaggy green mass. He'd made the ghillie suit himself, something he'd never share with his colleagues. As a child, he'd spent eight years in a sweatshop making clothing, work he'd detested with a passion. He never believed he'd use such a menial skill ever again, but life tended to be unpredictable.

Franco didn't need the ghillie suit to conceal himself from anyone in the center of town, about nine hundred meters distant, but it offered an extra layer of stealth. Several months ago, he'd dug a small, level pad into the mountainside and covered the excavated area with a branch he'd cut from a madroño tree. He'd dug similar pads in other strategic locations in the mountains surrounding the town. It was always best to have multiple options.

Since he still had thirty minutes until the church meeting would end, he figured he ought to use the extra time to practice his low-crawl technique. After checking for ants, he dropped to his belly and inched forward along the trail, maintaining a pace of three meters per minute. It was painstakingly slow but an essential talent for jungle combat. When he reached the area directly above his shooting position, he slowly pivoted on his left hip and began a downhill crawl. The terrain wasn't overly steep, but by going headfirst, he could control his speed more precisely. He eased the cut branch aside and checked for snakes, then, like oozing molasses, poured himself onto the excavated pad. Franco preferred shooting from a prone position, but the terrain dictated he use a sitting, cross-legged technique.

He maneuvered into position and pulled his coat out from under him. Unslinging his rifle, he checked its box magazine by pulling the bolt back halfway, careful not to eject the live round he kept in the chamber. All good. He closed the bolt and disengaged the safety with his thumb.

Although the clouds made the ambient light patchy, the sun hadn't yet dropped below the mountains. Now it became a waiting game. He scoped the flag above the general store and estimated the wind at just under ten kilometers per hour from the northeast. Using an expensive range finder, he took a reading to the general store and dialed the elevation into his scope. Next, he added a small wind correction. He didn't need much—the wind was coming from his one o'clock vector.

He returned his eye to the scope and began a series of slow deep breaths.

***

Inside the small brick church, Pastor Tobias finished his closing prayer and opened his eyes. The fear and uncertainty he saw in his congregation concerned him. News of Mateo's punishment made everyone edgy; Mateo wasn't the only miner who kept a personal stash of gold dust. Although the miners were allowed to pan gold for themselves on Sundays, technically the gold didn't belong to them, and they were required to exchange it for cash at the end of the day. One thing was certain, at next Sunday's cash-out, the payouts would be larger than normal. These people may be impoverished, but they weren't stupid. Anyone who owned a secret stash of gold would add a little extra over the next few Sundays so it wouldn't look like they'd been hoarding.

Poverty in the village created a vicious circle Tobias knew all too well. The poorer these people became, the more desperate for menial work they became, which only made them poorer. In remote areas like Santavilla, public schools, hospitals, and fire and police stations didn't exist. There was no infrastructure to create a better way of life. Their lives were mundane at best, downright dreary at worst. Most of them toiled seven days a week—they had to. Seventy-five córdobas a day—about four US dollars—didn't go far.

Perhaps that's why Tobias had chosen this town. If he couldn't help them financially, at least he could help them spiritually and educate them on the dangers of working with mercury.

Mrs. Perez approached him. She and her husband owned the general store near Mateo's house. "Bless you, Pastor Tobias. I heard about last night. Will Mateo be okay?"

"If he doesn't get an infection, he should be all right, but he'll be disfigured for the rest of his life."

"My husband and I have some money for him. It isn't much." She handed Tobias five hundred córdobas.

"That's quite generous. I'll make sure he gets it."

"I keep telling everyone to wear rubber gloves, but only a few of the ore workers are buying them even though we're selling them at cost."

"We can only make people aware of the danger. We can't force them to do anything."

"I wish I could give them away for free."

"You do plenty. Please don't feel guilty."

He thanked Mrs. Perez again for the donation, gave her a hug, and left the church.

The sound of a diesel engine broke the town's silence. The work bus had arrived with the first load of miners.

Franco focused on the bus as it entered the far end of town. When it stopped in front of the general store, he moved his scope to the south and spotted Antonia leaving the church. "What are *you* doing there?" he whispered.

He watched Mateo's daughter walk up the street toward the bus. He couldn't see her facial expression, but her body language seemed stiff. She didn't move with the confidence he usually saw in her stride. She kept glancing nervously back toward the church. Seeing her father punished last night had angered her—that much was clear. But rules were rules, and he intended to question her about her father's secret stash of gold.

Franco trained his crosshairs on Tobias as he walked toward the bus.

He subconsciously checked the safety with his thumb and continued his deep breaths. A surge of adrenaline coursed through his body. He loved the feeling and wished he could experience it more often. Perhaps he would. Antonia had some explaining to do.

Franco swung his scope to the flag above the general store. Watching its movement, he decided to add an additional half minute of angle to his wind correction. He returned the crosshairs to his target, blew half a breath out, and began a controlled pull of the trigger.

***

Seeing his friend's bandaged ear angered Tobias, but he fabricated the best smile he could. "How's the ear?"

Mateo stepped out of the bus. "It stings a little, but I'm okay. Thank you for helping me last night."

"Mrs. Perez made a donation to your family." He reached into his pocket and removed the money.

At the same instant he extended his hand, Tobias heard a loud crack. It sounded like a giant bullwhip.

An invisible hammer struck his chest.

He clutched his right side and fell backward.

When his head hit the ground, his vision spun, then went dark.

***

The discharge bucked Franco's body and slammed his ears. He reacquired Tobias in the scope and saw the man on the ground.

Screams of confusion and panic reached his position as the reverberating concussion of the report crackled off the mountainsides. People scrambled in all directions. None of them wanted to be the next victim.

***

Somewhere in the red haze of Tobias's mind, he knew he'd been shot. He also knew he'd never survive this. Overwhelming sadness washed through him . . . His work here wasn't finished.

Disconnected from his body, he had a vague sense of lying alone in the middle of the road. Blinding pain erupted along his chest and neck, slamming his mind and body back together.

"Tobias!"

He turned his head and opened his eyes. Mrs. Perez . . . Running toward him. *No, don't* . . . He didn't want her exposed out in the open, but he didn't want to die alone either. He sensed her kneel at his side and take his hand.

"I'm here, Tobias."

"Please go back, there's nothing you can—" He coughed and tasted blood.

"I'm sorry. I'm so sorry . . ."

He felt her tears fall onto his face and managed a smile. "Please don't mourn for me. I'll see you again . . . Tell the ore workers to wear . . . their gloves."

"I will. I promise. I'll give them away for free."

"You . . . have a kind soul, Mrs. Perez."

"I love you, Tobias. Everyone loves you."

"Please . . . forgive them." He coughed up more blood.

When he felt his consciousness begin to fade, Pastor Tobias began a silent prayer to God for living a blessed life.

***

Franco watched the touching exchange with mixed emotions. He didn't feel especially good about killing the pastor, but orders were orders, and he wasn't willing to question Macanas's authority. Doing El Jefe's bidding had made him a small fortune, enough to live comfortably for the rest of his life. He didn't plan on dying centavo-less like the rest of the peasants in that cursed town.

He slung his rifle over his shoulder and crawled out of the hole. After replacing the branch and covering its cut end, he made his way up to the trail and took a final look toward town. The woman remained at Tobias's side. A few people stood next to the buildings lining the road, but they didn't approach. His instincts told him to hurry, but he kept slinking at a slow pace until he reached the deeper cover of trees. He had an hour before the SUV returned, so he took his time removing his ghillie suit and tying it to his backpack.

In many ways, the miners would be better off without Tobias. All that old man did was give them a false sense of hope. Macanas didn't force them to work the mines. Any of them could leave Santavilla any time they wanted. They stayed because Macanas gave them employment.

Although Franco didn't feel guilt over killing Tobias, he did feel a nagging sense of apprehension. *Get a grip*, he told himself.

The foolish beliefs of that old man were meaningless, based on superstition and ignorance. He had nothing to fear. But as he hiked up the trail, Tobias's words echoed through his mind.

You will answer to God for this.

CHAPTER 3

Nathan McBride swung the ax with precision and power. The blade cleaved through the twelve-inch-diameter log, splitting it cleanly. He placed one of the halves upright on the stump and split it again. He'd been at this all afternoon and had worked up quite a sweat. A troubling sense of uneasiness had invaded him, and to make matters worse, he couldn't pinpoint its source. Nathan had no illusions about his nature. He possessed a conflicted personality, but his mood had been predominantly dark for several days. It felt like a mental splinter he couldn't remove. Whatever the cause, he knew from past experience the only way to purge the anxiety was through physical exertion, and making firewood did the trick. Nathan didn't understand why it worked; it just did.

Nathan was a big man and used all of his six foot five, 240-pound bulk to generate a lot of power. He didn't just swing the ax—he hammered it through the wood with a vengeance.

Nathan never removed his shirt in public, but here in the privacy of his backyard he'd tossed it aside. The late afternoon sun glistened off his upper body. His build mirrored that of an NFL linebacker, but no football player had dozens of long scars crisscrossing his torso at one-inch spacing. As punishment for not cooperating, his former tormentor had methodically sliced his skin with a searing knife, being careful not to make gouges deep enough to be fatal—just excruciating painful. Nathan had gotten used to the wicker-basket pattern on his skin, but the marks were a brutal reminder of a battle against insanity he'd once fought—a battle he'd nearly lost. Below graying hair that used to be reddish brown, his face also held grisly souvenirs. From forehead to chin, three lengthy scars dominated his expression. A plastic surgeon had repaired them, but they were still plainly visible. When people stared, he was often tempted to say, *What's the matter? Haven't you ever seen a man with a giant N carved on his face?* Coupled with his dark-blue eyes, the scars gave him a "don't mess with me" look.

Three weeks. That's how long he'd endured the twisted musings of a sadistic interrogator after his botched mission . . . Had it really been more than twenty years ago? Shouldn't two decades have been enough time to recover? Apparently not. He still woke up drenched in sweat, ready to kill anything that moved. The physical aspect of enduring pain had been manageable, but the hatred he'd discovered within his soul had produced a deeper, much more savage wound.

In the early years after his forced retirement, he'd become addicted to alcohol. In bars, he'd often been challenged by drunk "tough guys" wanting to test themselves, and Nathan had been more than willing to administer their exams. He remembered looking at his bloody knuckles one night and thinking, *This isn't who I am. Why am I doing this?* He'd experienced an epiphany, realizing he'd actually been seeking confrontations. He'd falsely believed that beating the tar out of a bully would make him feel better. Hurting other people—even jerks who deserved it—had put him on a corrosive journey. He'd felt like a wounded insect that could only crawl in a circle.

As for Nathan's current issues . . . well, it probably said something that over a five-day period, he'd produced eight cords of firewood. The source of the wood was a ranch in east San Diego County, where Harv and he owned fifteen hundred acres of pristine oak and pine forest. Harv, an expert at felling trees, had brought the 120-foot giant down with surgical precision. Seeing the massive tree fall had been an awesome yet sad sight. By controlling the direction of the fall, they'd preserved several oaks that wouldn't have survived otherwise. Such was a tenet of nature: some die so that others might live.

His thoughts drifted to Holly. When he'd first met her a few years back, she'd been the special agent in charge of the FBI's Sacramento field office. They'd connected with each other in an unguarded way Nathan hadn't thought possible. He missed her. Maybe he'd take a trip back east and rekindle their friendship. Harv had been urging him to do it for several months.

He felt his cell vibrate in his pocket, wiped his hand on his jeans, and pulled it free. He squinted at the screen but decided to take the call.

"The answer's no," he said.

"Charming, as always. No names."

"To what do I owe this honor?"

"Not over the phone."

"Well, that kinda limits our communication."

"I've arranged your transportation out here. You're both on a chartered flight."

"My friend's a family man. He can't just drop everything like I can."

"He needs to be on that jet."

"We're retired."

"You're never *retired*."

Nathan wiped sweat from his forehead. "Can you at least give me something?"

"Central America."

"Are we talking about the location I think we're talking about?"

"Yes."

Nathan didn't know what to say, didn't trust himself. After a few seconds, he asked, "Is this about our old friend?"

"No, it's something else."

"May I assume we wouldn't be talking if the situation wasn't urgent?"

"You assume correctly."

"Are we going down there?"

"Yes."

"How much time do we have before the charter?"

"A few hours. I'll text you the details after we hang up."

"What do we bring?"

"Overnight bags. We'll supply the rest."

"I'll bet that's an expensive flight."

"It is."

"Okay, we'll be there."

"Take something to help you sleep during the flight."

"I doubt I'll be sleeping anytime soon."

Nathan ended the call and stared at his phone. Ignoring the call hadn't really been an option. When the director of the CIA called, you answered. Besides, he liked Rebecca Cantrell. His trust in her wasn't absolute, but she'd never done anything to make him question her integrity. Still, he had to wonder: What on earth required a face-to-face with the director of Central Intelligence? Nathan didn't like the implications. Could this be about a potential leak? He and Harv weren't operations officers anymore, and surely Cantrell had people she could send to Nicaragua. So why involve them? It didn't make sense. One thing was certain—he and Harv weren't doing any wet work. Those days were long past.

He needed to call Harv right away. When he got thrown into voice mail, he sent a text.

call me asap

That would get his friend's attention. Harv would drop everything and call back right away, probably within—

His phone rang with a familiar tone. "Harv."

"Nate."

"Thanks for calling me."

"How's the hand holding up? I hope you're not overworking it."

"It's doing okay."

"What's up?"

"I just got off the phone with our friend on the Potomac."

"And . . . ?"

"We're going out there tonight."

"Did she say what it's about?"

"Central America."

Harv hesitated for a second. "Tell me we aren't talking about what I think we're talking about."

"I'm afraid we are."

Harv asked, "Are we going in?"

"She said yes."

Harv waited a moment before responding. "I hope you reminded her we're retired."

"I did. She told me . . . us . . . that we're never retired."

"With all due respect to *your* beloved friend, that's complete and utter horseshit. It has to end sometime. If we help her, it's because *we* made the choice, not the reverse."

"Come on, Harv. You know how it works."

"I'm just venting. I have no desire to step foot in that hellhole ever again."

"On that, we agree."

"What do we bring?"

"Just overnight bags." Nathan's phone chimed with a text message. "Hang on, I've got a text coming through . . . looks like we've got . . . two hours."

"Two hours?" Harv asked.

"We're leaving from Monty."

"This isn't about our old friend, is it?"

"She said it isn't."

"Well, at least that's something."

"Let's just find out what's going on and take things from there."

"I'll meet you in the lobby of Corporate Helicopters."

"Ninety minutes."

"See you there," Harv said.

CHAPTER 4

Just before 1800 hours, Nathan and Harv rode out to the flight line in a Corporate Helicopters shuttle cart.

Like Nathan, Harv maintained himself in top physical condition. Half-Hispanic, half-white, Harv was a handsome man. Behind a tan complexion, his light-hazel eyes and graying hair gave him a distinguished look. Although Harv wouldn't take it as an insult, Nathan thought his friend looked like a politician.

They exchanged smiles when they saw their ride. Its engines whining with power, the white Challenger was a beautiful jet and looked to be about sixty feet long. The first officer introduced herself and asked to see their IDs. She took a little too long looking at Nathan's face but recovered with a warm smile. She told them the flight would take a little under five hours with a local arrival time of 0200 hours. She showed them the amenities, gave them a safety briefing, and disappeared into the cockpit. He and Harv settled into their seats and buckled up. Five minutes later they were climbing into a twilight sky and turning east.

Nathan resolved to try to get some sleep but didn't feel optimistic. Unpleasant memories kept surfacing. *Mind over matter*, he told himself and took another look at the booze cabinet.

"Don't even think about it."

"Huh?"

"You keep glancing at the liquor cabinet."

"You'd never let me do it."

"You got that right."

Nathan grinned. "Think you could take me?"

Harv issued a half laugh. "You're falling apart at the seams. You may be four inches taller and outweigh me by forty pounds, but I know all your vulnerable spots. It'd be over in ten seconds."

"Sounds like your bedroom."

"Hey, watch it. Besides, I'm good for at least two minutes with Candace."

"How often are you getting it?"

"More than you."

Nathan waited, trying not to smile.

"Okay, lately? Hardly ever. I've been guaranteed a minimum of three times a year. Christmas, my birthday, and Groundhog Day."

"Groundhog Day?"

"It's best if you don't ask . . ."

"What did you tell Candace about this sudden excursion?"

"I told her it has something to do with an old mission and that it's just housekeeping—which hopefully, isn't far from the truth. She didn't like it, but she's okay. She knows the acronym we used to work for."

They enjoyed a companionable silence for a few minutes.

"This is a nice ride," Harv said, reclining his leather seat a little. "These things go horizontal for snoozing. I could get seriously spoiled flying this way."

"I'm gonna grab a water, you want one?"

"I do. Thanks."

Nathan unbuckled and raided the small refrigerator near the lavatory. He chose two sparkling waters.

"Do you think Cantrell's going to meet us at Dulles?" Harv asked.

"Yeah, I do."

"At zero two hundred?"

"She basically ordered us to drop everything and respond. It would be bad form to send a driver or make us take a cab somewhere."

"Yeah, you're probably right. I'm going to crash for a few. I know you have a hard time sleeping on planes, but try to get some shut-eye anyway."

"Thanks, Harv, I will. I'll wake you when we start our descent."

Nathan knew there was no point in further speculation about the face-to-face meeting. He'd have his answer in a few hours. He closed his eyes and reclined his chair. If he fell asleep, he hoped he wouldn't dream of Nicaragua.

***

A sudden jolt awoke Nathan. Feeling disoriented, he quickly sat up and looked around. The bump he'd felt was the landing.

"I didn't want to wake you."

"I can't believe I fell asleep. You?"

"A couple of hours, you know the adage . . ."

"Sleep when you can."

The Challenger turned off the runway and began taxiing.

"It's really tempting to time-share one of these jets," Harv said, "but it would be hard to justify."

"I was thinking the same thing, but as little as we fly, it wouldn't make economic sense. It's infinitely cheaper flying commercial everywhere."

Nathan and Harv owned a highly profitable private-security company. They'd founded First Security Inc. a few years after they'd retired from the CIA. Their firm specialized in sophisticated alarm systems and countersurveillance measures for homes and businesses. They also taught personal-security awareness and tactical-combat classes to VIPs and corporate executives. So far, they'd done extremely well. Last year, Harv started an armored SUV line, and he'd already secured a five-vehicle contract with three more big clients ready to sign.

"Well, at least you didn't have to go through a TSA checkpoint. I know how much you love doing that, Nate."

"It's not that bad—it just makes me want to break a few arms."

Harv smiled. "You've come a long way. Twenty years ago, you would've wanted to break a few *necks*."

"Don't remind me."

Nathan heard his phone chime with a text message.

How was your flight?

Very nice, thx . . . Are you meeting us?

Yes. I'm inside the Dulles Jet Center. See you in a few.

"Cantrell?" Harv asked.

"She's waiting for us in the jet center."

"Good call."

"Well, I wasn't one hundred percent sure."

When the Challenger stopped in the transient parking area, the first officer emerged from the cockpit and lowered the fuselage door, which also served as a ladder. They grabbed their overnight bags, complimented the crew on a pleasant flight, and stepped down to the tarmac. A jet center employee escorted them over to the automatic glass doors.

Director Cantrell was waiting inside with two men— presumably operations officers doubling as bodyguards. Both men wore business suits and had small ear speakers with lapel mikes. Cantrell was dressed in a dark pants suit. In her early fifties, her shoulder-length brown hair had a touch of gray. She stood at least a foot shorter than Nathan but possessed a commanding presence. Harv and he approached Cantrell and shook hands. Introductions were made. Nathan noticed that the woman behind the jet center's counter seemed to recognize Cantrell. When the woman made eye contact with Nathan, he winked. She forced a smile and quickly averted her eyes.

"It's good to see you guys," Cantrell said. "Thank you for coming."

"Glad to do it, Rebecca. You're working late."

"I'm on graveyard for a spell. We've got an operation going on the other side of the world. We're about to collar a major bad guy."

"Aren't you in more of a political position?" Harv asked.

"I've been resisting it." She smiled, then gave each of them a look, up and down. "You guys look sharp."

"Five Eleven Tactical line," Nathan said.

"It looks good on you."

"Thank you." Nathan wanted to ask what was going on but knew it had to wait until they were clear of any potential eaves-dropping equipment.

"We're parked out front," she said. They began walking toward the street-side entrance. At the door, Rebecca stopped and let the two operations officers leave the building. Nathan watched them through the glass as they visually searched the immediate area. One of them spoke into his lapel mike. *Tight security*, he thought. The director of the CIA was undoubtedly in the cross-hairs of countless assassins, with al-Qaeda fanatics topping the list. Although he gave it low odds, a sniper could be out there. He suspected Cantrell was being guarded by at least six officers at any given time—some of them they'd never see.

Rebecca acknowledged nods from her men, and they stepped through the doors.

Two charcoal-gray SUVs waited at the curb. Nathan noticed the ballistic glass right away. No doubt they were fully armored with environmental protection from gas or biological attacks.

"Does it wear you out? The twenty-four-seven security?" Nathan asked.

"You kind of get used to it, but to answer your question, at times, yes."

An officer slid out of the driver's seat, surveyed the immediate area, and opened the rear door of the second SUV. Rebecca thanked her, and they got in. Behind the soundproof glass separating them from the driver's compartment, two sets of opposing seats greeted them. One of the officers they'd met inside the jet center got into the back with them; the other climbed into the passenger seat of the lead SUV, and they were on their way.

"Why are we here, Rebecca?" Nathan asked. "And why you? Whatever the situation is, it's got to be below your pay grade."

"This requires my personal involvement."

Nathan waited.

"As you've surmised, we have a development in Nicaragua. Video cameras at the US embassy in Managua recorded a man throwing a paper airplane over the fence. The marines guarding the post didn't approach it. They were concerned it might've been laced with something. I've seen the surveillance video, and it's obvious the man had purposely disguised himself. He appeared to be Latino with dark hair, probably a wig, oversized dark sunglasses, ball cap—you get the picture. His size and build are consistent with ninety percent of men on the planet. Here's where it gets cryptic, and it's the reason I asked you guys to come out here. The note had only ten words."

She pulled a folded piece of paper from her coat pocket and handed it to Nathan.

ECHO FOUR: YOUR HELP IS NEEDED. RAVEN IS ACTIVE AGAIN.

Nathan looked at Harv but didn't say anything.

"Echo four was Harvey's designation," Cantrell said. "You were Echo five. I'm hoping you guys can give me something on the raven reference."

Nathan didn't say anything. He looked at the man sitting next to Cantrell.

"You can speak freely. Bill's my personal assistant, and he's been thoroughly briefed on the Echo program."

"Raven was the best shooter we trained down there."

CHAPTER 5

"Give me everything, Nathan. I want to know all there is to know about this man. Being trained by you makes him extremely lethal. I'm assuming he graduated and didn't wash out?"

"Yes, he graduated." Nathan said. "I remember him well. *We* remember him well. We had our doubts about Raven, but we didn't pick him for the program. That decision was made by his commanding officer, a lieutenant, as I recall. As you know, the candidate selection process was kept secret, even from us. Not just anyone could enlist in the program. Over a five-month period, our recruits underwent an intensive program designed to make them proficient in hand-to-hand combat, small arms, IEDs, surveillance, and countersurveillance. We also taught basic field-interrogation technique, tracking, and stealth, you name it. When our recruits finished the program, they had the equivalent of recon training with a strong emphasis on sniper skills. They didn't come to us green, they were hardened Contra rebels who'd been fighting a nasty civil war against the Sandinista regime. They already knew much of what we taught them. We just sharpened their skills."

"Since no paper exists on any of this, I'm relying on my memory, but I don't recall reading anything about a code name 'Raven.'"

"That's right. You wouldn't have," Harv said. "We gave all of our recruits nicknames. The CIA teams were called Echo units, and the Contra teams were kilo units. But we found calling them K1, K2, K3, and so on was too impersonal. We spent five months with them."

"So Raven was a shooter, not a spotter?"

"That's right," Nathan said. "And a good one. He had the gift. It's hard to explain how some people just have what it takes to be shooters. I never doubted he'd make it through. He was in great condition, had all the physical prerequisites, and had a good mindset . . . Maybe a little too good." Nathan looked at Harv, then said, "I can't swear it happened, but when he made his first kill, his face lit with . . . I don't know . . . exhilaration, I guess."

"The guy smiled," Harv said. "There was no guessing about it. No one ever smiles. We've seen men become everything from withdrawn to physically ill over their first kill. This guy loved it."

"Harv and I don't necessarily agree on this. It's the Mona Lisa question—is she smiling or not?"

"I know what I saw," Harv said.

"You're saying he enjoyed it?"

"In my opinion, he absolutely did."

"While you were flying out here, I reread many of your mission reports from pre-Nicaraguan ops, and it's clear: you always expressed regret at the actual taking of a human life. You were damned good at your jobs, but you didn't like pulling the trigger."

"Rebecca," Nathan said, "we're getting into personal introspection here that I'm uncomfortable talking about."

"Before Bill became an operations officer, he spent several years with the ATF as a special response team sniper."

Nathan raised a brow.

"Two," Bill said.

Rebecca continued. "I also read your report on the emotional aspect of being a shooter."

"You're talking about the second kill being the hardest?" Nathan asked.

"You both agreed the second kill was more difficult, because it meant you were willing to do it again."

Nathan looked out his window before refocusing on Cantrell. "We can't speak for anyone else, but that was true for us. Our first kill went by in a blur. It didn't . . . I don't know, seem real. It almost felt like we were acting in a play. It took us a few days to decompress and really think about what we'd done. When we went out for the second op, it felt different . . . like a job, I guess. Every sniper has to deal with the job in their own way. There's no book to consult on the psychological impact of being a shooter. Is it cowardly to kill someone who has no clue he's about to die? Is it fair? What *is* fair in war? Harv and I have talked about this at great length, and we've concluded that we saved American, coalition, and civilian lives. If a friendly position is being overrun and the commander on the ground calls in an airstrike, is that a cowardly act? In our opinion, it's clearly not. That commander used an available asset to save the lives of his troops and hold his position. There's an undeniable callousness associated with being a sniper, because it's up close and personal through the scope. You just have to disconnect from it. Think of it like an emotion switch that you turn off and on like a light. To make a kill, you disengage by turning the switch off."

"It's not unique to snipers," Harv added. "Think about the crew of an Ohio: if they didn't emotionally disengage, they'd never be able to launch their Tridents. The same thing applies to artillerymen, fighter pilots, you name it."

Bill nodded in agreement. It was clear he understood the concept.

"Raven's switch was always on, but he had no problem pulling the trigger."

"So why didn't you wash Raven out?" Cantrell asked.

Nathan looked out his window again. He'd been hoping she wouldn't ask.

"Look, I'm not trying to second-guess you guys, but it's a fair question."

"We created hardened and efficient killers. That was our assignment. If I'd insisted, I could've sent him down the road, but truthfully, I liked him. He was a good combat soldier, and I trusted him."

Harv jumped in. "In 1990 when the Sandinistas lost political power, most of rural Nicaragua was very much like our early Wild West. The government had little or no control over the remote areas. There were leftover Sandinista warlords committing horrible atrocities against civilians in those mountains. Anyone perceived as a Contra sympathizer, whether they were or not, was rounded up, tortured, slaughtered, and buried in mass graves. Our job was to teach the kilo teams how to take out the warlords without collateral damage to the civilian population. We were in a time-critical situation."

"Understood," said Cantrell. "As always, circumstances dictated what we had to do. Many powerful people in the media and on Capitol Hill wanted Reagan's head on a platter. I was neck-deep in Operation Echo. Atrocities against the civilian population took a sharp nosedive. There's no way to definitively gauge how many lives you guys saved down there, but it's probably in the hundreds, if not thousands."

Nathan nodded. "Thanks for saying that, Rebecca. We did our jobs as best we could. I don't like the idea of Raven misusing or selling his skills . . . if that's what's going on."

"All we know is what's written on that piece of paper, and it isn't much. Not surprisingly, there were no fingerprints. I think it's fair to assume whoever threw that note over the fence wanted to get our attention, and he succeeded. I also think it's reasonable to assume he'll make contact again."

"So how do we fit in?"

"When I said you're never retired, I was speaking figuratively, not literally. I can't force you to do anything, but I think I know you guys pretty well. If Raven's gone bad, he'll have to be dealt with, and the job should be yours."

"Because we trained him."

"I'm not saying that, and I don't think it's fair to you. If a cop goes bad, no one blames the academy instructors. It's more a matter of who's best suited to handle this. I don't need to tell you how dangerous he could be if he's aligned himself with a criminal organization like a cartel or gang."

"Agreed," said Nathan. "If he's become a gun for hire, he's more than capable of taking out VIP targets."

"Which is all the more reason to deal with this quickly to avoid any kind of Raven-CIA connection. Do either of you have any idea who our mysterious messenger might be?"

Nathan shook his head. "Not immediately. It's interesting he used only Harv's designation, though."

Harv added, "I think it's reasonable to assume we've either met him or know him."

"That's why you're here."

"Nathan doesn't exactly have the fondest memories of that place. Neither do I. You're asking a lot, especially of Nathan."

"I'm aware of that."

Harv looked at Nathan. "There's also a possibility this whole thing is a trap."

"I'm aware of that too. I'll be able to give you limited support, but metaphorically, don't call in any air strikes. Also, you may not discuss this with your families. Nothing goes any further than the two of you."

"So what's next?" asked Nathan.

"You guys are in the Hyatt tonight. Sit tight for now, but be ready to deploy at a moment's notice. When we're ready to move, I'll send you a text on this." Cantrell reached down to the floor and came back up with a plain cardboard box about the size of a hard-cover novel. "It's a special phone that comes with a few important rules. Always keep it on, and keep it with you. And never let its charge drop below thirty percent. If it falls below thirty percent, it erases itself and becomes unusable. It has a special battery that should last for three days if you don't use it too much. It also monitors and records your GPS coordinates in real time. If you lose track of it, let me know right away. We can remotely kill it. There are also instructions on how to erase it. It doesn't store recent calls or have a contact list, so you'll have to enter all phone numbers manually. It also has no voice mail. We either speak live or text."

Nathan and Harv nodded.

"I'll text you if you don't answer. If you call me and I don't answer right away, give it ten rings before hanging up. I'm either on the phone or unavailable. I'll see that you attempted a call, and I'll get back to you ASAP. In the event the phone falls into the wrong hands or you're being coerced, we'll need a code word. It will be the first thing you say to me after I answer. If I hear any other word, I'll hang up and kill it. Pick a word, something uncommon, anything you like."

Harv thought for a moment. "How about . . . chromium."

"That works. It's an international phone, so it will work in Nicaragua. Memorize Bill's cell number, just in case you can't reach me." She gave them the number, an easy one to remember because only the last four digits were different from Cantrell's.

A brief silence ensued as Cantrell pulled out her cell, looked at the screen, and tucked it away.

"We passed the Hyatt a few minutes ago," Nathan said.

"You don't miss much."

"Neither do you, Rebecca."

***

After dropping McBride and Fontana off at the entrance to the Hyatt, Rebecca Cantrell moved to the opposite side of the passenger compartment so she could face Bill Stafford.

"What did you think of him?" she asked.

"McBride? He's hard to read, but the word capable comes to mind."

"That's a good assessment."

Bill shook his head.

"What?"

"Those scars on his face . . . People must stare."

"I'm sure they do. He doesn't like being in public much. But I have a feeling he'd be reclusive even without the scars. He fits the profile of an operations officer perfectly; it's why I handpicked him for Echo. He and Harvey were ideal for the job. It was my brainchild. I built and operated the program. I've never told McBride and Fontana, but I suspect they know. The Reagan administration wanted to stop the atrocities being committed against the Contras and their families, but they didn't know how to do it. When I proposed surgical strikes using sniper teams, they loved the idea but didn't want the risk of having Americans on the ground in Nicaragua. We compromised by training Contra teams in neighboring Honduras. I can't help but feel a shared responsibility for what happened to McBride."

"You mean his capture and interrogation?"

She looked out the window. "I should've pulled them out of there sooner."

"That's the problem with hindsight, it's always twenty-twenty." Bill thought for a moment. "For what it's worth, they were dead-on about how it feels becoming a sniper. When I got home after my first kill, I was physically ill. I'd never shot anyone. Nothing Judy said to me that night helped. The guy was a first-class turd and deserved a bullet, but it bothered me for a long time. I guess it still does."

"Imagine multiplying that by a factor of sixty."

"I can't."

They went silent for a few miles. Cantrell liked that about Bill—he didn't ruin the quiet moments with small talk. McBride and Fontana were the same way.

"I didn't tell them, but we've already heard back from our messenger. He's requested a face-to-face."

Bill didn't say anything.

"I wanted a read on them first. I'm planning to tell them tomorrow morning."

"Do you think they suspect you're holding back?"

"Absolutely."

"I'm assuming it's going to be reconnaissance only? They meet with the messenger, determine what's going on, and report back to you? You aren't expecting them to engage, are you?"

"No, they aren't operations officers anymore. Don't get me wrong. They're still capable, but for obvious reasons, we can't risk them falling into the wrong hands. Besides, they'd never allow themselves to be captured, but I doubt it would come to that. I agree with Fontana's thought: they'll likely be meeting with some-one they already know."

"How are they getting down there? They can't—well, shouldn't—fly commercial, and Nicaraguan customs agents are thoroughly inspecting private jets and charters upon landing."

"I've already set it up with JSOC. All the assets are on the move."

CHAPTER 6

Later that same morning, Nathan and Harvey finished their thirty-minute jog and reentered the Hyatt's lobby. Despite being jet-lagged, neither of them had slept especially well. Just four short hours ago, they'd been inside an armored SUV with Cantrell. They strode into the bar and had no trouble finding a quiet spot. At 0615 the place was all but deserted. They grabbed a couple of plates and helped themselves to coffee and a continental breakfast.

"I expect we'll hear from Cantrell today," Nathan said. "I have a feeling she's already heard back from our messenger. Think about it—ten hours of chartered jet time for a ten-minute conversation, plus an encrypted phone? It's a safe bet she's already got a plan."

"The question is, what is the plan?"

"Well, there's no way we're flying into Managua under any circumstances. If that's her plan, we aren't going."

"I'm glad to hear you say that. I feel the same way."

"We go in covert, or not at all. Meanwhile, we should find out if anything major's going on in Nicaragua, politically or otherwise. Since Cantrell didn't mention anything, I doubt there's any serious trouble, but let's not rule it out."

"Do you really think Raven would sell his services to a cartel or criminal gang?"

"I honestly don't know. I hope not. We spent a lot of time with him, but how well did we really get to know him? Like I told Cantrell, I trusted him back then, but people can change."

"Money can be a powerful lure, especially in a poor country." Harv fell silent for a moment. "We can't go to war against a cartel."

"I couldn't agree more."

"And if we find out that's the kind of thing Raven's involved with?"

"Then we communicate it to Cantrell. Job done."

Harv took a sip of coffee. "I wish it were that simple. I don't trust her as fully as you do."

"I'm aware of that. We'll just make sure we stick to the plan, whatever it is."

"How can you be so calm?"

"I guess I just—"

Their special cell phone chimed once. They looked at the text screen.

Call me

"Here we go."

Nathan punched in Cantrell's cell phone number, engaged the speakerphone function, and turned the volume down low. Out of habit, they adjusted their chairs a little so they could keep an eye on each other's backs.

"Thank you for getting back to me so quickly," Cantrell said. "You secure?"

"Yes, we're inside the lobby bar at the Hyatt. No one's around."

"Several hours ago, our messenger made contact again," she said. "The specifics are just landing on my desk."

Nathan exchanged a glance with Harv.

"Embassy cameras captured a compact white vehicle pull to the curb at the bus stop. Without getting out, the driver, presumably our messenger, tossed a baseball over the fence. A folded piece of paper was attached with rubber bands. The vehicle's plates had been removed. From the footage, it looks like a million other compact cars. The video is virtually worthless for IDing the driver. The note was a little longer this time. Basically, our mystery man wants a face-to-face with Harvey and says he won't talk to anyone else."

"If Harv goes, I go," Nathan said. "It's not negotiable."

"Agreed. Since he left no way to contact him, we'll just have to assume he'll be okay meeting with both of you."

"If he knows Harv, he probably knows me as well. We were together the entire time."

Cantrell went silent for a moment. "What does the term 'scatter point alpha' mean to you?"

Nathan made eye contact with Harv and nodded an okay.

Harv answered. "It was one of four regrouping locations we'd planned to use if any member of an Echo or kilo team got separated from the group. In other words, if the shit hit the fan and we all had to bolt, we'd meet up at the closest scatter point and await retrieval."

"Would you be able to precisely locate it for me if you had good aerials?"

"Definitely," Harv said. "All four scatter points were on either ridgelines or mountaintops along a northeast to southwest axis. We purposely avoided choosing the highest or most prominent peaks, but each location provided a 360-degree defensible position with clear lines of sight to the north for radio communication."

"Is that where the messenger wants to meet Harv?" asked Nathan.

"Yes," said Cantrell. "Which means our messenger is likely one of your kilo grads. Who else would know about your rendezvous points?"

"No one," Nathan said. "It's entirely possible Raven himself tossed both notes over the fence."

"I've considered that. And if true, we need to know what he wants."

Harv continued, "It could also be the opening move of an extortion scheme. Pay me money, or I go public with Echo."

"I've considered that as well, but if extortion were his thing, I think he would have tried it long ago. In two days, Nicaragua's hosting an economic summit in Managua. Central American commerce ministers from Mexico to Colombia will be there. Not surprisingly, the United States is not invited. Security will be tight but not out to a thousand yards. All Raven would need is a little inside information to make a hit. As you know, even our own president isn't one hundred percent safe from a truly great shooter."

"And you think Raven might have his sights on one of the ministers?" Nathan asked.

"The timing of Raven's reemergence, if we can call it that, is highly suspect. But that's not my worst-case scenario."

"What is?" asked Nathan.

Their conversation paused for a few seconds. Nathan waited, hoping Cantrell would be forthcoming.

"There's a distinct possibility this whole thing is being staged to lure you into Nicaragua. There's no way to know why. It could be anything from revenge to extortion."

"Thank you for being candid," Nathan said. "We've already talked about the risk of it being a trap, but we can't address any tactical or security issues until we hear your plan for getting us in and out. We know those mountains well, and we can disappear if we have to."

"It's my job to make sure it doesn't come to that."

"You're the only person we trust, Rebecca."

"I appreciate that. Do you happen to remember a town called Santavilla?"

He exchanged another glance with Harv. "Yes."

"Then you also remember a Pastor Tobias?"

"He helped us during a tight situation. We may not have survived without him."

"Five days ago, he was shot and killed by a sniper. Presumably Raven."

"Was that in the baseball note?" Harv asked.

"Yes."

"That's a bad deal," Nathan said. "He was a good man."

Harv asked, "Do you think the murder of Pastor Tobias could somehow be connected to the approaching summit?"

"I don't know, probably not. All we know is that the shooting seems to have prompted the messenger to request this meeting with you."

"When?"

"He wants to meet you in just over . . . thirty-three hours."

"That's going to be tight," said Nathan, "especially if we have to hoof it through miles of jungle. Alpha was the westernmost point in the scatter point chain. Rebecca, you know that area. It won't be easy or quick getting there. We are *not* making a HALO insertion. Those days are long gone."

"I'd never ask that of you, especially at night."

"Also," said Harv, "your special cell phone isn't likely to get a signal in that area. How will we communicate with you?"

"I'm working on that too. Right now, though, I need current photos of you for your fake passports and visas. I don't anticipate you'll need them, but it's better to be on the safe side."

"It looks like there's a camera built into this phone," said Harv. "We'll text you some headshots in a few minutes."

"One question," said Nathan. "Exactly how are we getting down there?"

"I thought you'd never ask," said Cantrell. "The US Navy is giving you a ride."

CHAPTER 7

Driven by a primal desire, Franco returned to Santavilla in search of human prey. It had been too long since his last indulgence. Although one of the girls at the Silver Sands Club in Managua could've served his every need, she could never give him what he craved. Having his way with a prostitute was like feeding a dead rat to a boa.

He currently traveled alone but without concern. Everyone knew El Jefe's men drove metal-gray Range Rovers, and no one would dare challenge him. Besides, he was well armed. Whenever he made a solo trip to the village, he wore a sidearm and kept an Uzi under his seat.

His timing perfect, he drove across the wooden bridge at 1955 hours. He wanted to roll into town just as the general store closed. The town looked asleep, no activity to be seen. No doubt the peasants were well into their marijuana and moonshine.

At Tobias's church, a pit bull mix wandered into the street—he'd seen the dog before. If Tobias had been feeding it prior to his death, no one seemed to have assumed the job. The emaciated animal stopped and stared, its eyes pleading. Franco eased off the gas and rolled the passenger window down. The dog cringed and backed up a step.

"Easy boy, it's your lucky evening." He tossed his barbecued pork sandwich out the window. The animal flinched, then sniffed the air. It ran to the sandwich and consumed it in several violent chomps. Franco had planned to eat the sandwich on the way back to Managua later tonight, but this poor creature needed it more than he did. The dog looked up as if to thank him before retreating back toward the church.

Not wanting to draw attention, Franco applied just enough gas to keep the Range Rover moving. The Perezes' general store was just ahead on the right. In twenty more meters, he ought to be able to see the store's side door. He had the sensation of being watched from the windows of every building lining the street but dismissed it as paranoia. No one was around. This town's collective light switch was flipped off after 1900 hours.

He saw her then—a bluish-white blur at the right edge of his vision. Just after his Range Rover passed the local tavern, she'd dashed from the general store's side door toward the rear of the building in hopes of not being seen.

Nice try, sweetheart. Franco peeled around the corner into the vacant lot south of the store and spotted her in the gap between the two Conex containers the Perezes used for dry storage. She jerked her head back, but it was too late. Scratching the tires, he accelerated across the vacant lot. He didn't want to make it too easy, but he didn't want to lose sight of her either.

He skidded to a stop just short of the containers. In a fluid move he slid out, swung the door closed, and hit the lock button on the remote. The Range Rover chirped in response.

He circled to the far side of the containers just in time to see her hop the chain-link fence and take off in a full sprint toward the river. *Oh, no you don't.*

She had a good head start, but she'd never outrun him. Her only hope of evading him would be to reach the cover of the trees and hide in the undergrowth. Her odds weren't too bad, because the deepening twilight worked to her advantage. Franco never used night vision or thermal imagers for hunts like this. He considered it cheating. Even though she hadn't eluded him yet, she deserved a fair chance. And she might get away this time—there was always a first time for everything. If she did, he wouldn't punish her later. Franco had many faults, but fair was fair, and he never blamed others for his own shortcomings.

He allowed her an extra few seconds before beginning his pursuit. The girl was fast—he gave her that, but he was faster. Enjoying the challenge, he watched her drive her legs as she bounded across the knee-high grass. When he caught her, it would be a sweet victory, in more ways than one. Her attempt to escape heightened his desire, and he felt a stirring in his groin. He hoped it wouldn't be too easy. The last time she'd run away, he'd caught her almost immediately. Easy prey wasn't nearly as rewarding.

She glanced over her shoulder and changed direction, angling to the right. He guessed she was heading for the dam of rocks that allowed foot traffic to cross. On the opposite side of the pond, she'd probably turn left and try to hide in the thicker foliage. If he guessed wrong about this, she might get away.

Franco changed direction and ran straight toward the dam. If he could reach the trees before she crossed the dam, he'd be able to see what direction she went on the other side. He slowed his approach and crouched behind a rusted car near the top of the bank. He spotted her halfway across the dam, marveling at her balance and agility as she leapt from boulder to boulder. Knowing she'd look back once she reached the far side, Franco remained motionless. What she did next surprised him. Rather than look back or turn left, she stayed on the trail that led to Tobias's cabin and sprinted up the mountainside into the trees. Three seconds later, he lost sight of her.

Clever girl. But this hunt was far from over. He scrambled down the bank, crossed the dam, and followed her into the trees.

He slowed his pace and looked for movement. The girl wasn't more than twenty seconds ahead of him, but that had given her plenty of time to disappear. Maybe he shouldn't have given her such a large head start. Not wanting to give up, he continued up the trail. If all else failed, he could lie low and wait for her to reemerge. He had no illusions about it—she knew this forest better than he did. Rather than dwell on his disadvantage, he scanned the trees to his left. It was possible she'd turned east with the intent of crossing the river above the pond where the water wasn't deep.

Playing a hunch, Franco veered to his left and paralleled the mountain's contour. If she'd come this way, she'd been stealthy. The crickets and toads hadn't stopped their singing.

There!

He saw it then, fifty meters away, a flash of white that stood out like a cigarette on a putting green. She must've stopped running and gone to ground. He took a step to the right for a clearer line of sight.

Got you!

He could see her white blouse between two smaller trees. Like a predatory cat, he eased from tree to tree, being careful to avoid any sudden movements or noise. His camouflage fatigues blended perfectly into the colors of the forest. Even if she looked his direction, she'd never see him. She would've been better off trying to put some distance between them.

He closed to within ten meters and froze.

Something felt wrong. Her blouse didn't look right, and the forest had gone quiet.

It could only mean one thing.

Franco pulled out his handgun and whipped around.

The skin on his arms tingled at the same moment he knew he'd been tricked.

He heard her before he saw her. With a shrill cry, she flew at him. Dressed only in her bra and shorts, she looked incredibly sexy, but now wasn't the time to admire things. He jerked his head to dodge her fist coming at his face. He avoided the worst of it, but two knuckles still connected. He pivoted low and swept his leg. Anticipating his move, she jumped and his boot passed harmlessly beneath her. She squared off and assumed a low stance, her fists held in a defensive position. She was feisty but no match for him. *Why not toy with her a little?*

He lurched forward, deliberately moving more slowly than necessary. She sidestepped and tried to kick him in the groin, but he was ready for her move. He stopped short, and her foot found only air. He smiled when she lost her balance and fell.

The sweet taste of victory at last.

He pounced on her and pinned her hands over her head. She tried to head butt him, but his arms were several inches longer than hers, and he easily avoided contact.

Knowing she'd been beaten, she stopped struggling.

Franco lowered his voice. "You gave it a good effort. You're definitely getting stronger and faster, but I think you need another . . . private lesson."

She laughed and wrapped her legs around his waist. They'd gone through this mock chase many times. He lowered his head and gently kissed her. "Try not to make it so easy next time."

"Easy? You walked right past me!"

"I'll reluctantly admit your ruse worked, but I would've found you eventually."

"I'm getting better. I almost nailed you with that left jab."

"True, but your eyes gave you away. You should've looked at my chest, not my face."

"You can't see my eyes, it's too dark."

They both felt the carnal desire now. Franco removed his shirt and unbuttoned his pants. "I believe it's time for your lesson to begin."

They made love without concern for each other's needs. Franco liked the challenge. The girl's selfish desires heightened his excitement. Because she was half his age, she had twice his sexual energy—a good combination. Just before she climaxed, she whispered how much she enjoyed being his mistress. He found the comment amusing but didn't let on. Why ruin her fun?

Fifteen minutes later, drenched with sweat, Franco wanted to ask her what she'd been doing at Pastor Tobias's church meeting the day of the shooting, but it could wait. At least she'd told him about the meeting. Although Franco hadn't directly said it, he'd implied Tobias's days were numbered. Perhaps she'd felt some guilt. Understandable, but he didn't want her second-guessing her role as his personal spy. He had no emotional connection to her. They shared nothing beyond the physical relationship, and she'd never asked for anything more. She had to know she was being used as a tool for information, but her desire for a life outside Santavilla overrode her sense of self-worth.

Of course, Franco knew he too was being used. And just as she sought to leave Santavilla, he planned to leave Nicaragua one day. He had his sights on Las Vegas. Now *there* was a town. Nightlife. Women. Gambling. Booze. You name it, Vegas had it. If Macanas could keep a penthouse in the Trump Tower, why shouldn't Franco as well? That was the only life worth living—to be your own boss, make your own decisions, and not be held accountable to anyone else.

CHAPTER 8

Skimming the treetops at 160 miles per hour in a state-of-the-art, blacked-out HH-60H Rescue Hawk, Nathan rested his head against the bulkhead. Were they really doing this? It seemed surreal. For a frantic second, he could almost imagine demons in the forest below, waiting to hunt them. He took a deep breath and relaxed his hands and jaw. He and Harv were about to be delivered into unfriendly territory that held hideous memories of unspeakable pain and anguish.

Nathan looked at his watch—2100 hours—right on schedule. There was no turning back at this point. Service members had risked their lives getting them down here, and scrubbing the mission wasn't an option. The plan was to drop them four miles north of scatter point alpha, so there'd be no possible way the helicopter's noise could be heard at that distance. If an ambush waited for them up there, they planned to sneak up on it undetected. Nathan estimated their four-mile trek would take about five to six hours.

The Navy supplied all of their equipment, including his ghillie-wrapped M40 sniper rifle built from a Remington 700 model. He'd requested the optical be predialed to a 300-yard zero and that it employ external one-quarter minute-of-angle adjustments for windage and elevation. He'd also requested Lake City match ammo, because he knew its ballistic curve well. Dressed in MARPAT woodland uniforms, they'd meld perfectly into the environment. Their faces and the backs of their hands were painted in dark shades of green and brown. The half-moon wouldn't be a problem, as most of its light didn't penetrate the forest's multilayered canopy.

Through their headsets, the pilot announced they'd just crossed the Rio Coco and welcomed them to Nicaragua. They were also told to stand by—they'd be rappelling in just under two minutes.

Harv sat motionless, looking at him. Nathan nodded an okay.

The Hawk's crew chief and gunner didn't see their silent exchange. Wearing night-vision goggles, they were glued to their M-240D machine guns watching for any signs of human activity, most notably the twinkle of weapons fire. Nathan wasn't concerned; the ship's crew could deliver a few hundred pounds of high-speed copper and lead to anyone foolish enough to take a potshot at them.

He heard the turbine engines change pitch, then released his four-part seat belt. He kept his headset on, powered on his night-vision goggles, and pivoted them down to his eyes. Harv mirrored his moves.

Nathan's world turned into multiple shades of green. He leaned across the cabin and checked Harv's rappelling harness, backpack, waist pack, and sidearm holster.

Harv did the same for him. All secure.

Nathan moved his rifle from a chest position to his back where it fit snuggly against the side his backpack.

The pilot slowed gradually at first, then flared for a hover, being careful not to create blade slap.

The pilot said, *"You're good to go. We'll be orbiting on the border until you send us on our way."*

"Copy," Nathan said. "Thanks for the ride."

"Safe hunting."

Just before Nathan removed his headset, the crew chief told him they were fifty feet above the jungle floor. Nathan nodded an acknowledgment.

Without hesitating, Nathan grabbed the rope in the brake-hand, guide-hand technique. Keeping a tight brake grip, he quickly maneuvered into the L position, placing both of his boots on the edge of the deck with his butt hanging out the door. He held that position until the crew chief gave him the final hand signal to jump.

Nathan bent his legs, sprang backward, and loosened his brake-hand.

Gravity did the rest.

His stomach tightened as his body zipped toward the ground. He hadn't rappelled in quite a while, and it took several seconds to get a controlled descent going.

When he landed on the damp Nicaraguan soil, he unhooked the rope and drew his Sig. Crouching, he scanned his immediate area before looking up. Harv was already coming down. Nathan inwardly flinched at the tremendous noise. The sensation of being directly below such a thunderous machine felt humbling. The ground vibrated from the Hawk's energy. Whipping back and forth, the surrounding treetops protested in anger at the intrusion. Every low-growing plant within a thirty-foot radius was laid flat from the downwash.

Although he didn't see any footprints, trash, or other signs indicating human presence, he now wished they'd made that HALO jump after all but knew they were both too rusty. Landing in the canopy of an eighty-foot tree would've ruined his evening.

The pilot had chosen a good spot, but there wasn't much room for error. Their landing zone was a thirty-yard clearing on the forest floor where the ground wasn't quite level. Nathan estimated it had a downward slope of about 20 degrees to the north.

Harv unhooked and gave a thumbs-up to the crew chief, who was leaning out the door.

The Rescue Hawk made a 180-degree pivot and paralleled the downward pitch of the mountainside as it flew away, its deafening noise quickly abating. The insertion had taken less than fifteen seconds.

Nathan pointed to his NV goggles, then gestured toward the far side of the clearing. He remained crouched as Harv carefully worked his way across the uneven terrain to the east side of the LZ. After Harv was safely under tree cover, Nathan mirrored the move to the east, knowing Harv had his back. Inside the tree line, Nathan stopped next to a small rock outcropping. He took a knee and surveyed his immediate area. The trunks of massive trees dominated the mountainside like sentries. Their dark forms seemed to scrutinize him, looking for flaws and weaknesses. Nathan felt like an intruder who'd stumbled into an enemy camp. Closing his eyes for a few seconds, he forced the anxiety aside. He needed to focus on the task at hand: determining if their insertion had been detected.

Over the next sixty seconds, the helicopter's clatter faded until an eerie silence enveloped them. The air was still. Nothing moved at all. Adding to the isolation, the forest was totally quiet. The helicopter had frightened every animal in the area, including insects.

A few seconds later, a faint echo of the Rescue Hawk reached their position.

Their transition from technology to nature was absolute.

Nathan looked across the clearing at Harv, brought his hands together in an interlocked finger hold, and pointed to the south. Staying inside the tree line, they circled their way to meet at the southern edge of the open space.

Keeping his voice low, Harv said, "I don't know about you, but that rappel triggered an adrenaline rush I hadn't felt in years. I wasn't sure I remembered how to friggin' do it."

"I know what you mean. I experienced the same thing when my ass was hanging off the deck. Let's take a few minutes to settle our nerves. We've got time. Let's also power down our NVGs to preserve the batteries."

"I'll call our ride and tell them we're five by five."

Nathan turned around so Harv could access his pack.

"This is a perfect LZ. We should have a clear line of transmission out to the Hawk."

From what Nathan could gather, the pilot had dropped them in the precise spot Cantrell had identified on the aerials. They were about a third of the way up the north side of a small mountain. Scatter point alpha should be four miles directly south-southwest of their position.

Harv powered on the handheld radio and pressed the transmit button. It was preset to the right frequency. "Good to go."

They received an acknowledgment click.

Harv turned it off and returned it to Nathan's pack. "Whatever they're paying us, it ain't enough."

Nathan half laughed, knowing this was a gratis mission. "Our pilot did a good job. I wish I could've looked over her shoulder on the flight." He hadn't been able to see the flight deck because of the bulkhead separating their compartment. Rescue Hawks employed terrain-following software, and he'd never seen it in action.

"I wonder how many pilots are women these days."

"Probably more than we'd imagine. She's got the best job in the Navy."

Harv said, "Spoken like a true helicopter pilot."

"On our feet-wet leg, we were never higher than fifty feet."

"Driving Hornets may seem more glamorous," Harv continued, "but helos are where it's at."

"I don't think we've landed on a Perry-class frigate before. The seas had to be ten to twelve feet. The *McClusky*'s helipad looked really small during the approach. Did you notice how she hovered above the deck and let the ship come up to her? That was a good trick. She timed it perfectly."

"Fixed-wing landings on carriers are tough, but I'd be willing to bet that landing a helicopter on a missile frigate that's rolling and pitching is just as difficult, maybe even harder."

"No argument here," Nathan said. "It's incredible they do it at night on blacked-out ships. Squid aviators are a rare breed."

They fell silent a moment. Some of the forest's sound had returned, mostly insect buzzing. The birds and amphibians would take a little longer to feel secure again.

"I'll take point," said Nathan. "You ready to go?"

"Not really, but we're a little short on options. Let's just make sure we get to our extraction point on time. I don't relish spending more than one night down here."

CHAPTER 9

Nathan and Harv had been hiking for nearly three hours, and both were soaked, though not from rain. This northern area of the central region didn't have enough elevation to get them above the heat. In neighboring Honduras, it got plain cold in cloud forests. According to Harv's GPS reading, they'd traveled slightly more than three miles. The device supplied their current location along with a vector to their destination. It also calculated the remaining straight-line distance.

Four hundred yards up a fairly steep slope, Nathan pivoted and issued a low warbling whistle. He couldn't see Harv, but gave the form-up hand signal. His friend would be along shortly. Thirty seconds later, Harv seemed to materialize out of the undergrowth. *He's still got the touch*, Nathan thought, impressed with Harv's stealthy approach. They were nearly certain their insertion hadn't been detected; otherwise they would've been intercepted by now. Still, they never spoke above whispers.

"Let's take a breather and drink more water," Nathan said.

"Sounds good. We should chow down a couple of energy bars. This is a serious calorie burn."

"Listen to it, Harv. It's incredible."

"I think it's noisier at night."

"It definitely is." Nathan knew this jungle was teeming with life with a common goal: to reproduce itself. The combined drone from hundreds of frogs, buzzing insects, and high-pitched bird calls created an eerie sonata. Adding to the mood, a musty rotting odor hung in the air. Nathan didn't care for jungles much. Even though desert temperature changes could be extreme, Nathan preferred them over jungles. He also liked conifer forests. This place was beautiful in its own way, but its randomly entangled environment didn't suit him. It seemed like organic chaos.

Harv looked around and shook his head. "I keep thinking about Jesse Ventura's line from *Predator*. 'This place makes Cambodia look like Kansas.'"

"Amen to that."

"The going's a little easier under the canopied areas where the ground vegetation is thinner. So far, we haven't had to make many significant detours. I've noticed a lot more cleared areas that weren't here before. Think it's from illegal logging?"

Nathan peeled the wrapper from an energy bar. "Probably. It makes our slog a little easier in places, but it's a shame to see."

"Enforcement of preservation is probably spotty at best. I wouldn't imagine Nicaragua has a large budget for forest rangers."

"It definitely doesn't. Sadly, it's the honor system out here. I'm no expert on the subject, but I imagine Nicaragua has the same problem as many other parts of the world. People need wood for cooking."

"That was a beautiful stream we crossed down there with the waterfall into the pool and all the moss-covered rocks. There must be hundreds of places like that in these mountains."

"No doubt there are."

"How're you doing?" Harv asked.

"I'm okay. You?"

"I keep flashing back to carrying you through two miles of this stuff. I don't think I'd ever been so exhausted."

"I don't remember it."

"You were mostly unconscious and damned close to dying." Harv grinned. "You told me you loved me . . . several times."

"Don't ever repeat that, or you'll die slowly . . . It's true, though."

"I know," Harv said.

"You want to take point for a spell?"

Harv took another bite from his energy bar. "No problem. Alpha is just beyond this next ridgeline. At the top, we'll take a few minutes to look the area over, but I doubt we'll see anything."

"I keep wondering who we'll find up there."

"We might find no one."

"We're outta here then," Nathan said. "We aren't hanging around. We'll make the best possible speed back to the extraction point."

"Let's do another TI and RF sweep."

Nathan removed the handheld thermal imager from Harv's pack and placed its rubber flange tight on his face before powering it on. He conducted a slow 360-degree sweep of their immediate area. It wasn't supereffective in this environment because of all the layered plant life, but it confirmed there weren't any warm human forms within its reach.

Nathan untied Harv's ghillie suit coat and draped it over his friend's head. The thick shaggy garment would block the illumination on Harv's face from the radio frequency detector's small LCD screen. Even though the brightness had been adjusted to its lowest setting, it could be easily detected by a night-vision device. Nathan waited for Harv to give him the okay before removing the ghillie top.

"We're good," Harv said. "Just to be on the safe side, I'm setting it to vibrate and leaving it on." Harv tucked the device into his thigh pocket with the LCD screen facing in, toward his thigh. Third generation night-vision scopes were so sensitive, they could pick up invisible light bleeding through fabric. Even with the device facing inward, its bleed light could still be detected but not as brightly. "Okay, I'm on point. Let's close it up to a ten-yard separation until we reach the ridgeline."

Nathan waited until Harv moved out before following. Harv was a good point man. Like Nathan, he knew to avoid stepping on certain types of exposed roots because of their softer skin. They weren't overly concerned about leaving footprints, because no one was following them. Every one hundred yards or so, Harv would pause and hold up a closed fist. It was standard practice to stop and check for human presence, but the unbelievable din of the forest drowned out a lot of sound. It took a practiced ear to hear something that didn't belong. Jungle stalking was a double-edged sword. It was easy to conceal yourself, but equally difficult to spot someone with the same intent.

They arrived at the top of the ridgeline twenty minutes later and had to move laterally to get a clear line of sight through the trees to the south. Across a thousand-yard canyon, scatter point alpha wasn't more than a bump in the next ridgeline, but it had a distinctive shape, like a bowling pin lying on its side.

"There's alpha," Harv said.

"If anyone's waiting for us over there, we'll never see them unless they want to be seen."

"I'll take a look with the field glasses anyway. Our half-moon is getting low on the horizon. We'll use NV from here on. At the bottom of the canyon, we'll put on our ghillies for the ascent."

"I hate to admit it, but I'm kinda hoping no one's there."

Harv nodded. "Yeah, me too. It wouldn't break my heart to beat feet outta this place."

As predicted, Harv didn't detect any human presence. All was quiet. On par with the weather report the Navy had given them, patchy clouds were moving in, but they didn't look heavy enough to produce rain.

Harv took point again, and they started down the slope. Although they could've gone faster, they maintained a slow pace, careful not to make any discernible noise. Nathan felt as though they were being watched from across the canyon but dismissed the thought as paranoia. No one should be able to see them through all the undergrowth. Up ahead, Harv diverted to the west to avoid a dangerously steep section left over from an old landslide.

At the bottom of the canyon, they found a stream flowing to the northeast that would ultimately join the Rio Coco. The trickle of its water had a soothing sound, but neither of them felt especially relaxed. If there was going to be an ambush, it would likely occur up at alpha.

After slipping into their two-part ghillie suits, they looked each other over, making sure their coats weren't snagged on their backpacks or waist packs. Their jacket hoods wouldn't completely conceal their NV goggles without hampering their use, but only the last inch or so of their dual scopes would be visible. Using black elastic straps they'd sewn to the inside tops of their hoods, they secured the straps under their chins to keep their hoods from being pulled back by brambles and low-hanging branches.

"We'll make the ascent in parallel formation," Nathan said. "I'll take the left. Thirty-yard separation. Harv, we aren't being taken prisoner."

"Understood." His friend pulled his Sig and deployed out to the right.

Nathan mirrored the move to the left, envisioning himself as a wraith, slowly moving in for the kill. He used this mindset to keep his senses focused and sharp. In nature, most predators employed some form of stealth, and this situation was no different. They didn't plan on killing anyone tonight, but they wouldn't hesitate if the situation required it.

After fifteen minutes of climbing, it was impossible to determine how close to the ridgeline they were—the canopy prevented them from seeing its dark outline. The sound of the jungle was slightly less pronounced up here, but it didn't concern Nathan. It was always noisier in basins and canyons near water.

Taking steps every three or four seconds, they climbed for another five minutes. It was a tediously slow pace, but it prevented a potential enemy from detecting their movement. Nathan kept looking up, hoping for a glimpse of the summit.

Then he stopped cold, frozen by the sudden sound of a helicopter.

CHAPTER 10

Nathan looked for Harv, but saw no sign of him.

The unmistakable thumping of a main rotor echoed in from the northeast. And it was definitely getting louder.

Nathan felt his entire body tighten, and he forced himself to think before moving. He looked through the treetops, hoping to catch the flashing beacon of a commercial bird but saw nothing.

Without warning, the noise tripled in intensity. The helo was flying low, and it must've just cleared the ridge they'd traversed.

Abandoning all stealth, Nathan hustled over to a massive tree and put its trunk between himself and the threat. He unslung his rifle, thumbed the safety, and steeled himself for a fight.

If the helicopter were merely passing through, he'd have his answer within the next fifteen seconds. He pressed his chest against the tree, hoping it wasn't crawling with ants. Fighting two battles didn't seem fair. Time seemed to stretch as the whooping slaps of the helo's main rotor pulsed up the canyon.

Nathan breathed a sigh of relief when the noise quickly faded. From what he could surmise, the helo had been on a westerly course, and it had just ducked behind the ridge they were climbing.

If that had been a military bird, he knew they wouldn't have been spotted by night vision, but a thermal imager might've nailed them. It was impossible to know why it had crossed the area, but the Honduran border wasn't more than six or seven miles away, so it could've been a routine patrol. Their current location was only an hour's flight from Managua. The Rescue Hawk had flown well under the radar, and even if it had been seen, a Nicaraguan patrol bird should've scoured the area hours ago.

He looked for Harv and saw his friend standing on the south side of a tree, also in an effort to visually screen himself from the helicopter's line of sight. Nathan issued a closed fist and then spread his fingers. Harv acknowledged with an okay gesture. They'd sit tight for five minutes to make sure the helo didn't return. The NV-capable weapon sight on his M40 was zeroed for three hundred yards, so if the helicopter reappeared and things turned ugly, Nathan was more than capable of accurately shooting at its crew or engine compartment. If the bird was one of the Nicaraguan air force's Mi-24 Hind attack helicopters, Nathan knew the Hinds employed armor plating to protect their vital areas, which meant he'd have little chance of shooting it down. The best he could hope for would be a wounding shot to make it withdraw. He felt fairly confident it hadn't been a transport; its rotor noise hadn't been throaty enough.

There was no sense in speculating further, but he wasn't convinced the helo's passage across the canyon wasn't connected to them. Hearing several helicopters at the same time could've meant serious trouble, because each Hind had the capacity to carry eight combat troops and all their gear.

He didn't deny his previous ordeal down here made him edgy, but it was prudent to hold their position for a spell. They had time. If all went well, they'd have alpha thoroughly scouted before their mysterious messenger arrived, but he suspected the reverse was true. If their messenger possessed formal Echo training, he would've arrived by now to secure the area himself. And he might not be alone—there could be more than one person up there.

Before five minutes had elapsed, Nathan gave Harv the form-up gesture, and they moved laterally toward each other.

"Talk about a pucker factor," Harv said.

"Yeah, no kidding. Think it was a Hind?"

"Probably. It didn't sound like a transport, and it was definitely a single rotor. Its noise was never constant, so I don't think it hovered and deployed troops. If it did, we could be facing a squad-sized force."

"Quit trying to cheer me up." Nathan looked toward the west where the helicopter had disappeared. "We'll stay a little longer."

"The helo could've spooked our messenger. He might bug out thinking he's been blown."

"If we don't find anyone up there, I suspect it would only delay the inevitable. I'd like to solve this mystery tonight and be done with it."

"Agreed."

"Did your RF detector vibrate?" Nathan asked.

"No, I didn't feel anything. You're thinking if it saw us, it would've radioed our location. If it did, the detector should've picked up its transmission. Nate, we can't rule out the possibility it rappelled troops on the north side of that ridge we just came from and then blew through the canyon to deceive us. To make matters worse, Raven could be with them."

"How long would that have taken?"

"If they're seasoned combat troops, less than twenty seconds."

"How much time do we have if that's the case?"

"If they take a direct route over the summit like we just did, thirty minutes to an hour, depending on how stealthy they want to be. It would take them considerably longer to traverse the mountain to the east or west."

Nathan didn't respond.

"Do you want to leave?"

"I think we're okay. Like you said, its noise never sounded constant from a hover. Just because it was dark, doesn't make it a Nicaraguan air force bird. It could've been a drug runner or a private ship."

"That's true."

"We have several options, but all of them terminate with two possible outcomes. We either complete the mission as planned and meet with the messenger, or we don't. Cantrell won't second-guess us either way. A helicopter's passage through the area doesn't seem like a strong enough reason to scrub the mission. I think we should hunker down right here and see if anyone shows up. We can't worry about meeting our messenger until we're certain we're not being pursued."

"Sounds like a plan."

They separated again to give themselves the best chance of detecting intruders. The next thirty minutes seemed to stretch into thirty hours. Nathan didn't like being immobile, but it was the right thing to do given their situation. Sometimes no action was the best action.

Nathan tapped his memory of the mission briefing Bill Stafford had given them. The Nicaraguan air force had several Mi-8 Hip military transport helicopters and at least five Mi-24 Hind attack birds in its arsenal. With skilled pilots, the Hinds were capable ships, and Nathan had no desire to engage one of them. If a Hind had bored down on them, they would've had little chance of surviving, even with all the cover. Trees were no match for rockets and large-caliber machine guns. There was an outright terror associated with being hunted by a helicopter, especially a Russian-made gunship.

With five minutes to spare, he looked over at Harv's position, issued the form-up signal, and started in that direction.

"I think we're good," Harv said. "If anyone's tracking—" His friend stopped midsentence. "Someone's talking. The RF detector just vibrated."

Nathan pulled his Sig and crouched. Harv followed suit. Were they blown? How? And who was it?

"Nate, it's going off again."

"Shit."

The next thing they heard was a voice from somewhere above. It had a Southern drawl.

"US Marines, one-one."

CHAPTER 11

What the hell? Nathan exchanged a stunned glance with Harv and quickly considered their options. He needed verification in a big hurry. That voice could belong to anyone.

He called out a question. "Where're you stationed?"

"Pendleton."

"Where did one-one see its first major campaign?"

"Guadalcanal."

"What's great about *Sports Illustrated*?"

There was a brief pause. "The swimsuit issue."

"What cities have the Raiders played in?"

"Oakland and Los Angeles."

"Do you like them?"

"No."

"Copy that. We're coming up."

"Shit, Nate. You're a piece of work, you know that?" Harv mocked his question. "'What's great about *Sports Illustrated*?'—what kinda question is that?"

Nathan shrugged.

Harv shook his head. "Cantrell said we'd be supported, but I sure as hell didn't expect this."

"Let's beat feet up there."

Since their USMC friend had been vocal, it could only mean the immediate area was secure. They made their way up to the summit without haste.

Slightly winded, they arrived at the highest point of the bowling-pin formation but didn't see anyone. The tree cover up here was modest, but it obscured most of the moonlight. Waist-high ferns and shrubs dominated the area. Like something out of a video game, six ghillie-suited figures materialized from crouched positions. Within seconds they were surrounded. Nathan had his Sig in his hand but kept it lowered.

One of them approached, presumably the marine who'd made contact. In the dim light, he looked identical to Nathan and Harv, just not as tall. When the man pulled his hood back, Nathan saw his face was also painted. The other marines formed a defensive perimeter. Nathan and Harv released the elastic straps and pulled their hoods back.

Nathan extended his hand. "You guys are a damned welcome sight."

"Thank you, sir. I'm Staff Sergeant Lyle, one-one. We don't know your identity, and we won't ask."

"Understood. Sorry about the interrogation, but we weren't expecting you. I had to be sure you were the real deal."

"That's not a problem, sir."

"Did you get a good look at the helo? Was it a Hind?"

"Yes, sir. A twenty-four. Nicaraguan air force."

"Is there any chance it inserted troops?"

"No sir, at least not within our visual range. We monitored its thermal signature. It never hovered, and it wasn't high enough for jumpers. It was probably just a routine patrol. They're used mostly for drug interdiction."

"A long time ago, we were with one-eight," Nathan said.

"Recon?" Lyle asked.

Nathan nodded.

"Outstanding."

"Sorry you guys got dragged out here."

"Are you kidding? We love deploying."

"How long have you been here?"

"Corporal Ramirez and Sergeant Birdsall have been with you since the LZ. The rest of us have been up here for the last twelve hours."

"Are you serious? We were followed?"

"Yes, sir."

"We never saw or heard anyone."

Lyle smiled. "No sir, you wouldn't have."

"How'd they beat our TI sweeps?" Harv asked.

"When you stopped for thermals, they ducked behind trees to hide their signatures."

Harv shook his head. "We were too predictable."

"No, sir. Rammy and Bird lost you several times and had to reacquire. You weren't easy to track."

As if on cue, two more men rounded the summit from the north, making Lyle's group a squad-sized unit.

Very tight, Nathan thought. "You guys find anyone up here?"

"Yes, sir, he arrived five hours ago. He made a good approach, but we bagged him. He's been tight-lipped. Says he won't talk to anyone but one of you. We haven't interrogated him. Our orders were to secure him and maintain a perimeter until you arrived."

Lyle looked to his left and issued a hand signal. Two of Lyle's men appeared, and sandwiched between them was a third man who appeared to have his hands secured behind his back. The man didn't seem nervous, just the opposite. Dressed in a wood-land combat uniform with a light coating of face paint on his exposed skin, he walked with confidence.

The moment of truth had arrived.

They were about to meet the mysterious messenger from the embassy.

A ray of moonlight hit the man's face, and Harv took a step forward. "Viper? Is that you?" he asked in Spanish.

"Mayo!"

Harv embraced him. No words were spoken.

Nathan smiled at hearing Harv's old nickname. During their Echo operations, Harv had procured an entire case of the little squeeze packs. He used to put mayonnaise on everything, even his hot dogs. The kilo teams settled on *Rojo* for Nathan. *Red.* Back then, his hair had lacked any traces of gray.

Lyle pulled a knife, cut the disposable binds around Viper's wrists, and gave him his handgun back.

Viper tucked the gun into his holster.

"I apologize for cuffing you," Lyle said, "but we had to be sure you weren't a threat."

"It's okay," Viper said. "No harm done."

"You speak English," Harv said.

"A lot has changed over the years."

The two marines who'd brought Viper over lowered their handguns and withdrew.

"It's good to see you again," Nathan said. He too gave the man a hug. Being a good ten inches shorter, Viper nearly disappeared inside Nathan's grasp. They couldn't reminisce in front of the present company, but Viper had played a critical role in Nathan's rescue.

"I need to get on the SATCOM and update our status," Lyle said.

"How do you do that?" Harv asked. "I didn't see a dish."

"We use a backpack unit for LEO birds. We can type or dictate messages into a terminal, and the unit sends an ultra-short encrypted burst."

Nathan wondered how many low-earth-orbit satellites the US military had . . . probably dozens. Joint Special Operations Command had many resources at its disposal.

Harv said, "So the burst transmission minimizes your RF signature."

"Exactly, sir. It's not foolproof and can be jammed, but the unit rotates frequencies in that event. We're currently in a dark period until the next bird clears the horizon. We usually have a twelve- to thirteen-minute window before it drops back down. We can talk to JSOC in real time with an HEO bird if we have to, but that's not as stealthy, and it depletes the batteries faster. I'll give you guys some time alone."

Nathan said, "Thank you, Sergeant. Do we need to move out?"

"Not just yet, sir. I'll let you know what JSOC comes back with."

They waited until Lyle rejoined his men.

"Damn, it's really good to see you again," Harv said.

"Yeah, you guys too," said Viper.

"I never had a chance to properly thank you. You helped Harv save my life. I've never forgotten it."

"I felt terrible about what happened. I'm really sorry you went through it."

"It happened. I've moved on."

"I'm sure you guys are wondering why I asked for your help."

Nathan lightened the moment, knowing Viper felt uneasy about all of this. "The thought had crossed our minds."

"We kept our real identities secret, even from each other. I haven't used Viper since I saw you guys last. My real name is Estefan Delgado."

"We can only give you our first names. I'm Nathan. That's Harv."

"It's okay. I don't need to know more than that."

Harv said, "In your second note to the embassy, you said Pastor Tobias was killed by a sniper, presumably Raven."

"That's right. Tobias was his first name. His *apellido*—" Estefan had trouble finishing his sentence, emotion catching in his throat. "His surname was Delgado."

CHAPTER 12

"He was your father," Harv said.

Estefan nodded.

"Man, I'm really sorry."

"He was a servant of God who never questioned his faith. He gave away nearly all his money. He never asked, but I sent him all I could. He'd dedicated the latter part of his life to helping the people of Santavilla."

"You're his legacy," said Harv. "You and the other kilos saved countless lives, and you didn't do it for money. If your dad had known about that, he would've been proud."

Estefan shrugged. "I never told him I became a sniper. We weren't very close until recently. I have a hard time letting go of old anger. We sort of patched things up last year. My wife kept pressuring me to make the effort. I wish I'd done it a long time ago."

"Tell us what you know," Nathan said, concerned they didn't have much time. "Why do you think Raven's the shooter, and why was your father murdered? We didn't see the second note you tossed over the fence into the embassy, but we know you mentioned Santavilla. What's going on?"

"Gold."

"Gold?" Harv asked. "You mean literally?"

"My father was murdered because of greed. There are several rich veins very close to the surface near Santavilla, but the locations are too rugged for larger commercial operators to access without destroying a significant area of forest." Estefan's tone sounded lifeless and flat. Clearly, he was still reeling from his father's murder.

"We don't have to talk about this now," Nathan said.

"It's okay. One of the mines produces a very high yield. Before he was killed, my father told me the mine was producing nearly three ounces of gold per ton. The spot price of gold has hovered at $1,400 per ounce, and it's resurrected the industry here. In fact, gold is one of Nicaragua's new economic engines. It could even become one of our country's biggest exports within a few years. There's huge money involved."

Harv said, "Three ounces per ton doesn't seem like a very big number to me."

"Three ounces per ton is a lot. Trust me, it's a big number. Many large commercial mines yield less than a quarter ounce per ton. They make up for the smaller ratio through sheer volume. You've seen those huge Komatsu dump trucks, the ones with the giant tires where the driver has to climb a ladder and take a staircase to drive it? An average-sized Komatsu can haul one hundred tons of ore. If you do the math using 0.2 ounces per ton, that's twenty ounces per load."

Nathan ran the calculation in his head. "So every truckload of ore is worth $28,000?" Nathan asked.

"That's what I meant when I said there's huge money involved. Keep in mind, 0.2 ounces per ton is on the low side. Some commercial mines yield four or five times that number."

"We're in the wrong business," Harv said.

Nathan glanced over at Staff Sergeant Lyle, who was huddled in a clump of ferns with one of his men. Lyle made eye contact and nodded an okay. Nathan looked toward the eastern horizon but didn't see any traces of morning twilight reaching through the canopy yet. "How do you know so much about this?"

"I live in Managua now. I'm a government attaché. I work with foreign mining companies, mostly Canada and the US, that want to do business in Nicaragua. I negotiate the larger contract points before the lawyers hammer out the finer details. I wine and dine them, put them up in the nicest hotels, and give them tours of existing mines and processing plants. It's a competitive business. We have to contend with South American countries to attract the commercial operators, but we can't give the leases away. My job is to find a balance between concessions and benefits. My father did the same thing before he became a pastor. I think that's why he was adamant about helping the miners of Santavilla. He felt guilty."

"I'm no expert," Nathan said, "but I would imagine starting up a large-scale mining operation requires millions of dollars."

"It absolutely does. As an example, one used Komatsu dump truck can cost close to $1 million by itself. Just changing a single tire costs tens of thousands, but the payoff can be huge. Several of our larger mines down here are producing over a hundred thousand ounces of gold annually."

"Are you serious?" Nathan asked.

"Yes, and they're not even monster mines like in South Africa, America, and Canada. Some of those overseas mines yield over a million ounces of gold annually. The US production of gold in 2012 was around two hundred thirty metric tons, that's over eight million ounces."

"It's hard to wrap my mind around that," Nathan said. "Eight million ounces?"

"Remember, it's far from pure profit. Like you said, mining gold on a large scale is expensive. It all boils down to production cost per ounce versus spot price. Big mining operators can produce gold for around five hundred dollars per ounce, so with today's spot price, it makes economic sense. Another thing to remember, gold ingots from mining operators aren't refined. The gold has to go through a refinement process before it can be sold to bullion companies or jewelry manufacturers. I always make it a point to show my clients a video of molten gold from Nicaraguan mines being poured into molds. That usually does the trick. Foreign-based mining is a hotly contested debate in our national assembly. Don't get me wrong—our country needs the gold industry, but it has to be balanced with preservation. Sadly, the worst offenders are our own people, not foreigners."

"You're a good spokesperson for the industry," said Nathan. "Your English is completely fluent."

"Thanks, it has to be. I spend a lot of time with Americans and Canadians. I've worked hard to lessen my accent. It's a lot better than it used to be."

"Didn't you raid and destroy gold mines and equipment before you were assigned to us?" Harv asked.

Estefan nodded and looked down. "Many of those mining contracts were negotiated by my father. He never even suspected I was destroying his life's work. He'd aligned himself with the Sandinistas. It's why we weren't close. Back then, he hated the Contras and everything we stood for. He had a change of heart later in life, but he never acknowledged my military service. I think he was ashamed of it."

Estefan went silent. Out of respect, Nathan and Harv waited for him to continue. The situation felt surreal. They were on the summit of a Nicaraguan mountaintop in the middle of nowhere at 0430, discussing multimillion-dollar gold-mining operations with a former student they hadn't seen in more than twenty years.

"Anyway, these local, rogue gold-mining operations are brutal," Estefan said. "I guess I never fully realized it until Raven took my father. It doesn't sting as much when it's someone else's dad. I can't believe I'll never see him again."

"I'm really sorry," Nathan said.

"We used to take lives. I guess this is what it feels like to be on the other end."

"We killed rapists and murderers. Neither Harv nor I feel the least bit guilty about what we did, and you shouldn't either. The comparison isn't valid. Your dad wasn't hurting anyone. Just the opposite. It sounds like he'd devoted his life to helping people."

"He did." Estefan fell silent again.

Nathan wanted to ask about the situation in Santavilla, but Estefan needed some time to vent. Losing a family member to murder had to be horrible—it must be sudden and jarring. Nathan knew the conversation would change direction, and it seemed rude to force it. For the moment, they had time. Without the marine recons, Nathan would've been much more anxious to get off this mountain, or at least become mobile again. He attributed some of his edginess to the horrid memories Nicaragua held for him. But, he also knew everyone up here would fight to the death for each other, and that went a long way in alleviating his angst. The expression "Once a marine, always a marine" wasn't just lip service.

"Are you okay?" Nathan asked after another silent minute.

Estefan nodded. "So what's happening is this: In Santavilla and many other remote areas, crime families and gangs are in control of small independent mining operations. They operate unpermitted sites and make kickbacks to the local authorities who look the other way. Every so often the police raid an unpermitted mine, confiscate the heavy equipment, and shut down the site, but it's usually just for show. The situation never really changes. The operation simply relocates to a different mine for a while. Small mills, like the one in Santavilla, can process about a ton of ore a day and yield three ounces of gold."

"That's a nice chunk of change," Harv said. "How many córdobas is that?"

"Last I checked, one US dollar equals around twenty-five córdobas. So it's over a hundred thousand córdobas. And that's only the income from one mill. The local mills have a production cost per ounce, but it's nowhere near a commercial operation. The cost is mostly cheap labor. My father was doing his best to educate the miners about the dangers of working with mercury."

Nathan exchanged a glance with Harv. "Mercury? What's that used for?"

"It's a crude but cost-effective way to extract the gold. Mercury amalgamates with gold."

"It does?"

"Mercury and gold are right next to each other on the periodic table. As you know, mercury's a liquid at room temperature, but because it has nearly the same atomic weight as gold, the mercury just kind of swallows the gold particles. I don't think anyone knows exactly how it works—it just does. It's still a common method of extraction used by small-scale placer mines, particularly in developing countries like Nicaragua. Using mercury to create amalgam isn't new; it's been done for thousands of years. Mercury won't combine with black sands and other heavier minerals, so it's ideal for gold panning and sluicing."

"Are you talking about gold panning, like the old forty-niners did it?"

Estefan nodded. "But the local operators do it on a bigger scale. They wash crushed ore down a slanted trough containing riffles that act like a series of dams. Because the gold is significantly heavier than the surrounding material, it gets caught behind the riffles, but it's still mixed with other heavier minerals that need to be separated out. That's where the mercury amalgam comes into play. Keep in mind, we're not talking about industrial operators—they extract gold from ore quite differently, mostly through a chemical-leaching process."

"And this crushed ore comes from a mine, I'm guessing?" Harv said.

"Right. After the ore is removed from the mine, it's broken into smaller chunks, usually by laborers with sledgehammers. Then it's hauled by mules or men to pickup trucks and driven to processing mills, where it gets tumbled in crushing drums to pulverize it. Sometimes huge grinding stones are used. The crushed ore is then run through large sluice boxes, and some of the leftover material gets panned by hand. Mercury is often added to the sluice boxes to create the amalgam."

"This all sounds pretty rough on the workers," said Nathan. "I understand why your dad got involved."

"It's terrible. There are all kinds of physical injuries. My father kept warning the workers about wearing eye protection, but few of them do it. Eye injuries are common. The laborers also suffer from hearing damage. The crushing drums are deafening. Steel balls the size of watermelons are rotated in huge steel drums to crush the ore for sluicing and panning. And then there's mercury poisoning. Women do a lot of the panning, and their hands come into contact with the mercury."

"Incredible," Harv said.

"The main processing mill is on the north side of Santavilla near the lumber mill. I remember driving past it when I visited my father several years ago. The crushing drums were loud, even from fifty yards away. The mercury poisoning represents the worst danger to the mill workers. After sufficient quantities of amalgam are made, there are several ways to separate the gold from the mercury. The best way is with a retort. The amalgam is placed in a steel capsule and heated with torches. The mercury evaporates leaving fairly pure gold behind."

Nathan asked, "What happens to the mercury? It's not lost, is it? Isn't it expensive?"

"It's actually fairly cheap. In large quantities, it costs less than fifty cents an ounce, and an ounce of mercury can go a long way because it can be used over and over. The retorts are supposed to capture and condense the mercury for reuse, but they're often not sealed properly and mercury vapor escapes. The mill workers are breathing that stuff all day long. Eventually, the mercury becomes what's known as 'dirty' and stops amalgamating with gold. It has to be discarded then."

"And I'm sure everyone disposes of it safely," Nathan said with sarcasm.

"Sadly, they don't. It gets buried or tossed in a river, or it just sits around in open containers, mostly jars and cans. Unscrupulous types try to resell it, but everybody knows dirty mercury when they see it: it doesn't have its original luster."

"This sounds like a recipe for disaster," Harv said. "Mercury around rivers and streams? It's got to create an environmental mess."

"It's an environmental disaster. The freshwater fish around here are toxic, but people still eat them. Then the mercury moves up the food chain to other animals."

"Let's get back to Raven," said Harv. "Why do you think he's the shooter?"

"My father isn't the first sniper victim near Santavilla. Other people have been killed in the same area. I had a long call with him the night before he was killed. He used the phone at the general store. We talked for over an hour. He told me there had been at least five long-distance shootings this year alone. He had specific details about a murder several months ago at the lumber mill. One of the miners who lives at the base of the mountain where the shot originated told my dad he heard the report come from somewhere above his home. The lumber mill where the man was killed is eleven hundred yards away from the mountain."

Nathan looked at Harv. "That's a good shot, but it doesn't mean Raven did it."

Estefan didn't say anything.

"Who got nailed?"

"The manager of the lumber mill. My father said the mill became profitable again after that. He thinks the manager had been skimming."

"Who owns the lumber mill?" Harv asked.

"Guess."

"The same man who owns the mines," Nathan said.

"His name is Paulo Macanas. He's known simply as El Jefe, The Boss. I'm willing to bet he's connected to a larger cartel. He conducts legitimate businesses like the lumber mill and some cattle ranches and coffee farms, but he's dirty. He either owns or directly controls everything in Santavilla. The last thing Macanas wants is for his revenue stream to be interrupted. I'm convinced that's why my father was murdered."

"I'm only speculating," said Nathan, "but don't you think killing your father just because he was educating the miners is . . . I don't know . . . extreme? Would your father really be murdered for that?"

"You're right. It doesn't make a lot of sense. He was certainly no threat to anyone. All he wanted to do was save people's lives, the very people who are needed to work the mines."

"Estefan, don't get me wrong, and I'm not suggesting anything, but I think it's reasonable to assume he wasn't killed just for trying to help the miners."

Estefan looked down and didn't respond right away. "Actually, I'm afraid *I'm* responsible for my father's death. Once I suspected Raven was the shooter, I asked my father to see what he could dig up on Macanas's gold-mining operation. I told him to be careful, to only talk to people he trusted. I shouldn't have done that. I should've known something like this would happen."

"Don't beat yourself up, Estefan. You don't know the reason why he was murdered. If Macanas's love of money goes deep enough, he might've been killed solely for the reason you suggested, for meddling in Macanas's operation. Macanas might've killed him to send a message: mess with me and you pay the ultimate price. People have been murdered for far less."

"I guess that's true, but the timing is highly suspect. A week after my father starts asking about Macanas's operation, he gets killed by a sniper."

"Does Macanas know the connection to you? Are you or your wife in danger?"

"I've considered that, but I don't think so. If Raven knew I was Tobias's son—a former kilo—I'd already be dead."

"How do you know so much about Macanas?" Nathan asked.

"I'm friends with the deputy chief of police. His office is near mine in Managua; we go to lunch a few times a year. I asked him to look into my father's murder, but I'm not holding my breath. It's no secret Macanas is a huge landowner in the area. He's got around forty square miles."

Harv asked, "Are we on Macanas's property right now?"

"No, it's a few miles farther east. Big landowners annex more property by disputing property lines. They're often successful because smaller owners usually don't have title insurance and have no way to prove they own it, and they can't afford a lawyer to defend the claim. It's a pure land grab. My friend in the police department told me Macanas has been expanding his holdings over the years. As a concession, Macanas lets the people stay in their homes, but he takes ownership of the land."

"How generous of him," Harv said.

"It's like that everywhere in the remote areas outside of the forest preserves. Nobody cares what happens. Forests are slowly being destroyed. Everyone's on the take. It's a cash society. It's the reason there's a lack of infrastructure. Not enough taxes are collected. It's getting better, but it's a difficult problem to solve."

"The problem isn't exclusive to Nicaragua," Harv said. "It's like that all over the world."

Nathan caught movement to his left.

"We've got company," Lyle called.

CHAPTER 13

"What's going on?" Nathan asked.

"Rammy spotted bleed light coming from the northeast. He thinks it's two vehicles, possibly three. His NV picked up the glow. We can't see it with the naked eye yet. ETA is seven to ten minutes."

"What's over there besides the road?" Nathan asked.

"Nothing that we know of, sir."

"How close does the road come to our position? It looked pretty close on the aerials."

"About eight hundred yards due east."

"Whoever they are, they have their headlights on . . ."

Lyle nodded. "Yes, sir. But we're still going to monitor this closely. Be ready to bug out just in case." He looked at Estefan. "Sir, is your vehicle concealed?"

"Yes, it's parked off the road. No one will see it, even in daylight."

"Stand by," Lyle said and rejoined his men.

Nathan didn't need to ask Estefan if he'd been followed—it would be an insulting question, and Estefan likely came from Managua, in the opposite direction from the vehicles. And

Estefan's kilo training had included spotting and losing tails. Nathan and Harv flipped their NVGs down to their eyes and looked to the northeast. A mile or so distant, the canopied slopes of the canyon glowed with varying intensities as two or more vehicles negotiated turns along the road. They couldn't hear any sound yet. In these conditions, Nathan expected to hear the vehicles when they closed to within a thousand yards.

"You still haven't explained why you're convinced Raven's the shooter," he said to Estefan.

"Using information my father gave me about the shootings, I plotted the kills on a map. All of the kills are within Raven's old territory—Jinotega. My territory was farther east in Atlántico Norte, where the large commercial mines are."

"Okay, that's something, but it's still not conclusive."

"Excluding military special forces, how many shooters can make a kill from over eleven hundred yards?"

Nathan didn't answer, but Estefan had a point. Aside from some highly skilled big-game hunters who didn't normally shoot people, he believed it couldn't be more than a handful. "Have you kept in touch with the other kilos over the years? Couldn't it be one of them?"

Six kilo teams, totaling twelve men, had been trained—six snipers and six spotters. Nathan and Harv had trained all twelve men.

"I've had contact with only three of the snipers over the years. Stinger moved with his family to Panama after the election. Zebra lives in Spain; he's a lawyer now. Jag lives in America. He and his wife were lucky and got work visas. Last I heard, he was a gunsmith in Texas. I'm pretty sure he got his citizenship."

"Excluding you, that leaves Raven and . . . I can't remember the last kilo."

"*Martillo*," Estefan said. "The Spanish word for hammer."

"Marty. That's right," Harv confirmed. "I remember he played the guitar and sang. He had a good voice. He was always so lighthearted and positive. I can't see him turning bad, which kinda leaves Raven."

"I've had no contact with Raven or Marty at all. If you're asking me to tell you it's Raven with one hundred percent certainty, I can't."

Nathan looked toward the source of the vehicular light, but it still wasn't visible without NV. "But you feel it," he said.

"Yeah, I do."

"That's good enough for us. Harv's trusted my instincts over the years, and he's never second-guessed me. You've earned the same respect, Estefan. I wouldn't be alive if you hadn't helped Harv. So what's your plan?"

"I don't really have one yet, but one thing's for sure: if Raven killed my father, one way or another, he's going to die."

Nathan didn't know how to respond, so he kept quiet.

"My father wrote tons of letters over the years." Estefan looked down again. "I kept all of them, but I was busy . . . and he wrote so many. I was getting three or four a week for nearly a year at one point. Lately, he'd been writing often again."

"You didn't read all of them?" Harv asked.

"I didn't care about his missionary work, but I should have. I should've visited him more too. I really regret that now. My father wasn't a scholar by any means, but he wasn't stupid. He knew what was going on in Santavilla. I guess he hoped the letters would serve as some kind of written record of his life, of what he was trying to accomplish. Some of the letters I did read had information on Macanas's mining operations. Once a week, one of his men would fly up from Managua and collect the gold. There's a helicopter pad in town somewhere. My father said everyone in Santavilla knew why the helicopter came and went. It wasn't hard to figure out. If we can find—"

"Estefan," Nathan interrupted, "what you're proposing sounds complex and will likely require extensive surveillance."

"I understand."

"Look," Harv said, "our presence down here is dangerous for a lot of reasons. We don't exactly look like locals. Except for this immediate area, we don't have aerials or road maps. How well do you know the area around Santavilla?"

"Fairly well. Because of my work, I have access to detailed topographic maps and aerials. The area around Santavilla has been identified for potential large-scale mining operations."

"I'm assuming these aerials are in Managua?" Nathan asked.

"My office is in a government building."

"How long does it take to drive down there?"

Over the sounds of the forest, they all heard a distant clank of metal on metal, followed by another noise with a slightly different pitch. To Nathan it sounded like the pickup beds being jarred by potholes in the road. They turned toward the sound and saw the glow of the headlights. Nathan glanced in Lyle's direction and saw the recon had his NVGs on. Like a statue, Lyle was totally focused on the source of the sound. The sound of two more clanks reached their position just before the vehicles the recons had spotted earlier came into sight. Their high beams looked incredibly bright against the dark background. Through clearings in the canopy, the illumination bounced and changed direction as the trucks drove closer.

They lost sight of the headlights as the trucks moved laterally below them. Nathan wondered how often this road was used. The clanking and banging from the trucks grew louder, but the noise didn't stop, which was a good sign. Gradually, the glow from the headlights started to dim as the vehicles moved away to the south.

"It takes about four hours to reach the Pan-American Highway," Estefan said. "It's another hour from there. It hasn't rained heavily, so the stream crossings won't be bad. The road those trucks just used intersects a paved road about thirty miles away, but it winds all over the place, and it's pretty rough going and slow."

Nathan needed a moment to gather his thoughts. When Nathan had been captured in Nicaragua, Estefan had dropped everything and risked his life to help Harv rescue Nathan. Although the final day of Nathan's ordeal escaped him, he recalled the rest of it with clarity. He'd endured three weeks of relentless torture before being suspended in a vertical bamboo cage that had forced him to stand. By the third day without water or food, he'd welcomed death. That kind of thirst can't be described to someone who's never experienced it. Time itself became the enemy. His tormentor had teased him by spitting water on his lacerated skin. Rage had sustained him, fueling his soul with the energy it needed to survive. Traces of that anger still haunted him and always would.

Now, Estefan needed their help, and they'd deliver. It was as simple as that. The bond they shared wouldn't be broken. Time hadn't diminished or diluted it. If Nathan died helping this man, so be it.

"It's okay," Estefan said with resignation. "I shouldn't have asked Harv to come. I didn't think it would be both of you, but I should've anticipated that. I'm sorry."

Nathan looked at Harv. No words were necessary.

"You aren't doing this alone," Nathan said.

"I can handle it."

"No, I mean you aren't doing this without *us*. Estefan, you're family to us and you always will be. We're going to help you, but we don't have unlimited time."

"That means a lot to me. Besides you guys and my wife, I don't have any family."

"No kids?" Nathan asked.

"No. My wife can't have children. I knew that when I married her."

"Harv?" Nathan asked.

"Even though we both speak Spanish, we don't have the local dialect or accent. We'd never blend in. Nathan's a good foot taller than everyone down here. At six one, I'm still a head above most of the locals."

"I blend in perfectly," Estefan said with some renewed energy. "I'll do all the legwork."

It was good to see Estefan's mood improve, but Nathan needed to make something clear. "Our help isn't unconditional."

"Okay."

"Harv and I are in command."

"That's okay with me."

"I need you to fully understand the situation. Command decisions are ours unless we ask for your input. Think about it carefully, Estefan. There will be no second-guessing us."

"I can live with that. It worked before when I was a kilo . . . I never questioned your orders."

"That's true, you didn't. Now you said you read some of your father's letters. We'll start there, with all of them, and glean what we can. But before we go down this path, Estefan, you have to really think about it. You've got a good thing going. Are you sure you want to risk everything you've accomplished? It sounds like you have an important job and a wife you love."

"Raven murdered my father."

"We don't know that for sure."

"He did it."

"All I'm saying is we need to avoid impulsive decisions and do this right. Engaging Raven in a long-distance shoot-out might not have a favorable ending. We need to take him by surprise on our terms. If what you suspect is true, he's still quite lethal. We're going to need a whole lot more information on Macanas's operation in Santavilla. When we asked if you had a plan, you gave us a goal, not a plan."

"I need to say something for the record here," Harv said. "We can't go to war against any cartels. We don't have the firepower or the ammunition for a prolonged engagement. We either make a surgical strike, or nothing at all."

"Harv's right, Estefan. You all right with that?"

"Yes."

"Now about your father's letters . . . I'm assuming they're in your home in Managua?"

"Yes."

Harv asked, "Have you had a chance to look through your father's things? He might've kept a journal or an address book."

"No, I guess I should've done that right away, but my father didn't really have much. He gave all his money to the church."

"Then it's possible whoever killed him has already looked through his belongings," Nathan said. "Especially if he was killed because he knew something critical or important about Macanas's operation. We should search his house anyway. The church too."

"That's a good idea. Whoever killed my father may have missed something."

"If all else fails," Nathan said, "we can always grease some palms. We have a hundred thousand córdobas with us; that's around $4,000 US. At the right price, everyone's for sale down here, especially the police, and it's a good bet they know something."

"What you're proposing is risky," Estefan said. "Especially if we try to bribe the wrong cop. It would be just our luck to pick someone on Macanas's payroll."

"Hell, they're probably *all* on Macanas's payroll," Harv said. "I don't like the idea of bribing anyone. That could backfire. Someone in Santavilla must know what's going on. We just have to find out who it is and get them to open up. Thinking about it more, I doubt any of the locals will cooperate. They'll be worried Macanas will get word of it."

"Leave that to me," Estefan said. "They'll talk."

"Okay, but keep this in mind: I am not in favor of hurting anyone to get what we need," Nathan said. "It's bad enough these people are dirt poor. I don't want to contribute to anyone's misery. Let's try offering some money. I have a feeling it might go a long way. You're Tobias's son. From what you told us, the town thought highly of your father. You wouldn't be perceived as a complete outsider. I'm willing to bet some of them want to see his murderer brought to justice."

"I'll try it your way first," Estefan said.

Nathan continued, "We just need to convince them they have nothing to fear from talking to you. You can use some of the info in your father's letters to gain their trust. If they realize you're on their side, they might cooperate."

"Macanas is their employer," Harv said.

"You think they'll protect him to keep their jobs? That's entirely possible. We won't know until we make the attempt." Nathan looked in Lyle's direction. "Harv and I didn't get here on our own, and we need to relay our change in plans."

"Will she be okay with it?"

"She?" Harv raised his eyebrows.

Estefan kept a neutral expression.

Nathan knew it was common knowledge a woman sat in the director's chair of the CIA. Before he could deny Estefan's comment, he heard a low whistle. Sergeant Lyle issued a hand signal to form up.

"I'll be right back."

Harv stayed behind as Nathan wove his way through the ferns to Lyle's position where the radio transmitter operator had a small keyboard deployed. The backlit screen was dimmed to a super-low setting.

"We're up," Lyle said. "We just received this."

Nathan bent down to read it. The small screen displayed one word.

STATUS?

Nathan said, "Send this: Situation stable. Messenger familiar. Extraction delayed. Expect further contact within twenty-four hours."

Lyle's RTO typed the message and sent it. A few seconds passed before a new message arrived.

COPY. NO UNNECESSARY RISKS. DO NOT ENGAGE.

"Copy that, please," Nathan said.

Lyle's man complied.

"We'd like to get off this mountain," Nathan said. "I don't know how far away our ride is, but I'll find out. We'd appreciate a tail if you have time."

"That shouldn't be a problem, sir."

"Thanks, sergeant. Did our man have NV goggles when you intercepted him?"

"No, sir."

"Do you have a spare set?"

"Yes, sir, we always carry extras." Lyle motioned to one of his men. The recon came over and took a knee. Lyle accessed the man's pack and pulled out a pair of goggles—an expensive gift. "Do you have plenty of ammo? Do you want anything else? Some stun or frag grenades? We've also got a couple of Claymores."

"You know, that's not a bad idea, but we don't have a lot of backpack space. We'll take a few stuns and frags. They might come in handy."

Back at Estefan's position, Nathan handed him the goggles and gave the explosives to Harv.

"Nice," Harv said, packing them away.

"Okay, we're bugging out. How far is your truck?"

"About a mile to the south."

"Lyle's team is going to escort us."

Estefan adjusted the NV visor to fit his head.

Nathan nodded at Estefan's hip. "Your handgun isn't suppressed."

"Understood."

"Okay, let's move out."

They shook hands with Lyle and his men and started down the mountain to the south. Nathan hadn't asked how Lyle and his men were going to be extracted. It wasn't something he needed to know and asking would've been inappropriate. He had no doubt the recons would exit Nicaragua as covertly as they'd entered.

Nathan and Harv maintained a five-yard separation; Estefan followed twenty yards behind. Even though they had a recon escort, they'd still make a stealthy approach to Estefan's pickup. The passage of the two trucks ten minutes earlier had probably been harmless, but it was tactically sound to remain on high alert. One or more men could've exited the vehicles and set up an ambush. Nathan thought that scenario was unlikely, but he didn't rule it out.

Nathan logged a mental note to thank Cantrell for the support. Finding the marines had been a pleasant surprise, and their presence reflected favorably on Cantrell's commitment to get them in and out of Nicaragua safely. Although they wouldn't see or hear Lyle's team now, knowing it was back there felt good.

Once they reached a cellular signal closer to Managua, he'd contact Cantrell using the phone she'd supplied and give her a complete update. He'd also ask her to thoroughly look into Paulo Macanas. With a little luck, the CIA might have a file on him. The murder of Estefan's father—seemingly for educating the miners on basic safety precautions—didn't seem reasonable. Something else had to be going on. Could Estefan's father be connected to Macanas? If so, how? He hoped the letters in Estefan's house would give them some answers.

He had his reservations about helping Estefan, but as long as he and Harv stayed in a support role only, their presence down here should remain secret. Cantrell had told them not to engage, but her meaning could be loosely translated into not to *actively* engage. As of now, their plan was to retrieve Pastor Tobias's letters before heading to Estefan's office for the topos and aerials. They couldn't plan much more until they had a better picture of the situation. Harv's point was well taken regarding the townsfolk not wanting to betray their employer, but there had to be somebody willing to talk.

Nathan pushed his thoughts aside. For the moment, he needed to focus on getting off this mountain safely. Although the undergrowth wasn't as thick on north-facing slopes, he maintained a slow, deliberate pace. It was easier to miss footholds going downhill. Most of the exposed rock was covered with moss and quite slippery.

As it happened, it wasn't the footing that stopped them.

Without warning, the forest erupted all around.

CHAPTER 14

A loud growl followed by a snarling yelp came from directly over Nathan's head.

What the hell!

"Harv, get down!" He instinctively dropped into the ferns and brought his Sig up.

He toggled the laser and aimed into the tree directly above him but saw nothing in the green image of his goggles.

A single voice became two, then tripled, and tripled again. Within five seconds, the entire area echoed with obnoxious grunting and barking. It sounded like a pack of rabid Rottweilers right on top of him.

His mind took a second or two to process the sounds.

Nathan looked upslope and saw Harv put Estefan on hold.

Harv's voice came through his ear speaker. *"Howler monkeys. An entire family unit."*

"So much for our stealth."

Nathan remained motionless, still recovering from the shock. The monkeys' din sounded like something out of a demented haunted house filled with screaming psychopaths. It gradually ebbed, then stopped altogether. The ensuing silence lasted a few seconds before the insects, birds, and frogs started up again. Nathan shook his head in awe at the exotic environment. He wished this place didn't hold such bitter memories.

At a small stream at the bottom of the mountain, Nathan took a knee and motioned for Harv and Estefan to advance.

Keeping his voice low, Estefan said, "Those howlers are crazy. I've heard them a lot, but it still freaks me out."

Nathan acknowledged and asked Estefan to take point for the final leg. As Estefan led them, Nathan watched his former student closely but didn't see anything alarming about his technique. The man hadn't lost his edge. He seemed acutely aware of his surroundings while being careful where to step. He was also cautious to avoid letting the undergrowth snap back after pulling it aside. If Estefan had traversed along this stream on his way up to alpha, Nathan saw no signs of it.

After a hundred yards or so, Estefan issued a form-up signal. Harv and Nathan joined him.

"My pickup is just ahead. I drove up this stream. It's around the next bend. I cut some branches to conceal it. There's no place to turn around, so I'll have to back out to the road. It's a little tricky in one place where the rocks are bigger, but I shouldn't have a problem. It's a four-wheel drive."

"We'll stay on your six. When Harv and I reach your truck, we'll keep going and scout the road. We'll climb in down there."

Estefan smiled. "I'm glad I bought a crew cab."

"Yeah, me too," Nathan said. "Stay dark and use the NVGs to drive."

"The brake and reverse lights will come on. There's no way to prevent it unless we break the bulbs."

"I think we'll be okay. After you reach your truck, give us a few minutes before you start backing out. Harv, give Estefan one of our spare radios. It's preset to our frequency, but it's not wired for stealth. We'll do that later. I'll give you a heads-up if I want you to stop for any reason."

"Just like old times," Estefan said.

Nathan and Harv reached the concealed truck and kept going. Well screened behind the cut branches, the vehicle appeared to be a fairly recent-model Ford. They couldn't see its color with the NV, but it wasn't overly bright. A minute or so later, they heard Estefan toss the cut branches aside and open the truck's door. Nathan glanced back to make sure Estefan had disabled the cab's dome lights—he had.

If all went well, they'd be on their way toward Managua in a few minutes. Nathan wished he could thank the marines again, but Lyle and his men would remain concealed. One thing was certain—they couldn't have missed the howler monkeys. Hell, anyone within a half-mile radius had heard them.

The stream followed a sweeping left turn, and they lost sight of the truck.

"Should we leave our face paint on?" Harv asked.

"At least until the sun comes up."

"What do you think about Estefan's situation?"

"We'll help him, but we can't get too involved. We'll be unsupported from this point, and I don't want to kill anyone just to avoid being taken into custody. That wouldn't sit right with me. If we help Estefan, we'll have to trust him with our lives—there's no way around it."

"I think he's already proven himself."

Nathan didn't respond. He hadn't realized until he'd said it aloud how much they'd be depending on Estefan from here on. If things spiraled out of control, they could always bolt and work their way north into Honduras, but that could take weeks. A helicopter ride from the US Navy would be infinitely preferable.

"I trust Estefan," Nathan said. "I don't think he's hiding anything from us, and I don't think he's been dishonest."

"Me either. Here's our road."

Their Nicaraguan "highway" was a single-lane dirt track that looked as primitive as any they'd ever seen. In some places, it might be possible for two vehicles to pass each other—barely. They weren't getting any sleep in Estefan's crew cab. Its potholed surface was going to rattle their fillings. A ten-foot-wide swath filled with rocks channeled the stream across the road. Two sets of muddy tire tracks trailed away from the stream toward Managua. Nathan turned his NV to maximum gain and looked in both directions. He hadn't expected to see any headlight glow and didn't.

They looked toward the sound when Estefan started his truck; it had the unmistakable drone of a diesel engine.

"NV off," Nathan said. They needed to protect the phosphorescent screens inside their devices.

Half a minute later, the bright glare from the pickup's reverse lights reflected off the water as it came into view. After their friend maneuvered onto the road, Harv climbed in next to Estefan and Nathan slid into the back, taking the middle position of the bench seat from which he could see the road ahead. Nathan turned his NV back on, and just like that, they were leaving the area.

"Leave your headlights off. NV only until the sun comes up," Nathan said. "It's tempting to use the AC, but let's leave the windows down."

"These goggles are awesome," Estefan said. "Can I keep them?"

"They're yours."

The truck jolted, and Nathan's head nearly hit the cab's roof. He hoped the road improved soon. Enduring several hours of this would grate on his nerves. In another hour or so, morning twilight would be in full effect. Although Nathan had a modest tan, his skin was significantly lighter than the locals. He'd use the brown paint stick to darken his complexion. He could also slump down in the seat to conceal his size. The tinted rear windows helped. Harv wouldn't need face paint—the Latino half of his genes was dominant. Nathan wasn't overly concerned. As long as they didn't have any close contact with law enforcement during their drive south, they'd be okay.

"What do you know about the Central American summit next week?" he asked Estefan.

Cantrell had told them not to share anything they'd discussed prior to coming down here, but bringing the subject up couldn't hurt as long as he didn't mention any specifics.

"A lot actually. Why do you ask?"

"I'm just curious." Nathan saw Harv shift his weight.

"It's not common knowledge, but it's going to be focused on the gold industry and its growth in the region. There's more gold in Nicaragua than most people know. A lot more, actually. According to my best estimates, I think there's five to six million ounces fairly close to the surface in Atlántico Norte alone. Most of the world's gold remains undiscovered or unreachable. We're probably finding less than a tenth of a percent of it."

"Why is the summit happening in Managua and not Bogotá or Caracas?"

"President Torres arranged it, and he's footing the bill. There's prestige associated with hosting the summit. He also wants to put everyone on notice that Nicaragua intends to be a player. We've already secured some big leases, and there are more in the works. The reemergence of gold mining has triggered concerns that South American countries with bigger mining operations, like Colombia and Venezuela, will try to corner the market in this part of the world. Torres doesn't want Nicaragua to lag behind."

"So by hosting the summit, Torres is telling the gold industry that Nicaragua isn't going to be bullied by the larger-producing countries."

"Yeah, that's basically it. We'll never be able to compete with super producers like the US, Canada, and China, but we can compete with South America. We also don't have all the red tape."

Harv asked, "You're talking about environmental concerns?"

"We're not irresponsible when it comes to the permitting process, but it doesn't take years and dozens of costly studies either.

Labor costs are significantly lower. It's easier and more cost effective to set up shop down here."

They rode in silence for a few miles.

Millions of ounces of gold? It seemed surreal. Nathan hadn't given it much thought before now, but that kind of money had to invite corruption. And probably did.

"We need to find out where Macanas lives," Nathan said. "If Raven's a gun for hire, there's a good possibility he's working for the man."

"It's not a coincidence all the sniper murders are in or around Santavilla," Estefan said. "Think about it. The man who ran Macanas's lumber mill was murdered, and the mill suddenly started producing again. My father was murdered, because he was trying to help the miners who work at Macanas's sites. A helicopter comes and goes regularly from Santavilla. It's not hard to figure out what's being taken out of there. All roads lead to Macanas. If we find him, we'll find Raven."

"Is there any way you can discreetly ask your lunch partner in the police department for an address? Do you know him well enough?"

"I can try, but he'll want to know why I'm asking."

"Yeah, you're right. It's a red flag. My instinct says hold off on doing that for now. If word gets back to Macanas that Estefan Delgado is asking about his personal information, bad things will happen. If we run out of options, you can talk to your police friend as a last resort. We may be able to make that work for us, not against. You said you've already mentioned your father's murder to him, but you didn't name any suspects, did you?"

"No, I didn't."

"Then so far, no one knows you're Tobias's son. I'd like to keep it that way."

"There are people in Santavilla who know, but they have no reason to mention me. From what I remember reading in my father's letters, they don't like Macanas much even though he gives them work."

After a few seconds Nathan said, "Pull over at the next open store or roadside stand you see. We all need food. Harv and I haven't eaten much since yesterday. We'd prefer to save the MREs we brought with us. We'll wait in your truck. Grab a case of bottled water too."

Over the next half hour, Nathan watched the landscape gradually brighten, revealing the forest's true nature—a mixture of every shade of green imaginable. The landscape looked similar to that of other tropical forests. Every so often they passed a rusting sheet-metal hut or decaying barn, but there was no sign of human presence. Small farms and ranches lined the road, but from the look of things, most of these people lived in abject poverty.

"It's getting pretty light out," Nathan said. "We should change clothes and remove our face paint."

Nathan pulled Harv's clothes from his backpack and handed them forward. Both of them swapped their MARPATs for cargo shorts, T-shirts, and flip-flops. Aside from their height, they ought to blend into the civilian population fairly well. Bill Stafford had made the wardrobe suggestions based on what the majority of Nicaraguan locals wore. Blue jeans were popular but bulkier, and they had limited space in their backpacks. Although they hadn't anticipated needing civilian clothes, they were glad they'd brought them. Nathan also applied a fair amount of brown skin paint in an effort to darken his skin and cover the contours of his facial scars.

Finally, Estefan made the right turn onto a much better road. Its surface, although rough, looked to be regularly bladed by a road grader. They drove through village-like pockets of civilization where no more than several dozen people lived, while other towns looked to be home to several hundred. None of them qualified as cities in the traditional definition. Unfortunately, none of the places where they could buy food were open yet. Their hunger would have to wait. Nathan expected Santavilla to look similar to one of these towns. Most of them had churches, general stores, small shops, taverns, cafes, and painted-plywood roadside stands.

Nathan kept checking his cell, but it didn't register a strong signal yet. They were still in a predominately rural area. He didn't want to make a call to Cantrell until they had at least two bars of coverage. Nathan was sure he'd get a better signal further south. Until then, Cantrell would have to wait. The delay turned out to be fairly short. Fifteen miles closer to Managua, his phone picked up three bars.

"We've got coverage, but it may not last," Nathan said. "Estefan, see if you can find a place to pull over where Harv and I can get out without drawing too much attention."

"I'll turn onto a side road and drive a safe distance away from the highway."

"Sounds good."

"Harv, will you grab my cell from the glove box?"

"Hey, no texting and driving," Nathan said.

"I never do," Estefan said. "I'll check it when you guys climb out to make your call."

Estefan found a good spot and made the turn. Barbed wire lined both sides of the road, but no animals were present. The primitive dirt track didn't show any signs it had been used since the last rain.

"There doesn't appear to be any place to turn around. How far do you want me to go?"

"The road curves to the left in that valley up ahead. We don't want to drive into someone's front yard. Let's go another five hundred yards. Backing out to the highway shouldn't be a problem."

"For who?" Estefan said with a smile.

Although their friend was emotionally frayed, he seemed to be in good spirits. Nathan didn't want to ruin the mood by talking about the difficulty of what Estefan planned to do, but sooner or later, Nathan would need to reaffirm they didn't have unlimited time down here to conduct a prolonged surveillance of Macanas's gold-mining operations. At this point, they didn't even know where the guy lived. If Macanas possessed the kind of wealth Estefan suspected, he probably owned several homes. Unless Estefan had a reliable source within law enforcement, they'd have to rely on Cantrell, and if she couldn't produce anything on Macanas, they'd have to start from scratch and learn what they could from people who lived in Santavilla. Nathan didn't like their odds.

Harv grabbed Estefan's cell from the glove compartment, handed it to his friend, and got out of the truck. He and Nathan walked several pickup lengths farther up the road. They were well screened from the highway by chest-high weeds and bushes growing along the base of the fence. The fields on both sides of the road had been plowed, but whoever did the tractor work had kept a safe distance from the wire.

Nathan tapped Cantrell's number and waited, allowing her phone to ring ten times before hanging up.

Within seconds, their phone received a text from Bill Stafford's number.

ten minutes

Nathan looked at his watch. "Let's get going."

"We may lose our cell signal farther down the road."

"The sun's coming up. We're not hanging around here. Besides, the call isn't that urgent." They walked back to the truck.

Estefan backed out to the road. "When you guys get your return call, I'll pull over and get out."

"Good idea," Nathan said. "I guess we should've done that back there."

"No harm done," Estefan said.

A few miles farther south, they entered the outskirts of a larger town that looked to be home to several thousand people. Nathan checked his cell. Three bars. "It's still early, but with a little luck we'll find a place to grab a bite. Keep an eye out for a diner or roadside stand. At this point, I'd settle for anything other than an energy bar." Near the center of town at a major intersection, Nathan looked around and saw what they needed. "Make a right here."

"I see it," Estefan said.

They pulled up to a curio and fruit stand where the owner was still setting up shop. Estefan rolled his window down and asked if she was willing to open a little early. She nodded and continued unloading wares from her van.

"I'll get a good mix of fruit. If she's got some pork jerky, I'll get some. Nuts too."

"Sounds good," Nathan said. "Offer her a nice tip for opening early but not too big. We don't want to be remembered."

"No problem. Give me a wave if you get your call while I'm out there. I'll delay getting back in."

After Estefan climbed out, Harv suggested sending a text to Stafford saying now would be a good time to talk.

A few seconds later, Nathan's phone rang. He issued a single word. "Chromium."

"I've got you on speaker. Bill's with me." Cantrell's voice sounded clear and unbroken.

"We're secure. Thank you for sending in the recons."

"You're welcome. I wouldn't have inserted you without them, but I couldn't let you know ahead of time. Their presence in-country is as unofficial as yours."

"We appreciate it and understand."

"What's your status?"

"As we suspected, our messenger is a former kilo grad. A shooter, not a spotter. His name is Estefan Delgado. He's the man who helped Harv rescue me from Montez's camp. His father was Pastor Tobias."

"Do you trust him?"

He exchanged a glance with Harv. "Yeah, we do."

"What about Raven?"

"That's where it gets complicated. Estefan can't tell us with one hundred percent certainty that Raven's responsible for his father's murder, but he's given us a strong argument." Nathan relayed all the information about the sniper killings in the area.

"Given everything I just heard, I'm tending to agree with Mr. Delgado. It sounds like Raven's your man."

"Estefan wants to kill him."

"And . . . ?"

"The man risked his life to rescue me."

"I'll take that as a yes."

From the fruit stand, Estefan looked over. Harv simulated a phone to his ear. Estefan nodded understanding.

"If you're willing," said Nathan, "we could use some help. We need whatever you can dig up on a man named Paulo Macanas. He's a landowner who runs some legitimate businesses. He owns a lumber mill in Santavilla and operates some cattle ranches and coffee farms. He also owns several gold mines. Gold is the reason Estefan asked for our help."

Nathan gave Cantrell a quick overview of what Estefan told them about Santavilla, the gold-mining operation, and the connection to the slaying of Tobias Delgado.

She said, "On the surface, it doesn't sound like a good enough reason for murder."

"We thought the same thing and pushed Estefan a little. Because there were multiple shootings in Raven's old territory, he told us he'd asked his father to see what he could learn. I think it's fair to assume Tobias discovered something and got himself killed over it."

"Based on everything you know at this point, is there a national security risk?"

"My gut says no. On the surface, it appears to be a personal issue between Raven and Estefan." Nathan filled her in on what Estefan had shared about the summit.

"We'll look into that. So what's your next move?"

"We're heading down to Estefan's house in Managua. His father wrote hundreds of letters about what was happening in Santavilla. We're going to read them and hope they give us something useful. We're also going to access some maps and aerials to get a better handle on Macanas's operation."

"How much additional time do you need?"

"I don't know, maybe a few days. We made it clear to Estefan we can't conduct a prolonged surveillance of Macanas's operation."

"I've got your current GPS location around eighty-five miles northeast of Managua."

"We've been driving for a while. In a straight line, that distance sounds about right."

"I want you to give Bill Stafford regular updates. He'll brief me."

"No problem."

"Give me as much lead time as possible for your extraction. I'll have to set it up again. Unless something happens to change it, your extraction point will be the same coordinates as planned."

"Are you giving us the nod on Raven?"

"That's your call. I won't second-guess you on it."

"Understood."

"I'll have Stafford update you if we find anything on Macanas."

"Apparently he owns a helicopter. I wouldn't be surprised if he has a helipad at his house. From what Estefan told us, he's fairly wealthy."

"I'm making a note. We might be able to do something with it. Try to keep your profile as small as possible."

Nathan sighed and rubbed his eyes. "Will do. We'll check in with Stafford after we've looked at the letters."

"When was the last time you two slept?"

"It's been a while. The road leaving alpha was pretty rough. We should be okay from here on. We'll catch a few z's on the drive into Managua."

"Make sure you do."

Nathan ended the call. "Any doubts about her at this point?"

"Honestly, it's hard not to like her."

Nathan waved Estefan over. "But liking and trusting are two different things, right? Come on, Harv. She didn't have to arrange the marines. I think it's a clear statement. Setting that up with JSOC couldn't have been easy."

"Easy enough. All she did was make a call or two."

"You know what I mean. She put troops in harm's way. Yes, that's her job, but that doesn't make it easy. Cut her some slack. She's earned our confidence."

"If you say so."

"Yeah, I do. And so do you."

Estefan climbed in and handed the box of fruit back to Nathan.

"Good job, Estefan. Keep the change."

"How generous of you. Our merchant was quite thankful for the tip. She had some homemade pastries, so I bought a couple dozen. We'll stop for some jerky closer to Managua. I know a good spot."

"How long to your house from here?"

"From here . . . maybe two and a half hours, depending on traffic."

"Harv, we should try to get some rack time."

"Yeah, that sounds good."

They all saw and heard it at the same time.

A Nicaraguan National Police pickup turned right at the center of town and drove straight toward them.

CHAPTER 15

"Everyone stay calm," Nathan said. "Estefan, be ready to punch it. We aren't being taken into custody. If we have to bolt, we'll head back toward alpha and try to lose him on the far side of town through those S turns." Nathan began formulating a plan. If they had to evade the cop, they'd need to disable his vehicle without injuring him.

The NNP pickup's front end lifted as it accelerated down the narrow street. They all collectively held their breath as the pickup screamed past. Its driver didn't even look at them.

"Damn it," Harv said. "I really hate that feeling."

"Let's get going," Nathan said. He looked behind and saw the cop make a left about a hundred yards farther down the road.

"No argument here," Estefan said. He made a U-turn and drove back to the intersection.

"We're all on edge," Nathan said.

"We'll be able to relax a little when we reach my house. We can pull into the garage. No one will see you guys. I'll call my wife and ask her to head over to her sister's and spend the day over there. She knows I get nervous when she's alone for more than a few days."

"Is your house somewhat secluded?" Nathan asked.

"It's not extremely close to other houses. Most of the lots are about three acres. I'm in a semirural area at the top of a ridgeline overlooking Managua. It has a nice view of the city. Don't worry. We'll have the place to ourselves."

Nathan handed a banana to Harv. "Won't it be . . . I don't know . . . a little awkward? Asking your wife to leave for the day?"

"Not really. She's been wanting to visit her sister for a few weeks. We just talked about it before I left to meet you guys. I'll tell her I got delayed. She'll be fine with it."

"Sounds good. Nate and I could use showers and some serious rack time. That hump through the jungle took a toll on us."

"Getting old?" Estefan asked.

"Just drive, amigo."

***

When Estefan pulled into his garage and closed the door, Nathan felt a tremendous sense of relief at not having to worry about prying eyes any longer. It would be nice to unwind for a spell. All three of them needed hygiene and sleep—in that order. Neither he nor Harv had gotten more than six hours in the last two days. They couldn't function indefinitely like this. Sooner or later, fatigue would win the battle and shut their brains down. Nathan had been through longer periods without sleep, but there was no reason to push it right now. As tempting as it was to dig into Tobias's letters, it could wait. Estefan agreed and threw their MARPATs and underclothes into the washing machine. Since none of Estefan's wardrobe would fit Nathan, he had to settle for a pair of Estefan's tighty-whities, and the damned things were two sizes too small.

When he stepped out of the bathroom, Harv gave him an amused look.

"Don't even think it."

Harv feigned innocence. "What?"

Estefan's expression registered shock, but he recovered quickly.

Nathan held up a hand. "If either of you say anything, you'll die slowly."

"What's there to say?" Estefan said. "I think a couple of things speak for themselves. What do you think, Harv? Can he get a job downtown?"

"In a heartbeat."

"I'm going to kill you guys."

Estefan crossed his arms. "What are you going to do—dance us to death?"

"That would do the trick," Harv said. "The man has no rhythm. It's an ugly thing to watch."

This was hopeless. Until the load of laundry was finished, Nathan would have to settle for looking like a male stripper. He issued a dismissive wave and left the room, heading for the kitchen. He knew anything he said could and would be used against him, so he chose to remain silent.

In the kitchen, he powered down a couple of pastries and chased them with a glass of milk and two mangoes. Feeling more composed, he found Harv in one of the spare bedrooms, stretched out on top of a beautiful quilt. If Estefan's wife had made it, she was a skilled artist.

"I'll be on the couch," Nathan said.

"Don't forget to warn Estefan about waking your ass up with a broom. I'm pretty sure he wants to keep all his teeth."

"Cute, Harv. I can always count on you for moral support."

"Sleep well, partner."

"Yeah, right."

Thankfully, his inner demons took the afternoon off. Sleep came in chunks, an hour or so at a time, but sleep was sleep, and Nathan took it.

Right on time, the cell's alarm awoke him at 1700 hours.

He needed coffee; they were facing another long evening. He found Harv in the kitchen, standing at the counter next to the range-oven combo.

"How did you sleep?" Harv asked.

"Not too bad, thanks."

"Your MARPATs are on the dining room table. I've been thinking about something."

"What's that?" Nathan asked.

"When you got out of the shower, you could've gone commando in your cargo shorts."

"Yeah, I know."

"So why didn't you?"

Nathan lowered his voice. "I think Estefan's more torn up about his father than he's leading on. I figured I'd lighten the mood."

"That was quite selfless of you, but it doesn't surprise me. You've always been a giving person."

"You too, Harv. Let's go sort through those letters."

"We still need to retrieve the aerials and topo maps and look into the public records on Macanas. Like Estefan said, if we find Macanas, we'll find Raven."

"Estefan's already got them." Harv handed him a cup of coffee.

"I didn't hear him leave."

"We pushed his truck out of the garage. We didn't want to wake you. He parked it on the curb when he got back."

"What about an address for Macanas from the public property records?"

"Estefan told me how it works. It's not that easy to get down here. Well, it kind of is, but there's no centralized database in Managua. Each city has its own cadastral office with survey records of the land. Nicaragua's a small country. He said if he went into the Jinotega office and pointed to Macanas's property on a big map, it's a safe bet the staff will already know the book and page numbers. He said he works with the various cadastral offices to determine ownership on land bordering the forest preserves all the time. He uses the information to contact the owners about pending road improvements through their property."

Estefan entered the kitchen. "What're you guys talking about?"

Nathan said, "Getting a home address on Macanas."

"Yeah, that might not be easy," Estefan said. "He's likely hidden his personal information by using shell companies as the owners of record. And those companies might be owned by second-tier shell companies. He's probably got attorneys on retainer who handle all the real estate paperwork for him. If that's the case, all inquests about ownership would have to funnel through his attorney's office. Macanas would then know someone was snooping into his property, and he'd want to know who and why."

"We definitely don't want that. Do you think it's worth a try? I mean, looking at the survey records?" Harv asked. "Do you have to sign a logbook or anything to look at the books?"

"No, but the cadastral office staff is often bored to tears. They'd be looking over my shoulder the whole time. I've been in the Jinotega office many times. We could hire an attorney to dig into Macanas's land-ownership holdings, but it would take time and be really expensive."

"Wouldn't that also raise red flags with Macanas?" Harv asked.

"It definitely would. He'd find out about it for sure. I'm fairly certain we won't find a residential address for Macanas in any of the cadastral surveys."

"Tell Nate what you told me about that large property purchase two years ago."

"A large chunk of land bordering Macanas's property was jointly purchased by two corporations. Jinotega Norte Corporation and EMI. I remembered doing a Google search. Nothing came up for Jinotega Norte, but there were a bunch of listings for EMI, and one of them jumped out at me. Edmonton Mining Industries is a medium-sized Canadian company that primarily extracts copper, silver, gold, and uranium. It operates several sites around the world."

"Uranium? Is that being mined in Nicaragua?"

"No," Estefan said.

"Could a uranium mine be in the works?"

"Absolutely not. I'd know about it for sure."

"Is there uranium in Nicaragua?" Harv asked.

"Technically, yes. It's found all over the world, but concentrated uranium ores are rare. Australia, Kazakhstan, and Canada are some of the bigger producers. Super-high-grade deposits are only found in Saskatchewan."

"What about copper and silver?"

"It's quite common for gold mines to also contain copper and silver in the ores. Some of the mines in Atlántico Norte are producing silver, but extracting copper isn't as cost effective."

"Estefan, don't take this wrong, but why didn't you look into Jinotega Norte? Didn't the connection to EMI make you curious?"

"I *was* curious, but two years ago before any of the murders, it didn't look out of place. It was before I suspected Raven was working for Macanas. EMI hadn't approached any landowners about leasing, and neither company applied for any mining permits. It looked like an investment or land-banking purchase."

"I see what you mean. The purchase seems suspect now, but back then . . ."

"That's right. Unless specifically requested, my office . . . well, me . . . I don't generally get involved in private-party sales or leases. My jurisdiction is over government-owned land, mostly forest preserves. It's like the Bureau of Land Management in the US. If a logging company buys some private property bordering BLM land, the BLM would get involved to make sure streams and rivers were protected from silt damage. Rivers cross from private to public land and vice versa. It works the same way down here, but many mining sites are bootlegged, so there's no environmental oversight."

"Are any of Macanas's mines permitted?" Harv asked.

"Yes, but not very many. He permits just enough to keep the heat off."

"What would you bet that Jinotega Norte is a Macanas-owned shell company?"

"I'd bet a lot," Estefan said. "If Macanas owns Jinotega Norte, the question becomes, why did he buy the land jointly with EMI?"

"That's a good question. Do you know how much land was purchased? Maybe it was beyond his reach alone."

"I don't remember exactly, but it was a pretty sizable chunk. I remembered it because it was within my overlay area of potential high-yield sites in Jinotega."

Nathan broke into the conversation. "Maybe the question should be reversed. Why would EMI need Macanas to make the purchase?"

"Yeah, I see what you mean. A company like EMI would pursue a long-term lease rather than make a purchase."

"Do other mining corporations buy land like that?" Harv asked.

"It's not unheard of, but most of the landowners don't want to sell. They're way better off leasing than selling. They get a bunch of money and get to keep their land."

"Is EMI currently operating any mines in Nicaragua?"

"No," Estefan said, "but we're being looked at by dozens of commercial operators, including EMI. It's the primary reason Torres is hosting the gold summit. Nicaragua is a hot prospect right now."

"It seems we've got more homework to do."

They followed Estefan into his office. Inside the closet, concealed by a long raincoat, Nathan saw a gun safe. It looked capable of storing ten or twelve long guns with enough room for an upper shelf. It employed a combination dial and a brass handle on its door.

"Why do you keep the letters in your safe?" Harv asked.

"It's fire resistant." He shrugged. "I guess they're important to me, even though I didn't bother to read most of them." Estefan opened the safe and removed two shoe boxes from the shelf. Behind the shoe boxes sat half a dozen boxes of various ammo and several handgun cases.

Nathan pointed. "It looks like you kept your Remington 700."

"I offered to buy it when our kilo unit broke up, but no one could tell me who to pay, so my lieutenant told me to keep it. All of us kept our rifles. I haven't used it in years."

"You still keep a three-hundred-yard zero?" Harv asked.

"Just like you taught me."

"Let's talk about how we're going to tackle these letters. Did your father date them?" Nathan asked.

"I think so, but I'm not positive."

They carried the shoe boxes out to the dining room table.

"We'll start by making sure all the letters are opened. Then we'll put them in chronological order as best we can. Let's reserve reading them until we have them organized."

"I'll get us a couple of kitchen knives." Estefan returned a moment later.

Nathan grabbed a stack that was secured by a rubber band. "Once we have them in order, we'll dig in. Each of us should have a pad of paper for making notes. Estefan, do you care if we color code the letters with a highlighter? I'm thinking we should put colored dots on the letters based on their relevancy to Macanas's operations. A green dot for important, a yellow dot for maybe, and a red dot for not relevant."

"Sounds good," Estefan said. "I'll get the highlighters from my office. I'll also grab a stapler for any letters with more than one sheet."

After Estefan left the room, Nathan shook his head. "He wasn't kidding about these letters."

"Looks like there's several hundred, and some of the envelopes look kinda thick. This might take a while."

"Hopefully, we can knock it out in a couple of hours. Not all of them will have what I'd consider tactical info. Most of them will probably have a mix of personal and tactical; we'll just have to sort through them."

"I'll start opening the sealed envelopes."

It took about fifteen minutes to get the letters in chronological order. They ended up with three stacks, each stack spanning a one-year period. Everyone grabbed a pile and began reading.

"Let's look for common elements," said Nathan. "If you see a name or place, like Macanas or general store, write it down on your pad. Every time you see the same name or place again, put a check mark next to it with the letter's date in parenthesis. With a little luck, we'll find people and places that are mentioned with some frequency. There's got to be someone in these letters we can talk to. It's reasonable to assume your father had the confidence of someone who fed him information on Macanas. Either that, or he overheard stuff. People love to talk."

"I remember reading some pretty detailed letters. I can't remember any specifics, but there were definitely names mentioned."

"We'll know soon enough," Nathan said. "After we've got them color coded, we'll use our notepads to make lists of names and places. Each of us can take a stack."

An hour later, a pattern emerged. Most of the letters expressed Tobias's concern for the safety of the mill workers and miners. Several key people and places were mentioned over and over. The two people mentioned most often were the general store's owner, Mrs. Perez, and the work bus driver, a man named Mateo. The three most referenced locations were the church, the general store, and the lumber mill. The open-pit mines north of town were chronicled with some frequency as well. About a third of the letters made some kind of reference to Macanas's bootleg operations and the periodic helicopter visits. Everyone in Santavilla seemed to know that gold was being flown out of there on a regular basis.

Mateo appeared to be a semiprominent figure in town. Although Tobias hadn't actually said so, it was clear he thought Mateo knew a fair amount about Macanas's gold-mining operation. If Mateo would be willing to talk to Estefan, they might get somewhere.

"Did you guys see a telephone number for Mateo anywhere?"

Neither of them had, but Estefan had seen Mrs. Perez's home number written on the back of one of the letters. He'd written it down in his notes.

"Apparently, Mrs. Perez and Pastor Tobias were close friends," Estefan said.

Nathan thought he heard a little resentment. He wanted to question how close but decided discretion was the right play. Besides, it didn't matter. "Let's give her a call," Nathan said. "She's probably got Mateo's number. Think she'll talk to you, Estefan?"

"Based on everything I read, I'm pretty sure she will."

Estefan put his phone on speaker and made the call. Mrs. Perez answered, and a minute later they had a phone number to Mateo's house. During the call, Mrs. Perez's biggest concern was over secrecy. Estefan assured her they were both in the same boat and that their conversation would never be repeated to anyone. Mrs. Perez also told them Mateo should be home, but it would be better to call him earlier than later. It seemed Mateo suffered from severe alcohol impairment after 7:00 PM. When Estefan called Mateo's house, a young woman answered. A few seconds later Mateo was on the line. They heard him issue a muffled command, presumably to the same young woman to go outside and give him some privacy. It took some convincing, but Mateo agreed to meet Estefan late tonight, especially after Estefan referenced some monetary compensation. No surprise there.

Nathan had no doubt the young woman who answered the phone was Antonia, Mateo's daughter. She was frequently mentioned in Tobias's letters. Tobias hadn't said anything too specific about her, except that she seemed to be somewhat reserved. One of the letters from last year mentioned Mateo's concern about some creepy looks Antonia had received from one of Macanas's white shirts.

One thing became clear from Tobias's letters: Estefan was right about Macanas controlling the town. It had little to no police presence, and even when an NNP officer cruised through town, no one spoke to him. It seemed like Macanas and his men maintained an iron-fisted reign over Santavilla.

It surprised Nathan to read that for the most part, the residents of Santavilla seemed somewhat content. Tobias often wrote about their indifference or lack of ambition. It seemed they'd given up and resigned themselves to a life of poverty. Antonia, however, was one of the few exceptions. She'd argued with her father extensively about wanting to leave Santavilla. But where could she go? Without money, her options were limited. Many of Tobias's letters mentioned her resentment about the situation. She seemed unwilling to accept the idea of living the rest of her life in a crappy little town full of losers and drunks. Quite honestly, Nathan didn't blame her. Life in Santavilla lacked any kind of excitement or change. It had to be tough, feeling like things were hopeless with no way out.

It seemed many families were being torn apart by substance abuse, and it wasn't always the men who were the problem. Some of the women in Santavilla could drink and smoke their men under the tables. Since Mrs. Perez and her husband owned the general store, most of the letters containing her name also referenced their store. Many of them mentioned how devoted Mrs. Perez was to Pastor Tobias's church. She was one of its biggest donors.

After they had a fairly clear picture of the key players and locations, they turned their attention to the aerial photos. Over the last five years, Estefan said he'd been to Santavilla fewer than ten times but had a pretty good idea where the major buildings were. He'd always stayed in the local motel rather than his father's hut. Nathan didn't think it was a statement of Estefan's social status; he simply preferred having running water and a functioning toilet.

Estefan grabbed the cardboard tube containing the aerials, pulled them free, and laid them on the dining room table. There were three, each map was about one meter square. All of them were centered on the small church. The 1:500-scale sheet offered the best detail, but it didn't include the lumber mill to the north or the wooden bridge to the south.

"Estefan, I'm a little rusty on this stuff. What distance does one inch cover on this 1:500 aerial?"

Estefan closed his eyes, concentrating. "Let's see . . ."

"Your phone should have a calculator," Harv told Nate. "We need to be as precise as possible. Since these maps use the metric system, we'll make some conversions. A meter isn't much longer than a yard."

Nathan pulled it from his pocket. "Give me the numbers, Estefan."

"Okay, like Harv said, one meter is 39.3 inches. So divide five hundred by that number."

"Got it. It's 12.72. So every inch equals 12.72 meters. One meter is 1.1 yards, so each inch equals . . . 13.9 yards." Nathan crunched a few more numbers. "Okay, so on the 1:500 scale aerial, one inch equals forty-two feet. The 1:2000 aerial is going to be four times that. Each inch becomes 168 feet or so, or just over . . . fifty-six yards. Let's be conservative and say it will take seven seconds to run one inch on this aerial. That means it will take one minute to sprint from the church due east to the river. The lumber mill is just over a one-minute dash. Let's calculate and memorize some additional numbers using the church as the anchor point."

They spent a few minutes marking the aerial with an orange highlighter and wrote the sprint times in black marker next to the colored lines. They allowed for changes in direction and unforeseen obstacles like fences and walls by padding the numbers slightly.

"As you can see, the topographic lines are only on the 1:10000 aerial. These are Macanas's open-pit mines." Estefan pointed to the top edge of the map. "As the crow flies, they're about one mile from the church and about half a mile from the lumber mill. I should be able to identify some of the prominent buildings in town." He moved his finger along the main road bisecting the town on the 1:2000 aerial. "Pretty much everything's along this road."

"That's definitely the church," Nathan said. "You can see the shadow of its steeple on the roof below. Let's study the basic layout of the town, so when we get there we can minimize our radio chatter."

Nathan was a quick study. Based on Estefan's input, he had a pretty good idea of the town's layout within a few minutes. The valley containing Santavilla was mostly flat. Although much larger in scale, the basin below the surrounding mountains was roughly the same shape as a football stadium field—a giant oval. The river followed the east side of the valley along the base of a sickle-shaped mountain. Everything had a gentle slope toward the river. Santavilla basically sat atop a thick alluvial buildup—higher on the west, lower on the east. Small farms and ranches surrounded the buildings near the center of town. Houses were interspersed across the valley like randomly thrown pebbles. It looked like a thousand other small towns nestled in mountainous valleys. The topo map indicated the town's elevation was two thousand feet. The open-pit mines were about five hundred feet higher, and the wooden bridge to the south was two hundred feet lower. As Estefan had indicated, the town was bisected by a thirty-foot-wide dirt road running north and south. Beyond the town to the north, the valley pinched down to a narrow gorge where the road wove its way up the canyon to the open-pit mines.

"Okay," Nathan said. "Let's make sure we've got this right. On the right side of the road, the prominent buildings are the church, some larger homes, Mateo's place, a vacant lot, the general store, and then the motel. On the left, we've got the Laundromat, the post office, the tavern, an abandoned building, and a small gas station. The northeast quadrant of town is where the ore-processing plant and lumber mill are located. Farms and ranches surround the outskirts all the way out to the river. It may only be a stream by most standards, but let's call it the river. At the river's south end, about two hundred yards from the wooden bridge, it looks like there's a sizable pond created by a dam that doubles as a crossing. It looks kinda marshy in these photos near the water's edge, so let's be sure we check that out before getting bogged down in the mud. Although the church isn't the commercial center of town, it's the geographic center, so let's call it our zero and vector all other buildings from there. Everyone aboard with my assessment?"

Nathan received nods.

"Estefan, anything you want to add?"

Their friend pointed to a curved line heading away from the river to the ore-processing plant. On the other side of the plant, it curved back to the river, but it looked wider on the south side. "That's the supply canal to the sluice boxes in the ore-processing plant. Freshwater enters the plant; silted water leaves. The exit canal has to be constantly dredged to keep the flow going."

"Can we get across the canal?" Harv asked.

"Yes, but I don't advise going across the exit side—it's muddy and soft from the constant supply of silt runoff. Lots of miners pan for residual gold along the exit side because the sluice boxes don't catch all of it. Some slips through."

"When we enter the valley, drop us here." Nathan pointed to a spot below the wooden bridge. "Harv and I will head up this mountain to the east and find a place that overlooks the town. The trees look thick down by the water, but the north-facing slope higher up looks less dense. We'll find a good spot to hunker down and watch your back. We'll be in constant radio communication with each other. We'll wire you for stealth—"

Estefan's cell rang. "It's my wife. I asked her to call around six thirty. I should take this. I'll be right back. Two minutes." With his phone still ringing, Estefan left the dining room.

"What do you think?" Harv asked.

"If you're asking what I think you're asking, I'm not real thrilled about this op."

"Me either." They remained silent for a long moment. "Look," Harv said, "I know you don't want to interrogate anyone, but we need a lot more information than we found in the letters. If greasing some palms doesn't work, we should consider . . . alternatives."

Nathan didn't respond. He didn't have to. Harv was right. There was more at stake than either of them wanted to admit. Even though no national security issue existed, it didn't diminish the fact that Raven was a product of their training. They created him, and they now needed to destroy him. He was their responsibility. Why else would Cantrell have sent them down here? As Nathan had noted in the armored SUV after they'd landed at Dulles, Cantrell had Central American assets available to her. Younger and better trained—

"What are you thinking about?"

"Huh?"

"You were gone," Harv said.

"I felt a brief lapse of faith. It was unsettling."

"Cantrell?"

Nathan nodded. "I dismissed the thought. She's not withholding anything we need to know. I'm certain of it."

"I admire your resolve, even though I don't share it. Don't get me wrong, she'd never betray us, but she'll never be completely honest either. She can't—her job description doesn't allow it."

"On that, Harv, we agree."

Estefan reentered the dining room and apologized for the interruption. He said his wife was coming home around 7:30 PM, which gave them another half hour to study the aerials.

Before leaving, they grabbed a few more things that might come in handy. Estefan's camera and telephoto lens topped the list. They wouldn't be taking any photos until daybreak tomorrow, but it couldn't hurt to bring it along. They split up the grenades Sergeant Lyle had given them and secured everything in their packs. To make room for all the tactical stuff, they removed their civilian clothes and put them in one of two spare backpacks that Estefan had. They loaded the other spare pack with canned food, fruit, and bottled water. Finally, Estefan added a few more camping items, including a charcoal water-filter kit and a small folding shovel.

"If you're planning to bury Raven," Nathan said, "you might want something a little more substantial."

Estefan shrugged. "I'll let him rot. The ants need food too."

Five minutes later they were on their way.

CHAPTER 16

This had to be one of the worst traffic jams Caracas had ever seen. Juan Batista, Venezuela's minister of basic industry and mining, couldn't believe the timing. If this mess didn't clear up soon, he'd miss his flight to Managua. What a pain in the ass. He'd have to charter a jet, assuming his staff could even find one available. The Central American summit was two days from now, and it would be very bad form to arrive late.

There must have been some kind of accident ahead. He looked at his watch—a little after 7:30 PM. The traffic shouldn't be this snarled. His limousine was stopped dead, and his lane of traffic hadn't moved more than ten meters in the last half hour. Tempers were short. Horns were blaring, and the collective din added to his irritation. At least he didn't have to brave the heat. The air-conditioning kept his environment at a comfortable 20 degrees Celsius.

He pulled his cell and made a call.

"I'm stuck in traffic a few kilometers from the airport," he told his secretary. "See if you can book me on a later flight tonight. If nothing's available, find me a charter-jet service. I want to be in Managua tonight."

"Yes, sir. I'll get right on it."

He ended the call and turned to his aide. "What's the expression? Shit happens?"

"Don't worry. We'll get you there on time for tomorrow's reception breakfast. Carmen's a resourceful woman. She'll take care of everything."

"I guess this is the price of progress."

"Indeed it is."

Juan looked out his tinted window. The entrepreneurial spirit was plainly evident. Dozens of street vendors were taking advantage of the stopped traffic. Children were selling gum and other trinkets, and they seemed to be doing well. Juan smiled, knowing no tax would be collected from these cash sales.

Selling bottled water from their waist packs, two bicyclists worked their way toward Juan's limousine. They didn't look especially young, maybe midtwenties. Juan smiled. The lead bicyclist had the jump on the guy behind him. The first guy stopped at the SUV in front of their limo and made a sale. The SUV's driver handed a bill to the cyclist and received two bottles in return. The street vender approached and rolled to a stop at Juan's window. Juan knew the young man couldn't see inside the tinted windows—all he'd see was his own reflection.

Juan leaned over, removed his wallet, and rolled his window down. Warm air assaulted his face. "How much for three bottles?"

"For you, minister, they're free."

Minister? Juan doubted a common street vendor would recognize him. But he had been on TV a lot lately, so perhaps being recognized wasn't too much of a stretch.

"You know who I am?"

"Of course I do." The young man smiled, but it didn't reach his eyes.

When the vendor reached into his waist pack, Juan saw a forearm covered with expensive tattoos. A street vendor could never afford something like that. It looked like gang ink.

"I think I'll pass on the water. Thank you, though."

The man's smile widened. "But I insist."

Before Juan could roll the window up, the man pulled an odd-looking brick of tan clay from his waist pack.

What the hell are those wires? Juan thought.

The man pressed something attached to the brick.

Then, as casually as throwing birdseed, the guy tossed the brick through the open window and sped away.

That's when Juan saw the batteries.

"Shit! It's a bomb!"

His aide reacted quickly but fumbled with his seat belt.

"Throw it out the door! Hurry!"

Five seconds after the device entered the limo, it detonated.

Juan's mind couldn't register the event. He had a vague sense of searing heat and impossible pressure.

Two pounds of plastic explosive tore him apart, vaporizing most of his flesh.

In a millionth of a second, the warm air entering the limousine reversed its course.

The explosion ripped through the sheet-metal floor and careened off the concrete.

As if suspended by an invisible cable, the limo lifted off the road. Before it came back down, fire erupted from every window, including the windshield.

Juan's driver had managed to get his door open, but it was too late. The force of the blast sent his charred body cartwheeling across several lanes of cars.

Tempered glass from hundreds of car windows shredded flesh. Storefronts blew inward, awnings went up in flames, and scorched pedestrians tumbled down the sidewalks.

Ten seconds after the blast, an eerie calmness descended, broken by blaring car alarms, the crackle of flames, and moans of agony.

***

Bill Stafford knocked on Cantrell's door before entering. Seeing she wasn't on the phone, he told her there'd been an explosion in Caracas. "Some kind of car bomb. Local authorities are saying it was a limo."

"A limo?"

Stafford nodded. "It went off in the middle of a traffic jam."

"Contact our station chief down there, and see what he knows."

"I'm on it."

"Anyone claim responsibility?"

"Not yet."

"How many?"

"At least several dozen."

"When was the last major terrorist bombing down there?"

"I'll find out."

"Keep me updated." Cantrell turned on her TV and started channel surfing. Most of the cable networks were covering it. A helicopter shot showed a circle of destruction at least a hundred feet wide. A black smoke column leaned toward the ocean. She picked up her phone and called the director of national intelligence. She had to wait several minutes until he came on the line.

"We're on it, Rebecca. It's probably overkill, but I'm going to recommend that Secretary Martinez quietly lock down the embassy there until we sort this out."

"How many marines do we have guarding it?" she asked.

"I don't know, but I'll also ask her to increase the number just to be on the safe side. The last thing we need is another Benghazi. I want to be able to tell the president we took immediate action to secure the place."

"Any official statement from Caracas?"

"Nothing yet . . . Rebecca, I've got to take another call. I'll get back to you once I hear something."

She hung up and tapped Nathan's phone number.

After ten rings, she sent a text.

call me asap

CHAPTER 17

At 8:25 PM, Franco stepped out of his hot tub, toweled himself dry, and strolled toward his house. Compared to his boss, he lived in a modest place, but it still ranked inside the top 1 percent of Managua's elite homes. The plantation-style villa was surrounded by exotic landscaping, complete with ponds and small waterfalls. He'd paid a small fortune re-creating the old-growth forest that once thrived here. Although his trees were significantly smaller because they'd been grown in a nursery and transplanted to his yard, they were still the correct species. Following the path of flagstone pavers, he glanced toward the lights of Managua below. He didn't resent civilization; he just didn't care for it much. He wondered if he could be just as happy living in a remote cabin with no bills to pay, cars to maintain, or telephones to answer.

Answering the phone wasn't always annoying because he'd just received an intriguing call from his well-paid insider within NNP's headquarters. Several years ago, she'd installed a sophisticated tickler program designed to alert her to inquiries on specific individuals. He and Macanas were two of the names she'd linked to her program. The woman was highly skilled, and the program she'd written was nothing short of ingenious. Franco knew his way around computers, but this woman's abilities were downright scary. She'd called to tell him that earlier this morning someone had accessed the NNP database, seeking personal information on his boss and a second person within the same inquiry. That in itself wasn't overly alarming, what had gotten the technician's attention was the fact that the IP address associated with the inquiry was a bogus number in Malaysia. It had looked too suspicious to overlook, so she'd called Franco.

The second person within the data stream was none other than Pastor Tobias Delgado.

Franco knew this couldn't be a coincidence. What were the odds of an inquiry with only those two names occurring at the same time? Hundreds of millions to one? For now, he'd keep this morsel to himself and not share it with Macanas.

He turned the music down and located his prepaid cell phone. The cheap flip phone had been purchased and registered to a wholly owned Paulo Macanas shell company created by a crafty lawyer who'd left no ties back to Macanas or himself. Franco knew he should drive a few kilometers away from his house before using the phone, but he wasn't in the mood. Besides, he'd used the phone all over Managua. No single cell tower would show more activity than any other one. He wasn't worried.

He opened the phone, powered it on, and made the call to Santavilla. As always, he let the other end of the line ring once before hanging up. Thirty seconds later, he did the same thing again. It usually took just under two minutes before getting a return call. He began locking the house. Methodically moving from room to room, he closed all the windows and left the interior doors in precise yet random positions, depending on their locations within the house. He used the pattern on the hardwood floors to act as a guide. If anyone entered his house in his absence, they might return the doors to their approximate positions, but they'd never be able to get them back into their precise locations. He had a state-of-the-art security system, but as with any electronically based system, it could be defeated. As he'd learned long ago in kilo training, old-fashioned security methods remained the best, and such methods included his two tactically trained Belgian Malinois. The dogs weren't big, but they packed plenty of punch. They followed him through the house during his routine, having seen it hundreds of times.

His flip phone rang ninety seconds later. He relayed his instructions to Antonia about thoroughly searching the church. "Call me back within the hour no matter what you find." He ended the call and looked at his dogs. "Good boys." Their expressions relaxed.

In the kitchen, he poured himself an iced tea and leaned against the counter. The call from his NNP insider about the dual inquiry required immediate investigation. Perhaps there had been more to the good pastor than met the eye. He settled into his easy chair, looked at his watch, and turned on the TV. He smiled when he found the breaking news in Venezuela.

Poor Minister Batista. I guess you weren't as popular as you thought.

***

With twenty minutes to spare, Franco received his return call. Antonia's search of Tobias's office inside the church had yielded an interesting piece of information. Someone sharing the pastor's last name—Estefan Delgado—had written a large check to the church, but it hadn't been cashed. Instead, Tobias had left it sticking out of a Bible like a bookmark. The check was over a year old. If Tobias never intended to cash it, then why keep it? Sentimental value? It had obviously come from a family member. Adding to the mystery, the address on the uncashed check lay only four kilometers from Franco's own house.

It was time to do some fieldwork. He grabbed his prepacked tactical bag, locked the house, and drove to Estefan Delgado's address. His first cruise past the residence confirmed the presence of a security system—a keypad was visible near the front door. Franco also noticed a large dog in a fenced backyard.

The outer suburbs of Managua were a mix of everything from tin shanties to brick-and-mortar mansions, and this place ranked somewhere in the middle—a modest three- or four-bedroom home.

With nothing more to learn from inside his vehicle, Franco drove to the opposite side of the canyon and parked in a vacant lot overlooking Delgado's house. Most of the trees atop the ridgeline were gone, leaving a clear view of the city below. From the type of trash present, it was obvious this place was frequented by party animals and amorous couples. For now, his Range Rover was the only vehicle present. He took a moment to study Delgado's house with field glasses but saw no movement and no lights on.

Franco rolled his windows down and listened for any sounds coming from the immediate neighborhood. All quiet. He also inhaled deeply through his nose. Detecting no cigarette odor, he donned a plain black ski mask, grabbed his tactical backpack, and started down the canyon's slope. The descent was steep, if not particularly difficult, but he found the bottom of the gulley loaded with hazards. A long time ago, the canyon had been used as an illegal dumping site. Before the houses were built on the ridgeline, people had dumped all kinds of trash. Everything from construction debris to abandoned cars had accumulated down here. The thick foliage, coupled with the steep slope, made seeing the smaller pieces of debris difficult. There were hundreds of objects to trip over down here. Once he ascended the other side, he'd emerge at the rear fence of Delgado's property. He had no misgivings about the danger of tonight's operation. Going against an unknown opponent held inherent risks, but he had the element of surprise on his side. He didn't feel overly concerned.

A little winded, Franco stopped at the tall chain-link fence and scanned the rear yard with his NV goggles. The collective glow of the city provided plenty of light, so he adjusted the gain down to a lower setting. He didn't think anyone would be in the yard but didn't assume that. Moving in slow motion to avoid making any noise, he pulled his suppressed Sig from his waist pack and powered its laser. The red beam wouldn't activate until he squeezed the button on the weapon's butt. On the far side of the manicured lawn dotted with banana trees, all of the home's windows remained dark. Ditto the security light above the sliding glass doors. The view from neighboring houses was screened by vines growing on the chain-link fence. In the middle of the grass, a small water fountain created a trickling sound. Several chairs encircled a fire pit, but he didn't see any light from it. Had there been any hot coals present, the NV would've detected them.

He issued a barely audible whistle and waited.

After thirty seconds nothing happened, so he repeated the whistle.

He heard it then—the clack, clack of a dog door.

Silhouetted against the house, the dog he'd seen on his drive-by bounded toward him. A few meters away it stopped, lowered its head, and issued a growl. As planned, thanks to the wind at his back, the dog had caught his scent. He backed up a few steps to give it a false sense of domination. Without warning, the animal charged the fence. Franco toggled the laser and sent a subsonic bullet through its nose. The dog collapsed to the grass and convulsed for several seconds before going still. Franco didn't feel good about killing it, but he didn't feel terrible either. In fact, he didn't feel anything at all. It was simply a phase in tonight's operation. Knowing the trajectory of spent shell casings from this pistol, he quickly found the warm brass shell and secured it in his thigh pocket.

Five seconds later, Franco was over the fence.

He wasn't worried about motion sensors or infrared beams because of the presence of the family pet. Dogs and motion detectors didn't go well together. He took a knee next to the dog and removed its collar.

Moving from tree to tree, he kept his head up, looking for any sign his suppressed shot had been detected. He also watched for dog shit because he didn't want to waste time cleaning his boots before entering the house. He wasn't worried about making a mess, but the odor might be a problem. It's hard to be stealthy when you smell like dog droppings. At the garage wall, he found the dog door. He held the electronic collar low and was rewarded with a disengagement click. After removing his backpack, he'd have no problem crawling through its opening. And, as with the nonexistent motion detectors, if the dog door had been tied into the security system, it would've set off the alarm when the dog passed through.

Inside the garage he caught the faint odor of gasoline and found only one car, a white SUV. Could the other vehicle be out front on the street or in the driveway? Using the NV, he crossed the slab, being careful to avoid the oil stain, and looked through one of three small windows in the garage door. Nothing. Maybe it was in a shop for service. Nicaraguan roads took a heavy toll on vehicles. The presence of oil on the concrete indicated there was normally a second car in here. He reached down and touched the slick, definitely fresh. He was tempted to leave, but he'd committed himself by killing the dog. Coming back later wouldn't work unless he hauled the carcass over the fence and dragged it into the canyon. Even so, the dog's absence would be noticed and create suspicion.

He was here; he'd stick to the plan.

The security keypad on the wall showed a red LED, indicating the system was armed. Franco used the collar to unlock a second dog door leading to the interior of the house. Moving slowly, he eased through the opening and stayed on his stomach, quashing the adrenaline rush from invading an unknown home. He held that position for a moment longer before gaining his feet. From somewhere ahead, the Westminster chime indicating 9:45 PM broke the silence. He smiled. Their clock was running fast.

Holding his Sig tightly against his chest, Franco moved deeper into the dwelling, which had an aged tobacco odor, probably from cigars. He liked the smell. Maybe he'd help himself to a few on the way out. The living room, dining room, and kitchen were all one continuous space. The furniture seemed modest, and the walls appeared mostly bare. Whoever lived here didn't appear to have excessive wealth.

He knew the hallway at the far end of the living room led to the bedrooms. Although he thought it unlikely, there could be a second dog. Franco entered the corridor and saw four doors, all of them open. The first exposed an unoccupied bedroom, the second led to a bathroom, and the third door revealed an office. The last door would be the master bedroom. A stroboscopic blue glow highlighted the rectangular opening. Franco had a sudden visual of a coffin, eerily lit from the inside.

He peered around the doorjamb.

On her side in a nightgown, a woman lay half-covered by a single sheet. Long dark hair covered her pillow.

On the muted flat-screen TV, a black-and-white western aired to a sleeping audience. An empty wineglass sat on the nightstand along with an ashtray containing several cigar butts. He also saw a cell phone.

Franco eased inside and approached the bed. The tobacco smell was stronger in here.

He stood over her motionless form for half a minute, soaking up the feeling of power, of owning this woman.

Time to get down to business.

He tucked his Sig into his waist pack and circled to the opposite side of the bed.

In a quick move, he clamped his right hand over her mouth and yanked her to the floor. Staying behind her, he wrapped his left arm around her torso and hauled her upright. In the mirrored closet door he saw her eyes register confusion first, then abject terror.

"I'm not going to hurt you. If you resist or scream, I'll make you regret it. Do you understand me?"

Completely overwhelmed with panic, she issued a muffled whine. When she tried to shake her head back and forth, Franco tightened his grip on her jaw. He pressed his groin firmly against her hip and moved his head in close. In the event she possessed self-defense training, he didn't want his balls grabbed or crushed, and he didn't want to be head butted. A broken nose would require an explanation.

Franco wasn't completely devoid of compassion. He knew this woman was terrified beyond all control. He had the power to ease her fear or enhance it.

"I know you're frightened, but I'm not going to rape you. All I want is information. Now I'm only going to say this one more time. If you scream or try to run, I will hurt you. Do you understand?"

The woman nodded.

"I'm going to uncover your mouth."

"Please, I don't have much money in the house."

"I'm not here for your money. I want you to sit on the edge of the bed and answer my questions. Do you think you can do that?"

She nodded.

"Don't try anything stupid. If you attempt to run, you'll be punished. Now please sit down."

The woman complied, keeping her legs together with her hands in her lap.

"Where is your husband? You're married, yes?"

"I don't know where he is."

"How long has he been gone?"

"He left yesterday morning."

"Did he say when he'd return?"

"Tonight," she said, but it sounded forced.

"Please don't lie to me."

"He said it might be a few days."

"So he didn't tell you where he was going?"

She shook her head.

"Where does he work?"

"At embassies."

"Your husband works at embassies? In Managua?"

"Yes."

"Which ones?"

"Mostly United States and Canada."

"What does he do at the embassies?"

"I don't know. He never talks about his work."

Franco turned on the nightstand light; he wanted to see her face more clearly. That's when he saw it, a small framed photo. He stared in shocked disbelief, then picked it up.

"This is your husband?"

"Yes."

"This guy, right here." He pointed to a clean-shaven man with a full head of dark hair standing next to several US Marines in dress blues.

"Yes."

Viper!

Franco felt his stomach twist. "Was Pastor Tobias your husband's father?"

"Yes."

"How long have you been married to him?"

"Twelve years."

"How long has he worked at the embassies?"

"Seven years."

"Does he work for the government?"

"I don't know."

"What *do* you know about his work?"

She wiped a tear and didn't answer.

"I know you're frightened, but you're doing fine. You said he doesn't talk about his work much. Have you overheard any of his phone calls, anything that might give you a clue about his work?"

"I've heard him talking about American and Canadian companies."

"What kind of companies?"

"I'm not sure. Mining, I think."

"Mining?"

"Yes."

Intriguing. "What else can you tell me?"

"I don't know. He travels to America and Canada a lot. Sometimes he's gone for weeks."

"Do you think he's up north now?"

"No."

"Why not?"

"He didn't pack for a long trip."

"Is that your SUV in the garage?"

"Yes."

"What kind of vehicle does your husband drive?"

"A truck."

"A pickup? What color and make?"

"A tan Ford."

"What is your security code to the house?"

She gave him the number.

"Does his office computer require a password?"

"I don't know. He never lets me touch it."

"What about you? What do you do for work?"

Her voice cracked again. "I'm a volunteer at the hospital. I also manage a nonprofit program there."

Questioning this woman further would be useless. She was either a really good liar or she truly didn't know much about her husband's line of work. He had no desire to torture her in order to find out.

Franco pushed her backward and straddled her with his thighs. He pulled his handgun and struck her on the side of the head. The trick was hitting hard enough to cause unconsciousness but not hard enough to kill or cause permanent damage.

She managed a yelp of terror before going limp.

He eased off her and checked for a pulse. Faint, but present. He'd stay put a little longer to be sure the woman didn't regain consciousness too quickly. He glanced at the TV. A black-and-white western showed a posse of mounted lawmen chasing a lone bad guy through a rocky canyon. The bad guy kept pivoting in his saddle and firing at his pursuers.

Franco pocketed her cell phone and left her bedroom.

Down the hall, he entered the office, closed the blinds, and turned on the desk's light. He powered on the computer, and not surprisingly, he was greeted with a log-in password screen. He made several attempts to log in using common passwords, but the system locked up after five attempts. It was worth a try, but getting information out of his old kilo friend would have to be obtained the old-fashioned way—through an interrogation. Franco conducted a quick search of Estefan's office, looking through file drawers and opened mail for anything that might shed light on the man's profession. Verifying what his wife had said, he saw several textbooks on mining in a small bookcase.

Back at the door leading to the garage, he punched in the security code. The LED turned green.

He returned to the bedroom and hoisted the woman over his shoulder in a fireman's carry technique. She felt light, no more than fifty kilograms. Hauling her through the house and out the sliding glass doors to the western edge of the property took less than a minute. Back in the garage, he grabbed one of the five-gallon gas cans he'd smelled earlier and returned to the master bedroom. He left it there and began scanning the ceiling for smoke detectors. He found four.

Using a chair from the dining room, he reached up to the ceiling and removed the battery from the kitchen's detector. He repeated the procedure in the other three locations, including the garage. If the devices were wired into the security system, the fire department's response would now be slower. Someone would have to see the fire and call it in. Because of the late hour, the house would probably be fully involved before anyone noticed it. Franco knew modern homes didn't burn easily unless they had some help—such as an accelerant. The gasoline would speed things up nicely. To give the fire more oxygen, he opened some of the windows. Next, he located the attic access in the first bedroom and stood on the bed to push the cover up and aside.

Satisfied he'd prepped the house for the quickest possible burn, he began sloshing gasoline around the interior of the master bedroom. Franco knew the fire would eliminate all traces of forensic evidence he may have left behind, but more importantly, it would rattle his former kilo colleague. A distracted and unfocused enemy was a vulnerable enemy.

He returned the depleted can to the garage and grabbed a second. He emptied most of its contents around key areas of the living room, dining room, and kitchen before creating a wet trail out the garage door and over to the dog door. The last of the gasoline went on the wall above the dog door where it cascaded down to the concrete.

All was set, but he felt as though he were forgetting something . . .

The cigars.

Being careful to avoid scuffing his boots on the carpet, Franco reentered the office and raided the cigar box. He tucked his Sig into his belt to make room for the smokes and stuffed his waist pack to the bulging point. Before leaving the office, he removed a piece of paper from the printer.

Outside at the dog door where he'd first entered, he felt his exhilaration build. He rolled the piece of paper into a long tube, folded it flat, and inserted it about a third of the way under the sill of the dog door, creating a time-delay fuse. Standing off to the side, he struck a match, lit the paper, and ran toward the fence. At first nothing happened, and he thought he'd have to go back.

But just as he turned, the house seemed to exhale a collective breath.

The sound was amazing, as if from a giant organ pipe.

All the fumes ignited simultaneously in a low-pitched *whoof.* Glass flew outward like orange glitter.

Within seconds, the entire house glowed from every window.

Resisting an overwhelming urge to flee the scene, Franco scaled the fence and calmly walked over to the canyon's rim.

Smoke was already billowing from the window frames and gabled roof vents.

As tempting as it was to stay and watch from this distance, he needed to clear the area before the police and fire department arrived. Viper's wife would be okay. He'd laid her down far enough away to avoid a radiant burn from the fire. Letting her live was the right thing to do.

A few minutes later, he finished his ascent on the opposite side of the canyon. He bent at the waist and rested his hands on his knees for a half a minute to catch his breath. He felt the pressure of time but stayed to watch the fire. An impressive sight, the flames towered more than six stories high. At one point, the inferno transformed into a cyclonic form, twisting skyward in a macabre dance. Swirling out from the top of the mushroom cloud, embers rained down on the surrounding neighborhood like amber-colored snow.

The fire department's reaction time surprised him. The first engine rolled on scene at the twenty-minute mark. Given the distance from the fire station and the time of night, he hadn't believed such a quick response was possible, but it was too little, too late. By the time the volunteers deployed, the roof and walls had already collapsed. Reduced to a smoldering pile, the house wouldn't give up any forensic evidence.

After putting his backpack into the backseat, he shook his head at the connections he had discovered between himself and Estefan Delgado. Seeing Viper in the photograph had been startling. They'd had no contact over the years. And yet somehow, Pastor Tobias had been Viper's father. And Viper worked for the government in the mining sector. Franco shook his head again. All coincidence, to be sure. But Viper wouldn't see it like that— just the opposite.

At least when Viper's wife regained consciousness, she wouldn't be able to give the police anything beyond being questioned and attacked by a man in a ski mask. Killing her would've been easier and cleaner, but he didn't believe in offing women and children.

For now, Franco held the advantage. He thought it unlikely Viper knew of his involvement in Macanas's organization. He'd never let anyone photograph him. In retrospect, perhaps killing Tobias without a thorough interrogation had been a mistake. He'd suggested as much to Macanas when they'd discussed Tobias's interference with the discipline of Mateo, but Macanas had been adamant about eliminating Tobias as quickly as possible.

He began formulating a plan to further complicate Viper's life. He intended to call the emergency number 118 from a pay phone and report seeing a man run away from the fire and get into a tan Ford truck. Once his former comrade learned of tonight's little bonfire, things were going to escalate, and Franco didn't intend to be on the defensive. Viper was a potentially dangerous man and could become a serious threat. He might be a mere paper pusher now, but he possessed training equivalent to his own, and Franco had no way to know whether Viper had kept his skills sharp over the years.

For now Franco would stay put, watch the barbecue, and wait for the ambulance to arrive. He felt confident Viper's wife would be taken to the nearest hospital, but he intended to follow the ambulance to be sure. Once he began his stakeout, he'd use the time to contact his police snitch and get a current driver's license photo. Once Viper showed up to visit his wife, he'd be an easy target. With a little luck, Franco could end the threat to Macanas's empire tonight.

Like a nagging fly, Pastor Tobias's comment circled around to pester him again. *You will answer to God for this.* Whether he believed it or not, he silently cursed the old man for planting a seed of doubt.

CHAPTER 18

Estefan's phone chimed. "That's my voice mail alert," he said.

"I'll retrieve it for you," Harv said. "Concentrate on your driving." Harv worked Estefan's iPhone and handed it to him.

Estefan's expression became a mask of panic. "We have to go back!"

"What's wrong?" Nathan asked.

"My house burned down!"

"What do you mean your house burned down? When?"

"Two hours ago! We have to go back."

Nathan immediately suspected foul play. "Estefan, calm down. We can't go speeding all the way back to Managua. We can't risk getting pulled over."

"But my wife. She was home!"

"You don't know that for sure—she could've been delayed."

"Then why hasn't she called? There are no messages from her."

"Look, I understand you're upset, but driving recklessly for several hours won't accomplish anything but land us all in jail, or worse. I have no desire to test the quality of our counterfeit passports."

"Okay, okay. No speeding."

Estefan scratched the tires, making a U-turn in the middle of the road. No cars were in sight, but it still seemed a little reckless. Nathan understood Estefan's urgency, but if Estefan couldn't calm down, Harv would need to drive.

"Who told you about your house?" Nathan asked.

"I don't know. Some damned NNP lieutenant."

"Is he calling it arson? Can we listen to the voice mail message?"

"Sure . . . Why not," Estefan said with a sarcastic tone.

Now clearly wasn't a good time to try to talk with Estefan, so Nathan silently considered the implications of the event. If the fire was arson, the timing couldn't be denied, and Nathan didn't like the odds if Estefan's wife was home. He knew Estefan had to be thinking the same thing. Would Raven murder an innocent woman in cold blood? If so, why? To distract Estefan? Put him under stress? Classic military strategy involved mentally battering your enemy. There were a lot of *ifs*.

The truck's speed was steadily climbing. "Raven did it," he said. "The sick bastard always liked fire."

"I'll concede the timing's highly suspect," Nathan said. "We have to assume Raven knows you're Tobias's son, but it doesn't necessarily mean he also knows you're Viper."

"If he went into my house, he would've seen photographs of me." Estefan pounded the steering wheel. "Shit!"

"We don't know if he went inside. We don't even know if he did this. Estefan, please slow down."

"I had an argument with my wife before I left. We were mad at each other."

"Estefan, slow down!"

"Okay! Damn it."

Harv said, "Try not to assume the worst."

"She would've called or left a message. 'Hi, Estefan, how's your business trip going? Oh, by the way, our house just burned down.'"

Nathan didn't respond. Estefan was right. She would've called—assuming she could.

With Estefan's permission, Harv took Estefan's phone, put it on speaker, and played the voice mail message.

"*This is Lieutenant Enrique Mauro of the Nicaraguan Police. There was a fire at your house this evening. Please call me back as soon as you can.*" The lieutenant left his number.

Harv opened the glove box. "Do you have a pen and paper in here?" Estefan didn't answer, but Harv found what he needed, played the message again, and wrote the phone number.

"It's probably best if you call back right away," Nathan said. "If they suspect the fire was arson, the police will automatically put you on the short list of suspects. Is there any way it could be an accidental fire? Does your wife smoke?"

"We both smoke cigars, but she knows she's not supposed to smoke in bed."

"Please don't take this wrong, but does your wife drink?"

Estefan didn't answer right away. "Our marriage isn't doing so well. I'm gone a lot."

"Then she could've been drinking and fallen asleep with a lit cigar?" Nathan avoided using the term "passed out."

"Cigars don't keep burning like cigarettes do. They go out."

"That's true, but they burn for a while. All I'm saying is that we can't rule it out as an accidental fire. Did your house have a security system or smoke alarms?"

"It has both. We also have a Rottweiler. The bastard probably killed my dog. He'd never get past him otherwise."

"Again, we don't know Raven did it," Nathan said. "I'll admit the timing's bad, but it's still not conclusive evidence. You should call the police back while we've still got a signal. Did you tell anyone you'd be out of town for a while? Anyone at work?"

"No. I really will be a suspect, won't I." It wasn't a question.

"It's standard practice for the police to look at family members."

"And I'll have no way to prove I didn't do it. It's not like you guys can come down to the station and vouch for me."

"You don't have to prove you didn't do it. I'm assuming your justice system works like ours?"

Estefan didn't say anything. His mind was clearly in turmoil over his father's murder, his house burning down, and the uncertainty of his wife's condition. This had to be tearing him up.

Harv said, "I'll dial the number for you." When it rang, Harv put it on speaker and handed the phone to Estefan. Not surprisingly, he got dumped into Lieutenant Mauro's voice mail.

"This is Estefan Delgado calling you back. Please return my call as soon as you can." Estefan recited his phone number twice.

"Okay," said Nathan. "That's good. Now we need to think about what you're going to say. Can you tell him you went up north on business? You said the area around Santavilla is identified for potential leases. Can you say you came up here to look the area over?"

"I can do that, but I didn't say anything about it at work."

"I don't think that's a major problem," Nathan said. "You can say it was a last-minute decision. Come to think of it, your cell phone might contain proof you weren't in Managua when the fire broke out."

Harv said, "I think the work-related angle's a good approach, but we don't want Estefan's answers to sound too rehearsed. It might be best if you don't have an answer for every question this Mauro might throw at you."

"I agree." Nathan said. "You weren't in Managua when the fire started. Beyond that, you'll just have to see where his line of inquiry goes."

Estefan smacked the steering wheel again. "This fucking sucks!"

"We'll get through it," Harv said.

Nathan didn't respond. There were times it was best to be silent. The next few miles seemed endless. They got stuck behind a semitruck and couldn't pass. Nathan felt Estefan's anger building.

When Estefan's phone rang, it startled him. His nerves were frayed, exactly what Raven would want and hope to accomplish.

"That could be my wife. Give me the phone."

"Pull over," Harv said.

Estefan did the opposite. He laid on his horn, hit the gas, and recklessly passed the semitruck on a blind curve.

"Shit, man!" Harv said. "That was dangerous. Getting us all killed won't help your situation."

Nathan was more firm. "Don't do it again."

"Calm down," said Harv, "and I'll put your phone on speaker."

"Harv, you hold the phone," Nathan said.

Estefan turned his head and said, "Hello?"

"Is this Mr. Delgado?"

"Yes."

"This is Lieutenant Mauro from the Nicaraguan National Police."

"Is my wife okay?"

"That's why I'm calling."

Estefan clenched his jaw.

"Are you there, Mr. Delgado?"

"Yes."

"Your wife is in the hospital. We found her in your backyard. She has a blunt-force head wound."

"What are you saying, she's alive?"

"Yes, she's unconscious, and she's in critical condition. The doctors don't think she's in danger of dying, but she might need surgery to relieve pressure on her brain. Her sister is at the hospital with her. You might want to be there as well."

Estefan hit the steering wheel hard enough to break it. The pickup swerved.

Harv tapped him and silently mouthed the words "pull over."

"Mr. Delgado, are you okay?"

Nathan leaned forward and poked Harv—hard.

"Mr. Delgado?"

Understanding Nathan's silent prod, Harv ended the call.

"Estefan! Pull over," Nathan yelled.

"That cocksucking son of a bitch! He didn't have to hurt her!"

"Pull over. *Now!*"

Estefan cut the inside corner of a curve too closely and lost control. The pickup fishtailed into the oncoming side of the road.

Estefan recovered but too late. They grazed a barbed-wire fence, crossed back onto their own side, and ended up halfway in the ditch with the tailgate of their truck protruding into the road at an angle.

"Damn it, Estefan!" Nathan whipped around, looking for the semi they'd passed a few seconds ago. It would emerge from the blind corner at any moment. "Get us the hell out of here!"

In horror, Nathan watched the trees next to the road burst with light.

"Estefan!"

Two seconds later, piercing headlights barreled straight toward them.

The blast of the semi's air horn penetrated their cab as the rig's driver veered to the left to avoid hitting them.

The truck roared past, missing Estefan's rear bumper by less than a foot.

In what seemed like slow motion, the semi's left wheels found the shoulder.

The rig began leaning.

Rather than go straight into the tilled field, the driver tried to recover and stay on the road—a bad move with a worse result.

Nathan felt a glimmer of hope as the rig teetered on its left wheels. His optimism ended when he realized the trailer's lateral momentum was too great, sealing the rig's fate.

Rocks, dirt, and shredded plant life erupted as the overturned trailer plowed into the earth and came to a violent stop.

Estefan threw the pickup into four-wheel drive and backed onto the road.

Nathan knew he intended to flee the scene.

"No!" Nathan said. "We aren't leaving until we know the driver's okay."

"He's okay," Estefan said and hit the gas.

"Harv!" Nathan yelled. "Make him stop!"

Harv reached over and grabbed the steering wheel. "Estefan, you either stop right now or we're done."

"Okay, damn it! Okay."

Harv kept iron in his voice. "Now pull over onto the shoulder—safely."

Nathan scanned the road in both directions but didn't see any other vehicles. Because of the curvy terrain, there was no way to see more than fifty yards in either direction. A car could come up on them at any moment. Their only warning would be the headlight glow.

"Harv, go see if he's okay. Double-time."

"I'll do it," Estefan said with resignation. "We don't want the driver to see either of you guys."

Even though Estefan sounded calm, Nathan said, "We're a little short on confidence right now."

"I'm sorry. I'm really sorry."

"No BS, Estefan. We want the truth. Hang on a sec." Nathan fished a bundle of cash from his backpack. "Tell him you're sorry and give him the money. Stay on this side of his windshield and make voice contact only. Don't let him see you. Get going. Turn on your flashers first."

Nathan watched Estefan jump out and follow the fan-shaped swath of destruction. Even in the bleed light from Estefan's headlights, Nathan noticed the truck's exposed underbelly was caked reddish brown with road scum.

Nathan heard Estefan's voice as he yelled to the driver, asking if he was injured. He didn't hear a response. Estefan repeated his question.

"Nate, are we scrubbing?"

"I don't know yet. Let's see how Estefan recovers. He just learned his wife was bludgeoned and might need surgery. How would we feel?"

"The same way."

"We'll cut him some slack, but it's not open ended. I just hope the driver's okay. If his window was open, he might have a crushed arm, or worse."

"I smell diesel, but I don't think the rig's going up. At least I hope not."

"We aren't leaving a seriously wounded man here. If we have to take him to a hospital, we'll scrub the mission and head back to alpha."

"Agreed. If the guy's a wildcatter and doesn't have insurance, we just bankrupted him."

"There's nothing we can do about that. Hop out and take a quick look at our tires. I'm too tall. If anyone drives by, they'll remember my size."

Harv was back five seconds later. "We're good, but he's got a ruined paint job from clipping the fence."

Nathan was tempted to say Estefan deserved it. He watched his friend toss the bundles of cash in front of the rig's windshield and hustle back to the pickup.

"He's really pissed off, but he's okay."

Nathan waited.

"I swear! He told me he wasn't hurt."

"Okay, punch it. We don't want him to get your license plate when we drive past."

They drove in silence for a few seconds.

"Estefan, this will be difficult for you to accept, but we can't go back into Managua."

"What? Why the hell not?"

Nathan kept his voice even. "Whoever attacked your wife probably intended to kill you. We have no idea how many people were involved. If it was Raven, he might not have been alone. Even if all three of us had been there, there's no guarantee we could have changed the outcome. We might all be dead. We also have to consider that your house and your office are now under surveillance by Raven."

"So what do we do? Nothing?"

"The endgame is Raven, and we need to fight him on our terms. We need to slow down and think things through. I'm really sorry about everything that's happened to you. I can't imagine how you're feeling right now."

"I'd like to personally thank Raven for turning my world to shit . . . before I beat him to death with a tire iron."

"All right, all right. Now listen, you aren't going to accomplish that in Managua—for a lot of reasons. We need to set up an ambush and force him to come to us."

"And how do you propose we do that?"

"By sticking to our plan. We can't fight him in an urban environment. Your sister-in-law is with your wife. As brutal as this sounds, there's nothing you can do besides sit at her bedside and hold her hand. Under different circumstances, a car wreck or other injury, sitting at your wife's bedside wouldn't be an issue, but our circumstances are anything but normal. Metaphorically, we're in the middle of a battle. We can't abandon our positions and go home. If we don't nail Raven, your family will never be safe again."

"So hurting my wife and torching my house down is just a statement that he owns the situation and can fuck with me anytime he wants?"

"Essentially, yes. But we won't play by his rules. We have to do the unexpected. Right now, he expects you to visit your wife in the hospital. You'd be out in the open, an easy target. He could nail you from hundreds of places. Up close or from a distance. Take your pick. Now let's turn around, head into Santavilla, and stick with the plan. Your wife's in the best hands possible."

"Has Nate always been like this, Harv? Calmly assertive?"

"Yeah, pretty much. I've learned to adapt."

"Shit," Estefan said. "All right. I hear you. So let's do the world a favor and blow this asshole away."

"Now that's the Viper I remember."

CHAPTER 19

They arrived on the outskirts of Santavilla at 2315 hours.

"Slow down to a crawl but don't stop," Nathan told Estefan. "We want to minimize your vehicle's signature. Your father wrote that he could hear vehicles entering the valley, especially at night."

After Estefan complied, Nathan continued, "Let's go over the plan one more time. After you drop us off, find a place to park no more than a hundred yards beyond the bridge. Follow the river like we talked about. You can use the tree line and undergrowth along its bank for cover. Give us a ten-minute head start before you head over to Mateo's. We'll be sure to pick a location where we can see Mateo's house and your approach from the river, and we'll radio you when we're in position. Now Mateo should be expecting you, but that could be a good or bad thing. We don't know this guy from Adam. Just because your father liked him doesn't mean he's not an informer for Macanas. Let us know if you see anyone, or if anyone sees you, on your way to meet him. Use your NV. If we lose radio communication for any reason, we'll meet near the south end of the bridge in exactly one hour. If things go completely to hell and we all get separated, we'll meet a half mile south of the bridge at the stream crossing.

"No problem," Estefan said.

"Are you okay?"

"I'm still pissed, but I'm okay."

"Well, just be sure to keep your head in the game. Remember, we don't know Mateo. We don't know anyone here. Never let your guard down, not even for a few seconds. Stay sharp."

"You can count on it."

"I want regular updates no more than ten minutes apart. We showed you where the radio's emergency transmitter button is. If you activate it, stay put. We'll come and find you."

"Let's hope I won't need it," Estefan said.

"Unless something requires a verbal response, we'll give each other acknowledgment clicks only. When you get close to Mateo's house, remove your NV and radio and secure them in your backpack. We want him to think you're alone. Keep your radio turned on, but pull the earpiece and microphone wires. We'll transmit only if there's any kind of trouble. The radio's speaker will be active without the earpiece connected, so turn its volume down to a whisper. Once you leave Mateo's place, your dad's office is next. Leave your NV and radio in your pack until you reach the church. Leave the lights off and use your NV to take a look around inside. Then, from the church, hike south along the trail until you reach the dam and rewire your radio inside the cover of the trees. Head up to your dad's house and conduct a quick search. We won't initiate contact, so make sure you make your update calls. We won't be able to see you once you're south of the pond."

"Sounds good," Estefan said. "How hard do you want me to press if Mateo isn't forthcoming?"

"Use your best judgment. Be sure to reinforce that anything he tells you will be kept confidential, okay? Tell him about the letters from your dad, and use something personal he shared with your father, like his favorite fishing spot on the river."

"Estefan should give him some cash," Harv said. "Tobias said Mateo needs money for his wife's opium, and you've already hinted we'd do that."

Nathan nodded agreement. "Estefan, grab twenty thousand córdobas from the pack. It's only eight hundred dollars, but I'm sure it will be a small fortune to Mateo."

Estefan said, "Thanks for the money. I'm sure Mateo will appreciate the cash."

"It should go a long way to earning his trust."

Nathan had them all perform a final wiring and radio check. Not only did their radios need to function properly, but their wiring also had to be tucked away securely. It was all too easy to snag a cord in a jungle environment. A loss of communication at a critical time could cost someone his life.

As planned, Nathan and Harv got out just before the bridge at the south end of the valley. They waited for Estefan to park before starting up the west-facing slope of the mountain. About halfway to the summit, they'd turn 90 degrees, head north, and start scouting for a good location overlooking the center of town. Judging from the tree density, Nathan gave it short odds of finding a single place that would work. Santavilla was fairly spread out. The lumber mill, ore-processing plant, and helipad were about a mile from their current position on the far end of the valley.

***

Estefan parked on the shoulder just past the bridge. He locked his truck and set out on foot, following the contour of the river. Off to his left he could see the dark outlines of a few small farmhouses beyond plowed fields, but all their windows were dark. Using the NVGs, he easily negotiated the dense foliage along the river's bank. The half-moon didn't concern him too much, because the trees lining the river created deep shadows. Every so often, beams of pale light penetrated down to the damp ground cover.

The symphony of the forest was in full effect, with frogs the dominant instruments. Adding to the amphibian groans, thousands of crickets chirped in the background. *An American banjo wouldn't sound out of place here*, he mused. The noise grew exponentially louder as he neared the pond. Just ahead, he could see the horizontal form of the dam. It looked to be about ten yards long. Upstream of the pond, the river's black water moved silently. Every so often, he passed the rusting hulk of an abandoned vehicle. Burned trash piles dotted the area. Any plastic bags not yet burned had been ripped open by scavengers—presumably animals. It was a shame to see such a pristine environment treated so carelessly.

He stopped, cleared his six, and pressed his transmit button. "I'm on the river's southwest bank, past the dam. There's no activity down here at all. I'll check in just before I head across the open ground toward Mateo's house. You should see me emerge due east of his house."

He received an acknowledgment click and kept going. In approximately six hundred fifty yards, he'd leave the tree line and head due west toward the work bus parked next to Mateo's house. Finding Mateo's house on the aerials hadn't been difficult; it was the only structure in town with a yellow bus parked next to it.

As he'd been taught, Estefan paused every hundred steps or so, held perfectly still, and scanned his immediate area. He also smelled for cigarette or dope smoke.

Detecting nothing, he kept going.

***

Halfway up the mountainside, Nathan and Harv intersected a footpath and followed it north where they found a good spot to watch the town through a horizontal window of open canopy. A few yards above the trail, their location wasn't perfect, but it gave them an unobstructed view of the center of town where the majority of the buildings were. They'd opted to leave their ghillie suits behind. The woodland MARPATs offered ideal colors to blend them into the landscape. Nathan's rifle, equipped with its powerful NV weapon scope, provided a great way to keep an eye on things. Harv broke out his NV binoculars. Unlike their visors, the binoculars magnified the image. Between the two of them, they'd be able to watch Estefan's back while he paid Mateo a visit. Nathan checked for ants, then sat in a cross-legged position before powering on his scope. He rested his elbows on his knees, shouldered the M40, and swept the immediate area surrounding Mateo's home. All quiet.

"See any movement anywhere?" he whispered to Harv.

"No. I think the town's asleep."

Mateo should already be at the rendezvous point at the bus's rear bumper, but Nathan saw no sign of him. Some sort of delivery van was parked between their position and the rear of the bus, and it blocked his view.

Nathan saw an unmistakable flare of light. The NV made it look incredibly bright. The area between the delivery van and the bus lit up like a small sun had briefly emerged, then went dim.

"We've got activity," Nathan said. "Someone just lit a cigarette."

"Near the rear of the bus?" Harv asked.

"Yes. I saw the flare." Nathan pressed the transmit button. "Estefan, I just saw the glow of a cigarette being lit. It's probably your man."

Nathan received a click.

"This will probably go one of two ways," Harv said. "A long meeting or else a quick one, meaning Mateo won't talk to him."

"Yeah, I see it the same way. We'll know soon enough."

"We'll make Mateo's house our zero and vector from there," Harv said. "I can't use the range finder at the same time as my binoculars, so you'll have to walk me onto Mateo's house."

Nathan made a mental note to upgrade his scope to include a range-finder feature. He waited for Harv to activate the range finder's laser, then said, "I've got you. Move slightly higher and to the right. A little higher . . . Good, now slightly back to the left . . . Keep going. A little more . . . Now down just a little. Right there."

"Six hundred seventy-two yards," Harv said.

"Copy at six seven two. Give me a correction from the rifle's three-hundred-yard zero."

"We've got a drop in elevation, so I'll factor that in." Harv paused for a moment. "I thought we weren't going to kill anyone."

"It's just a precaution. Estefan could be walking into a trap. We have no way of knowing if Mateo contacted anyone from Macanas's organization after we called him."

Harv gave him the elevation correction, and Nathan clicked it into the scope.

"Wind is calm," Harv said. "Less than three miles per hour from ten o'clock. Hold left two inches."

"Copy. Two inches left. We aren't letting anyone take Estefan into custody."

"Does that include police?"

"Yes."

"In for a dime, in for a dollar."

"No one's down there but Estefan and Mateo."

"Let's hope so."

***

Estefan reached the point along the river where he could see the yellow bus directly to the west. "Okay, I'm going to step out from the trees for a second. Before I leave the river, I'd like to know exactly where you guys are. I've got my NV on max gain. Paint the canopy directly above your position with a laser."

Estefan's earpiece sounded off with Nathan's voice. *"Stand by."*

Estefan looked about halfway up the north-facing slope of the mountain. Two seconds later, the interior of a tree glowed brightly for an instant, then went dark. Contrasted with the dark mountainside, it stood out like a camera flash, although one that would be invisible to the naked eye.

"Okay, I've got you. You're about a third of the way up the slope."

Estefan received a click in response.

"I'm about to go radio silent. Removing NV now."

"Let me know when you're ready to do a speaker check."

"Stand by, ten seconds . . . Okay." Estefan heard Nathan repeating the word "check" over and over. He adjusted the volume to where he could barely hear Nathan's voice coming from the radio's speaker. He pressed the transmit button and held the radio to his mouth. Without the lapel mike or earpiece attached, the radio worked like a regular handheld.

"Good to go. Leaving the tree line now."

A few seconds later, his radio crackled to life. *"We've got you."*

"I'm stashing the radio in my thigh pocket; it will be quicker to access there. Going silent."

Estefan received a click, turned his NVGs off, and capped their apertures. He tucked the device into his pack. A deep breath later and he was walking across open ground. He could see the black outlines of houses to his left and right, none of them closer than one hundred yards. The town wasn't completely dark. A few windows glowed with yellow light, probably from candles. Most people couldn't afford much of an electric bill.

Estefan felt naked out in the open but maintained a casual yet quick pace. If anyone happened to see him, he wanted to look like an insomniac out for a midnight stroll. He'd considered jogging the four hundred yards, but dismissed the notion. No one jogged in the middle of the night around here.

***

Nathan followed Estefan's progress across the field, alternately looking toward Mateo's house every few seconds. He still couldn't see anyone, but the incredibly sensitive NV weapon scope detected the periodic waning and ebbing of the cigarette's glow.

He swept back toward Estefan. "Shit! He just went down."

"I didn't hear anything," Harv said. "Was it a suppressed shot?"

"Hang on . . . He's back up."

"I see him." They watched Estefan issue a wave before making a more elaborate hand gesture.

Nathan half laughed.

"Did we really just see that?" Harv asked.

"Yep. Apparently our boy's a hockey fan. He just gave us the tripping penalty signal that referees use."

"Well, isn't old Viper just full of surprises. A Nicaraguan who follows ice hockey."

***

After dusting himself off from the embarrassing fall, Estefan had made it halfway across the field when a rustling sound startled him. He'd barely heard it over the crickets' noise.

Slowly pivoting, he focused his eyes just to the right of the sound. Peripheral vision worked better in near darkness.

There it was again! Quick measured footsteps, like someone hurrying toward him.

Damn, he really wished he had a suppressed weapon.

He pulled his Sig, took a knee, and waited for the intruder to arrive.

CHAPTER 20

Estefan held perfectly still and kept his Sig leveled at the source of the sound.

There! A waist-high plant shuddered from being bumped.

Some kind of animal was weaving its way over here, coming straight toward him.

Estefan put three pounds of pressure on the trigger, hoping it was just a dog. A two-hundred-pound wild boar with razor-sharp teeth and a bad attitude would try to ruin his evening. Whatever the threat, Estefan didn't want to blow his stealth by discharging his weapon. A gunshot would reverberate through this valley like a fireworks explosion. He should've switched pistols with Nathan or Harv. It was a careless mistake—perhaps a costly one.

He sighed with relief when a short-haired dog appeared. It stopped about fifteen yards away, lowered its head, and held still. Estefan had plenty of experience with dogs and knew what to do. Now wasn't the time to make friends. He issued a low growl and took an aggressive step forward. The animal jumped back and ran back the way it had come. Alone again, he resumed his trek across the field. He liked having his former instructors watching his back. He could almost feel Nathan's rifle scope track his progress. Night shooting was a fine art, much more so than daylight shots. It was far more difficult to gauge distances and make wind corrections.

He smelled it then, the cigarette Nathan had seen near Mateo's house, but it wasn't tobacco. It had the distinctive odor of marijuana. It would seem that Mateo wanted to be in a good mood for their meeting.

***

"I've got movement at the bus," Nathan said to Harv. "Looks like our man. He's looking toward Estefan . . . Okay, they see each other. Estefan waved. Keep eyes on the lumber mill area. I'll cover Mateo and Estefan."

"No problem."

"They're shaking hands. So far, so good. They're walking out toward the river. Someone else stepped outside. It's a woman. Mateo's saying something to her . . . She's going back inside. Looks fairly young. Late teens or early twenties."

"Probably Mateo's daughter, Antonia," Harv said.

Nathan remembered her name from Tobias's letters. He tracked Estefan and Mateo out to the tree line, making sure they weren't followed. "I just lost sight of them at the river."

"We're all quiet at the lumber mill. No movement."

"As long as Estefan's with Mateo, he won't be able to check in. Let's hope he doesn't keep us waiting too long."

"Nate, you should take a scope break. I'll watch for a spell."

"Sounds good." He powered off the scope before pulling its rubber boot away from his eye. He rubbed his eyes and took a few deep breaths. This whole operation, if it could even be called that, still seemed surreal. He thought back to Cantrell's comment. She was right: even if they had created a hardened killer, they shouldn't be held accountable for Raven's actions beyond his kilo missions. Still, there'd been signs of instability. Raven's demeanor hadn't been extremely unusual, but he'd been overzealous about his sniper training. As much as Nathan hated to admit it, Harv was right. Raven enjoyed his work a little too much. Cantrell's difficult question about why he hadn't washed Raven out had been valid, but the answer was moot now.

The next ten minutes passed without incident. Harv's voice broke the silence.

"Mateo's walking back to his house," Harv said.

Nathan shouldered his rifle and turned the scope back on. "We'll let Mateo get fifty yards away from Estefan before we make radio contact. I'd like to know how the meeting went."

A few seconds later, Estefan broke the radio silence.

"You guys copy?"

"Affirm. What spooked you earlier?"

"Just a stray dog."

"How did it go with Mateo?"

"He didn't know a whole lot about Macanas's day-to-day operations, but I learned a few things that might be useful."

"Do you think he was being truthful?"

"It's hard to say. He didn't want to accept it at first, but he was super grateful for the cash. We definitely scored some major points."

"We'll talk about your meeting later. Since you're in tree cover, go ahead and wire your radio back up. Follow the creek until you're abeam the church and head over there."

"Do you want me to break in if it's locked?"

Nathan looked at Harv. He hadn't considered that. "This isn't a big-city church with valuables inside. Aside from Bibles, there's probably nothing worth stealing in there. Besides, anyone who steals the most-printed book in all of mankind's history definitely needs to read it. If it's locked, look for a key in some obvious places near the door. But don't break in, okay? I don't like the idea of vandalizing God's house."

"Well, well, well, there may be hope for you yet."

"Just get going."

"Aye, aye, sir."

"If it's locked, head up to your dad's house and have a look around. Searching the church isn't as important as looking through your dad's possessions. You're primarily looking for letters he hadn't sent you yet. I think we can reasonably assume he discovered something Macanas didn't want anyone else to know."

"*I've kind of come to the same conclusion. He wasn't killed solely for helping the miners.*"

"On your way over to Mateo's, did you see the dam we located on the aerials?"

"*Yes, the trail goes across it and up the canyon to my father's house. I've hiked it a couple of times.*"

"We'll be able to see you once you reemerge north of the trees. One of the farmhouses between you and the church has a light on."

"*I saw it. I'll give it a wide berth. I'll stash my NV in the pack. If anyone sees me, I don't want to look too suspicious.*"

"Estefan, you're in a woodland combat uniform with a sidearm and face paint."

"*Yeah, I guess you're right. I already look out of place.*"

Nathan gave him a click and swung the scope toward Mateo's house.

All quiet.

***

Estefan retraced his steps along the creek. The damp fallout allowed him to move quietly. He didn't think anyone had come out here in the last fifteen minutes, but he'd never assume that. As he had on the way over, he stopped every so often and looked around. He knew he was approaching the pond because the frogs were getting louder. Crossing the riprap dam wouldn't be difficult. Allowing the water to flow between them, five-hundred-pound boulders were strategically placed like stepping stones. River crossings like this were common around here. After heavy rainfall, the water rose above the stepping stones, but it always receded back to a manageable flow. Every so often a hurricane would devastate the area, washing out the dams. Sometimes it took years before they were replaced.

Estefan looked to the west and spotted the church's abbreviated bell tower. If he left the creek here, a little sooner than he'd planned, he could avoid getting too close to the farmhouse with the glowing window. Not everyone in Santavilla was dirt poor; a few people had TVs with satellite subscriptions. Analog TV and cell signals weren't available this far north.

"I'm leaving the tree line. You should see me in a few seconds. Give me a click when you've got me in sight." Because of the towering trees between himself and Nathan's perch on the mountainside, he'd have to traverse more than seventy-five yards before he'd be visible.

Estefan received his acknowledgment click about where he'd estimated. Maintaining a northbound vector, he followed a narrow dirt track with barbed-wire fencing on both sides. The nearest he could tell, all the farms were approximately four acres in size. Estefan didn't see any livestock, but some of the fields had been plowed recently. Always scanning the immediate area, he maintained a steady pace. If all went well, he'd reach the church in the next three minutes.

***

Nathan kept his eye firmly against the rubber boot of the scope and aimed his rifle back toward Mateo's house.

He saw movement and froze.

There it was again.

A human form—moving slowly toward the main road.

"Harv, we've got movement."

"What've you got?"

"That girl I saw before. She's walking west toward the main road. She keeps looking over her shoulder."

"I see her. Can she get eyes on Estefan from there?"

"Not yet, but if she turns south toward the church on the main road, she'll be able to." Nathan pressed the transmit button. "You've got company. I'm pretty sure it's Mateo's daughter. She's walking toward the main road. I want you to do an all-out sprint for the stone wall east of the church. I think you can get there before she gets a clear line of sight to you." He heard his radio click and watched Estefan hustle down the dirt track. He hoped his friend's footfalls wouldn't be heard. Although he doubted any people would hear them, dogs were a different matter.

"Crap, she turned south at the road."

"Can he make it in time?" Harv asked.

"I'm not sure." Nathan kept alternating from Estefan to the girl, gauging her visual line of sight. Estefan needed to cover another two hundred yards which ought to take around twenty seconds. At the girl's current pace, she'd have a clear line of sight at about the same time. Her visual window wouldn't be large—an opening between a couple of houses lining the road—but if she looked in Estefan's direction, she might see him. Seconds counted.

"Nate, he's not going to make it."

"Estefan, drop!" Nathan watched his friend sprawl out on the ground and hold perfectly still.

"I'm on Estefan, Nate. What's the girl doing?"

"She stopped walking. She's just standing there, staring in Estefan's direction."

"Think she saw him?" Harv asked.

"I don't think so, but I'm not sure. At best she might've seen movement in the corner of her eye. Estefan, did you mention you were heading over to the church during your meeting with Mateo?"

"No, not really."

"Not really?"

"I just asked if it was locked at night. That's why I asked about breaking in."

"And . . ."

"Mateo didn't know."

"Did you see the girl before you went prone?"

"No."

"I want you to low crawl due north for about twenty-five yards until you reach the cover of the waist-high rock wall. It's about forty yards east of the church's playground. You should be able to see it."

"Copy. I've got it."

"Once you reach the wall, take a look over it. You'll see some abandoned vehicles. Hold your position east of the wall until you hear from me." He checked Estefan's position but detected no movement. The only indicator that his friend was making forward progress was the slowly decreasing distance between Estefan's prone form and rock wall. It seemed their friend hadn't lost his low-crawling skill.

"The girl's walking south along the east side of the street. At her current pace, she'll be at the church in less than a minute."

Harv asked, "Is she empty-handed? Do you see a gun?"

"No, I doubt most people own them here, besides farmers and ranchers. She keeps looking behind, like she's worried she's being followed."

"Maybe she snuck out of the house. How old is she?"

"It's impossible to say. Best guess, maybe twenty."

"That's a little old for sneaking out, don't you think?"

"Not in the Hispanic community."

"Then she could be going out to meet someone. Maybe a boyfriend."

"Stay on Estefan, Harv, I've got the girl. Under normal circumstances, I'd agree, but her timing is suspect. Give me a correction to the church."

"Seven down. No wind correction, just hold two inches left."

"Copy." Nathan clicked his elevation and answered Harv's unspoken question. "No, I'm not planning to shoot her. If she does anything weird, I'll put one at her feet."

"We'll need to relocate if you have to shoot."

"Let's see how this plays out." Nathan pressed his transmit button. "Estefan, you're good to go. I want you to hop the rock wall and advance to the abandoned vehicles. They'll screen you from the girl's position. You should have an unobstructed view of the church from there."

His radio clicked.

"What's your plan?" Harv asked.

"I'm open to suggestions."

"I've got an idea to determine the girl's intentions, but it means blowing Estefan's stealth."

"You want Estefan to let her see him?"

"She'll either make her presence known or try to avoid detection. She already knows Estefan's out there. She saw him back at the house."

"That's a good idea, but since we have no idea what her intention is, I want Estefan to keep a safe distance. I doubt it's a coincidence she's walking toward the church, especially after Estefan asked Mateo if it was unlocked."

"What do we do if she's spying on him?"

"We give Estefan a chance to practice the field-interrogation techniques we taught him."

"You serious?"

"Yep."

"I thought we weren't going to add to anyone's misery in Santavilla."

"Let's just say I have a personal distaste for snitches. Hang on, Harv. Estefan, we've got a plan. When I give you the word, I want you to double-time over to the east wall of the church. We're going to let the girl see you and see what she does."

"Copy. She doesn't have a gun, does she?"

"We don't think so."

"You don't think so? What do you mean you don't think so?"

"Relax. Stand by."

"He's still high-strung," Harv said.

"He'll be okay." Nathan had to time his command precisely. "Harv, as soon as the girl reaches the front door of the church, I'm going to tell Estefan to make his sprint to the rear wall. It's less than twenty yards from the wrecked cars to the church, so Estefan should be able to cover that distance in about five seconds. She's almost there . . ." He pressed the transmit button. "Now!"

Nathan watched Estefan weave his way through some playground equipment before dashing across the rear yard of the church and flattening himself against the east-facing wall.

"Hold position there."

His radio clicked.

"Okay, on my command, walk around the corner and head in a southwesterly direction across the vacant lot. At the main road, turn left. I want it to look like you're leaving town. She should be able to see you."

"Copy."

"Don't look behind. I'll keep you updated."

"If she shoots me, I'm going to be really pissed."

"I can't see a gun."

"You're six hundred yards away looking through an NV scope!"

"I've got your back. If she makes a threatening move, I'll drop her."

"Well, that's reassuring. When was the last time you made a—"

"Now!" Nathan said.

As instructed, Estefan walked around the corner and angled away from the church toward the road.

"She's trying the front door. It opened and she went inside. Keep going. She'll see the sanctuary's empty and come back out. Move your radio around to the front of your belt. We don't want her to see it."

Estefan needed to trust Nathan's ability to take the woman down if she made a threatening move. He felt insecure with a potential threat behind him, but if Nathan missed the shot, he'd have time to whip around and drop the girl in less than two seconds. Very few shooters possessed handgun skills equal to his own. His long-range rifle skills had waned over the years, but he'd practiced with his Sig often enough that he'd shot out its barrel. He'd replaced the barrel and the firing pin last year.

Estefan's earpiece sounded off. *"Okay, she's back outside. She sees you. Maintain your current pace, and don't look back."*

He casually reached down and clicked the radio. Since the girl was now twenty yards behind him, she'd have to speak somewhat loudly to be heard, assuming she wanted to make her presence known. So far, she hadn't said anything. He felt her eyes bore into his back and wondered what was going through her head. Like Nathan said, she was either out here to make contact or to spy. Maybe both. Either way, it was a bold move on her part. For all this girl knew, he could be a rapist, or worse.

"Anything from her?" Nathan asked.

He kept his voice just above a whisper. "Not a word."

"Let's see if she follows you. Did you mention your father's house?"

"No, but Mateo did. He asked if I'd been over there to look through his things. I said I hadn't."

"Then she might think you're heading up there."

"It's possible Mateo mentioned it to her after I left, but she didn't hear that part of my conversation with him. We were down at the river."

"Either way, heading up to your father's house is a reasonable next move on your part. Turn east at the next road, then turn south at the trail leading up to your father's house. If she follows you, ambush her in the tree line. Restrain her quickly and don't let her

scream. Reassure her you're not going to hurt her—you just want to know why she's following you. Nothing rough, okay?"

"Copy. Nothing rough."

"Estefan, when you get to the creek, remove your radio again. We want the girl to think you're alone."

***

Nathan studied the girl's movements carefully. Using the waist-high foliage to conceal her pursuit, she followed Estefan confidently, often running in a crouch.

"Estefan, she's definitely on your six. I want you to look left and right, but don't look behind."

Nathan's ear speaker clicked. He didn't relish the idea of shooting this girl, but he'd do it without hesitation if she produced a weapon. Dressed in only shorts, open-toed shoes of some kind, and a T-shirt, she still didn't appear to have a handgun, but at this distance, he couldn't see enough detail to rule out a compact weapon in her shorts pocket. There was something about her demeanor that concerned him. She wasn't acting nervous, just the opposite. She advanced with a confident stride, and her movements looked almost . . . what? Rehearsed? Could she be an off-duty cop? Nathan thought that unlikely. This wasn't the US, female officers here were extremely rare. She also looked too young. At this distance, Nathan couldn't accurately estimate her age, but he trusted his first impression. She was late teens to early twenties.

He felt confident Estefan could restrain her silently. During their Echo missions, it was something they'd practiced countless times. A large part of Estefan's training had involved taking prisoners for interrogation.

Nathan watched Estefan turn right at the trail and walk at a good clip toward the creek.

"She's still behind you. One hundred yards. She keeps looking over her shoulder, clearing her own six."

"I'll set up my ambush once I drop below the river's bank."

"Be ready for a struggle. Watch for a head butt and guard your groin. We don't want to carry your ass back to the truck."

"Thanks for the vote of confidence."

"I'm serious. Something tells me she's more capable than she looks."

***

Estefan reached the tree line a minute later and hustled down the sandy slope. He chose a large tree two yards to the right of the trail and used it for cover. He quickly removed his pack and stashed the radio and wiring. When the girl passed his position, he would take her from behind, clamp his hand over her mouth, and get her off balance at the same time. He hadn't done this sort of thing in many years, but it was a simple enough technique. Nathan was right though: if by chance she was a skilled fighter, she'd react quickly and try to head butt him. Maybe it would be best to wrestle her to the ground and use his weight.

"Stand by, Estefan. I'll let you know when I lose sight of her. We'll go radio silent right after that. Do you have eyes on her from your current position?"

"No, the river bank's too high."

"Okay, sit tight and wait for her to come to you."

***

Nathan watched the girl sprint toward the river. She obviously knew that anyone down at water level wouldn't be able to see over the bank. Her actions suggested she was trying to advance before Estefan crossed the dam and climbed the opposite side. She was playing a dangerous game against an unknown opponent. What was worth taking such a risk? Perhaps she thought Estefan hadn't given all of his cash to Mateo, and she planned to rob him. Was that likely? Estefan looked like a special forces soldier, complete with face paint and a sidearm. Challenging him to a physical contest didn't seem like a wise move unless she were highly skilled in hand-to-hand combat. What were the odds of that? Anything was possible, though. A few years back, Nathan had come close to losing a wrestling match against a woman half his weight.

***

Estefan peered around the tree but saw no sign of the girl. He ought to be able to see her by now.

Something felt wrong.

The crickets behind him had gone quiet, which could mean only one thing.

He slowly pivoted to his left.

Incredible!

The girl was standing a mere thirty feet away with her arms crossed. She'd managed to maneuver down the bank and get behind him undetected. If she'd been armed . . . He couldn't see a lot of detail, but she was beautiful, that much was clear. Long black hair accented strong cheekbones, and her shorts and tank top were tight in all the right places.

Estefan spoke in Spanish. It was unlikely this girl knew English. "That's a good trick, sneaking up on me, but it's also a good way to get yourself killed."

"I knew you'd hide down here."

"How's that?"

"On your way over here, you weren't looking over your shoulder to clear your six. You knew I was behind you. You're Tobias's son, aren't you." It wasn't a question.

"And if I am?"

"He talked about you, said you were a soldier."

Estefan brought his gun up. "Do I need this?"

"Hardly, I'm not here for a fight."

"What's your name?"

"Antonia."

"Well, Antonia, 'clearing six' is a military term."

She raised her chin slightly. "I know. I have a friend who's teaching me."

"And . . . ?"

"I saw you give my father some cash."

"I see . . . What are you offering?"

She sucked her teeth. "Not that."

"It's past your bedtime, sweetheart. I'm over twice your age and not interested. Let's try again. What're you offering?"

She didn't say anything.

"Nice meeting you, Antonia." He turned to leave.

"I know stuff."

"You'll have to do better than that."

"Something's happening tomorrow."

"Such as . . . ?"

Again, she didn't respond.

Estefan nodded toward the road. "The money's in my truck. I trust twenty-five hundred córdobas will do?"

"It's a good start."

"So tell me about your friend."

She cocked her head impatiently.

"Right . . . I'll be back in a few minutes."

Estefan picked up his pack, climbed the bank, and walked at a good clip toward the road. He could make better time along the rim of the bank. He knew Nathan couldn't see him because of his proximity to the trees lining the river. Nathan had to be wondering what was going on. When he reached a safe distance from Antonia, he pulled the radio.

"I'm heading back to my truck. The girl wants cash for information."

"What kind of information?"

"She's tight-lipped until she sees some green."

"I guess the entrepreneurial spirit is alive and well in Santavilla."

"I'm heading over to my pickup to get it."

"We'll keep eyes on the area and make sure no one else approaches her position."

"I'd appreciate it. I'm reluctant to admit this, but she got behind me."

"How close did she get before you heard her?"

"That's just it—I didn't hear her at all. But to answer your question, ten yards. She said she has a friend who's been teaching her. She knows what 'clear your six' means."

"Interesting."

"Tell me about it. She must know someone who's a cop or in the military."

"Your father's letters spoke of her desire to leave Santavilla. Maybe this guy's her ticket out of there. He must be the white shirt your father mentioned. How much money does she want?"

"I offered twenty-five hundred córdobas, and she told me it was good start."

"Her friend could be Raven," Harv added.

"Harv's right. She could be the break we're looking for. Tell her there's more if she keeps the info flowing. What's your take on her?"

"She's confident but hard to read. If I had to bet, I'd say she knows a lot."

"Play up to her ego, then. Keep her talking."

"That shouldn't be difficult."

***

Eight minutes later, Estefan descended the creek's bank and found Antonia in the same place, finishing a cigarette. She flicked the butt into the water.

He handed her a wad of bills. "We'll start with this and see how far it goes. If I like what I'm hearing, there will be more."

She tucked the money into her waist.

"A helicopter's going to land at the lumber mill tomorrow. Everyone knows why."

"Enlighten me."

"It takes the gold out of here."

"How do you know that?"

"The man who's teaching me stuff is one of El Jefe's white shirts. All the other white shirts report to him."

Estefan knew about the white-shirt reference from his dad's letters. El Jefe's lieutenants wore white buttoned shirts to distinguish themselves from the other men. "Did he tell you that?"

She nodded.

"How many white shirts are there?"

"Five, I think."

"How many men does El Jefe have?"

"Maybe twenty, but only a few stay in town."

"At the lumber mill?"

She nodded.

"How many?"

"Usually five."

"Do any of his white shirts stay in town?"

She made a *pshh* sound. "Hardly, they might get their shoes dirty."

"The white shirt who's teaching you stuff, what's his name?"

"Franco."

"Last name?"

"I don't know it—he never told me."

"What happened to your father's ear? I didn't ask him."

"Franco came into town with a bunch of his men the night before Tobias was killed. They cut my dad's ear off, because he was hoarding gold to pay for my mom's medicine. Tobias tried to stop them, but they beat him up."

Estefan took a deep breath and tried to remain calm. None of this was in the letters.

"What does Franco look like?"

"I don't know. He just looks like a guy."

"How old is he?"

"Maybe forties. I'm not really sure."

"Is he tall and thin, short and fat, what?"

"He kinda looks like you. You know, the same build. He has really dark eyes. He thinks they make him look tough."

Estefan felt his skin tighten. "Does this guy have a small round scar above his left eye?"

She hesitated, then nodded.

Raven.

Her eyes had changed, confidence giving way to fear. "He'll kill me if he finds out I'm talking to you."

"He won't find out from me."

"Are you going to kill him?"

"And if I am?"

"That's going to be difficult by yourself. He has lots of men."

"I'm used to working alone."

She pulled a pack of cigarettes from her pocket. "You mind?"

"They're your lungs . . ."

She seemed to sense his next question. "Franco gives them to me." She cupped the match with both hands, took a deep drag, and blew the flame out with her exhale.

Estefan recognized the technique. "Did he teach you that?"

"What?"

"Shielding the flare of the match."

"He's always paranoid someone's watching him. When we're together, he's always looking around, even when . . . you know."

"For what it's worth, my advice is to steer clear of him. Whatever he's told you is a lie. Let me guess, he said he's going to take you out of here someday."

She nodded.

"Do you honestly believe that?"

"He's never lied to me."

"Trust me, he doesn't care about anyone but himself. Look, all I can do is warn you. You have to decide what to do. How do I get ahold of you later?"

"If you call the house at ten in the morning, my dad's up at the mines. My mom's in the gold mill. There's nobody there but me, but I have to go to work at noon."

"Where do you work?"

"At the Perezes' store. I work the late shift until eight at night." She went quiet for a moment.

"Does he give you money?"

"I'm not a whore!"

"Hey, calm down. I didn't say you were."

"I'm a mistress."

Estefan nearly laughed. *Is that what you are?*

"He gives me nice clothes and stuff. We have a flat TV and a satellite dish. We even have a dishwasher. He's teaching me how to shoot guns. I can hit a beer can at fifty meters."

"You're using a scoped rifle?"

"He says it's his favorite gun of all time. A 'remilard,' or something."

"Remington?"

"Yeah, I think so."

Another piece of the puzzle. "You said a helicopter's coming tomorrow. Franco told you that?"

"He flies it himself. He said he'd give me a ride someday. I've never been in one."

"Do you know when he's coming?"

"He always comes before I go to work."

"So sometime before noon?"

She nodded.

"How do you contact each other?"

"He calls the house twice, but he only lets it ring once each time. It's our secret code. I'm supposed to call him back from the pay phone."

Estefan waited.

"No way. I'm not giving you his number."

"When does he call?"

"We usually talk really late when everyone's asleep but not always."

"Aren't you worried people will find out? You know, that you're his mistress?"

"I'm not the only one. All of the white shirts have girls here. It's not really a secret."

"I'm sorry for what I said. I didn't mean to suggest you were a prostitute."

"It's okay. Don't worry about it. Nearly all the girls my age are selling themselves to the miners. Younger ones too. They trade sex for gold and turn it in on free Sunday."

"What's free Sunday?"

She took another hit. "It's why my dad got in trouble. El Jefe lets the miners pan gold on Sundays, but they have to trade it in for cash at the end of the day. Some of the miners don't turn all of it in. El Jefe calls it hoarding."

"How much gold can they pan in one day?"

"I don't really know, but Franco told me most of them get around two or three hundred córdobas for it."

Estefan took a step forward. "Antonia, why did you come out here? Was it just for the money?"

She looked down. "I liked your father—everyone did. He was a really nice man. I was there when he got shot."

"Will you tell me about it?"

For the first time, she showed some emotion and wiped a tear. "I was at the church meeting just before it happened. He went out to the work bus to greet the miners like he always does, and he handed something to my father. It looked like money. That's when

I heard it. There was a loud sound, like a whip. I didn't know what the sound was."

"It's a supersonic bullet. It makes a small sonic boom. How long was it between that sound and report of the rifle?"

"What do you mean?"

"You should've heard a thud sound right after the crack."

"I did hear it. I remember because it echoed like thunder."

"Was it about one second?"

"I think so, but I'm not sure."

"But the two sounds weren't really close together, right? There was a delay?"

"Yes, I remember it. Mrs. Perez ran over to your father and held his hand. Everyone else was too scared. I think he died pretty fast. She held his head and said a prayer. I felt really bad for him. It took the police forever to get here, and nobody would talk to them."

"Thank you for sharing that with me. I'm glad he didn't die alone."

"Mrs. Perez really liked him. She's been really sad lately. She hardly comes into the store anymore."

Estefan needed to up the stakes. "You're in a dangerous relationship. The man who considers you his mistress is the sniper who killed my father."

"Because he knows about rifles?"

"Other things too. He also shot the manager at the lumber mill a few months ago."

She didn't say anything.

"Look, Antonia, you seem like a smart girl. I don't know what you've got going with him. It's none of my business, but I don't want you to become his next victim. I'm serious. He's not what he appears to be. Don't trust him at all; he's just using you until he doesn't need you anymore."

"Maybe I'm using him."

"Then you're playing a very dangerous game. Think about what I told you, okay?"

She didn't react.

"I have to go. The nice stuff Franco's buying for you? The money and clothes? His promise to take you out of here? It's not worth selling your soul. Deep down, I think you know that."

He couldn't see her face, but her body language suggested she was about to cry again.

With that, Estefan walked away. When he looked back a few seconds later, she was gone. She must've climbed the bank, but he needed to be certain she wouldn't follow him. Estefan pulled his radio and turned the volume up a little.

"You guys copy?"

"We're here."

"Do you have eyes on the girl?"

"Affirm. She's heading for the church."

"I'm ninety-nine percent sure her boyfriend, who goes by Franco, is Raven." He told Nathan and Harv about the scar—the scar he had given Raven during a fistfight when they'd both been drunk right after the war.

"This is gold," Nathan said. *"She's our connection to Raven. Good work, Estefan."*

"I think she'll stop at the general store and call the guy."

"Let's hope she does. We want Raven to know you're in town asking questions. Harv?"

"Yeah, I agree. It's possible he'll try to neutralize Estefan using men from the lumber mill without coming up here himself."

"Not a nice thought," Estefan added.

"Then we'll just have to make sure that doesn't happen," Nathan said.

"Maybe I should drive into town and check into the hotel using my real name."

"That's a good idea. We might be able to set a trap."

"I'll camp with you guys up there tonight. We'll take turns keeping watch. Three sets of eyes are better than two."

"Okay, she turned right at the church, she's heading toward the general store. Do you think she suspects you were playing her?"

"It's hard to say, but my gut says no. She was too busy playing *me*." Estefan took a minute to update them on most of the stuff he and Antonia talked about, especially the part about the helicopter and Raven keeping some of his men at the lumber mill. "I'm a pretty good judge of BS, and I was just hip deep in it. She even faked some tears."

"Then you think she'll call Raven?"

"Absolutely."

"She just passed the store. It looks like she's heading home without stopping at the pay phone."

"I trust my instincts—she'll call him."

CHAPTER 21

"Let's drink more water," Harv suggested.

He and Nathan downed a pint each. Neither of them felt dehydrated, but given the heat, they should be sweating more than they were.

Nathan kept his eye to the scope, scanning the area surrounding Mateo's house.

"Well, at least this confirms what Estefan believed all along. Raven's definitely our shooter," Harv said.

"It pisses me off he's sold his skills to someone like Macanas. I never saw this coming."

"Don't beat yourself up, Nate. People change, but I'd like to know how he got hooked up with Macanas."

"Yeah, that's a good question." Nathan couldn't conceal the bitterness in his voice. "He sure as hell didn't respond to a help-wanted ad in the paper. Sniper needed, past experience preferred."

Harv didn't respond.

"I'm just venting. We held people's lives in our hands, and it took a heavy toll. We've never killed anyone for monetary reasons or for personal gain. We literally had licenses to kill, even domestically, but we held ourselves to the highest possible standard. We never killed an innocent to make our jobs easier. You remember the damned chain-smoker who kept us from entering that warehouse in Romania?"

"How could I forget? We froze our asses off. Look, I know you feel we're partially responsible because we trained him, but Cantrell's right. Raven has free will. As far as we know, no one's forcing him to murder anyone. Like Cantrell said, you can't blame the academy's instructors if a cop goes bad. Life doesn't work that way. I mean, how far do you take it? Do you blame the makers of Jack Daniels for drunk drivers? If a guy kills someone with a baseball bat, do you blame the tree it came from?"

"I get that, Harv. I guess I'm . . . I don't know . . . feeling betrayed."

"You *have* been betrayed, both of us have."

"He seemed okay at the time. Yeah, he liked his job a little too much, but I never doubted his loyalty. He was an extremely dedicated combat soldier who never complained or made excuses. When he made a mistake, he didn't deflect the blame. I meant what I said to Cantrell. I liked the guy."

"Maybe you saw some of yourself in him."

Nathan went silent and knew Harv would give him a moment to collect his thoughts. He liked that about his friend. "Without knowing anything about Raven's activities after the kilo units broke up, there's no way we'll ever know how he got connected with Macanas. Hell, for all we know, they met at the local racquetball club or strip joint."

"We could take Raven alive and wring it out of him."

"It's going to be hard enough just killing him. And I guess it really doesn't matter how he went bad. I'd just—"

"I'll be at my truck in thirty seconds."

Estefan's voice brought Nathan abruptly back to the mission at hand.

"Wait there for Harv. I'm sending him down to collect the rest of our gear. We don't want to leave anything in your truck."

"*Since I'm already down here and you guys can keep an eye on my six, I should head over to the lumber mill and have a look around. I'll do it after I check into the motel. We also need to scout the area where the helicopter lands.*"

"Make it quick. If Antonia calls Raven from her house, you might have unexpected company down there. Raven might use his men from the lumber mill to go after you."

"*Do you guys have eyes on the place from there?*"

"Yes, but it's a lot farther away. From our current position, it's got to be over thirteen hundred yards. That's beyond the limit of my NV weapon scope. We'll need to relocate to cover you. Your diesel's loud, and Mateo's house is about fifty yards from the main road. Even if she doesn't see it, Antonia will hear your truck for sure. Let's keep playing her. Leave your headlights off. She'll think you're trying to sneak in there. Like I said, we have to consider the possibility she'll use the phone inside her house to call Raven, but I'm pretty sure Raven wouldn't want her to do that. The call would show up on her father's phone bill."

"*What if she makes the call when you guys are on the move?*"

"I see what you mean. After you check into the motel, find a spot to keep an eye on the pay phone while we're relocating. You should be able to see it from the post office or the tavern across the street. We don't need to be super stealthy up here, so it shouldn't take us that long to reposition. We'll give you a laser when we reach our new shooting position."

"*Sounds good. When I get to my truck, I'll check my cell, but I've never gotten a signal in this valley.*"

"We don't have a signal up here either."

"*It might be possible to get a connection at the top of the mountain.*"

"I know you're worried about your wife. I promise we'll try to get a signal later. Sit tight until Harv gets there. He'll grab your rifle and all the ammo. We shouldn't leave any of the cash in your truck. If there's anything else you want Harv to take with him, have it ready to go."

"There's nothing. My wife makes me keep the truck immaculate . . . Shit."

"Estefan?"

"It's just . . . my wife, she hates clutter. She's always getting after me about it."

"She'll be okay. Harv's on his way down."

***

Proud of herself, Antonia stopped at the work bus and lit a cigarette. If she'd had any doubt, it was now dispelled. The techniques Franco had taught her worked perfectly. The excitement she'd felt sneaking up on Tobias's son had been intoxicating. She'd never felt so powerful. Her mom got high on opium, her father on alcohol, but Antonia had discovered a much more addictive drug—adrenaline.

The day after Tobias was murdered, Franco had asked her to watch for anyone new showing up in town, especially anyone asking questions. During their call earlier this evening, he'd reminded her to stay alert. Well, Pastor Tobias's son definitely qualified as someone asking questions. He wasn't new to town. She'd seen him before, but he'd never been dressed like a soldier. She wanted to call Franco right away and give him the news, but she didn't know where Delgado was. She didn't want him to see her use the pay phone—that would look suspicious. The call to Franco would have to wait for the right moment.

Something else required the right moment as well. When the time was right, she planned to ask Franco for a job. Surely El Jefe's organization could use a tactically trained female in its ranks, and she was the perfect candidate. She already had the confidence of El Jefe's right-hand man. If she played this right, her ticket out of Santavilla was certain. She wanted a convertible, a house on the hill, and a closetful of clothes to show off her figure. She hated dressing in hand-me-downs. Nothing would stop her from getting a better life, certainly not Tobias's son. The guy had been laughable, especially that fatherly crap about being concerned with her safety. She'd nearly given him a hug, but that would've seemed forced. She'd gained his trust well enough without a phony show of affection.

Antonia was many things, but naive wasn't one of them. She knew Franco was using her, but he didn't know she was using him too. When they'd first started seeing each other, he'd been reluctant to teach her anything. Over the course of several months, she'd gradually worn his defenses down through crafty manipulation. When he was aroused, she'd tease him and promise a little something extra in exchange for tactical training. It had been all too easy. Everything he'd taught her, from surveillance to bomb making to personal combat skills, was all neatly tucked away for future use. Maybe she'd even replace him someday. She felt confident she could apply her feminine wiles on El Jefe as easily as she had on Franco.

First things first. She needed to find Estefan Delgado before calling Franco. He wouldn't like getting a call this late, but he'd be grateful once he heard the news.

She finished her cigarette, slipped inside her house, and looked at the ugly clock on the wall. It was just after 12:30 AM.

What a dump. She resented everything about this place. The beat-up furniture, stained curtains, and bare concrete made her feel cheap and dirty. Even though they had some nice stuff, a shanty was still a shanty. Her father spent all his money on booze and opium. She felt bad about her mom's condition, but there was nothing she could do for her. If she didn't leave this place soon, she'd end up just like her, or worse.

She'd wait a few more minutes before going outside to scout the area.

***

Estefan reached his truck and conducted a quick survey of its tires. He didn't trust the girl and wanted to be sure she hadn't flattened any of them.

"I'm at my truck," he said.

"*Go ahead and pack up everything and be ready to go.*"

"You got it."

"*We'll keep eyes on Mateo's house and let you know if we see Antonia head for the pay phone.*"

Estefan removed his face paint and briefly used the dome light to see if he'd missed any areas.

Harv arrived a few minutes later and grabbed all their gear. He let Harv know he kept some of the money for the motel. Fifteen seconds later, Harv disappeared into the foliage. Now it became a waiting game. Estefan didn't doubt Antonia would contact Raven—the question became when? He sat in his truck, staring straight ahead. He almost felt sorry for the girl, but she was old enough to make informed decisions. If she ended up in an unmarked grave because her priorities were screwed up, so be it. Sadly, the world wouldn't miss her.

His earpiece came to life with Nathan's voice. "*Stand by, Estefan. Antonia just stepped outside.*"

CHAPTER 22

"She's lighting a cigarette and looking around. I'll let you know if she makes a move for the pay phone. Harv, did you copy?"

"*Affirm.*"

"Where are you?"

"*Two mikes.*"

"Go ahead and double-time it. I'm confident we're alone up here."

His radio clicked.

"Antonia appears on edge. She keeps looking from side to side and turning around. She knows you're out here, Estefan. She just doesn't know where."

"*She'll know soon enough.*"

"I'm counting on it."

Nathan froze when he heard Harv's approach. To be sure it was Harv, he issued a warbling whistle and received the same whistle in return, lower in pitch. Had Harv's return whistle not been lower in pitch, Nathan would've gone into high alert.

Nathan said, "Stand by, Estefan. Harv's back. We'll get his eyes back on the lumber mill."

"I'm on it," Harv said, breathing heavily.

Nathan removed his finger from the transmit button and kept his scope on Mateo's house as he spoke. "Maybe we should interrupt Antonia's call. If we time it right, Estefan could drive into town right after she gets on the phone. She'll duck for cover, and she'll think she's eluded Estefan. It would be unsettling to Raven to have her call suddenly end like that. Put yourself in Raven's shoes. You just learned Viper's in town, snooping around and asking questions. What would you do?"

"I'd get up there as soon as I could, find a good SP overlooking the town, and drop the guy from a safe distance."

"Exactly," Nathan said. "But here's the kicker. Raven doesn't know we're with Estefan. He thinks Estefan's alone. If we can get eyes on Raven, even for an instant, we can drop him."

"That's a big *if*," Harv said.

"Here we go." Nathan pressed the transmit button. "Estefan, Antonia's on the move. Start your roll into town. You're about a mile from the general store, so it will take about three or four minutes. Turn on your high beams. I'm hoping she'll see them in the distance and alert Raven that someone's coming—presumably you. Turn off your lights just shy of the church. We want Antonia to think you're trying to sneak in there. Your engine noise works in our favor. You copy all that, Estefan?"

"Affirm. On my way."

Echoing in the distance, Estefan's truck rumbled to life. Despite all the trees and undergrowth lining the mountainsides, sound traveled amazingly well through this valley.

"Harv, keep eyes on the lumber mill."

"Will do. Besides the meltdown on the road, Estefan's done well."

"He's worried about his wife, so I doubt he's totally focused down there."

"You're probably right, but he's a vet. I'm okay with Estefan." Nathan pressed the transmit button. "Estefan, she's heading straight for the phone. Pick up your speed a little."

His radio clicked.

Harv said, "If Raven has men at the lumber mill like Antonia said, he'll call over there after he hangs up with her. Things could get dicey for Estefan."

"I have an idea. I'll go over it in a minute."

***

Franco was watching the entrance to the hospital when his prepaid cell rang. Only Antonia had this number. "You're calling awfully late."

"It's important." She sounded breathless, quite unlike her usual phone manner.

"What's so important that it can't wait until tomorrow?"

"Tobias's son is here. He came to our house and talked to my father."

"When?"

"Maybe half an hour ago."

"What did they say?"

"I didn't hear them. They walked out to the river. I wanted to follow them, but my dad told me to stay in the house."

He started his car and grabbed a notepad and pen from the glove compartment. "Okay, slow down. How do you know it's Tobias's son?"

"After my dad came back from the river, he told me Tobias's son was going up to his father's house. I followed him, but I think he knew I was there. He was waiting for me near the dam, but I snuck up on him. He didn't see me." She paused. "You aren't mad, are you?"

"What happened next?"

"We talked for a while. He asked all kinds of questions, but I didn't tell him anything. He wanted to know how his father died. I told him Mrs. Perez was there and held his hand when he died."

"How touching."

"He wants to kill you."

"I hope you told him to take a number and get in line."

"He seemed really serious. He was dressed like a soldier, had a gun, face paint, and everything."

Franco needed a current description. All he'd seen in Viper's house was an old photograph. He was still waiting for his police insider to deliver a current photocopy of Viper's driver's license. "I need a good description of how he looks. Tell me as much detail as you can. Don't leave anything out. Actually, forget that—I'll ask you questions."

"You sound mad."

"I'm not mad. Now I want you to relax and take a couple of deep breaths. It's important you stay calm. When people are upset or nervous, they can't focus, and I need you really focused. I want you to close your eyes and think back to when you first saw him. You said he was dressed like a soldier. Let's start there. Was he in digital camouflage, like the ones I wear?"

"Yes."

"Did he have a backpack?"

"Yes."

"Did he have a rifle, like the one I taught you how to shoot?"

"No. He just had a handgun like yours. It was in a thigh holster."

"It wasn't at his waist?"

"No."

"Right- or left-handed."

"Right."

Franco asked a few more questions and ended up with a good picture of his old kilo friend. "This next question is really important. Did you ever see anyone else or suspect anyone else was with him?"

"No, he said he preferred to work alone."

"How did that come up in conversation?"

"I'm not sure. I think he said it after I asked if he wanted to kill you. Wait, I'm remembering now. I told him it would be hard to kill you by himself. I was trying to find out if he was alone. That's when he said it."

"That he preferred to work alone?"

"Yes."

"Smart thinking, Antonia. I'll make an operative out of you yet."

"Thanks, I was kinda nervous, but he couldn't tell. He told me to stay away from you—that you were dangerous and not to be trusted. I let him think I cared about his advice. He wanted to know when you'd be here next. I told him you'd be flying here tomorrow."

"You're incredible. More good thinking."

"Aren't you worried he'll . . . you know . . . try to kill you?"

"I'm not worried—"

"Someone's coming! I see headlights. I think it's him."

"Find out where he goes, and call me back as soon as you can."

"I will."

"Get going before he sees you. You did well, Antonia. I won't forget this."

***

Cantrell heard a gentle knock on her door before Stafford entered. "We've got an official statement from Caracas," he said. "It's not for public consumption yet, but the limousine was taking the minister of basic industry and mining to the airport. Guess where he was flying?"

Cantrell squinted in thought. "The Central American summit in Managua."

"You got it. But the situation's just become a lot more serious. Several hours after the bombing in Caracas, an attempt was made to kill the Colombian minister of mines and industry. The government kept it quiet, but one of our people in Bogotá got word. The minister survived, but he's in the hospital."

"Let me guess, he was also on his way to the Managua summit. How did it happen?"

"Several gunmen ambushed his vehicle right after it left the security gate of his residential community. His bodyguard killed the gunmen but died from multiple gunshot wounds. The Colombian minister was shot twice. He's in critical condition, but he's expected to live. No one's claimed responsibility. Both the ministers were going to be key players at the summit. There's been no official statement from Nicaragua, but so far, the summit hasn't been cancelled."

"There's no way any of this is a coincidence. Keep trying to contact McBride and Fontana. We're getting them the hell out of there. No arguments—they're leaving. Whatever's going on there, the last thing we want is any kind of connection to us."

"I'll get right on it."

"See if you can get the DNI on the phone. I'm going to give him a complete update on McBride's situation. I'm uncomfortable withholding it at this point. What's your take on it?"

"It sounds like someone's trying to sabotage the summit."

"My thoughts exactly. I want to know who, and why."

CHAPTER 23

"Estefan, I think she sees your headlights. Go ahead and kill them a little early."

"Copy. How's my speed?"

"You're looking good. She's on the move. Keep going."

Estefan slowed a little. He didn't want to wreck his suspension. The low half-moon gave him enough light to see the overall width and direction of the road but not its neglected surface. Considering the size of this town, he thought the road ought to be in better shape. He supposed getting FOMAV out here to make a few passes with a road grader was like expecting to find a short line at the unemployment office.

Rolling into the center of town, he saw no sign of the girl. On the same side of the street as the Perezes' store and Mateo's house, the motel stood about one hundred yards farther north. Estefan had stayed there a few times over the years. You didn't have to pay extra for clean sheets, but every room was multiple occupancy: one human and lots of cockroaches. It was a simple rectangular building with a hip roof. All the doors faced the street. Small windows on its rear wall allowed air to flow through. The owner would be grateful for his business, even if it meant getting up at 0100.

"Where's the girl?" Estefan asked.

She left the pay phone in a hurry and went across the street to the tavern. I lost sight of her behind the building.

"She should be able to see my truck by now, even with the lights off."

She can hear it coming for sure. Park behind the motel to keep the ruse going. Don't forget to remove your face paint before you check in.

"I already did. There's nothing I can do about my combat uniform; walking into the place in my underwear isn't a good option."

I don't know. You might get a package discount.

"Very funny. I'm the one in the shit down here."

You never had a chance to look around the church. When we saw the girl, our plans changed. You took her out to the river.

"You want me to check it out before I head over to the lumber mill?"

Hold off, I've got another idea. Let's see what Antonia does after she watches you check into the motel.

Driving past the tavern, Estefan felt the girl's surveillance, but he avoided looking in her direction. He pulled into the gravel lot behind the motel and parked next to some rusty cars that looked like they hadn't moved in years. After locking his truck, he walked around the corner to the office, making sure to look over his shoulder a few times. If Antonia were lurking at the tavern, she'd hidden herself well. He pressed the doorbell and heard a muffled chime. Half a minute later, he faked pressing it again and leaned in toward the door, pretending to listen. He was actually stealing a glance toward the tavern, but its north wall created deep shadows, and he saw no sign of the girl. As he turned his head, he caught the odor of a cigarette in the light wind coming from the southwest. She was definitely over there somewhere.

***

Antonia took a hit from her cigarette and helplessly watched the smoke drift toward the motel. She immediately put it out and hoped the guy wouldn't smell it. She should've tossed it when she'd first heard his truck coming. There was no recovering from this mistake; the smoke was on its way. She was about to relocate when a light came on inside the motel office. A few seconds later, Mr. Fernandez opened the door and waved the guy inside. The timing was perfect. She'd head up the street to the gas station. Although the tavern offered a decent view of the motel, the gas station was directly across the street. She'd be able to count doors and tell Franco the exact room number.

She ran north along the dirt alley paralleling the road and angled across a vacant lot. A glance to her right confirmed the light was still on in the motel's office. The gas-pump island offered an ideal place to hide. The pumps were big enough to screen her entire body, and the old convenience store blocked the moonlight. He'd never see her.

***

Nathan saw the girl reemerge on the north side of the tavern. "She's on the move again. She just ran up the street to the gas station. She's hiding behind the pumps. It looks like there's a clear line of sight from there to the motel room doors. I'll let Estefan know where she is once he enters his room." He watched for a moment, then saw Estefan leave the motel's office and head down the walkway lined with doors. After he lost sight of Estefan, he pressed the transmit button a couple of times, making Estefan's radio click in his pocket. He didn't want to say anything, because he didn't know if the motel room's window was open.

"Copy. I'm here."

"Antonia's across the street hiding behind the gas pumps. Pull the curtain and turn on a light. We want her to think you're settling in for the night."

"It's like an oven in here. I've gotta open the windows. I'll turn my radio down to a whisper. She'll never hear it from across the street."

Even with the curtains pulled, Nathan's scope registered a tiny amount of bleed light escaping the room onto the gravel. "Is there a rear window?"

"Yes, it's next to the bathroom, but it's fogged glass. There aren't any curtains."

"Does it open? Can you get through it?"

"Yeah, it opens. It'll be tight, but I can get through."

"Okay, sit tight for now. I have a feeling Antonia's next move is to the pay phone to report your room number. Wire up your radio, and be ready to move out."

"Should I leave the light on when I leave? There's no TV in here."

"No, turn it off when you leave, but keep it on for now."

***

This place is stark, thought Estefan. It looked clean enough, but all it contained was a bunk bed and a nightstand. The only place to sit other than the floor was the bed. The horrid purple carpet had been worn through in a triangular pattern between the door, the bed, and the bathroom. He supposed this room served its purpose. He'd been in worse, but this one ranked in the top five. At least the nightstand drawer contained a Bible.

Check-in had gone quickly. Estefan hadn't recognized the young man handling night-shift duties, but he'd opened the office, taken Estefan's money, and given him a room key without complaint.

Already a sheen of perspiration had formed on his face. Time to get out. He radioed Nathan to confirm he was leaving.

"Okay. On second thought, leave the light on. Do you have any cover behind the motel when you climb out?"

"Not really. My pickup is back there with some other cars, but if anyone's watching, they'll see me for sure. I'll be a silhouette in the bathroom window."

"Well, it seems unlikely that anyone but Antonia's out there, and she's in front. Harv has eyes on the lumber mill. Should be low risk. We'll keep eyes on the girl and let you know if she heads for the phone. Go ahead and slip out the back window, but hold position near your truck."

Estefan clicked his radio in response and reached for the rear window.

***

"There are a few lights on at the lumber mill and ore-processing plant," Harv told Nathan, "but I don't see any activity."

"If Raven's men are going to ambush Estefan, they'll need his room number."

"And they won't have it until Antonia relays that to Raven."

"Right. I need a break," Nathan said. "Alternate eyes between the tavern and lumber mill."

"You got it."

Nathan secured his M40 rifle, walked a few steps away, and stretched his arms over his head. He bent at the waist a couple of times and twisted his torso. "Maybe we should pick an SP over-looking the front of the motel, not the helipad and lumber mill."

"That would mean relocating to the west, across the river on an east-facing slope."

Nathan nodded. "That will take at least twenty minutes. I have a feeling Antonia will be on the move before that. Let's stay put for now. We're zeroed from this SP. I think we're good."

"If things turn ugly down there, Raven's men will probably disable Estefan's truck. Unless we steal a vehicle, we'll be looking at a long hump back to our extraction point."

"You're raining on our parade, Harv."

"Hey, I'm just trying to think everything through."

"Unless Macanas can mobilize dozens of men to canvass the entire area, we'll get back to our EP okay."

"What about Estefan?" Harv asked. "Assuming we kill Raven, Macanas won't be real happy about it. Estefan won't want to spend the rest of his life looking over his shoulder."

"You're making it rain harder."

"I know, but seriously, if we kill Raven, I don't see how Estefan could stay in Nicaragua with Macanas still in the picture."

"There's no way we're going after Macanas," Nathan said. "We made it perfectly clear to Estefan. We said we'd help him with a surgical strike against Raven, and that's the end of our involvement."

"Agreed, but I don't think Estefan's thought all of this through."

"We may have to pull some strings and get him a new life in the US."

"Think he'll want to do that?"

Nathan sat back down and shouldered his weapon. "I have no idea."

"We could offer him a job."

"Yeah, we could. He's more than qualified. I'm on the tavern. Switch back to the lumber mill."

"Do you think Estefan's hell-bent on killing Raven?"

"It sounds like it. Why do you ask?"

Harv didn't answer right away. Nathan gave him a moment to collect his thoughts.

"If we take Raven alive, he could cut a deal with the Nicaraguan authorities and put Macanas behind bars."

"That's an interesting idea, but it's going to be ten times harder taking him alive than killing him. And you assume the Nicaraguan justice system is ready and raring to go to prosecute Macanas. I think we're getting ahead of ourselves. If the opportunity presents itself to bag him alive, we'll let Estefan decide. Estefan knows Raven's just the trigger man. The true source of his father's murder is Macanas."

"Are you saying we let Estefan decide if Raven lives or dies? I'm not sure that will sit right with me, and I know it won't sit right with you, especially if he chooses death."

"You're right," Nathan said. "It won't. We're not killing Raven if he's out of the fight and in our custody. And we aren't looking the other way while Estefan does it. There will be no summary executions on our watch."

"So where does this leave us?"

"We need to talk about that. We can't exactly march Raven down to the nearest NNP station and say, 'Here he is.' And we obviously can't leave him in the care of anyone in Santavilla."

"Cantrell?"

"No way. She'd never agree to it, and I'd never ask."

"Then what?"

"Hell, I don't know. I really don't feel confident about him being convicted for murder here. Unless there's indisputable proof he killed Estefan's father and the others—and even if there is—he might very likely walk."

"That sucks."

"On the other hand, if we nail him in a fair fight, I'm okay with it too."

"I hate to say this, but any other outcome is going to cause considerable problems. If we have Raven in custody and Estefan's hell-bent on killing him, what do we do?"

"We walk," Nathan said. "I'm not going to disarm or fight Estefan over it. We'll do our best to dissuade him from killing Raven in cold blood, but if he ignores us, we're outta here without looking back. I'm really hoping he won't do that. I think I know Estefan. I'm fairly certain he won't execute a helpless prisoner, even if it's Raven."

"He seems pretty pissed about his wife and torched house."

"He won't pull the trigger on a helpless man."

"Let's hope you're right."

Nathan didn't say anything for a few seconds. "There's one other scenario we need to reinforce."

"Yeah?"

"We can't let Estefan be taken prisoner."

"Are we prepared to kill Raven and his men to prevent it?"

"Yes."

"I'm okay with that. If Estefan falls into Macanas's hands, he'll die badly and probably give us up. We could end up looking over our shoulders for the rest of our lives."

"More than we already do?" Nathan said dryly.

"You know what I mean."

"Sorry, Harv. I didn't mean to sound flippant."

"We're good, partner. Estefan isn't the only one stressing tonight."

"Amen to that."

"I guess we should've had this discussion with Estefan when we first decided to help him."

"Things happened quickly. Let's not worry too much about Estefan. He's a pro. Instinctively, he knows everything we just talked about. There's only one eventual outcome: Raven or us."

"Yep." Harv nodded. "And I choose Raven."

CHAPTER 24

"You okay, Nate?"

Harv's tone brought Nathan back to full alertness. Even after stretching and taking a break from scope duty, he was finding it hard to focus on his surveillance for extended periods. A sign of fatigue setting in, and it would only get worse. Not a good thing. He rubbed his chin, feeling the stubble that marked their time in-country.

"If you were Raven, would you want Estefan alive?"

Harv thought for a moment. "It's hard to say. I'm not sure he'd believe Estefan's motivation is anything other than to avenge his father's death. I mean, why think otherwise? We talked about this. I don't see any value in taking Estefan alive other than to find out who, if anyone, he's talked to."

"Us."

"Afraid so."

"Then let's proceed on the assumption that his men will have orders to capture Estefan alive if possible."

"Meaning . . ."

"Unless something changes, we shoot to kill."

"Copy that," Harv said.

"Picture Estefan strapped to a chair while Raven tortures the shit out of him. We'll never let that happen."

"Agreed."

"What's the fastest Raven can get up here if he flies?"

"I'm not sure . . . He'd have to round up some men, drive to the airport, preflight the ship, and take off. It's an hour of flying time, so I'd conservatively say . . . at least ninety minutes at a minimum. It might take longer if he keeps it in a hangar—he'd have to tractor it out to the flight line."

Nathan was silent for a moment. "Maybe I should be the one at risk down there."

"No way. We need you up here behind that M40."

As much as Nathan wanted to disagree, he couldn't.

***

"I'm through," said Estefan. *"I put the screen back and left the window open. If anyone looks inside, they won't be able to see the bed. The narrow hall leading to the bathroom blocks its line of sight. Where's the girl?"*

"She's still behind the gas pumps," Nathan said. "The general store is screening you from her view right now. Stay put and be ready to relocate to the north wall of the store. We still think she's going to report your room number to Raven. Can you see her house from there?"

Partially, the Conex boxes are blocking my view.

"If we see any of Raven's men emerge from the lumber mill or the ore-processing plant, we'll move you over to the boxes. You'll have better cover and a clear line of sight from there. You copy?"

"Affirm."

Nathan kept his scope on the area surrounding the gas pumps. "After Antonia makes the call, things might happen fast. Everything hinges on Raven's men believing you're in the motel room. They'll either try to ambush you and kill you outright or take you prisoner."

"Not a nice thought."

"Don't worry. We won't let you get taken prisoner."

"Well, that's comforting. I suppose you'd be doing me a favor."

"We would."

"Let's ah . . . make that a last resort."

Nathan spoke slowly. He didn't want Estefan to feel any doubt about his resolve. "Estefan, if things get heavy, you will be in a shoot-to-kill situation. Center mass or head shots. I doubt they'll be wearing armor. Anyone who approaches your motel room is fair game, whether you see a weapon or not. Clear?"

"Clear. Shooting to kill."

"What's the distance from the gas pumps over to the motel?"

"Around twenty-five yards."

"What's your laser's zero?"

"Fifteen yards."

"That works. You doing okay down there?"

"I'm still worried about Martina, but it won't be a problem. I'm okay. My head's in the game. If you're thinking about that truck wreck I caused, I know I acted stupidly. It won't happen again."

"Already forgotten. We're going to end this tonight. You'll be visiting Martina later this morning."

"I'll hold you to it."

"Antonia's on the move. You should see her walk past the south wall of the motel any second."

"I've got her."

"Hold position . . . Something's wrong. She's not walking toward the phone."

"I can relocate to the store's southeast corner without her seeing me. She might want a look around before making the call."

"It's possible, but it's really dark down there. Without NV, she'd never see you."

"She got the upper hand on me down at the river."

"We all underestimated her."

"I don't like the feel of this," Harv said.

"Me either. She should be updating Raven. Could someone else have eyes on Estefan?"

"It's possible, but we haven't seen anyone."

"I'm still on the lumber mill, Nate. What's she doing?"

"She's walking south toward the church."

"You want me to keep her in sight?"

"Negative, Estefan. We've got eyes on her. Is there another pay phone in town? At the post office or Laundromat?"

"I don't know."

"Stand by." Nathan's mind raced with alternate plans. Everything hinged on Antonia making the second call to Raven. Where the hell could she be going? He supposed she could still be planning to call him, but when? And why the delay? "Harv, switch to the thermal imager, and sweep the entire area surrounding the lumber mill."

"You got it."

"To be on the safe side, I'm putting more distance between Estefan and the lumber mill." He radioed to Estefan, "Divert east past the Conex boxes to the small road behind Mateo's house and turn south. Head over to the rear yard of the church. The small houses on the south side of the vacant lot should screen you. There are some abandoned cars over there. Use them for cover." His radio clicked. "Harv?"

"Hang on, I'm just powering it on . . . I've got nothing. No warm bodies."

"Check the river."

"I'm not seeing anyone."

"Verify if it sees the girl."

"Affirm. The TI shows her as a bright object."

"Okay, stay on the TI and keep eyes on the lumber mill. I don't know what Antonia's up to, but we're staying on the offensive. We're not going to fight Raven's men on their terms."

"She didn't make the second call. How do we get them where we want them?"

"We'll make the call for her. Loudly." He pressed the transmit button. "Estefan, change in plans. Double-time it across the vacant lot, and prepare to fire a shot in front of Antonia."

"Copy. How close do you want it?"

Nathan liked how Estefan didn't second-guess his orders, a trait of a good combat soldier.

"I'll let you know. You'll need to be mindful of bullet skip."

Nathan refocused on the street and felt a chill.

Antonia was gone.

CHAPTER 25

"Estefan, take a knee and hold position. We lost eyes on Antonia." Nathan remained focused on the area immediately surrounding Estefan in the event Antonia planned to ambush him. "Harv, I need eyes on the street."

"I've got her," Harv said. "She's running south, along the west side of the road. She just passed the post office."

Nathan focused where Harv indicated and reacquired her. "We've got her, Estefan. She's in a dead run heading south between the post office and Laundromat."

Nathan watched Antonia take a sharp right and disappear behind the Laundromat—the southernmost commercial building on the west side of the road. "She could be executing a surveillance detection route," he told Estefan. "Hold position until we determine that's what she's doing. If we're correct, she'll work her way north along the dirt track behind the buildings and head back toward the pay phone, but we're done waiting for her. We're going on the offensive." His radio clicked.

"It seems Raven's a good teacher," Harv said.

"It's a smart move doing a SDR. I might've done the same thing had our situations been reversed."

"It's interesting she doesn't assume Estefan's still in the motel room."

Nathan said, "Either that or she suspects he isn't alone down there."

"She's had no reason to think that. She hasn't seen or heard Estefan on the radio. Raven probably told her to make sure she wasn't seen using the phone."

Nathan expected to see Antonia appear again within the next few seconds. He wasn't disappointed. "Okay," he radioed Estefan, "she's on the move in the alley parallel to the main road. She's heading north, back toward the post office. Sighting from your position, there's nothing but open field behind the tavern. When I give the word, advance toward the street and be ready to fire a shot in the dirt in front of her. Use your NV in tandem with your laser. I'm hoping to flush Raven's men out of the lumber mill and spook Antonia into going home. One shot only. Clear?"

"She deserves a bullet," Estefan said.

"Are we clear?"

"Clear."

"You'll be able to see her when she runs between the post office and the tavern."

"I'm on it."

"Harv, I need your eyes back on the lumber mill."

***

Estefan moved laterally about a yard to take advantage of a small clump of weeds and focused between the post office and the tavern. He gauged the distance to where the young woman would appear at just over thirty yards, took a deep breath, and tried to relax. The more he thought about it, the more he knew Nathan was right. They needed to avoid killing or injuring an innocent person—apparently that sentiment included Antonia. Although he wasn't overly concerned about a stray shot from his pistol hurting someone, Raven's thugs would likely have machine guns, and they wouldn't be concerned about collateral damage at all.

Estefan hated to admit it, but he was rusty. The last combat he'd seen was over twenty years ago. He'd soon be mired in a game of cat and mouse where a mistake could prove fatal. Even though his trust in Nathan's shooting skill was absolute, he had no desire to test his faith. The closest hospital in Jinotega was several hours away, and limping in there with a gunshot wound wasn't a viable option. Secondly, he wanted to keep Nathan's rifle silent. As long as Raven believed he was facing a single combatant, he'd feel confident that he and his men could eliminate the threat and get on with business as usual. Conversely, if Raven discovered a second sniper in the area, he'd be ten times harder to kill—if not impossible. As Estefan had learned long ago—from Harvey and Nate, in fact—short of facing an insurmountable number of enemy soldiers, a sniper's worst enemy was another sniper.

***

Nathan was about to scan the lumber mill area when Antonia dashed from the northwest corner of the post office toward the tavern. "Estefan, she's on the move. Put a bullet in front of her. Shoot now!"

Nathan saw Estefan's gun flash.

A full second later, the sound reached his position, crackling off the valley's walls like a small thunderclap.

The girl froze, then crouched. She reversed course and ran back to the post office, where Nathan lost sight of her.

"That ought to wake up the neighborhood," Harv said.

"I'm not seeing any lights come on."

"Based on Tobias's letters, it's not surprising. Here we go. We've got movement at the lumber mill," Harv said.

Nathan swung his scope to the lumber mill and saw three men emerge from the building with the lit windows, presumably its office.

"Estefan, you're on. Three gunmen are headed in your direction from the mill. Looks like they've got assault rifles. You're out in the open. Make an all-out sprint for the abandoned cars behind the church. The gunmen are too far away to see you." He released the transmit button. "Harv, I'm still zeroed on the church. Give me a wind correction."

"No change. Hold left two inches."

"Copy. Hold two left."

"Do you think Raven alerted his men after Estefan interrupted her call? That was well over ten minutes ago."

"Either that or someone from the motel called over there. I doubt they were dressed for combat at one o'clock in the morning. It took them a few minutes to get ready."

"Hang on, Harv. Estefan, it looks like one of the gunmen is heading for the motel. The other two are running directly toward you. Sprint for the rock wall behind the church. Drop down on the other side and speed crawl over to the abandoned cars. The wall will screen you from their line of sight."

"Am I cleared to engage?"

"Negative." Nathan saw Estefan hustle south toward the church and knew it would be close. The gunmen were fast runners. "We want to avoid a firefight in the middle of town. Those houses have paper-thin walls."

"Antonia might see me running over here."

"Your shot spooked her. She's hiding somewhere on the west side of the post office, probably scared shitless. When you reach the cars, stay low and hold your position. Don't worry. I'll drop every one of them if they make a move to capture you. Fall back on your training and become part of the landscape. They'll never see you."

"Let's hope they don't have flashlights or NV."

"Stand by." Nathan saw lights come on inside Mateo's house. A few seconds later, Mateo stepped out to his porch and looked around. When the pair of gunmen reached Mateo's house, they stopped. One of them said something to Mateo, who held his hands out innocently before retreating back inside his house.

"Estefan, you're in good shape. Mateo just bought you a few extra seconds. You'll reach the cover of the abandoned cars well before they get there."

"Where are they?"

"They just passed Mateo's house. Maintain radio silence until you hear from me. It looks like they're going to pass very close to you. They'll be there in thirty seconds."

Harv spoke up. "One of those gunmen could be Raven. We shouldn't assume he's in Managua. Can you see a scope on any of their rifles?"

Nathan refocused on the gunmen, but they were carrying their weapons one-handed while running, which created too much motion for him to see any detail. "I can't tell, but I understand your point. If one of those guys is Raven, Estefan could be in trouble."

***

Still using his NV, Estefan lifted his head just high enough to peer over the hoods of the wrecked cars. From this distance, he couldn't see much detail, but whoever these guys were, they were hauling ass directly toward him. Wearing woodland combat uniforms, the two men hopped the waist-high rock wall and resumed their sprint.

Estefan didn't get a clear look at their assault rifles, but he was certain they weren't AKs or M-4s. Those rifles had distinctive shapes.

He ducked lower, pulled his Sig, and held it close to his chest.

The thuds of their boots changed to crunches as they reached the expanse of gravel. Nathan had called it pretty damned close. These guys were going to pass within two or three yards of his hiding place between the cars.

In slow motion, Estefan lowered himself to a prone position and pivoted onto his right hip. Ignoring the rocks grinding into his flesh, he aimed his gun through the gap between the cars and held perfectly still.

He could hear their breathing.

If either of them glanced in his direction as they sprinted past, things would turn ugly.

Time seemed to slow as the moment of truth arrived.

He exhaled when two dark blurs rushed past the crevice between the cars.

As quickly as it had come, the crunching from their boots receded. It would've been easy to pop up and nail both of them, but Nathan had made it clear he didn't want a firefight in the middle of town, and the third gunman was still out there somewhere. Estefan felt relief when Nathan's voice came through his ear speaker.

"*Good job. I want those men out of breath from their sprint before I send you out to the river.*"

"Where's Antonia?"

"*Still behind the post office. I want you to start a low crawl directly toward the river. That will keep the abandoned cars between you and the church. When you reach the rock wall, hold your position until I tell you to scramble over it.*"

"Do you guys have eyes on the third gunman?"

Harv said, "*I lost sight of him when he initially crossed the street near the motel. I think he's watching your room. Don't worry. There's no way he can advance toward your position without me seeing him.*"

"Copy. Starting my crawl now."

Nathan kept alternating his surveillance between the motel and the church. The third gunman's diversion to the gas station to watch the motel was an intriguing development. Since Antonia hadn't been able to make a second call to Franco, she couldn't have been the source of the information. For now, Nathan had to assume the info had come from whomever checked Estefan in to the motel. A second snitch on Macanas's payroll was hardly surprising. In all likelihood, that person reported all comings and goings in Santavilla to Macanas's local headquarters. Or perhaps Estefan's garb or manner had triggered suspicion. Either way, a gunman now watched Estefan's lighted motel room, wondering whether Estefan remained inside. As long as the watcher stayed in place, it worked to their advantage. Nathan's primary concern was the two men approaching the church.

On the east side of the church, the pair suddenly stopped running and huddled briefly. Now that they were a lot closer and holding still, Nathan got a clear look at their weapons.

"Harv, their rifles aren't scoped."

"Then it's highly unlikely Raven is one of them. He'd be using a scoped weapon."

"Agreed. Let's keep your eyes on the area around the gas station. We need to know if the third gunman moves south. I'll watch Estefan and the area around the church. Estefan, we're going to give those guys alphanumeric designations. G1 and G2 are at the church, G3 is behind the gas station watching the motel. Copy that?"

"Copy. You have eyes on me?"

"Affirm. I have you in a low crawl approaching the rock wall due east of the abandoned cars. Keep going."

Nathan saw G1 and G2 fan out in opposite directions and encircle the church. When they reformed a huddle in the middle of the street, Nathan saw an opportunity. Estefan had only crawled about half the distance to the rock wall. If he made an all-out sprint, he could reach the wall in under five seconds. Nathan decided it was an acceptable risk.

"Estefan, stop crawling and run for the wall. The church is screening you from the gunmen. Once you reach the wall, stay low and be ready to beat feet out to the river."

Nathan swung his scope back to the men in the street. They appeared to be frozen in indecision. Since they hadn't found anyone, they were probably trying to decide if conducting a search was worthwhile. No doubt they were pissed at having to run all the way over there for nothing.

"Did Estefan make it to the wall?" Harv asked.

"Yes. Estefan, stand up. I want the gunmen to see you. Okay, they're looking your direction. Move south along the wall . . . a little more . . ." Nathan watched one of the gunmen point in Estefan's direction. "Go now! All-out sprint to the river!"

Both gunmen joined the chase, but they weren't running as fast this time and Estefan had a hundred-yard head start. Short of Estefan injuring himself during his sprint, Nathan knew his former student would reach the cover of the trees well in advance of the gunmen.

"G1 and G2 are on your six. When you reach the river, turn right and head for the dam. Use your radio to coordinate your location with Harv. Your gun isn't suppressed, so find a good spot to lay low until Harv gets there. As far as I can tell, they don't have NV, and I haven't seen any flashlights."

"*Copy. Do I have a green light if things get ugly?*"

Nathan didn't hesitate. "Affirm. You are cleared to engage once you reach the river, but do your best to avoid it. Harv will be at the dam in three mikes. Copy that?"

"*Copy. Three mikes.*"

Nathan released the transmit button. "Harv, throw on your ghillie and get going. I'll be okay up here. Leave your pack. You've got spare mags in your pockets?"

"Four."

"That ought to be enough."

While Harv scrambled into action, Nathan made a quick calculation. Estefan would reach the trees with at least thirty seconds to spare. If the gunmen opened fire on the run, they'd have little chance of nailing him from that distance. If their orders were to take Estefan alive, they might not fire at all. Once the gunmen reached the tree line, he'd lose sight of them. It became Harv's show at that point, but Nathan wasn't worried. Harv possessed expert handgun skills—better than his own.

Nathan consciously slowed his breathing and kept G1 in the center of his scope as the man ran toward the river. He wanted to make sure G1 entered the tree line at the same point where Estefan had. Once he lost sight of G1, he'd switch his surveillance over to the gas station area. If G3 decided to join his comrades, he'd need to warn Estefan and Harv.

***

Estefan hated scurrying for cover like a field mouse. He'd rather face danger than run away from it. At least now he was cleared to engage his pursuers and get some payback for his torched house and bludgeoned wife. He'd personally deal with Raven later.

He pushed aside the distracting surge of anger and concentrated on his footing. If he twisted an ankle or sprained a knee, he'd have to shoot it out with a crippling and painful injury. Conversely, as long as he kept his feet, Estefan had little doubt he could kill both gunmen. The knee-high grass under the barbed-wire fence offered perfect cover from a prone position. Bushwhacking them as they approached would be easy, especially with a laser sight. They'd never see him in time. He toyed with the idea of faking a fall, but he'd never be able to face Nathan after such a disgraceful deception. Nathan and Harv had risked their lives coming down here, and he wouldn't betray their trust. In truth, he'd sooner take a bullet in the back. Estefan had many faults, but a lack of integrity wasn't one of them.

Still in a full sprint, he reached down and pressed the transmit button on the radio clipped to his belt. "Nate, where are they?"

"They just hopped the rock wall. You're about one hundred fifty yards ahead of them. Harv's on his way. He's using the trail leading down to the dam. I haven't seen any sign of G3. Since he hasn't joined the pursuit, I doubt they're using radios. There are multiple buildings between where I last saw G3 and the area behind the church. I doubt G3 saw you or his friends. Harv, unless something tactical happens, I'm going radio silent so you can coordinate with Estefan."

"I just reached the footpath," Harv said. *"I'm going to slow my pace when I get closer to the river."*

"It's me again," said Nathan. *"One of the gunmen just changed direction. He's running due south. I'm calling him G2. G1 is still on your six, Estefan. It looks like they're trying to flank you. When you reach the river, turn right, but find a place to conceal yourself well short of the dam. G2 is going to reach the dam before Harv gets there. He may set up an ambush while G1 tries to drive you over there. You copy?"*

"Copy. G1 is on my six. G2's heading for the dam."

"Okay, I just lost sight of you at the tree line. Harv's Sig is suppressed, so hold your fire if possible. I don't want G3 to hear any shots and join the fight."

"Copy that." Estefan needed to point something out. "The guy on my tail won't know which direction I went at the river. Do you want me to make it obvious I'm heading toward the dam?"

"Harv?" Nathan asked.

"Yes. I want them both in the same place."

"Okay, Estefan, take G1 west toward the dam. I'm going radio silent. I'll only come up if I see G3 or Antonia make a move."

***

The trail Harv followed was little more than a furrow carved into the slope. Because of all the tree cover, the aerials didn't show this footpath, but it served several dozen homes farther south overlooking the wooden bridge, including Pastor Tobias's house. Harv wasn't worried about being too stealthy until he got closer to the dam. His night vision, coupled with the ghillie suit, gave him a substantial advantage. In another hundred yards or so the trail would level out where the foliage grew thicker along the river. He would slow to an ultraslow pace then to avoid producing any discernible movement. Even in low light, the unaided human eye could detect sudden motion.

***

Estefan scrambled down the bank and turned right. He wove his way through the ferns and other bushes until he reached the same spot he'd used to watch Antonia's approach. Like he had before, he climbed just high enough to peer over the edge and saw G1 running in a full sprint toward the spot where he'd disappeared over the bank. He couldn't see G2. He grabbed a low-hanging branch and gave it a tug, making the outer reaches of its leaves shimmer in the moonlight. He ran another thirty yards and did the same thing. There was no way G1 could miss the shaking branches. The air was still. Nothing else moved down here.

He backtracked to a location well behind the spot where he'd shaken the second branch and saw what he needed. Lying against the bank, a fallen tree offered a good place to hide. Its splayed array of bare branches would conceal the sharp lines of his body. With a little luck, G1 would pass directly below him, believing he was headed for the dam. Since this hiding place was closer to the first branch he shook, G1 should be focused beyond this point, farther down the river. Estefan took a few seconds to make sure his NV visor wasn't leaking light. Satisfied its rubber boots were pressed firmly against the skin around his eyes, he turned the gain up to maximum. It was damned dark under these trees.

"Harv, I'm in place," he whispered.

"I'm one hundred yards from the dam and slowing my pace to a crawl. I don't have eyes on G2. He could be hiding on the north side of the river waiting for you. Has G1 reached the tree line yet?"

"Fifteen seconds." Estefan knew Nathan was hearing their communication.

"Are you concealed?"

"Affirm. I'm halfway up the bank. He'll pass directly below me."

"Give me a quick laser burst into the canopy above your position. I want to know exactly where you are."

He clicked his radio, aimed straight up, and tapped the button on the butt of his gun. His NV made it look as bright as a camera flash, but he knew it would be virtually undetectable to the naked eye.

"I've got you. You're about three hundred yards east of the dam. Sit tight. The gunmen will want to avoid shooting each other, so G1 will advance cautiously along the river. He'll be expecting you to ambush him, so be patient and stay low."

Estefan clicked his radio.

The collective buzz of frogs and insects was deafening down here. It had ebbed briefly when he'd disturbed the tree branches before returning to its former volume. At this point he could speak on the radio without much concern. As long as he kept his voice to a whisper, the gunman would never hear him.

He focused on the area to his left and watched super-slow movement turn into a human form.

G1 had his rifle leveled at the hip. Every so often he froze and looked around.

Decent technique, Estefan thought. *Keep coming.* When G1 closed to within fifty feet, Estefan eased into a prone position and used a small opening under the fallen tree to watch G1's legs—he couldn't see the gunman's upper body. *Crap.* He hadn't checked for ants. Lying in a fire ant nest would definitely ruin his evening. It was a careless mistake he hoped wouldn't prove costly.

Gun in hand, he watched the rise and fall of G1's boots. In a few more seconds, his pursuer would pass inside five yards of his hiding place.

Estefan reminded himself to breathe.

He wasn't prepared for what happened next.

The guy turned his direction and took two slow, measured steps.

Estefan watched in horror as G1's boots stopped moving. Could he have been spotted? How was that possible? Estefan could see the laces were double-tied—the guy was that close. *Shit!*

"I might be blown," he whispered. "G1 stopped right in front of me."

"Don't move," Harv said. *"Give it a few more seconds. Stay calm, Estefan. You've seen this before. He's probably just looking for movement."*

Estefan clicked his radio.

Time seemed to stretch as Estefan waited. What the hell was this clown doing? Maybe he should pop up and nail him before a deadly barrage of bullets sprayed his hiding place.

He was seconds from doing that when a stream of liquid bisected the guy's boots.

Estefan couldn't believe it and nearly laughed out loud. "The son of a bitch is taking a piss."

"I could crack a joke, but I'll spare you," Harv said.

"Good grief . . . This guy's raising the river."

"They left the lumber mill in a hurry. Your gunshot caught them off guard."

Estefan watched the waterfall continue for thirty more seconds. *Man, this guy really has to go.* "Okay, he's moving again. Do you want me to tail him?"

"Yes, but give me periodic lasers into the canopy so I can keep track of your advance."

"No problem. Whoever this guy is, he's moving pretty well. I suspect he's former military. The only mistake he made was taking that leak."

"When you gotta go, you gotta go. Keep eyes on him. G2's well concealed, but I have a feeling once they see each other, they're going to huddle at the dam to decide what to do. Nathan, did you copy our exchange?"

Estefan heard Nathan's click. For the moment, he remained motionless. From the opening under the fallen tree, he watched G1's boots recede toward the dam before maneuvering into a kneeling position. He leaned to his right to keep the gunman in sight. Every ten to twelve steps G1 stopped to clear his six, and Estefan saw the pattern clearly. Tailing him shouldn't be difficult.

Looking around, Estefan knew why G1 had chosen this spot to relieve himself. It was the same reason Estefan had picked it. The downed tree provided good visual protection from both directions. Years ago it had fallen from the top of the bank at a 45-degree angle to the water. It offered a mushroom-shaped area of deep shadow laced with patchy moonlight. The pattern of silvery light landing on the ground looked similar to the digital pattern of the guy's combat uniform. Had their situations been reversed, Estefan might've chosen the same spot.

He eased over the trunk, checked himself for ants, and began following. "I'm on the move. G1's about thirty yards ahead of me. I'll give you a laser into the canopy every thirty steps or so. Any sign of G2?"

"No. Until he makes a move, I probably won't see him. I left the thermal imager with Nate. I'll give you several rapid clicks once I have G1 in sight. Once you hear my clicks, hold your position. I don't want a stray bullet finding you if a firefight ensues."

"Good hunting," Estefan said.

***

After making a slow-motion approach down the footpath, Harv estimated his distance from the dam to be less than thirty yards. He moved off the trail to his left and took a knee. He'd like to be a little closer, but he wasn't comfortable going any farther because he had no way to know if G2 had already crossed. The guy could be anywhere within a hundred-yard radius. Harv was reasonably sure G2 would focus his attention to the east, along the north side of the river, because that was the direction from which Estefan would be coming.

Harv registered every laser shot Estefan sent into the canopy. Even though the beams weren't directly visible, the surrounding flash created from their penetrations were. Based on the number and frequency of Estefan's laser bursts, Harv knew he'd be able to see G1 within the next two minutes. Patience wasn't one of Harv's strongest traits. Despite outward appearances, Nathan possessed much better control in situations like this. His friend had an uncanny ability to disconnect his emotions. The light-switch analogy described it perfectly, and right now, Harv had to flip his switch. He couldn't think of Raven's gunmen as human beings. They were nothing more than armed thugs who'd readily deliver himself, Estefan, and Nathan into the hands of a sadistic interrogator. Thinking about it in those terms made it possible to kill. Like Nathan, Harv would never allow Estefan—or himself—to be captured and rendered. Not on this marine's watch.

A vicious image of Nathan's emaciated body invaded his mind. Not more than thirty miles from here, Nathan had endured three weeks of unspeakable pain and anguish before being left to die in a suspended cage. When Harv had rescued Nathan, his friend hadn't weighed more than 120 pounds, half his normal weight. Being in this dark jungle environment was a stark reminder of Nathan's ordeal. But now wasn't the time to reminisce; he needed to concentrate on his surroundings. Although he doubted there were more than two gunmen pursuing Estefan, he couldn't be certain. It was possible G3 had avoided detection and joined the hunt.

From his current location he had a pretty good view of the pond created by the earthen dam. In another ten minutes, the moon would sink below the horizon, and it was going to get even darker out here. Unlike cities, remote Nicaraguan villages had no streetlights, lit parking lots, storefronts, or other sources of artificial light. As far as Harv was concerned, Santavilla was one step above stone knives and bearskins.

About seventy yards from the dam, Harv saw the interior of another tree flash, indicating Estefan's position. If Estefan had gauged his separation accurately, G1 ought to be about forty yards from the dam. Harv focused at that approximate location but saw nothing. The underbrush, interspersed with the dark vertical forms of massive trees, was moderately thick on the north side of the river, but it wouldn't totally obscure a human body—especially someone walking upright.

Patience, Harv told himself. *Give it a few more minutes.*

There!

He saw G1's outline. The guy was holding his assault rifle at the hip and advancing in high, calculated steps, careful not to trip over anything.

Silhouetted against the random background, G1's sharp lines might've gone unnoticed, but his forward motion betrayed his location. Estefan was right, the guy was skilled. Harv thought he was doing well given the absence of an NV device. Harv repeatedly clicked his radio, looked in Estefan's direction, and saw a tree flash three times, indicating Estefan had heard the clicks.

Harv studied G1's progression carefully, making a mental note of which foot the guy used to resume walking after clearing his six. Not surprisingly, G1 was right-footed. Most right-footers were also right-handed. Harv wanted that info in the unlikely event he ended up in hand-to-hand combat. If all went well, the two gunmen would make their presence known to each other, but it may not happen until they were closer together. If some kind of verbal signal was used, it wouldn't be easily heard over the forest's noise unless it was pretty damned loud. Harv put himself into G1's shoes and knew he had to be feeling a high level of apprehension at this point. If Antonia or the motel owner had relayed Estefan's description to Raven, the three gunmen would know they were pursuing an opponent who had the appearance of a special forces soldier.

Harv remained motionless, waiting for G2 to reveal himself.

He didn't have to wait long.

Materializing like a black wraith no more than fifty feet away, G2 stood and started toward the dam.

Harv was no stranger to covert fieldwork, but he still felt his skin tighten at how close the guy had been. At that distance, a fully automatic rifle burst would've been fatal. His stealthy approach down the trail hadn't created any discernible movement or noise. He had no doubt his former recon training had just saved his life. Harv counted his blessings, said a silent thank-you, and thought of something Nate liked to say, "Luck favors the well prepared."

When G2 reached the dam, Harv eased over to the trail. Staying in a crouch, he advanced toward the dam and made a mental note of the gunman's tread pattern in the damp soil. He wasn't too concerned about being seen—the entire area held deep shadow from the massive trees lining the pond. As long as he didn't make any sudden movements, the ghillie suit would do its job.

"Nathan, Estefan, stand by."

He received two clicks.

The closer he got to the pond, the louder the frogs became. G2 began hopping from rock to rock as he crossed the dam heading for the far side. Harv thought that was risky given the other gunman hadn't yet made his presence known.

Or had he?

Harv instinctively froze.

He hadn't seen any radios, but that didn't mean they didn't have them.

Gun up, he slowly took a knee.

Be patient, he told himself again. *Do nothing and see what happens.* There were times when no action was the best action.

Thinking about it more, Harv seriously doubted they were using radios. Since Estefan hadn't reported seeing either of the gunmen use a radio, it was likely they had some kind of loose plan to meet at the dam and reassess their situation.

When G2 reached the opposite side, he stepped off the trail, crouched, and stared in the direction of his approaching comrade. Harv doubted G2 had seen any movement yet.

He heard it then, coming from Estefan's direction.

A high-pitched whistle overpowered the frogs' noise.

A few seconds later, Harv heard a similar whistle from G2.

Keeping both men in sight, Harv relocated to within thirty feet of the dam and hid behind a waist-high plant.

G1 picked up his pace and waved when he saw his friend. A few seconds later, they met next to the trunk of a massive tree. Harv noted G2 was bigger than his comrade. No doubt they were talking about their next move.

Harv waited, analyzing the situation. If they fanned out in opposite directions, he'd have to take them down separately. That would take time, because he'd have to wait until they were adequately separated before taking the first one down. He'd then have to backtrack and pursue the other gunman from behind. He supposed Estefan could silently kill one of them with his knife, but he didn't want to put Estefan in that situation if he didn't have to.

Harv's answer arrived when the gunmen walked in his direction. It became clear neither of them suspected their opponent had night vision. They were obviously relying on the near blackness down here to conceal their movement.

Harv aimed his Sig but didn't activate its laser.

With G2 on point, both men navigated the rocks and crossed the dam.

He confirmed G1 had his finger off the trigger. He could clearly see the man's forefinger in a straight position on the outside of the trigger guard.

He let them advance a few more steps.

Harv extended his Sig over the top of the bush.

Now!

He painted his laser center mass on the lead gunman and double tapped him. His expression confused, G2 collapsed.

Before G1 could react, Harv nailed him in the chest with two quick shots.

Even with two chest wounds, G1 managed to level his rifle at the source of the suppressed shots. Harv shot him in the face before he could discharge his automatic weapon.

He fired a final round into G2's head to end the man's writhing.

In less than four seconds, he'd fired six shots and scored six hits. His emotional switch remained turned off, but Harv felt remorse at killing two men like this. It hardly seemed fair. They never had a chance. *Them or us*, he reminded himself, then pressed his transmit button. "G1 and G2 are down."

He knew Nathan wouldn't say "good job" or "well done." Now wasn't the time for back-patting or compliments.

"No change in town," Nathan said. *"I don't have eyes on Antonia or G3 with NV or the TI."*

"Copy. Estefan, double-time over here. We need to conceal these bodies."

"On my way."

Harv approached the dead men and wished this hadn't been necessary. During their scout sniper missions and subsequent covert ops with the CIA, Nate had done 99 percent of the killing. Nevertheless, Harv had felt equally responsible for each death even though pulling the trigger was quite different from making range, wind, and elevation calls.

He reached down and confirmed both men were dead. At least neither of them had suffered longer than a few seconds.

"*I've got you,*" Estefan said. "*South side of the dam.*"

In that moment, Harv knew what to do next.

***

Cowering inside the recycle Dumpster behind the post office, Antonia hadn't heard anything in a long time and wondered what she should do. Thankfully, there was only paper and cardboard in here. She slid the flattened boxes she'd used for concealment aside, cracked the bin's plastic lid, and peered through the narrow opening. She didn't know how long she'd been hiding in here, but it felt like hours. One thing was certain, she sure as hell didn't want to get shot at again. She'd seen the red laser beam a split second before the bullet plowed the ground in front of her. Raw panic had seized her, a wholly unpleasant state of mind. She'd been panting like a dog when she'd scrambled into the bin. Ten seconds later, her body had begun an uncontrollable shiver, and she'd nearly vomited at the thought of the shooter opening the Dumpster's lid to finish her off. She'd been utterly helpless and thoroughly shamed. Franco could never know about this; he'd dump her for sure.

Once her mind calmed, she questioned who'd shot at her. It had to be Tobias's son, but why would he do it? He seemed to care about her. It didn't make sense. Could he have missed shooting her on purpose? If so, why? Maybe he wanted her to react exactly like she had. Maybe he was teaching her a lesson and wanted her to go home. If that was his intent, it worked. She'd had her fill of action for the evening. She climbed out of the recycle bin and followed the rear wall of the post office to its southwest corner. It took her a moment to build up enough nerve to peer around the corner.

Was that movement? She could've sworn she saw something on the south end of town. She held perfectly still and stared toward the bridge. There it was again. Thirty seconds later, the movement turned into two dark shapes walking down the middle of the road.

One of them was in front of the other, and it looked like the guy in front was a prisoner. His arms were behind his back, and he walked with a slight limp. The guy behind was holding a rifle at the hip. It looked like he had a backpack with something bulky dangling on the outside. As they got closer, she confirmed the first guy was definitely a prisoner. Then she saw him clearly, and despite her frazzled state, Antonia managed a smile. Perhaps the evening wasn't a total disaster after all. One of Franco's men had captured Tobias's son and was marching him up the road. It felt good to see Estefan Delgado caught and helpless. He certainly wouldn't be shooting at her again.

Without conscious thought, Antonia decided what she'd do: follow them at a safe distance wherever they were going. If Franco planned to interrogate the guy, she wanted to watch and learn how to do it.

***

"I've got the girl," Nathan said. *"She's at the southwest corner of the post office. Slowly angle to the west side of the street. We want her to recognize Estefan."*

Harv clicked his radio and jabbed Estefan in the back with the flash suppressor—hard. "Keep moving, you low-life scumbag," he said, loud enough for Antonia to hear.

"Asshole," Estefan whispered. "That damned thing better be on safety."

"It has a safety?" Harv asked.

"You're a real riot, you know that?"

Nathan watched Antonia advance up the street to the tavern. *"We're in business; she's following you. She's behind the tavern. Keep going at your current pace."*

Harv stepped closer to Estefan. "I'm glad you're in front in case this doesn't work."

"You're a double asshole."

"Don't worry. It's going to work."

"It better."

The motel's office appeared dark. The owner had probably gone back to bed after reporting Estefan's presence. The street looked nearly pitch-black. High, thin clouds reflected a tiny amount of moonlight.

If the third gunman was still at the gas station, he should be able to see them by now.

Keeping the assault rifle level with his left hand, Harv felt for the laser's tiny power switch on the base of his Sig's handle and moved it to the "on" position. He'd turned it off when he tucked the gun into his belt at the small of his back. The beam would remain dark until he pressed the activation button on the Sig's grip. Adding to the ruse, he gave Estefan a shove forward. At the same time, he diverted his hand to the radio. "Nathan, stand by."

Doing his best imitation of what he'd heard down at the river, he issued the high-pitched whistle.

Nothing happened.

"Let's go a little farther," Harv whispered.

Estefan kept his hands where they were, maintaining the deception they were bound behind his back.

Harv repeated the whistle. Louder. "Let's slow our pace. If G3 doesn't show up in the next few seconds, we'll go to plan B and divert over to the motel room."

"He might've relocated without Nathan seeing him. He could be anywhere."

"I'll tell Nathan that unless we see our guy in the next few seconds, we're going to plan B. Wait, I see motion. I think he's behind the gas pumps. Nathan, we've got G3. Do you have eyes on Antonia?"

"Affirm. She's watching from the tavern."

From twenty paces away, Harv watched G3 step away from the pumps. The guy waved.

Harv waved back and gave Estefan another shove forward.

Holding his rifle in one hand, the gunman kept coming. "You got him," he said in Spanish.

The guy took two more steps and stopped. His body language tensed.

"Jaime? Where's Tomas?"

Estefan moved to his left to screen Harv from the gunman's view, but it was too late.

Something had already spooked the guy.

In an aggressive move, the gunman grabbed the assault rifle with his other hand.

Estefan ducked.

Harv reacted before G3 could bring his weapon to bear. He dropped the rifle, pulled his Sig, and activated its laser.

He centered the red dot on the man's chest and fired a two-round burst.

The result wasn't glorious.

Twice punched by an invisible fist, the gunman's body shuddered as the subsonic slugs tore through his heart. He dropped his weapon and stood motionless. When reality hit home, he fell to his knees and crossed himself.

Harv rushed forward, but the guy had already slumped sideways onto his shoulder.

"Grab the rifles," Harv told Estefan.

As quickly as possible, Harv dragged G3 across the street to the motel. Estefan reached the room first and opened the door.

***

Antonia waited until Franco's man walked Tobias's son well past the tavern before following. She still felt uneasy about the way the two men were acting. She'd heard them whispering again.

Staying out of their line of sight, she crept along the back of the post office where she'd hidden herself in the recycle bin. She peered around the corner and saw the two men continuing up the street. Confident she wouldn't be seen, she ran north to the tavern. From there, she'd have a good view of the motel and gas station.

Franco's man slowed and whistled. A few seconds later, he did it again, only louder. She wondered who he was signaling. Her answer arrived when she saw a third man appear from behind the gas pumps. Carrying a rifle in one hand, he waved and stepped away from the pumps.

Something was wrong. The third guy suddenly stopped and brought his rifle up with both hands. Was he going to shoot them?

The next few seconds became surreal.

Estefan crouched and Franco's man grabbed a handgun from behind his back.

His gun flashed twice, but it wasn't very loud.

Antonia covered her mouth as the man from the gas pumps fell to his knees.

This whole thing was a trick. Estefan wasn't a prisoner at all. His hands weren't even tied.

For the second time tonight, Antonia felt fear, raw and deep. She needed to get out of here. Something terrible was happening, and she no longer knew who was who.

She pivoted to her right and found herself face-to-face with the biggest man she'd ever seen, his face painted like Tobias's son's.

"It's nice to meet you, Antonia."

She inhaled to scream, but the guy moved faster than she'd thought possible. She had a brief sense of feeling weightless before landing on her chest. The impact drove all the air from her lungs. She felt the man's weight lift off her back a little, which allowed her to suck in a labored breath. Completely pinned with her face jammed into the dirt, she couldn't move at all.

CHAPTER 26

"You're in a world of trouble, young lady," Nathan said in Spanish. "If you scream or try to fight, I'll hurt you. Are we clear on that?"

No response.

Nathan added some weight to his knee.

The girl grunted and nodded tightly.

"Good. I'm not planning to hurt you unless you try something stupid. If you scream, I'll make you regret it. We're going across the street. We can do it the easy way or the hard way. I never hit women, but I'm willing to make an exception in your case."

"Who are you?"

"I'm the guy asking the questions. Now would you like to walk or be dragged?"

"Walk."

"Good choice."

Nathan hauled her upright and forced her wrist behind her back. He walked behind and slightly to her left. He knew she was right-footed from watching her earlier.

"Hey, you're hurting me."

"Keep moving. The discomfort's a reminder to behave yourself. Don't worry. We aren't going to rape you, so you can put that out of your mind."

At hearing that, she seemed to relax a little.

Across the street, the motel room went dark just before Estefan and Harv disappeared inside.

If Antonia was going to make a move, it would happen within the next five steps or so. Nathan knew she'd have to pivot to her left to free her left arm, so he drove it higher and tighter to her body. She cried out but not loudly.

"Just making sure you still know who's in charge."

Inside the room, Nathan shoved her forward and kicked the door shut. "Estefan, close the rear window."

When Nathan heard the metallic scrape and subsequent thump, he verified the curtains were closed and flipped the light switch. The room filled with bland yellow light from the nightstand lamp.

Antonia pursed her lips when she saw Estefan.

Harv emerged from the bathroom, drying his hands with a blood-smeared towel.

"Sit her down," Nathan said.

Estefan pushed Antonia toward the bed.

She sat, keeping her legs together and her hands in her lap.

Staring at the girl, Nathan remained silent for ten seconds. Neither Harv nor Estefan said anything. It was a classic interrogation strategy. When Nathan finally spoke, his voice had an icy evenness. "I don't suppose you feel the slightest bit guilty about the men we killed out there."

She kept her head down and didn't respond.

"I didn't think so. I'm going to ask you some questions, and you're going to answer them truthfully. Here's my first question. Do you understand what I just told you?"

She nodded without looking up.

"In a few minutes, you and I are going to walk over to the pay phone, and you're going to call the man you know as Franco. I'll tell you what to say. If you deviate from the script, you'll end up like your father—with one ear." Nathan pulled his Predator from its ankle sheath and held it a few inches from her face. He twisted its menacing blade a few times. "I trust I won't have to use this?"

She shook her head and wiped a tear.

"Spare me," Estefan muttered.

Nathan looked at him. "Wire up. We need eyes outside."

Estefan looked like he wanted to object but didn't.

After Estefan slipped outside, Nathan continued. "You're in over your head, Antonia. I'm sure that's abundantly clear now. This isn't a kid's game of cops and robbers. You're in the big leagues now. Here's the deal. You're going to answer my questions. Refusing to answer or lying will result in pain. If you'd like to test yourself to see how tough you are, by all means try it. I'm willing to administer your exam. Try to imagine what it feels like having your skin peeled off in narrow strips. Personally, I think that kind of sacrifice is misguided, given who you're protecting, but that's an internal debate you can have once we get started." Nathan looked at Harv who crossed his arms. "Since we don't have any goggles or rain ponchos for blood spatter protection, we'll have to start with noninvasive methods, such as broken bones, dislocated joints, and soft-tissue trauma. I'll secure a folded pillowcase inside your mouth, so you won't crack your teeth during the process. Ready, Harv?"

Harv obliged with a solemn nod.

"Are you ready?" Nathan asked Antonia.

"I'm sorry," she whispered.

"For what?"

"About the men who died."

"Well, it's a start. Ask yourself this. Do you think your white-shirted boyfriend would suffer through horrible agony for you?"

From the look on her face, Nathan knew he was close to breaking her. "Quite frankly, you're in our way. We could make our lives a whole lot easier by adding your corpse to the bathtub. Maybe you have info we can use, maybe you don't—it's too early to say. I'm not going to ask questions that require long answers. If you go off topic, I'll be very unhappy."

"You don't have to hurt me. I'll tell you what I know."

"A wise decision. For the record, I don't think you're a stupid person. I think you've made some bad decisions, but that doesn't make you stupid."

"I'm really sorry about Estefan's father. He was a nice man."

"If all goes well here, you can tell Estefan that yourself. I'm sure he'd appreciate hearing it. The man you're . . . associated with burned Estefan's house down and put his wife in the hospital. Did you know that?"

"No."

"Did you tell him who Estefan was?"

She hesitated, then nodded.

"How did you get personal information on Estefan?"

She told him about the uncashed check from the church.

"If I were you, I'd pray Estefan never finds out about that."

"You aren't going to tell him?"

"No."

At this point Nathan knew she'd answer his questions readily, so he went methodically through a list of things they needed to know.

Three minutes later, they had a basic understanding of Macanas's operations in Santavilla. He also verified the information she'd shared with Estefan earlier. The lumber mill was the center of activity, and Franco never came into town without going there. Antonia didn't know why so many men were stationed there, but she said the number had grown from three to five or six over the last nine months. Franco's men lived there in a barracks type of setup. If her information was up to date, then they could count on at least two more men being at the mill.

Nathan did a quick calculation in his head. Estefan had fired the shot in front of Antonia around twenty minutes ago. The remaining men in the lumber mill would be wondering why their friends hadn't come back by now. He pressed the transmit button on his radio. "Estefan, we need you back in here."

"*On my way.*"

Antonia kept her head down and remained motionless while Harv let Estefan into the room.

"Watch our guest for a minute," Nathan said. "If she tries anything cute, break her arm . . . in two places. Cut up some strips of bedsheets to use as ties."

Estefan nodded. "My pleasure."

***

Walking across the street with Harv, Nathan thought about the call he wanted Antonia to make. A good idea formed, and he was surprised he hadn't thought of it earlier.

"So what's the plan?" said Harv.

Nathan found a place in the shadows where they could speak without being seen. "Well, we need to force Raven to come up here as soon as possible, if he's not already on his way. We can do that with a call from Antonia, but immediately afterward we need to cut off all communications between Santavilla and the outside world. That accomplishes a couple of things: Raven won't be able to coordinate with his men, and no one can report our presence to him."

"Good point," said Harv. "If he hears one of his former kilo colleagues is working with a couple of American agents, he'll put two and two together."

Nathan nodded. "We're pretty hard to confuse with anyone else. Especially me. And there's no way Raven would engage

Estefan *and* his two old Echo instructors, even with a small army of men."

"So we cut the phone line coming into town?"

"Basic military strategy. Sever the enemy's communication."

Harv looked to the south. "Yeah, it could work. There's no cell service in this valley, but didn't Estefan say there might be a signal at the top of that mountain?"

"'Might' being the operative word. If we have time later, we'll hustle up there and check."

"Cantrell could be trying to contact us."

"We can't worry about that right now."

"You realize we'll be isolating the town from the outside world. If someone calls one-one-eight in an emergency, no one will receive it."

"I don't like it much, but I think the odds are pretty low someone will have a life-threatening emergency during the next few hours."

"Nate, we create life-threatening emergencies."

"Come on. You know what I mean."

"I guess I'm okay with that too. Like you said, the odds are pretty low. So we'll need a pair of wire cutters."

"We'll ask Antonia if the general store has them. If not, we'll improvise. It might take a few bullets, but we can shoot the phone line if we have to."

"So what's our timing?" Harv asked.

"We sever the phone line right after I force Antonia to call Raven. Raven'll try to call the lumber mill for an update and be concerned when he can't get through."

"If our goal's to get him to come up here, we need him more than concerned."

"I have no idea if he'll get an out-of-service message or if the line will just ring indefinitely. Either way, he'll feel compelled to come up here and deal with Estefan. If we play things right with

Antonia's call, I'm ninety-nine percent convinced Raven will show up quickly. The wild card is, how he does it: fly or drive?"

Harv said, "He could do both. He could send some of his men in on the ground and fly himself in."

"He knows he's facing a former sniper. I doubt he'll land at the helipad wearing a fluorescent-orange shirt and yell, 'Here I am.'"

"He definitely won't do that. What would you do?"

Nathan thought for a moment. "I'd time the arrivals simultaneously. There are plenty of places to land a helicopter around here. Raven knows Estefan can't possibly cover the entire valley from a single location."

Harv went silent.

"What's on your mind?"

"Nate, we talked about this. We agreed we couldn't go to war with Macanas's cartel. We could be facing a small army of mercenaries."

"I can't deny that's a possibility, but I don't think Raven will be thinking that way. See, I think Raven needs to end this as much as we do. His boss would *not* want him getting into this kind of private war over something personal when it could jeopardize his business here. Chances are, Raven will be doing everything he can to keep this secret from Macanas."

"Then he'll only bring a handful of his best men."

"That's what I'm thinking."

"Okay, but are we going to bail if Raven shows up with a small army?"

"Absolutely, Harv. We aren't equipped for that kind of fight, and I have no desire to kill a bunch of men. I hate to say this, but one way or the other, we're calling for our ride home later today."

"I guess I needed to hear you say that."

"Our mission hasn't changed. We fight Raven on our terms in a limited engagement or not at all. We talked about this with Estefan. He knows the score."

"Something just hit me," Harv said.

"What is it?"

"We need to look for Internet satellite dishes at the lumber mill and ore-processing plant before you have Antonia make the call. There are ways other than landlines and cell phones for Raven to communicate with his men."

"Good point. Let's do this. You and Estefan split up. You'll head over to the ore-processing plant and lumber mill and check for satellite dishes. All you'll have to do is cut their coaxial lines or torque the dishes out of alignment. If they're out of reach, just shoot their feed horns. That should disable them. Estefan will head to the south end of town and stand by to cut the phone line. I'll wait here with Antonia until you guys are all set."

"Sounds good."

"Harv, if we can avoid killing anyone else tonight, we should do it. If it turns ugly over there, I know you won't kill unless it's absolutely necessary."

"What about the girl? We can't keep her with us after the call. She can't be hanging around during the fight, and we don't want her loose to talk about us being here. We'll have to confine her."

"We'll take care of that at the lumber mill. There's got to be a good place somewhere. A storeroom or janitor's closet. Something."

Nathan nodded toward the motel, and they began walking back.

"Then we're planning to neutralize the men over there?"

"Yes," said Nate. "With nonlethal force, if possible."

CHAPTER 27

Nathan and Harv reentered the motel room, planning to keep it brief. With all of them in here, they lacked eyes outside.

Antonia kept her head down. Her unmoving, stiff posture told all. Nathan knew the anguish and fear she felt. He'd experienced it firsthand no more than thirty miles from here. His initial captors had beaten him nearly unconscious, but that paled in comparison to what came later. He forced the corrosive memory aside.

Using English, he quickly updated Estefan on the plan to ensure Raven's arrival, then cut communications to Santavilla. Estefan took it in without questions and pronounced it a good strategy.

"I have a question for you," Nathan told Antonia.

She looked up at him, uncertainty in her eyes.

He asked what their chances would be of finding wire cutters at the general store.

They were in luck. Last year, after the hardware store had closed, Mrs. Perez bought its inventory. There would be plenty of wire cutters and pliers in the general store. Surprisingly, Antonia offered additional info Nathan had planned to ask for. Though the store was locked, a spare key was hidden near the cargo containers.

Nathan told Estefan to cover Antonia while Harv secured her ankles. The two-foot-long bond would allow her to shuffle along like a chain-gang prisoner, but she wouldn't be able to run. Antonia started to object, promising she wouldn't try to escape, but Harv silenced her with a look while he worked.

Outside the motel room, Nathan pivoted his goggles down to his eyes and activated the NV's infrared flashlight feature. He'd likely need it to locate the spare key. At the corner of the motel, he paused and scanned the area before hustling over to the cargo containers. He was considering what to do with Antonia if she'd lied about the key when he found its tarnished form exactly where she'd said it would be. Nathan had no trouble entering the store and finding two pairs of wire cutters. He grabbed a couple more items from the same aisle, left one thousand córdobas next to the register, and relocked the store. Outside, he returned the key to its hiding place and ran back to the motel room.

Harv had Antonia fully bound, hands tied behind her back.

"Where's Estefan?"

"I've got him on the north side of the motel watching the lumber mill area."

"How far away is the lumber mill from here?"

"As I recall from the aerials, around five hundred yards, give or take. The ore-processing plant is about a hundred yards closer."

"Okay, let's get you two moving." He handed Harv both pairs of wire cutters, shook the pillow out of its case, and looked at Antonia. "Hold still. I'm going to gag you."

"You don't have to do that," she said quickly. "I'm not going to scream."

"We're a little short on trust." Nathan didn't make the gag overly tight. There was no point in being cruel, and she'd earned the extra slack by volunteering the location of the hidden key.

"Tell Estefan I want three-minute updates, even if there's nothing to report." Nathan turned off the light and sent Harv on his way. "Well, Antonia, I guess it's just you and me for a while."

***

Harv pivoted his NVGs down and powered them on. He'd elected to take his backpack rather than fill his thigh pockets to their bulging points. Although he didn't intend to use them, he had plenty of spare magazines for his Sig. His pack also held the TI and NV binoculars.

The best way to approach the lumber mill was via the river. Because of his size, Harv couldn't pretend to be one of Raven's men and just walk into the enemy's camp. Estefan could've done it, but Harv understood Nate's desire to avoid killing any more men.

He pressed the transmit button. "Estefan, I'm on my way to your position. Ten seconds."

"Copy. I've got you."

Harv saw Estefan peer around the corner of the motel. He too wore NV goggles now.

An idea came to Harv as he walked north along the motel's doors. He keyed his radio. "Nate, if Estefan drives to the south end of town, I think he can stand on top of his cab to reach the phone line. After he cuts the line, he can park his truck behind the church with the other vehicles. It looks newer, but it's pretty dirty from the drive up here. It won't stand out too badly."

"His diesel is noisy. Think you guys can push it a couple hundred yards south before starting it? Estefan, is there gravel where you parked?"

"No, but we should be able to move it without too much trouble."

"Okay, push it down to the church before you fire it up. That will minimize the possibility of it being heard at the lumber mill. Maintain your perimeter. We don't know how many more men we're facing or where they are. Keep your heads up."

"Will do," Harv said and handed Estefan a pair of wire cutters. "The poles aren't more than four or five yards high. Power should be the highest wire. The phone line's below it and probably insulated and thicker. Don't get zapped. As you recall from your kilo training, phone lines can pack a punch."

"I'll be careful."

It took some effort to get Estefan's truck to the front of the motel, but once they had it on the main road, their job got a lot easier because the road had a slight downhill grade to the south. Once they got some momentum going, Harv glanced around but didn't see anything alarming. It was possible they were being watched from some of the dark residential windows, but the near blackness masked all detail. Their effort wasn't totally silent. The tires produced a barely audible hiss-like crunch from the decomposed granite surface.

"Let's keep going a little farther," Harv suggested. They pushed for another fifty yards. "Okay, I think we're good. Choose a location close to where you initially parked when we first arrived. You should hunker down outside your pickup." Harv keyed his radio. "Nathan, it might be best to give Estefan a heads-up when you're en route to the pay phone with Antonia. We need to minimize how long Estefan's out in the open. And we need a new scatter point. Let's use the wooden bridge."

"Sounds good."

"Estefan should be in place in the next thirty seconds. My ETA to the lumber mill is around ten mikes."

"Copy. Ten mikes."

"Estefan, give me thirty seconds before you start your truck. If anyone looks, they'll only see one person. Leave your headlights off. Once you're parked under the power line, you're in stealth mode again. Our radios are good for several more hours of active use. Stay sharp down there."

"I will."

Harv walked at a brisk pace toward the river. Dotting the landscape on either side of the one-lane track, all of the houses were completely dark. If Estefan's pistol shot had awoken anyone, there was no sign of activity. At the river Harv checked in with Nathan, eased down the bank, and turned north.

Estefan's voice overpowered the frogs and crickets. *"I'm in place under the power line. Standing by."*

Harv heard Nate's acknowledgment click.

After going twenty yards through impossibly dense understory, Harv decided to scale the bank and head north along its rim. It wasn't as stealthy, but it was five times faster. He removed the TI from his pack and scanned the area in front of him. Stationary combatants can beat NV, but the thermal imager nailed them every time. He detected no warm bodies within its range and switched back to NV. A few minutes later, he encountered the exit channel from the ore-processing plant, where the plant's runoff flowed into the river. As the aerials had shown, a thirty-foot-wide swath of mud delineated the zone. Getting across would be a messy slog.

His night-vision goggles were a godsend. Footprints like his own marched along both sides of the expanse, showing where miners had panned for leftover gold. Where the mud was wettest, it looked like quicksand. Rather than risk sinking down to his knees, Harv diverted to the west. The channel looked to be narrowing as it got closer to the plant. Every so often he passed a large mound of dried earth, no doubt the result of excavations to keep the water flowing toward the river.

Aside from some rusted farm equipment and abandoned cars, Harv didn't have any cover. Most of the small houses weren't much bigger than the Perezes' Conex containers. Harv slowed his pace, looking for any discernible movement. At this distance of just under two football fields to the plant, he hadn't expected to see anyone and didn't.

The light breeze didn't carry any traces of smoke, tobacco or otherwise. Fifty paces farther ahead he found a makeshift crossing. Side-by-side planks of old lumber bridged a stack of pallets. The pallets acted as a column in the middle of the muck. Harv tested his weight before venturing too far. The planks sagged under his two hundred pounds but held.

On the other side of the channel he resumed his trek, angling toward the ore-processing plant's office. His gut told him the place was deserted, but he needed to be 100 percent certain. He didn't want to worry about anyone moving in behind him when he continued over to the lumber mill.

So far, he hadn't seen any satellite dishes attached to the eaves of any of the buildings, residential or otherwise. Weeds and waist-high growth prevented him from seeing the ground next to the plant's office. If a dish was over there, he'd have to get a whole lot closer to find it.

He keyed his radio. "I'm fifty yards east of the processing plant. No activity or satellite dishes are visible so far. All the houses are dark. It's quiet out here."

Nathan's voice came through his speaker. *"You should be able to see the helipad from there. Look directly to the north from your current position. Do you see a wind sock?"*

"Affirm. I have it. It looks like there's some kind of screening fence surrounding it. The sock is attached to a post extending above the fence."

"Verify you're seeing a visual screen surrounding the helipad?"

"Affirm. Six feet high. It's probably chain-link with fabric attached. I almost didn't see it. The fabric's got some sort of camo digital pattern, like ivy or something."

"How did we miss this on the aerials?"

Estefan cut in. *"I don't remember seeing a fence. It must be fairly new."*

"Harv, locate the gate. It's probably on the west side facing the buildings. Best guess on the fenced area's diameter?"

"Forty yards, plus or minus. I didn't see it when I had eyes on the lumber mill. There are very small trees planted along its length. It just looked like a small orchard. I missed it."

"No worries, Harv. We're on the clock."

Harv issued a click. Nathan would never tell him to hurry, but "on the clock" meant proceed without haste. Harv was already at the ten-minute mark, and he hadn't cleared the ore-processing plant yet. The longer he delayed, the more suspicious Raven's remaining men at the lumber mill would become. Even so, he took a moment to make another TI sweep.

Something looked wrong, and it took Harv a moment to process what he saw. On the aerials, the processing plant looked like a rectangular building—its shape and shadow had been clearly visible. Looking at it from ground level revealed something quite different. It wasn't a building at all. It was essentially a large expanse of concrete covered by a roof structure. Log-cabin-style columns supported a system of crudely made beams and trusses. Flanked by two slanted sluice boxes, the ore-crushing drum dominated the middle of the slab. The drum looked like a converted concrete truck minus its wheels. A pulley system was in place to hoist five-gallon buckets full of crushed ore to the top of the sluice boxes. Harv cringed at the thought of working next to that thing without hearing protection. He'd expected this place to be a mess, but it wasn't. The plant's supervisor clearly ran a tight ship. All the shovels, rakes, and other hand tools were stored in racks. Even the water hoses were neatly coiled under their spigots. At the south side of the slab next to the office, a dozen stainless-steel sinks probably served as the panning area for the material recovered from the sluice boxes. Overhead cameras monitored the panning sinks.

Harv shook his head. Macanas was getting rich while these mine workers wrecked their backs, destroyed their hearing, and ingested toxic levels of mercury. He didn't see the retorts Estefan had mentioned, but he couldn't miss the five-hundred-gallon propane tank that supplied their fuel for cooking the amalgam. From the look of things, Macanas had a very profitable operation going. It was tempting to burn this place to the ground, but that would only hurt the people who worked here. Then again, maybe it would be doing them a favor and even save their lives in the long run.

Harv reminded himself that he and Nate weren't here to play God with these people's lives. They were here to help Estefan avenge his father's murder and now, his bludgeoned wife and torched house. They were here to stop a rogue killer, a killer they'd created. Harv had never liked Raven, though it was difficult to pinpoint why. Maybe it was a chemistry thing. There'd just been something about the guy he found unsettling. It wasn't normal to act so calmly all the time. Nothing ever seemed to rattle the guy.

He pushed the thought aside to remain focused. The helipad's fence became an asset. He could use it as a visual screen to approach the lumber mill. Beyond the wind sock, he saw the ominous black form of the mill's huge gabled roof. The main building had to be forty feet high and at least one hundred twenty feet long. His NV registered the glow of the trees to the east, which meant at least one exterior light was on over there. Confident he was alone, Harv advanced to the office wall and flattened himself against it. He reached over to the air conditioner's compressor and felt it for warmth. It was cool to the touch.

"I'm at the ore-processing plant's office. No satellite dishes present. Stand by."

Nathan gave him a click, and he eased along the wall toward the dark window. Before pivoting his NV goggles up, he took a slow look around. Even though the office was dark, he knew someone could still be in there. He placed his ear against the stucco wall and didn't hear anything. Surprisingly, the window's shade was only partially drawn. He leaned forward and used his NV to scan the interior. The tiny light on the computer's CPU blinked sleep mode, providing one-second intervals of illumination. Excepting the digital scale on the desk, presumably used to weigh gold, it looked like a moderately furnished office. Nothing out of the ordinary jumped out at him. A door on the west side probably led to a bathroom.

Time to move on.

Harv walked directly toward the helipad, planning to skirt the fence's eastern hemisphere. He wondered why the canvas covering the fence had an ivy pattern. Was it for aesthetic or tactical purposes? Whatever the case, it had prevented him from seeing it earlier. At the fence he peered over the top and saw the gate on its west-facing side. In the middle, a round concrete pad was surrounded by a sea of fist-sized river rocks. Smart, Harv thought. The rocks wouldn't be disturbed by the rotor wash. No vegetation was present—not even a single weed. The fence didn't screen the helipad from an elevated position, but it did offer privacy at ground level. Harv didn't think Raven would be overly worried about anyone besides kids scaling the mountainside to watch the helicopter land and take off—what would be the point? Everyone in town could clearly see it as it overflew the area. As Pastor Tobias's letters had indicated, it was no secret why it came and went.

Just north of the covered slab, Harv encountered the supply side of the canal and saw a well head and several large pressure tanks. Apparently, the pressurized water for the hose bibs came from here. Harv had no trouble stepping over the three-foot-wide channel. At the helipad fence he turned east and worked his way around to where he had a clear view of the lumber mill.

The illumination he'd seen earlier got increasingly brighter as he navigated the fence. Once he had a clear view of the mill, he made a TI sweep and didn't detect any warm bodies. He'd expected to see a sentry.

The mill looked a lot bigger than it had on the aerials. The main building towered over the other two structures. Harv estimated it was at least forty feet high with a rectangular footprint of fifty by one hundred fifty feet. The smaller of the two buildings was on the south side of the property, and Harv saw light leaking from drawn blinds or curtains. He also heard the drone of an air conditioner, its noise originating from the far side of the small structure. A larger freestanding building was on the north side of the lumber mill's property, likely the barracks where Raven's men lived. A large parking lot to his left held half a dozen lumber trucks, a backhoe, a front-end loader rigged with grappling arms for moving timber, and some smaller vehicles that appeared deserted. He studied the area surrounding the office and almost missed seeing the satellite dish mounted on the wall. Half of its oval form was screened by a light-colored Range Rover. Harv saw an opportunity to look inside. Superbright slits of light came from the upper parts of the windows. With a little luck, he'd be able to peer inside, but he'd have to climb onto the Range Rover's hood. First things first. He needed to disable the satellite dish. At this distance he couldn't see if the coaxial cable ran down the wall or if it punched directly through the wall behind the mounting bracket. He'd know soon enough. He also needed to check in with Nate, which he did.

He froze when he realized he'd forgotten something critical.

Dogs.

He should've checked for them at the ore-processing plant as well.

If there were dogs outside the lumber mill's office, they might hear his approach, even over the compressor's humming. The TI would be better to see their heat signatures, so he switched devices. Watching for movement, Harv pulled his suppressed Sig, crouched, and issued a soft, high-pitched whistle. He waited a few seconds before repeating it. He knew his whistle might be heard by humans, but it was a risk worth taking. A tactical dog, or even a junkyard mutt, could put a world of hurt on him if he missed shooting it during its attack run—not a nice thought. When no dogs appeared, he hustled over to the office's wall and nearly tripped over a rusted wheelbarrow concealed by weeds. He told himself to slow down. The fact that no sentries were present out here presented only two possibilities. They were either unwilling or unable to come outside. Perhaps Raven had given them orders to stay put. In a few minutes, they wouldn't be getting any more orders, period. They were about to be cut off from the outside world. Harv saw where the coaxial cable disappeared through the wall. Clipping it with the wire cutters would be easy.

"I'm in place at the lumber mill's office. There's a satellite dish. I'm standing by to cut its coaxial cable on your mark."

"Good work, Harv. Estefan, ninety seconds."

CHAPTER 28

Franco fully expected to have heard from his men at the lumber mill by now, and his patience was stretched to the breaking point. What were they doing up there? He didn't like being in the dark. The last update he'd received was fifteen minutes old. His bean-counting cousin inside the mill hadn't reported hearing any additional gunshots. The three men who'd gone outside to investigate the single gunshot hadn't come back yet. Franco felt uneasy about the situation, but getting irritated accomplished nothing. Santavilla was a small town, but it covered a huge area. Men on foot wouldn't be able to patrol its entire expanse quickly. It could easily take forty-five minutes to an hour. And it was possible the initial gunshot could've been a farmer shooting or scaring off an intrusive animal. He was about to call the lumber mill again when his flip phone rang. He patched it through his BluLink adapter.

"Antonia, what's happening up there?"

"I think he killed your men from the lumber mill. I'm really scared he's going to kill me too!"

"Antonia, slow down and tell me—"

"He just saw me! I have to go!"

***

Nathan slammed the pay phone into its cradle. He'd been holding it for Antonia so he could also hear it. He keyed his radio. "Cut the lines now. You both copy?"

"*Copy. It's toast,*" Estefan said.

"*Likewise,*" Harv added.

Nathan scanned the immediate area as he prepared to escort Antonia back to the motel. The call with Franco served its purpose, but not in the way he'd planned. Nathan had heard a distinctive humming noise coming from Franco's end of the call. It was a sound Nathan knew well and it came from a very specific place: the cockpit of a helicopter.

Franco was already in the air.

***

Franco heard a click, then nothing. "Antonia, are you there? Antonia!"

Shit. Things were spiraling out of control. Franco called the pay phone back and let it ring ten times. No one answered at the lumber mill either. Where were they? The answering machine should pick up the call—unless it can't. He called the mill again with the same result. The ore-processing center was also unreachable by phone. Like the lumber mill, its answering machine failed to pick up the call. The phone line had to be down, and Franco knew why.

Well played, Viper.

Using his other phone clipped to his knee-board, he sent an urgent e-mail to the lumber mill's office.

If Viper killed his cousin, he'd make certain the bastard died an agonizing death.

And what about Antonia? She said he'd seen her.

He called his second-in-command at Macanas's ranch in southern Jinotega. "Pastor Tobias's son has made some trouble for us. Get Jaime and our three best men ready to go. I'll be there in a few minutes. See if you can reach them by phone and patch me into a three-way call. Try to e-mail them. I want to know what's happening up there."

"*Right away, sir.*"

***

The air conditioner's compressor on the north side of the office worked against Harv, severely hampering his ability to hear the presence of the enemy. He looked inside the Range Rover. If the vehicle had an alarm, it didn't appear to be armed. He felt the hood for engine warmth and realized it was a pointless gesture—he'd done it purely out of habit. When he rounded the corner in a crouch, the drone of the AC unit grew even louder as he moved north along the office's east wall. Identical in size and height, two more windows glowed around their perimeters. He ducked beneath them, reached the northeast corner, and peered around the corner. From here he could see the compressor unit and the mammoth form of the lumber mill's main building. Rather than continue into the illuminated cone created by the light mounted on the building's wall, he backtracked to the SUV, where it was much quieter. He still needed to clear the west side of the office. Since he hadn't seen a door, it had to be on that side of the building. He was about to place an ear to the stucco when he heard the buzz of conversation. Whoever was inside didn't seem too concerned about keeping their voices low.

Nathan's voice on the radio interrupted his thoughts. "*We're gonna have company soon. During Antonia's call, I heard an unmistakable hum in the background. Raven had his phone patched into the helicopter's NavCom, I'm certain of it.*"

Harv took a knee. "I'm hearing voices inside the lumber mill's office. How much time do we have?"

"Antonia made her initial call to Raven around forty-five minutes ago. Depending on how accurate your estimate of ninety minutes is, we're halfway there. We can't assume the helicopter or Raven were in Managua when Antonia called, so we could be looking at a much shorter time frame. Hang on a sec."

Harv waited through twenty seconds of silence.

"Antonia doesn't know where Raven was when she first called. He could be incoming at any moment. Like we discussed, I doubt he'll land at the lumber mill, even with the screen fencing. It doesn't conceal him from an elevated SP."

"I need a few more mikes over here. I'll make it quick."

Nathan continued. *"Estefan, park your truck behind the church, out of sight as best you can, and double-time back here. I need eyes outside."*

"On my way."

"I'm going radio silent," Harv said. "Three mikes."

"Copy. Three mikes."

Harv heard the urgency in Nate's voice but returned his focus to the office. Surely Raven had called his men about Estefan's presence in town. Shouldn't they be concerned in there? Their three friends had been gone for a long time. Maybe they'd been drinking. Tobias's letters mentioned a chronic alcohol problem in Santavilla.

A more realistic and chilling explanation entered Harv's mind—they had a sentry out here watching the area. It would explain why the men inside weren't concerned about their voice levels, but it didn't explain why Harv hadn't been spotted by now. He ducked below the glowing windows and peered around the southwest corner. He was surprised when he saw no one. He smelled it then, the unmistakable odor of a cigarette.

Someone *was* out here.

He looked to the southwest and saw several houses, but the closest one sat at least one hundred yards away. The smoke he'd smelled seemed too concentrated to have originated from there, but the logging trucks were parked in that direction.

Harv tried to visualize the layout of the mill in relationship to the rest of the village. As he put the map together in his mind, he realized the mill's office, the truck parking area, and the motel were all roughly aligned on the same vector. If Raven's men did have a sentry posted out here, and if they believed Estefan was at the motel, then the trucks would provide a good position from which to monitor an approach from the motel.

Relying on the technology of his NV goggles, he turned the gain to maximum and kept his attention fixed on the area. He'd seen vehicle taillights reflect the glow of a cigarette before. *Come on*, he thought, *I need a break here.* He was about to do it the hard way and approach the lot without knowing where to start when the taillights of every truck came to life for several seconds before dimming and winking out. And the farthest left taillight was the brightest.

He switched to the TI.

"Got you," Harv said. He now knew exactly where the sentry was—sitting in a backhoe and facing the motel. As luck would have it, the machine was parked in the middle of an expanse of gravel.

He could attempt a stealthy approach to the sentry's position, but it would be next to impossible to traverse the gravel silently. Adding to the degree of risk, he'd be stuck out in the open for most of the crossing. If the sentry turned around to check his six, Harv would be blown and he'd have to shoot the guy, something Nathan wanted to avoid.

He keyed his radio. "There's a sentry in the truck parking area on the south end of the mill's property. I'll need Estefan's help if you want me to take him down without shooting him."

"Affirm. Nonlethal force unless absolutely necessary. Estefan, coordinate with Harv. I'll sit tight with the girl."

"I'm parking behind the church right now."

Harv said, "Estefan, bring G3's assault rifle with you. How long?"

"Two mikes."

"Standing by. Two mikes."

***

Raven made a flawless approach to Macanas's compound in southern Jinotega. He set the Bell 429 down on the concrete pad, throttled down to idle, and watched his men jog over from the small hangar. Ducking low, they climbed into the passenger compartment. The ship could carry seven passengers, but he wanted only five men, including himself, for tonight's operation.

Thirty seconds after touching down, he lifted off and flew a course of 18 degrees toward Santavilla.

Fortunately, Macanas spent the majority of his time at his mansion in Managua, and that's where he was right now. Raven didn't plan to tell his boss the Tobias situation had escalated. Antonia said she'd thought Estefan had killed his men. She hadn't said it with certainty, though. Either way, he intended to end this unfortunate chain of events tonight and bury Estefan Delgado.

***

Harv's ear speaker came to life with Estefan's voice. *"I'm ready to go."*

"Head north along the main road, and let me know when you have the lumber trucks in sight. Can you duplicate that same whistle Franco's men used?"

"Absolutely, it's not difficult."

"Practice a few times, but not loudly. The digital pattern on your combat uniform is slightly different from what Franco's men wear, but the darkness works in our favor."

"What do you think spooked the guy at the gas station?"

"It's hard to say, but it was probably my size. I'm not as big as Nathan, but none of Franco's men are over six feet. It could have been my body language. These guys know each other well. They've been living in the barracks together. Here's what we're gonna do to avoid what happened before." Harv laid out his plan. "Nate?"

"I think it's solid. Look, we don't have a book of rules in play here. I'd like to avoid more killing, but if the sentry makes an aggressive move, you drop him, Harv. Clear?"

"Copy that. I think if we play this just right, it should work."

"I'll let you know when I have the trucks in sight," Estefan said.

"You'll be able to see them once you're past the ore-processing plant. They'll be on your right at two o'clock—you can't miss them. The sentry is on the east side of the parking area, sitting in the backhoe's seat. He'll be able to see and hear you as soon as you're past the processing plant."

***

Guillermo was bored to tears. What a total waste of time. Jaime and the others were probably laying their girlfriends while he sat in this lousy backhoe and watched a sleeping town. Someone had fired a gun—big deal. Franco's paranoia went beyond ridiculous—the guy saw demons around every corner. Guillermo tossed his cigarette butt and fired up another. At least it wasn't raining. He was about to climb down and stretch his legs when he caught movement to his left and focused on the spot. It looked like someone was slowly walking up the road using a cane.

He leapt from the backhoe and hurried over to a lumber truck, taking cover behind it. What idiot would be walking down the road in the middle of the night?

Ducking slightly, Guillermo eased down the length of the truck's flatbed for a better look. When he reached the cab, he heard the familiar whistle Franco had taught them.

***

Harv keyed his radio. *"He's on the move, Estefan."*

Estefan had untucked the front of his shirt to conceal the radio clipped to his belt. Feigning a stomach wound, he bent at the waist and used the deception to respond. "I'm ready."

"He's coming around the truck nearest to you. You'll have a clear view of him in five seconds."

Estefan clicked his radio and used the assault rifle as a crutch to take another labored step. He knew the darkness prevented the sentry from seeing any real detail.

Weakly, he issued the whistle again.

The sentry called out, "Jaime? Is that you?"

Estefan dropped the rifle and fell to his hands and knees.

"What's wrong with you?"

Completing the act, Estefan collapsed to his left shoulder.

The guy cursed, slung his rifle over his shoulder, and ran out from between the trucks.

***

Harv couldn't have played it better himself. Estefan's act was totally believable.

The sentry ran over to Estefan and bent down.

In return, Estefan swept his foot and took the man to the ground.

Harv abandoned all stealth and sprinted across the gravel.

The two men were locked in a wrestling contest when Harv arrived. The sentry had a grip on Estefan's throat and drove his knee at Estefan's crotch, but Estefan closed his legs in time to avoid what would've been a crippling blow.

Estefan elbowed the guy in the nose and seized the guy's groin. The man howled under the sudden compression but didn't let go of Estefan's neck.

Screw this, Harv thought, and he pistol-whipped the sentry on the side of the head hard enough to draw blood.

The guy reacted by thrusting his foot at Harv's knee. The pistonlike move nearly caught him off guard. Had he not taken the weight off his leg in time, the blow would've sprained the joint. Fortunately, the force of the kick harmlessly swung his leg around. Harv recovered his balance and kicked the guy in the ribs. Amazingly, Estefan's throat remained connected to the guy's hand. Drawing on a hiss for strength, the guy tried desperately to twist away from Estefan's grip on his testicles.

Harv admired the sentry's toughness, but enough was enough. He clocked the guy again, producing a dropped-melon sound. *That sounded bad*, he thought and hoped he hadn't swung too hard. He didn't want the man unconscious, only stunned.

The sentry grunted before going limp.

Estefan coughed and spit blood. He shoved the guy aside and half laughed. "Damn, Harv, it's a good thing you got here when you did, I might've killed the SOB. How's my lip?"

"Not bad. Your teeth okay?"

Estefan tongued his mouth. "I think so. The asshole nailed me with an elbow on the way down. Shit, he was fast."

"I saw that. Do you have any concussion symptoms?"

"No, it just stings."

"Don't worry. You did okay."

"Let's just say I was glad to see you . . . And leave it at that."

"Deal. Let's get him out of the road. Grab an arm. I'll get his rifle."

They dragged him over to the trucks and sat him up against a tire.

Harv updated Nathan via radio. "We took the sentry down without shooting him."

"Can he answer questions?"

"Barely."

"Do whatever's necessary to obtain information you can use to secure the office and barracks . . . in short order."

Harv caught Nate's unspoken meaning. "Understood."

Their prisoner didn't want to cooperate at first, but two dislocated fingers convinced him otherwise. According to the sentry, there weren't any other men outside. The barracks was empty, but there were two more men in the office. One of them was a white shirt, in command of the men in Santavilla. The other was an accountant, a bean counter who wouldn't offer any real resistance.

Their field interrogation complete, Harv moved quickly, removing the man's pants and slicing the legs into long ribbons. He used them like makeshift lengths of rope to both gag their prisoner and tie his hands and feet together behind his back. He and Estefan then dragged him across the gravel and left him twenty feet short of the office.

Harv whispered, "I'll take the right. It's about the size of a two-car garage in there, so clear your nine o'clock first. Your head okay?"

"I'm good."

"NV off?"

Estefan nodded.

Both of them pivoted their goggles up and pulled their Sigs.

Harv reared back and kicked the office door with all his strength.

CHAPTER 29

The door flew open with a violent bang, breaking its shaded window.

Harv rushed inside and pivoted to his right. To their immediate left, Raven's white shirt sprang forward from a couch to grab an assault rifle just beyond his reach.

Estefan painted his laser on the man's chest and yelled, "Don't do it!" The man looked at the rifle lying on the coffee table before retreating back onto the couch. "Good boy."

Harv's threat was at his two o'clock position. A small man pushed back from a huge desk and made a mad dash for the corner of the room.

Harv knew right away. This was the bean counter.

More importantly, an open safe loomed in the corner.

Harv couldn't see any contents; its partially open door blocked his view.

Clearly, the bean counter intended to close it.

Harv yelled, "Stop!"

Ignoring his command, Bean grabbed the heavy steel door and began pushing with all his strength.

Harv painted his laser on a chubby forearm and fired a single shot.

The suppressed report sounded like a heavy book being dropped on carpet.

Two feet above the floor, a red splotch materialized on the wall next to the safe. The meaty arm fell away.

"Stop!" Harv yelled again.

With one arm, Bean continued pushing.

Harv adjusted his aim.

A metallic clank filled the room as a second slug passed through the guy's other forearm and careened off the green steel door. The bullet plowed into the side of the desk, splintering its wood.

The white shirt shielded his eyes.

Without the use of his arms, Bean's efforts were over. He collapsed to the hardwood floor and pulled his wounded arms into his stomach. Blood was oozing but not gushing.

The momentum of the safe's door kept it going. It clanged against its jamb and harmlessly bounced back a few inches. Its lever arm had to be cranked to engage the locking rods.

"You stupid motherfuckers!" Bean cried in Spanish.

"I've got 'em both," Harv told Estefan, also in Spanish. "Clear those doors."

Estefan rushed over to the north wall and kicked open the door. He darted inside and yelled, "Bathroom. Clear!" He yanked a second door open and pivoted to face it. "Empty closet."

Harv looked at Bean. "Had enough?"

The guy hissed through clenched teeth. "If you dumbasses walk away, I'll forget this ever happened."

"Get up."

The little man didn't move.

Harv aimed the Sig's shimmering laser on the floor between Bean's legs and fired a third round. More splinters flew.

"I'm not going to ask again. The next one finds that uninhabited melon you call a head."

With a hateful expression, Bean used his elbows to gain his knees, then ungracefully labored into a standing position.

"On the couch, next to your friend."

His fingers dripping blood, Bean moved across the room and plopped down, grunting from the jolt. The top of his bald head barely cleared the couch.

"Thank you for your cooperation," Harv said with mock sincerity. He took a few seconds to scan the room for security cameras but saw none. He had twelve rounds left in the Sig; no need to load a new magazine.

Estefan kept his laser locked on the white shirt's chest and moved to a better location to see the entire room. "Keep your hands where I can see them and stand up."

White was about Estefan's size, but ten years younger. The wispy mustache didn't do anything for him. The man complied, grudgingly. "Do you know who owns this place?"

"We'll be asking the questions from now on," Harv replied. "Keep facing me and reach back. Lift up the cushions."

White extended his right hand.

"Other hand," Harv ordered and kept a neutral expression at seeing a Beretta 92 concealed under the middle cushion. He told White to step away from it.

Taking a wide berth around Bean, Harv grabbed the pistol, ejected its magazine, and cycled the slide. A live round cartwheeled to the floor. After reinserting the 92's mag, he put the weapon in his thigh pocket. He unloaded the HK assault rifle before tossing it into the corner of the room behind Estefan. Blood had already pooled in Bean's lap. Without pressure bandages, blood loss would become critical in the next twenty minutes.

Harv looked at White. "Take your shirt off." When the guy just stared, Harv forcefully said, "Do it now."

White unbuttoned his shirt and peeled it off.

"Toss it over." Harv holstered his Sig, pulled his Predator, and cut the shirt into wide strips. Looking down at Bean, he said, "I'm going to tie off your wounds. If you try anything cute, I'll let you bleed out. Are we clear on that?"

"You're an asshole," Bean said.

"Lose the tough guy attitude."

"Better let his sex partner apply the field dressings," Estefan said. "There's no telling what diseases that little runt has. Personally, I'd let him die. You'd be doing him—and the world—a favor."

"Fuck you," Bean spat, then winced.

Harv knew firsthand that bullet wounds were hideously painful. He looked at White. "You know how to field dress those wounds?"

White nodded.

Harv threw the cloth strips onto the coffee table, swapped his Predator for his Sig, and pointed it at White. "Please proceed slowly," Harv said. "This weapon has a two-pound trigger, and we wouldn't want any accidental discharges."

Harv ignored the safe for now; his priority was getting these two men squared away. It took a minute for White to get Bean's arms bandaged, but the guy did a decent job.

He ordered White to have a seat next to his buddy and handed Estefan the knife. "Cut me some strips from the sofa's fabric, and test them for strength. Cut up as many as you need. We're going to secure our three guests back-to-back around the wooden post in the middle of the room. I want their wrists bound in front of them with their elbow joints secured to one another. Right to left and left to right."

"No problem."

Harv used this opportunity to update Nate on their break-in and the two additional men in custody. He told Nate about the safe and Bean's defiant effort to close it.

"It can wait until after you've secured the men. Who knows, there might be something we can use against Raven and Macanas. Maybe the bean counter keeps a ledger in there. We'll go through it later."

"The barracks are fifty yards away on the north side of the lumber mill's main building. I need to send Estefan over there to verify no one's home. If anyone's over there, I doubt they heard our entry into the office."

"You shouldn't be alone in the lumber mill's office with no eyes outside. Sit tight. I can be there in a few minutes."

"Antonia's feet are tethered."

"I'll carry her."

Harv could only imagine her expression at hearing that. "Nate, she's one hundred twenty pounds, and you've got five hundred yards to cover."

"You carried me through two miles of pitch-black jungle when I weighed one hundred twenty pounds."

"I was motivated, but it also took five hours . . . You'll need help humping our gear. Let me send Estefan after he's secured our prisoners. In a dead run, he could be there in ninety seconds. I'll kill the lights and wait just outside the door where I can keep eyes on the office and the barracks. He'll be on his way in under one mike." Harv released the transmit button. "Watch them for a sec."

"These two piles of pig shit aren't going anywhere."

"Easy, Estefan."

Harv stepped outside, grabbed the sentry by his collar, and manhandled him up the porch steps into the office. Estefan was slicing a second cushion and testing each strip by putting one end under his boot and yanking on it. The makeshift ties were quite strong—Estefan couldn't tear them.

Harv wanted to know something before Nathan brought Antonia over here. "Ask the girl if these are the guys who mutilated Mateo's ear."

"Stand by."

"We never touched that worthless drunk," Bean said.

Harv told him to shut up. After fifteen seconds of silence he was about to radio Nate when his ear speaker came back to life.

"She said no. The men who hurt her father came from Macanas's compound in southern Jinotega. For what it's worth, she says the small guy is Raven's cousin."

"His cousin?" Harv asked, purposely repeating aloud.

Estefan smiled, then winked at Bean.

The little man's hateful expression returned.

"That's what she said. His name is Raul Sanchez, and she hates his guts. She said he's a complete asshole."

"Yeah, we kinda gathered that. Estefan's almost finished securing our guests." Harv's radio clicked.

"I'll be right back." Estefan ducked into the bathroom and returned a few seconds later, dabbing his lips with tissue. He shook his head. "I hate the sight of my own blood. It really pisses me off."

"Double-time over to the motel. Switch Sigs with me—yours isn't suppressed." Harv also handed him an additional mag. "My laser's set to a fifty-foot zero."

"Not a problem," Estefan said, taking a last look at the bound men.

Harv knew his friend wanted their roles reversed so he could have some quality time with the prisoners, but they weren't here for that.

"Estefan's on his way."

"I'm ready to move out when he gets here."

Harv killed the lights and activated his NVGs. "I can see all of you clearly. If you try anything, you'll regret it."

"What are we supposed to do?" Bean said. "We're tied up, you dumbass."

"That's your third strike." Harv grabbed the remaining strip of fabric and silently moved in behind Bean. In a quick motion before Bean could react, Harv looped the gag into Bean's mouth as if using a garrote, then tied it tight. This pint-sized turd hadn't earned any respect.

Before stepping outside, Harv decided to take a quick look inside the safe and activated the infrared feature of his goggles. Bean's eyes reflected an eerie iridescence.

Moving silently across the pitch-black room, Harv approached the safe. He pulled the door and stared in disbelief. "Oh, man," he whispered. "No friggin' way . . ."

CHAPTER 30

"I'm outside your door," Estefan said.

Nathan let him in. "Grab those two packs and the rifles." Nathan looked at Antonia. "If I take that gag out and untie your hands, do you give me your word you won't scream or try anything stupid?"

She nodded.

"Good, because it's going to be an unpleasant experience being carried over to the lumber mill, even worse with your arms tied behind your back."

"You don't have to carry me."

"Afraid I do." Nathan cut her wrists free but left her ankles bound together with the two-foot strip. He didn't have time to chase her all over creation. He ordered her to stand and hold still. In a fluid move, he heaved her over his right shoulder, bending her at the hips. Outside, he and Estefan pivoted their NVGs down and took off in a medium-paced jog up the street. He couldn't ignore the sensation of her breasts bouncing against his back, and he knew she was embarrassed from being carried this way.

"You okay up there?"

"My ribs hurt."

"Try to relax. This won't take long."

After fifty yards, she used her arms to encircle his waist and her wrists ended up across his groin. Although awkward, it definitely created more stability. He was tempted to say something but didn't.

Nathan felt a good burn begin in his legs. He'd always liked physical exertion and never understood why most people tended to avoid it.

Fairly winded from hauling Antonia across five hundred yards, Nathan reached the lumber trucks and turned right.

"I've got you," Harv said.

At the office, Nathan set the girl down on the top step of the porch and took a few deep breaths. "Estefan, double-time over to the barracks. Make sure no one's home. Surveillance only. Do not engage. If you see anyone, come up on the radio. One-mike check-ins." Nathan saw Estefan was in great shape. The three-minute jaunt hadn't phased him. He took off and disappeared into the blackness.

Harv nodded at the open door of the office. "There's something you need to see in there."

"On your feet," Nathan said to Antonia. "We're going inside."

"But that creep's in there," she whispered.

"He won't be a problem," Harv said. "I'm turning on the lights. NV off."

Nathan powered his goggles off and pivoted them up.

The bound men squinted at the sudden brightness.

Harv pointed to the open safe.

"Am I seeing what I think I'm seeing?" Nathan asked.

"Indeed you are."

"Unbelievable," he said under his breath.

"It's no wonder I had to shoot our little friend over there. Twice."

Sitting on a thick plywood shelf, twenty-six gold bars the size of chalkboard erasers loomed like pirate's treasure. There were six columns, stacked four high, with a seventh column containing only two bars. The ingots were pitted and crudely made, but he had no doubt they were solid gold. Unrefined, but gold just the same.

Nathan ignored the two men secured to the post and looked at Antonia. "Did you know about this?"

The bitterness in her expression told all.

"Do you still think you and Franco were going to live happily ever after?"

Staring at the safe, she pursed her lips.

He heard muffled groaning and turned. The little man with blood-soaked bandages was whipping his head back and forth in a frenzy. The other guy looked on the verge of tears. *Understandable*, Nathan thought. He escorted Antonia over to the safe where he could keep an eye on her. Nathan hefted a bar. "Feels like two pounds."

"Probably one kilo each," said Harv. "That's a little over two pounds."

"How many ounces is that?"

Harv thought for a moment. "I think a kilo's around thirty-five or so."

Nathan tried to run the calculation in his head aloud. "Twenty-six bars times thirty-five ounces, what is that?"

"There's a calculator on the desk."

Nathan picked it up. "If we're right about each bar being . . . thirty-five ounces, then there are nine hundred ten ounces in there. Multiply that by $1,400 and you get . . ." Nathan made a whistle sound. "We're looking at more than $1.2 million. That's at spot price for gold bullion, so it's not worth that much, but it's still a small fortune."

"We can't let Macanas keep it."

Nathan lowered his voice. "We'll hump it into the jungle and use our special phone to take a GPS reading. What about Estefan? He's going to want some of this."

"We'll deal with that when the time comes."

"We're telling him about it, right?"

"Absolutely."

"If Raven's been skimming, it's possible this is his private loot."

"That's a boatload of skimming. Either way, we don't—"

Estefan's voice cut in. *"It's all quiet at the barracks. No one's home."*

"Double-time back here. There's something you need to see."

"On my way."

Estefan arrived half a minute later and walked over to the safe. "You're kidding me." Estefan picked up an ingot. "These are one-kilo bars. Each one is worth about $50,000. This is a major score!"

"We've only got two backpacks and they're pretty full, but if we split it evenly, we'll be okay. I think we can handle adding . . ." He worked the calculator again. "About twenty-eight pounds of gold each. Can you manage that, Harv?"

"I bet I could." Harv nodded toward Bean. "What about him?"

Bean's makeshift bandages were fairly soaked, but they weren't dripping.

"He's not in danger of bleeding out. We'll deal with him later after we get this gold squared away."

"And her?" Harv asked, loading their packs with the ingots.

"Please don't tie me up with them," Antonia said, genuine terror in her voice.

Nathan grabbed her wrist, took her outside, and lowered his voice. "I have no reason to trust you, but you have every reason to trust us. Do you doubt we could've easily killed you tonight?"

"No."

Nathan pulled his knife and cut the tether binding her ankles. "You need to choose sides right now, Antonia. I don't know what kind of a person you are, but if you stay on your current path, it won't have a happy ending. I hope you don't dismiss what I'm about to say as patronizing or condescending, because it isn't meant to be. All the things you think are important—money, power, material possessions—none of them will make you happy. There's no correlation between wealth and happiness. Absolutely none. It's one of society's biggest lies. You may not fully understand what I'm saying right now, but if you live long enough, someday you will." Nathan put a hand on his chest. "True happiness comes from helping others who are less fortunate than you. It comes from doing the right thing. Nothing else works."

"What happened to you? In the office, I saw scars under your face paint."

"Life happened to me."

"You're not from around here."

Nathan didn't respond.

She hugged herself. "There's nothing left for me here."

"That's where you're wrong. You just haven't figured it out yet." In the amber light spilling out of the office, Nathan watched her face. She was so incredibly beautiful. Perhaps she could find inner beauty as well.

Antonia lowered her voice. "Raven always keeps two men with him. They're like bodyguards or something. I guess not always, just when he comes up for business stuff."

"We'll keep that in mind," Nathan said. "Why'd you share it?"

She shrugged.

Estefan and Harv joined them.

"I'll be right back," Nathan said. He went inside the office and told Bean in no uncertain terms to leave Antonia and her family alone or he'd come back and put Bean in a wheelchair.

They all looked to the south at the same time.

A helicopter's thumping echoed through the valley, then went silent.

"Shit," Harv said.

"Antonia," said Nathan, "I need the truth, right now. Does Raven fly helicopters?"

She nodded.

"Does that sound like the helicopter you always hear?"

"Yes."

"We're out in the open, people," said Estefan.

They ran over to the office's porch.

The helicopter's drone returned, louder this time.

"You're all dead now!" White yelled from inside the office. "You hear me? He's gonna kill every one of you stupid fucks!"

Estefan slipped past Harv into the office and hurried over to White.

White cringed when Estefan pulled Harv's suppressed Sig from his waist.

"Estefan, no!" Nathan yelled.

Nathan watched Estefan point the pistol at White and activate the laser. A crimson dot marked the top of White's head. Time seemed to slow as Estefan held the man's life in his hands.

"It's not who we are," Nathan said.

Estefan swung the weapon like a hammer, delivering a haymaker. The man slumped sideways against Bean's wounded arms. Bean whipped his head back and forth in agony.

"Pull him off," Nathan said. "Harv, kill the lights."

The helicopter's drone tripled when it entered the south end of the valley.

Rather than slow down and drop in altitude, the helicopter screamed over their heads at five hundred feet. Completely dark with no beacons or landing lights, it banked hard to the left, sweeping across the valley to the west. If Raven intended to land, he wasn't doing so at the helipad.

On the lower slopes of the mountains, Nathan saw a few residential lights come on.

He aimed his rifle for a look but had a hard time acquiring the helo. He took his eye out of the scope and looked down the length of his barrel, lining up on the sound as best he could, but he still couldn't find it.

"Harv, track for me."

Harv moved in behind and placed a hand on his back. They'd done this before, many times. "Move left and up a hair, a little more . . ."

"I have it," Nathan said. "Looks like a Bell. Six or eight seats."

In the NV image of his scope, Nathan didn't see anyone in the left seat, but there were men facing each other in the rear compartment.

"How many?" Harv asked.

"At least four in the back, but no one's in front with Raven."

"He doesn't like anyone sitting next to him," Antonia offered.

Harv said, "If he's wearing goggles, we're visible right now."

"Shit, I didn't think of that." He lowered his rifle.

The Bell kept going south.

"He's descending," Harv said. "Hear him cut power?"

"Yeah."

The sound changed again as Raven reapplied power.

"He's going to land at the south end of town," said Nathan, "probably west of the bridge in the open field where the power lines aren't a factor."

"He's on the ground," Harv said. "He just throttled down to an idle."

"How do you guys know all of that?" Estefan asked.

Nathan said, "We're both pilots. *Shh.*"

A few seconds later, they all heard it—a sudden increase in power, followed by the growing *whoop-whoop-whoop* of blade slap.

"He's in the takeoff curve," Nathan said. "Heading straight for us."

Harv nodded. "It's a good bet he just unloaded some of his men."

The helicopter roared over their position and continued north without changing direction.

"He's going for the open-pit mines to bracket us in this valley. Harv, you stay with Estefan and engage the men coming up from the south."

Nathan took off in a dead run for the road.

"Wait!" Harv yelled.

Nathan stopped and turned, counting precious seconds. "If Raven gets eyes on us first, we're all dead. I need you and Estefan to cover my six."

"Damn it. Take the TI." Harv shucked his pack.

Nathan shook his head and resumed running. "Keep it," he yelled back, "I'll be okay."

Harv's voice boomed through his ear speaker. *"I want your word you won't do anything heroic or reckless up there."*

"You have my word. Shoot to kill from now on, Harv. Anyone carrying a weapon is fair game."

"Shit, Nate. I hate it when you do this."

"I'll be okay. We've got the radios."

"You gave me your word."

"Absolutely, you have my word."

"Estefan and I are going to lay low and let our enemy come to us. Good hunting, partner. Don't get your ass killed. I like my world with you in it."

"Relax, Harv. Raven doesn't stand a chance."

CHAPTER 31

Nathan Daniel McBride ran.

He knew this would push his physical endurance to the limit. *Mind over matter*, he told himself. Although he could run faster than his current pace, he wouldn't be able to sustain it. He had to find the right balance between going too slowly and exhausting himself prematurely.

In less time than it took for Raven to land and shut down the helicopter, Nathan needed to sprint more than nine hundred yards up a steep road, in unfamiliar territory, in the dead of night, and face an unknown number of enemy combatants—one of whom was a sniper who'd been trained by none other than himself.

Although he'd told Harv that Raven didn't have a chance, he didn't believe it for a second. Barring some kind of miracle, if Raven saw Nathan first, it was over.

Though it bore its own risks, separating from Harv and Estefan had been the best tactical decision. If all three of them pursued the helicopter, the men Raven had dropped to the south of Santavilla would retake the lumber mill and add an extra man to their numbers. Raven's cousin was out of the fight, but the white shirt could still join the fray, assuming his brain wasn't hemorrhaging from

Estefan's pistol-whipping. Harv's plan to remain at the lumber mill's office was solid. Nathan had no way to know if Raven had actually dropped gunmen off at the south end of town or not. His brief landing there could have been a ruse. If Nathan had taught Raven anything, it was to use deception to his advantage, especially when facing the unknown. Still, if Raven had dropped men on the south end of town, they were no more than ten minutes away from Harv's position.

"Harv, you copy?"

"I'm here."

"Can you still hear the ship?"

"Barely. As far as I can tell, it hasn't descended yet."

"You and Estefan should switch Sigs so you have the suppressed weapon."

"We already did."

"Where's the girl?"

"She's still with us. She doesn't want to go home."

"It's your call, Harv."

"She won't make trouble."

"Raven's men might approach from the river."

"We'll be ready. We need a new scatter point."

"If I go silent for more than thirty minutes, give White Shirt a flesh wound in the leg, lose the girl, and take Estefan up to our original SP. Wait there for me."

"Silent for thirty minutes? As in . . . you're dead?"

"Don't assume the worst . . . it may only be a radio issue."

"A lot can happen in half an hour."

"Confirm for me what you remember about where I'm headed from the aerials."

"The photos only covered the south half of the pit mines. The road you're on turns right at a small pass between two peaks up there. It follows the side of the mountain and begins a gradual descent into the open-pit-mine area. I recall seeing some wide, flat

sections on the road that looked like fill areas. The right side of the road looked really steep, nearly vertical in places."

"Could Raven land on the road up there on those wider areas?"

"I don't think so, but I'm not one hundred percent sure."

"Those are spoil dumps," Estefan added. *"From adits."*

"Adits?" Nathan asked.

"Raven just throttled down," Harv cut in, *"but I seriously doubt he's landed yet. If I'm right, I should hear him increase power for the landing."*

Nathan spoke between breaths. "I can't hear much over my breathing."

"Save some energy, Nate."

"Yeah, I have to slow down . . . or I'll be trashed at the top."

"Nate, we don't have to engage Raven and his men right now. We can easily slip away and wait for a better opportunity."

"Let's play this out . . . We can fall back on that . . . if things go south."

"Your ghillie won't help you much during your sprint up the middle of the road. Keep your head up as best you can and stop running near the top. If you don't get immediate eyes on Raven, beat feet into the cover of the trees and put it on. He might have an NV scope with TI capability. The ghillie will help mask your heat signature."

"Will I have a clear view . . . of the whole basin from the pass?"

"You should. There are some trees here and there, but it looked like the moon up there. Raven will have multiple places to land."

"Antonia told me that Raven . . . always keeps two men with him . . . I think you can count on facing two . . . possibly three men moving in from the south."

"Copy. You sound winded. Don't burn all your energy going up that road. You're carrying almost thirty pounds of gold."

"Don't remind me."

"Nate, you can pull your pack off and toss the bars while you're running. We'll find them later. They're not worth your life."

Nathan could only imagine Estefan's horrified expression, but he strongly considered doing it. With each stride, the gold banged against the small of his back like a meat tenderizer. "I'll deal with it . . . I'm going radio silent . . . to breathe."

He sucked in a few quick deep breaths to recover from talking. The burn in his legs returned in force as the road began a steeper ascent along the east side of the canyon. He caught a faint echo of Raven's main rotor, looked up, and nearly fell. He needed to watch his footing. The road had loose rocks, ruts, and potholes.

Concentrating on his breathing, he drew in a lungful every three strides and exhaled three strides later. The sounds of his footfalls became a metronome, and he used the rhythm to regulate his breathing. Step-step-step, inhale; step-step-step, exhale.

Mind over matter, he repeated to himself. He'd been through worse physical ordeals—a lot worse.

After two hundred yards the road steepened even more, forcing Nathan to slow in order to maintain the same energy output. To take his mind off the hideous muscle burn, he imagined himself in a helicopter watching the vertical speed indicator rise as he traded velocity for an increase in climb rate. He applied left cyclic and a tiny amount of left pedal to stay centered in the middle of the road as it took a hairpin turn toward the west. He envisioned the compass needle gradually rotating counterclockwise toward 270 degrees.

Harv's voice broke his trance. *"He must be down, Nate. I don't hear anything. He can't leave the helicopter until he shuts down, but his men can get out. How are you doing?"*

"I've got a rhythm going . . . I'm in the zone."

"Be careful, partner."

"Count on it."

On a whim, he pulled his cell and checked for a signal. Nothing yet, but he might get a connection at the rim. He'd check again later. Knowing it would cost a few seconds, he stopped running and held his breath for an instant. Hearing nothing but crickets and trickling water, he continued running.

His legs screamed for oxygen, and he increased the frequency of his breathing. He flashed back to his boot camp days and silently sang a cadence from *Full Metal Jacket* to control his strides. *Up in the mornin' to the rising sun, gonna run all day till the runnin's done. Ho Chi Minh is a son of a bitch, got the blue-ball crabs and the seven-year itch.*

After five repetitions, he estimated he'd been running for just over two minutes. At this pace he ought to be close to the halfway point. When Raven touched down—likely within the last thirty seconds or so—he'd have to remain in the helicopter during the engine shutdown. If Raven's ship were a Bell 429, the engine cooldown was amazingly fast. Nathan remembered reading that it only needed thirty seconds and its main rotor could be stopped inside of two minutes after landing. One thing was certain, Raven wouldn't risk striking his main rotor on the steep side of the road up ahead by trying to land in too small of an area. Crashing a helicopter, even a few feet in the air, can yield fatal results. The ship was filled with Jet-A fuel.

Nathan sensed this was going to be a close race.

He dug deeper and summoned some precious reserve energy. He had to arrive at the pass first. If he could get a bead on Raven, he could end this fight before it started, but he faced a major hurdle. His rapid heartbeat and breathing weren't conducive to making a precision shot. His sight picture would be jumping all over the place. He doubted he could make a kill beyond two hundred yards. The reverse was also true. If Raven bolted from the helicopter and made a mad dash straight up the basin's wall, he'd be winded as well. Nathan doubted Raven would follow the road on foot unless he landed somewhere on or near it.

He silently thanked Harv for reminding him to drink lots of water, because right now, it was pouring out of him. His shirt was plastered to his chest. He pumped his arms to keep his legs going, but with every stride a tiny amount of additional fatigue crept in. He returned to the cadence. Although his body screamed to slow down, he overruled it with willpower. He had to keep going. All of their lives depended on him seeing Raven first. He glanced up, looking for the pass Harv had described. He ought to be able to see it by now. If only he could—

There!

Nathan saw a wide area of exposed earth up ahead.

Starting about one hundred yards ahead, most of the trees had been cut down. That had to be where the road turned east between the peaks and followed the mountain before starting down into the open-pit basin. It felt good to be so close. The barren area ahead must be one of those spoil dumps Estefan mentioned. What was the word he'd used before Harv interrupted? Abit or adit? It didn't matter—he was nearly to the pass, and the road was finally leveling out. Rather than increase his speed, Nathan used the flatter terrain to maintain his current pace, which gave his legs a much-needed break. As tempting as it was to run faster, Harv was right. He needed to conserve energy, because he had no idea what he'd be facing up here.

He closed to within fifty yards and saw where the road curved sharply to the right, forming a vista point of sorts. If Harv were right, he should be able to see where Raven had set the helicopter down from there. He slung the M40 over his left shoulder and pulled the suppressed Sig from his waist. In his current state, he'd never be able to hold the rifle steady. And he might not be able to hold the Sig steady either.

Finally, almost fully spent, he slowed down to a fast walk and reached the overlook. To avoid being seen from below, he kept a safe distance from the edge. In the basin below, entire swaths of forest had been stripped away. Scattered randomly, huge open pits containing muddy ponds littered the area. The entire basin looked like a war zone. Dotting the mountainside on the far side of the valley, black mine openings were accented by man-made spoil dumps of blasted rock. He spotted Raven's helicopter near the middle of the basin but saw or heard no movement. He gauged the distance to Raven's helo at five hundred yards.

He'd done it! He'd beaten Raven up here.

His excitement ended when he heard footfalls.

In the green image of his night-vision goggles, two armed men followed by a third scrambled up and over the edge of the road like ants coming out of a hole. They all wore digital combat uniforms and looked like pros, not mercenaries. He whipped his head around for cover, but the entire right side of the road offered nothing but a vertical face. He glimpsed an area of deep shadow, but he'd never reach it in time.

A mere twenty yards away, they ran directly toward him, though it wasn't clear whether they'd seen him yet. The two men in the lead had M-4 assault rifles slung across their chests in the patrol carry position. They also wore right-handed sidearms.

Nathan focused on the third man. He didn't carry a sidearm, but he held a scoped rifle in the classic tucked-carry position under his right arm—in the exact way Nathan had taught him more than twenty-three years ago. He also wore a pair of NVGs. Nathan couldn't see the entire rifle, but he was sure it wasn't an M-4.

Raven.

Caught completely in the open, Nathan had no choice but to shoot it out. There wasn't time for any other course of action.

Suddenly sensing they were no longer alone, the two lead gunmen stopped running.

Raven yelled, "Shoot him!"

In a purely instinctive move, Nathan sucked in a huge lungful of air, dropped to one knee, and toggled the laser. But the man on Raven's left was faster. Before Nathan could level his pistol and acquire a target, the gunman's pistol came out of its holster in a fast-draw motion quicker than Nathan had thought humanly possible.

The handgun flashed twice, and Nathan steeled himself for the ugly result. Contrary to common belief, getting shot doesn't automatically end a firefight. The human body can sustain a fair amount of trauma and still function, at least for a while.

The darkness of night saved Nathan's life.

Both shots missed low and left, giving him the half second he needed.

He held his breath, painted Fast Draw's chest, and squeezed off a two-round burst. One of the bullets whistled away after finding the gunman's M-4, but his target's good fortune ended there. The second round slammed home. The man jerked from the impact but didn't go down. Nathan double tapped him again and released a labored breath.

Eleven rounds left in the Sig.

Raven fired from the hip and bolted for the edge of the road.

The concussion of sniper rifle report shuddered Nathan's body and slammed his ears. His NVGs showed a green javelin of fire reaching for him.

Five yards short and left, the rocky surface exploded. Even though he wore NVGs, he instinctively raised an arm to protect his eyes. The move saved his goggles. His left forearm took a stinging blow, from a chunk of rock, he hoped, not a bullet fragment.

Even with three center-mass wounds, Fast Draw managed to aim his handgun in Nathan's direction and get two additional shots off. Both bullets sailed high. The slower of the two men who'd preceded Raven up the slope had initially frozen in indecision, but he now joined the fight.

In eerie detail, Nathan saw Slow's forefinger enter the trigger guard of his assault rifle.

Had Nathan not been winded from his sprint up the mountain, he could've easily ended the threat. But as he sucked in a precious lungful of air, he realized he'd never be able to line up on Slow in time.

A split second before Slow's M-4 erupted, Nathan dived left, aligning his body to offer the smallest profile. The M-4's flash suppressor did its job, creating a menacing flower of hot gas and blinding light. Nathan felt his body vibrate like a guitar string from the concussions and braced himself for the crippling result. But the gunman's rounds—dozens of them—skipped off the ground where he'd just been.

Slow stood his ground, ejected the empty magazine, and reached for a new one.

Nathan was slow to return fire because his freshly injured forearm had landed on a sharp rock.

Shit!

He aimed from a prone position and squeezed off a fifth round.

At the same instant he fired, the laser's dot vanished from Slow's chest. His bullet flew wide. He'd pulled the shot.

His lungs screamed for air.

Holding the same breath, he ignored the hideous sensation of suffocating, fired again, and scored a hit.

His bullet plowed into Slow's hip before the guy could insert the magazine. The man shuddered and made a second attempt to jam the magazine home. Nathan shot him again. The laser had been dead center on the man's chest, but it drifted off target and found the outside edge of Slow's left shoulder. The guy's tactical sling kept his rifle from falling to the ground when he let go of it.

Eight rounds left.

Close to passing out, Nathan exhaled and took several quick breaths as he instinctively rolled away from his current location. He couldn't continue fighting like this—especially against Raven. He needed cover and needed it quickly, but he saw nothing available in this open expanse of gravel and rock.

Raven had dropped out of sight over the edge. Nathan felt certain the scope he'd seen atop his adversary's rifle was NV capable. At this very moment, Raven would be relocating below Nathan's line of sight. Within seconds, his former student would have a clear bead on him. He was tempted to finish off the men he'd shot, but he didn't have time. The stopwatch in his head was ticking down to zero. He couldn't wait out in the open for Raven to reappear, because he had no way to know where that would occur. If he didn't find immediate cover, he'd have no chance of surviving the next few seconds.

Nathan whipped his head around and scanned the area again. This expanse hadn't been created from a road cut, it was a flattened spoil dump from a mine. No more than ten yards behind him, the area of deep shadow he'd seen earlier was a dark opening into the rock face and it represented his only hope of survival. Without knowing where Raven was, running toward the edge of the road was paramount to suicide.

Gritting his teeth, he made a beeline for the pitch-black hole.

CHAPTER 32

Nathan ran in a zigzag pattern toward the opening. As he did so, he considered scaling the exposed rock face rather than going inside the mountain. In daylight he might've been able to climb the wall, but he'd never manage it now, especially in his fatigued condition. Like a fly on a window, he'd make an easy target for Raven.

Just inside the mine's entrance, an ore car sat atop narrow rails. Its rusty form would offer waist-high protection. He had no idea if rifle rounds would penetrate its iron plating, but his options were severely limited. He reached down and pressed the transmit button.

"Harv, do you copy?"

Nothing.

Four strides left.

"Estefan! Do you copy?"

Shit! The terrain blocked his transmission.

Just ahead, an area of finer, powderlike dirt covered the ground. Nathan purposely angled toward it and left Harv a footprint. He and Harv always removed specific cleats from the waffle patterns of their boot soles for this very purpose.

From behind him, where he'd shot the two men, Nathan heard the distinctive sound of an M-4 bolt being released and knew he had mere seconds to reach the ore car. An M-4 could be handled with one arm but not as accurately. He didn't know which of the two men he'd shot was wielding the rifle, and it didn't matter. He didn't think it was Raven, because Raven would be using his sniper rifle, likely his old Remington 700. If so, it packed quite a punch and its slugs might cleave through the ore car—at least one side of it.

Two strides from the car, Nathan's world transformed into a maelstrom of sparks, high-speed chips of rock, and choking dust as bullets slammed into the wall in front of him. Fortunately, the shooter was twenty yards away, and his bullets went high. Unfortunately, Nathan felt half a dozen wasplike stings as shrapnel peppered his chest and legs. None of the wounds felt too serious, and thankfully they'd missed his face and groin, but they were definitely going to draw blood, especially the deeper wound on his thigh.

From the length of the burst, he knew the shooter had emptied the magazine. He cried out and cursed loudly, faking like he'd been shot. He purposely fell, got back up, and hobbled the last two steps.

Nathan tucked the Sig into his waist, maneuvered himself behind the ore car, and got his feet on the steel rails just in time.

The shooter fired two quick bursts, more accurately this time. The ore car vibrated as bullets pinged off its surface. Several rounds whistled down the tunnel, reverberating in eerie whines. Nathan couldn't be sure, but he didn't think any of the bullets had breached the metal. He *was* sure his right calf had taken a fragment. Aside from the fresh puncture wound, he was otherwise unscathed by the latest barrage. Rather than expose himself over the top of the car to return fire, he used its mass as a moving shield and pulled it deeper into the mine.

Nathan heard a familiar *whoomp* as the wall of the mine exploded at knee level. The trailing end of the ore car absorbed the bullet fragments with a metallic thump.

Son of a bitch!

Before Nathan could shield his face, Raven fired again.

The ceiling ignited in a shower of sparks and dust, breaking a bare light bulb. Glass rained into the ore car.

As much as Nathan disliked backing himself into a tunnel, if he hadn't moved deeper inside, he'd have been bleeding even more. Or dead. Even though he'd retreated beyond Raven's direct line of sight, the man had aimed his shots quite deliberately. And the effect of those strategically placed rounds was unnerving. Nathan had been on the wrong end of gunfire many times, but this was different. With no place to go but deeper into the mountain, he'd just entombed himself in an oversized coffin.

Screw this.

Nathan pulled his Sig, leaned out from his hiding place, and activated the laser.

The result churned his stomach. The suspended dust turned his beam into a bright green vector, pointing directly to his position.

He released the button and returned fire, walking his eight remaining bullets across the open expanse outside the tunnel. Scoring a hit was a long shot, but it might buy him a few extra seconds. Each suppressed shot flashed in the narrow tunnel, producing stroboscopic vertigo. Nathan closed his eyes for his last four shots and ducked behind the car again.

A third bullet from Raven's weapon shrieked down the tunnel, impacting the mine's wall somewhere behind him.

Nathan coughed and hacked from the dust. He needed clean air in a hurry. Abandoning all stealth, he hauled the ore car even deeper into the mine.

Fifty feet inside the mountain he found better air—it was also cooler. He stopped pulling the car at a shallow alcove in the tunnel's wall. About the size of a household refrigerator, it held half a dozen sledgehammers, pick axes, and shovels. Estefan had said they broke the ore by hand before hauling it down the mountain. It would be cramped, but he was certain he could get his entire body into the indentation.

The near absence of light severely hampered his NV, but he wasn't willing to activate its infrared flashlight because Raven's NVGs would easily see it.

Using feel only, he took a few seconds to insert a new magazine into his Sig and evaluated his tactical situation. From this point on, he believed he'd be facing Raven only. Fast Draw had taken three rounds in the torso. If the guy wasn't down for the count, he soon would be. The other man had one crippling wound, possibly two, and wouldn't be any use to Raven except to guard the entrance to the tunnel.

What would he do if he were Raven?

Wait it out?

Collapse the tunnel?

Neither tactic would end well for Nathan, and the latter was too terrible to contemplate. No, he had to get Raven to come in here after him. And do it fairly quickly. A prolonged silence might mean he was retrieving explosives. Nathan had no way to know where the dynamite was or how long it would take Raven to go get it.

From the safety of the alcove, he took a deep breath and called out in Spanish, "Hey, Franco, I've got your gold from your safe. All twenty-six bars. Does Macanas know about your private stash? Maybe I'll just tell him."

Raven didn't respond.

Of course, Nathan was lying about having all the gold, but by simply proving his knowledge of it, he'd given Raven an urgent reason to come in here, neutralize the threat, and reclaim any gold that Nathan possessed.

Silence from outside the tunnel.

Nathan decided to up the stakes. "And that worthless cousin of yours? He's bleeding out."

Raven's voice echoed in the tunnel. "You aren't Estefan Delgado. So who are you?"

Knowing his foreign accent had given him away, Nathan said, "Only one thing matters for you. I'm the guy who's got the goods on your ass."

Raven's response arrived in the form of a fourth bullet. It whistled past his alcove like an angry hornet, followed by a concussive boom.

"Go ahead and waste all your ammo."

Provoking Raven gave Nathan a measure of satisfaction, but he felt terribly cramped inside the alcove and the air quality had degraded from the latest blast from Raven's sniper rifle. Worse than that, the tunnel seemed to be constricting around him. He jabbed his thigh wound and used the sensation of pain to ward off the illusion. Nothing had changed, the tunnel wasn't getting smaller.

From outside, he heard muffled voices but didn't see any movement. Because his field of vision was narrow, he could only glimpse a tiny portion of the outside world. The reverse was also true, Nathan reminded himself. His enemy saw only the black opening of the mine.

He decided to make a bold move, one that involved substantial risk. In the closed confines of the alcove, he managed to shuck his pack and pull out a single gold bar. To reinforce the ruse of being wounded, he pressed the ingot against his thigh and smeared it with blood. Keeping his Sig up and firing a round every third step, he dashed for the entrance. He stopped well short, threw the bar out of the mine, and hustled back to the alcove, firing over his shoulder as he ran.

Back in the safety of the alcove, he peered toward the opening. Nothing happened.

"There's your proof," Nathan yelled. "I've got twenty-five more."

Nathan saw a black form sweep across the entrance and simultaneously scoop up the bar, too quickly to make for a hittable target.

Bright light appeared on the ground near the entrance. Nathan knew Raven had likely activated a small LED flashlight. Nathan used the time to reload his Sig.

"Looks like you're leaking."

"I'll live."

"What do you want? Maybe we can make a deal."

Knowing his response wouldn't be well received, Nathan pressed himself as deep as he could into the recess. "I want you and your boss in a prison cell together for the rest of your lives for murdering Pastor Tobias."

Raven didn't respond; his mind was probably racing.

"Did you hear me? You're going to rot in prison with Macanas. You—"

Nathan's world erupted again, this time from a fully automatic M-4 that Raven must've taken from one of his wounded men.

The M-4's sound was beyond deafening.

Son of a bitch!

Nathan covered his ears and ducked his head away from the fireworks display tearing past his position. Bullets pinged off the ore car and more overhead light bulbs popped.

When the gunfire ended, Nathan felt as though he'd been run over by an eighteen-wheeler. His body buzzed from the teeth-fracturing barrage. No more than eighteen inches away, forty hypersonic slugs, each producing its own sonic boom, had quite literally pounded his eardrums into mush. With a little luck, blood wouldn't be oozing down his lobes.

Think, man! React and overcome!

With a start, Nathan realized Raven could be using the suppressive burst to advance into the tunnel. He stole a look around the edge of the alcove but didn't detect any movement. To hear Raven after that auditory assault would be hopeless. Still, to be on the safe side, he fired a blind round toward the entrance. It zinged off the wall.

He sucked in a dust-filled gulp of air and tasted burned gunpowder. "Nice try, numbnuts, but it's not going to be that easy."

Raven didn't respond.

Nathan peered in the opposite direction, but his NV couldn't see beyond ten yards or so. He didn't know much about underground mines but believed there'd be other tunnels connecting to this one farther down the passage. From talking with Estefan, he seemed to recall they were called crosscuts or drifts. Turning his NVGs to maximum gain, he looked deeper into the mountain and saw only telltale speckling on the tiny TV screens. The photocathode plates weren't receiving enough light to amplify the image.

If there were other tunnels deeper inside the mine, could he find another way out of here? The thought gave Nathan a glimmer of hope, but he dismissed it. Although he was no expert at judging cut and fill volume, there had to be several thousand cubic yards of blasted rock outside the mine's entrance. The flattened expanse had been the size of a tennis court. And even if there was an alternate exit, what were the chances he'd find it? It could be on a different level—higher or lower. Or nowhere. He'd be forced to use either his infrared illuminator or a light stick, either of which would give Raven a huge advantage. And escaping didn't solve the problem of neutralizing Raven. As unpleasant as the thought was, his best bet was to stay semiclose to the entry point and wait for his enemy to make a mistake. The trick was getting Raven to do it.

He focused on his immediate area and saw that the walls and ceiling were jagged and uneven from being dynamited. A thick layer of dust covered every surface. There were no timbers for support. He flashed back to a childhood memory of a Knott's Berry Farm ride into the depths of a mysterious and colorful gold mine, but this grimy place was neither mysterious nor colorful.

Pitch-black and dirty, it had a musty odor—probably from water dripping from the ceiling.

Nathan's blood and sweat had combined with dirt, thoroughly trashing his MARPATs. Adding to his stress, he was already experiencing the early symptoms of anxiety from being trapped in an enclosed dark place.

As he considered his options, an idea formed. He only hoped he had the strength—and time—to pull it off. He fired two more rounds toward the entrance, stepped out of the alcove, and put a shoulder against the side of the ore car. He pushed with all his strength and was a little surprised when it tipped over without too much effort.

It clanked against the rock wall and, to his horror, stayed like that. For his idea to work, Nathan needed it flat on the ground. He silently cursed himself for not anticipating this. Sensing Raven was about to unleash another salvo, he pulled his Sig and fired three shots toward the entrance, purposefully skipping them off the ceiling. He wanted his bullets to go whistling out of the entrance and hit the ground.

He tossed the handgun into the alcove and hefted the car just enough to unseat its side wheels from the rail. The ore car clanged as it fell onto its side. In two quick jerks, he muscled the ore car sideways across the tunnel so its wheels faced the entrance. As he'd hoped, it was a near perfect fit. He now had solid cover three feet high, and he'd be able to run in a crouch deeper into the mine. As he ducked behind the overturned car and prepared to reach for his handgun, a short volley of bullets slammed into his newly created cover. He crawled inside the cast-iron box as two more salvos hammered its exposed belly. Raven was firing in short controlled bursts that banged the ore car like a drum and filled the tunnel with the forlorn cries of deformed slugs. For the third time in as many minutes, he endured the horrid feeling of helplessness. At least he was protected on five sides. Flecks of rust pelted his exposed skin as the ore car took more impacts. He ran his fingers along the iron where fresh dents had formed. No holes, yet. If Raven switched to his larger caliber sniper rifle, though, the bullets might punch through.

The barrage ended and Nathan yelled, "You missed. I'm still here."

Raven came back with, "How are your ears?"

"What?" Nathan yelled.

"I said, how are your—" Raven stopped midsentence and huffed a laugh. "Why don't we compromise and split the gold. We don't need to involve Macanas. It's mine anyway."

"Feels like blood money to me. Sorry, not interested."

"A shame."

"Tell me about it."

He pressed his hand against his thigh wound and left several bloody prints on the wall. Contrasted to the dusty surface, the dark stains couldn't be missed. Next, he reached into the side pocket of his backpack and wanted to kiss Harv when he felt the package of light sticks that Staff Sergeant Lyle had given them. For a sickening moment, he'd thought Harv might have them. He tore the wrappers free from four sticks and pocketed three of them. He bent the first stick, felt the internal snap, and shook it violently.

Its chemistry was instant.

He hurled the light stick toward the entrance and ran deeper into the mine.

CHAPTER 33

The ambient glow reflecting off the walls and ceiling gave Nathan's goggles all the light they needed. He stole a look over his shoulder and fired a blind shot. The shadow cast by the ore car was perfect. It kept the lower half of the mine dark while providing reflected light up high.

He'd run thirty steps when Raven's M-4 erupted again. Nathan hit the deck as several bullets whizzed over his head. Their whistling frequencies changed as they ricocheted down the passage. He thought he heard solid thumping farther down the tunnel but wasn't sure. In an instant, the level of illumination plummeted. Raven must've shot the light stick. Its glowing liquid was now splattered over a large area, diluting its effectiveness. Leaving the Sig's laser dark, Nathan rolled onto his back and fired three angled shots at the ceiling beyond the overturned car.

With three rounds left in the Sig, he reached into his thigh pocket for his last full magazine. He carried a box of fifty more subsonic rounds in his backpack, but they needed to be loaded into magazines. He was about to resume running when Raven's muffled voice penetrated the passage.

"You're bleeding. It's not too late to call this off."

"That's not gonna happen, but I promise to visit you in prison. I'll bring flowers for your cell mate."

Anticipating another barrage, Nathan fell onto his stomach and wished he didn't know as much about ballistics as he did. Raven's next burst was long and sustained. He covered his ears again as chips of rock pelted him from multiple directions. Somewhere up ahead, a puddle of water erupted, splashing his head with grimy water. He cried out before the barrage ended, timing it perfectly. The tail end of his shriek of agony overlapped the waning reverberation.

"Die slowly!" Raven called.

Nathan added a grunt and a soft yelp, then went silent. Except for the bits of pulverized rock, he hadn't been hit. He ran his hand along his soaked pant leg and wiped more blood on the wall at hip level. Seeing it wasn't convincing, he rolled up his left sleeve, pulled his knife and drew its blade along the upper part of his arm above the elbow. The cut immediately began to drip blood. Keeping his elbow bent, he let the blood drip onto the rail. In the absolute silence each drop produced a barely audible tap sound. He then smeared the blood around a little. The rail wasn't wide—less than half an inch—but the dark stain looked authentic. He began a low crawl deeper into the abyss, trailing more blood from his arm and thigh as he progressed.

Despite the trail of blood he left—both manufactured and real—Nathan wasn't feeling any detrimental effects from blood loss. Of course, that could change, and quickly.

Still moving ahead, he called out loudly, trying to put pain in his voice. "Hey, Franco, you still want to talk?"

"Not just this minute. Let's see how I feel in say . . . twenty minutes. Sound about right?"

Nathan fired toward the entrance again but didn't use the same pattern of quick shots. He sent one bullet, followed by two delayed shots a few seconds apart—the futile efforts of a desperately wounded man.

The muzzle flashes betrayed his location, but since he wanted Raven to know he'd moved deeper into the mine, they worked to his advantage. Raven would see only the first flash; he'd get out of the way for the subsequent shots. Using his hand like a metal detector, Nathan swept the tunnel's floor for puddles of water as he crawled. He didn't want to dilute the blood trail he'd created, and he definitely didn't want to be soaking wet. The temperature already felt cold, and farther in, it would get even cooler. He knew there was more water up ahead because he heard drops landing in puddles. Not only was this place pitch-black, it was utterly silent as well. He kept spreading blood as he crawled until he reached the limit of his NV goggles. The only light his NV detected occurred when he looked toward Raven's end of the passage. The other direction was a black hole—completely void of light.

Darkness played tricks on the mind. He could've sworn he saw his hand sweeping back and forth but knew it was impossible. Even the best NV devices can't work in total blackness.

He reached up and activated the infrared flashlight for a split second and hoped Raven wasn't looking down the tunnel at that exact moment.

What Nathan saw during the brief flare was nothing short of glorious.

No more than fifteen yards ahead, the tunnel terminated in a T intersection. The rock wall facing him was peppered with fresh pockmarks from all the bullet impacts.

If he could reach that junction, he'd be able to get out of Raven's direct line of fire. He'd still be vulnerable to fragmentation wounds, but he'd take those odds any day over his current predicament. Thus far he'd been incredibly lucky to escape serious injury. His former student had unleashed at least one hundred twenty rounds of .223 and several larger-caliber rounds, probably .308. The sooner he crawled around one of those corners, the better.

Completely blind, Nathan continued creeping along the tunnel floor between the rails. Every few yards or so, he stopped and held perfectly still, listening for any sounds other than dripping water. He also glanced back toward the entrance, where the destroyed light stick would silhouette Raven against the soda-straw effect of light. So far, Raven hadn't come in. It was possible Raven had advanced to the overturned ore car, but Nathan didn't think so. He hoped the ringing in his ears had receded enough to allow him to detect any such sounds. Still, he couldn't dismiss the possibility that Raven was conducting his own low crawl toward the overturned car.

As he reached the T junction, Nathan felt something strange on the floor. With a little more blind exploration he knew what it was—a small turntable for the ore car to change direction. He chose the right side of the passage and crawled around the corner. After gaining his feet, he felt his way along the wall for several steps and removed a light stick.

He bent the stick with too much anticipation and accidentally dropped it. It immediately produced a tiny amount of light which allowed him to recover it without feeling around. He shook it, and his world turned bright green. Raven would see this for sure. He threw the stick farther down the crosscut, returned to the junction, and peered around the corner. The overturned ore car lay at least thirty yards distant, the entrance another fifteen yards beyond that. Nathan knew Raven could've already advanced to the car and tool alcove, but if he came any farther up the tunnel, he'd risk exposure. Just to be sure, Nathan activated another light stick and hurled it down the main tunnel. If Raven tried to sneak past the ore car, Nathan would see him now. Neutralizing the light source wouldn't be easy either. He supposed Raven could try to shoot the stick, but he had little chance of hitting it without taking a precision shot with the sniper rifle, and he probably maintained a three-hundred-yard zero like Nathan had taught him. No, to neutralize the stick's glow, Raven would have to block its light or toss it back toward the mine entrance. Either way, the change in illumination would alert Nathan to Raven's position.

Next, Nathan activated the fourth stick and hurled it into the opposite passage of the crosscut. His goggles now had plenty of light to work with, which created a double-edged sword. When Raven approached the junction, the same would be true for his goggles as well.

Satisfied, Nathan turned and kept moving deeper into the right-hand crosscut. He pressed his bloody pant leg against the wall, went a few more steps, and squeezed his self-inflicted arm wound. Enduring the pain, he dripped blood on the tunnel's floor in several places. He hurried over to the first stick he'd thrown and placed a couple of rocks in front of it so it didn't offer as much light toward the junction. Turning, he quickly returned to the main-tunnel junction as quietly as he could and again saw no sign of Raven.

Now that his nerves had settled a bit, he took a moment to evaluate his surroundings. Looking back and forth at the two branches of the crosscut tunnel, he saw they didn't intersect the main passage at a 90-degree angle. The right-hand side made a sharper angle, closer to 70 degrees. The left-hand side of the crosscut, however, angled slightly away from the mountainside, plunging deeper into the mountain. The left-hand side, with its obtuse angle, would be slightly more susceptible to ricochets from Raven's gunfire.

Nathan decided to stay in the right-hand branch of the crosscut for the moment. The rock was different here—lighter in color and shinier. Nathan thought it was some kind of quartz but wasn't sure. It looked as though the miners were concentrating on removing the light-colored plane of rock along the axis of this crosscut. Nathan believed he was looking at a vein of gold ore and the miners had blasted it free for as far as the light sticks on either side of the crosscut could illuminate. More jagged and crude than the entry tunnel, both branches of this crosscut passage obviously chased the vein. Reinforcing his conclusion, overhead light bulbs appeared more frequently in the crosscut. The miners probably used a portable generator to power them. He wondered how much gold in his backpack had come out of this mine. Nathan shook his head. This was a depressing environment. He couldn't imagine toiling in it all day.

He spread more blood along the wall and wondered how much time he had. What had Raven said earlier? Twenty minutes? Nathan didn't believe Raven would wait that long, but he might let Nathan stew for a spell. Without adequate lighting, most people would be extremely uncomfortable in a place like this, and Nathan included himself in that group. He didn't merely dislike enclosed places, he detested them. He'd felt a brief pang of panic when he'd crawled into the overturned ore car, and thinking about it now didn't help a bit.

He refocused his attention by looking across the main tunnel into the left-hand passage where he'd tossed the second light stick. On the far side of its sphere of light, he saw something dark. He checked the main tunnel before darting across, careful not to step on the three-foot-diameter turntable. He sensed Raven's presence lurking at the mine's entrance, but thankfully, no additional bullets arrived. Maybe Raven was conserving ammo for his final assault. Moving as quietly as possible, he eased past the light stick. Fifteen yards distant, another ore car materialized. Its size and shape differed slightly from the one he'd overturned, but it looked as though it would hold roughly the same volume. Just beyond the car on the right side, a secondary crosscut loomed. The black outline of its opening looked waiting like a frozen sentry. Looking for drop-offs or other types of ankle-breaking holes, Nathan stepped inside and activated the IR illuminator.

"Oh, man," he whispered. At first he had a hard time processing what he saw. The ceiling of this narrow tunnel seemed to disappear abruptly. Taking a second look, he realized it actually extended upward at an angle to the limit of his IR. This intersecting crosscut must have been blasted to follow a vein of gold ore. And clearly the vein had led upward at an unexpectedly steep angle—hence the rising tunnel floor and the extremely high ceiling above.

How the heck had the miners done it? They must've used some sort of scaffolding or blasted it from the top down. It boggled the mind, but it also gave him a new idea.

He turned off the IR, hurried back to the T junction, and saw no sign of Raven. It was puzzling that Raven hadn't come in here yet. In a situation like this, the defender usually had the upper hand, but Raven's M-4 gave him a huge firepower advantage. Nathan's suppressed 9-millimeter was a peashooter in comparison—a peashooter that needed its magazines reloaded.

He took a knee and removed his backpack. The ghillie suit was damp from being partially dragged through the puddles. Nathan had kept his body fairly dry, but the shaggy garment hung down when tied to the pack. Leaving his IR dark, he felt through his supplies, wishing he had a small mirror for looking around corners. He located the box of ammo and fed rounds into the partially expended mags. He swapped the Sig's current mag for a full one and topped off the one he'd removed. Since the Sig had a live round in its chamber, he didn't need to cycle the slide. To be on the safe side, he lowered the hammer using the decocking lever on the thumb side of the slide. The Sig was double action, so all he had to do was pull the trigger.

Raven's voice broke the silence. "Hey, you still alive in there?"

From the distant echo, Nathan knew Raven remained outside the mine's entrance and felt some relief. At least Raven was still around and not retrieving explosives.

He slipped across the junction over to the 70-degree crosscut on the right-hand side.

Because the light sticks he'd tossed into both sides of the crosscut were at least forty feet from the T junction, Raven wouldn't see much more than a dim glow in here. Like Nathan, Raven had two

NV devices: his goggles and the scope on his sniper rifle. Nathan supposed Raven could be lying in a prone position, scoping the tunnel for movement, but he dismissed the thought. The overturned ore car prevented a low line of sight. He seriously doubted Raven would risk aiming down the tunnel from a standing position for any length of time, if at all.

"Hey," Raven called again. "Are you there?"

Nathan projected strain in his voice, as if the effort of speaking drained his strength. "What happened to my . . . twenty minutes?"

"Doesn't sound like you *have* twenty minutes. Why keep fighting?"

"You're an asshole," Nathan said weakly. "Maybe I'll hide the gold."

"What?"

"I said, maybe I'll just hide the gold."

"Where's the sport in that?"

"At least you won't have it."

"I can assure you I'll find it. Why throw your life away like this? It's not worth it."

"I was about to—" Nathan issued a wet cough, purposely trying to keep it muffled. "I was about to ask you the same thing."

"This is your last chance."

Nathan fired a single round down the tunnel.

"Is that your final answer?"

"Yes."

"Then we'll do it the hard way."

Nathan used his pack like a shield and lay flat behind it. Raven fired a short burst of four or five rounds. *Well, at least he's consistent.* The bullets slammed into the wall of the T junction and more shrapnel whizzed over his head. Thankfully the thunderous roar was tolerable at this distance. Nathan took the short burst to be an indicator that Raven didn't have unlimited ammo. Nathan remained motionless for several more seconds before reaching into his pack for water. His mouth was super dry.

He chugged the water, making sure to leave plenty of bloody prints on the bottle, then set the bloody bottle down and rummaged around inside his pack until he found what he needed. He put the two M84 stun grenades into his pants pockets, but he didn't like how they felt, so he moved them to his thigh pockets. If he had to do more crawling, they'd still dig into his legs but not as badly. So be it—he'd deal with it. He decided to keep the two M67 frag grenades in his pack. Using high explosives inside a mine didn't seem like a good idea.

As he prepared to move, a better plan suddenly came to him. Better, yes, but it involved even more risk. He closed his eyes as his mind worked overtime, visualizing what he needed to do. It was a great idea if he had time to set it up.

Nathan picked up the bloody water bottle and darted across the T junction over to the left-hand crosscut. Listening for any sounds, he walked a few steps, took a knee, and went to work.

CHAPTER 34

Franco didn't relish going in after the guy, but he had little choice. When he'd first ordered his men to shoot, he'd seen the guy's night-vision goggles. They were hard to miss. Franco had initially assumed he was Viper, but the guy had a strong *norteamericano* accent. He'd also been too tall to be Viper. Now Franco had more immediate concerns—such as avoiding a bullet.

Whoever this intruder was, he was dressed in the same way that Antonia had described Viper: a special forces soldier. Antonia hadn't said anything about Estefan having a friend with him. He'd need to have a little chat with her about that. Whoever this mystery man was, he knew his way around a handgun. He'd dispatched two of his best men with relative ease. More remarkably, he'd seemed to appear from nowhere. Could he have hustled up the canyon after hearing the helicopter? It seemed unlikely but no other explanation fit. Franco didn't doubt it could be done, but there weren't too many people with the stamina to pull it off and still be functioning at the top. He included himself in that elite group.

And now, although Franco had the stranger pinned down in the mine, the stranger had his gold—and the ability to protect it.

Seeing the blood-stained bar had rattled Franco. He'd been stock-piling his private stash for years, constantly moving it around so it never remained in the same place for too long. As a supplement to his pay, Macanas let him keep 10 percent of all the gold extracted from Santavilla's mines. The problem was he'd amassed closer to 20 percent, and if Macanas ever found out he'd been skimming, he was as good as dead, or worse. Macanas had criminal friends in high places all over Central and South America, and Franco knew he'd die an agonizing death if his secret leaked. Over the last few months, he'd considered cashing it in, but the spot price of gold had really plummeted.

Which left him here, facing one of his worst fears: someone had stolen his retirement money. And he'd have to chase this jerk into the mine to recover it. Not an easy mission, especially alone. Franco would have preferred to conduct a leapfrog advance down the mine's main gallery, but one of his men was unconscious and the other couldn't walk. The two men he'd dropped near the wooden bridge were headed for the lumber mill, and their orders were to stay there until relieved. At the time he'd given that order, he hadn't known the lumber mill had been compromised and his gold stolen. Other than his bleeding cousin, which could be total BS, Franco didn't know the status of any of his men permanently stationed in Santavilla. Right now, he was strongly motivated to go in there, kill the guy, and find out what the hell was going on in town. He'd deal with Estefan Delgado then.

For a moment, Franco forced himself to imagine what it must feel like to be trapped in the mine, facing the business end of his M-4. It had to be hellish at best, pants-pissing at worst. He knew the foreigner had taken at least one bullet before going in there. Lucian had reported seeing the guy fall down and hobble into the opening. Franco couldn't be sure, but he believed he scored another hit with his second-to-latest salvo. He didn't know the seriousness of the stranger's wounds, but it must add to the pressure he was feeling in there. Alone in the dark, bleeding and trapped, the guy's outlook was bleak. Franco knew a hopeless situation often forced a man into making reckless decisions. He'd need to be mindful of it. A trapped and wounded animal could be unpredictably vicious.

He turned his goggles to maximum gain, aimed his M-4 from the shoulder, and silently slipped inside the mountain.

***

After finishing his task just inside the entrance to the left-hand crosscut, Nathan approached the ore car he'd seen before. Moving past the light stick, he held a hand out to block its brightness. Three yards short of the car, he pulled a ten-foot length of fine fishing line from the small spool he always carried with him on ops. Even though the light stick remained ten yards behind him, it provided plenty of light to work with. He tied one end of the line around a fist-sized rock and repeated the same procedure on the other end. Before placing the rocks, he dabbed his thumb and forefinger into his thigh wound and coated the length of fishing line with blood to darken and dull its surface. He also bloodied the areas where the fishing line encircled the rocks. Then he scooped up some powdery material from next to the rail and sprinkled it along the wet line. Next, he rubbed the rocks in the powder, camouflaging the fishing line around them. Finally, he smoothed the area he'd disturbed and covered it with gravel.

After placing one of the rocks inside a waist-high crevasse in the wall, he looked for a similar place on the other side of the crosscut and found one at knee level, a little closer to the ore cart. Perfect. He didn't want the trip wire to be level or straight across the tunnel. His initial plan had been to string the line across the top of the rails and connect it to a stun grenade, but that plan assumed Raven would be walking between the rails, not on top of them. Nathan had used the rails to move silently and believed Raven would too.

He finished rigging the trip wire and checked his handiwork. Both rocks were secure and wouldn't fall out of their small alcoves without being pulled. He placed a small flat rock on the rail eighteen inches short of the trip wire, so he'd know where to step over it when he returned. Moving silently, he eased back toward the T junction and picked up the light stick. Hoping Raven wasn't looking, he threw it across the junction and into the right-hand crosscut. It bounced three times and came to rest about halfway between the junction and the other light stick. Both of the light sticks now lay in the right-hand side of the crosscut tunnel.

Nathan kept going and slowly peered around the corner down the main tunnel. He thought he saw movement just past the overturned car but couldn't be sure. He turned around and eased along the rail back toward the other ore car. With no light sticks left in this side of the crosscut, the available light kept decreasing with every step. Soon, the telltale speckling in his goggles returned. Just ahead, he could see a dimmest outline of the ore car and a few ceiling crags, but the floor of the tunnel was pitch-black. When he closed to within ten or twelve feet of the car, he began sliding his foot along the rail, feeling for the rock he'd left.

And couldn't find it.

Where was it? It should have been right here. Could it have fallen off the rail? He didn't think so but wasn't 100 percent certain. Refusing to second-guess himself any longer, he dropped to his hands and knees and extended his sliced arm. Realizing his mistake, he quickly withdrew it and rolled his sleeve back down to avoid dripping any blood on this side of the crosscut. With the wound covered, he extended his hand again.

Still nothing.

Was he looking on the wrong rail? No way. He'd placed it on the left rail on the low side of the trip wire.

His Sig.

He could activate its laser for a split second without creating too big a flare. To be even safer, he put his left forefinger over the laser's aperture and pressed the button.

Nothing happened.

What the hell?

Then he remembered turning it off after leaving the tool alcove to avoid accidentally activating it while he crawled. The mistake hammered his nerves. He'd just forgotten something that might've cost him his life. Pursing his lips, he flipped the button on the base of his Sig and pressed the button a second time. The tip of his forefinger brightly glowed and an image from the movie *E.T.* flashed, unbidden, in his mind.

There. Just beyond his reach, the flat rock sat on the rail. Feeling relief that he was still grounded in some sense of reality, he pushed the rock off. Leaving the laser on, he held his glowing finger tight against his body to minimize the light and carefully stepped over the trip wire.

Before moving past the car, Nathan took off his pack and gently placed it where he couldn't possibly trip over it later. He leaned his rifle against the far side of the car so none of its form could be seen from the junction. Just past the car, he found the opening into the secondary crosscut where the huge slab of rock had been removed from the ceiling . . .

And stepped inside.

Now came the hard part.

***

Franco advanced to the overturned ore car and saw something flash at the end of the tunnel. He froze, not wanting to create any discernable movement. The ore car offered him cover, but he'd hoped to keep his presence inside the mine undetected.

Whatever flashed seemed to have come from the end of this main tunnel, but it had happened too fast to see properly. The glow down at the end looked about the same as it had before. This cat-and-mouse game would be much more difficult if it migrated deeper into the labyrinth of passages. He would have to guard against letting the stranger slip out behind him undetected, a difficult task given the nature of this system of tunnels. Although Franco hadn't been in this mine in several months, he had a fairly good idea of its layout. This main entry tunnel ended at a T junction, branching to the right and left. The left side held more secondary passages and would offer more places to hide. It was likely his prey would set up an ambush on that side. Even though he couldn't know where his enemy would conceal himself, Franco felt he had the advantage. He wasn't wounded, possessed a fully automatic M-4, and had a state-of-the-art pair of NV goggles, complete with an IR illuminator for pitch-black environments.

One thing was certain, the guy was bleeding and from the look of things, pretty badly. Blood was smeared everywhere. He smiled. With a little luck, he'd walk up to a dead body. If the guy carried through with his threat and hid the gold, finding it shouldn't be difficult. This linear environment didn't offer many hiding places. Franco wasn't worried.

He *was* worried about that damned light stick fifteen yards farther down the tunnel. Its presence prevented a stealthy advance. Shooting it from here wouldn't be easy. Throwing it down the mine had been a smart move on his enemy's part . . . On closer inspection, though, it also afforded him an opportunity. The light stick had ended up on the outside of the left rail, nearly up against it. If he hugged the right side of the wall, he'd be in the shadows when he got closer to the light stick. He considered a balls-out run to the light stick so he could hurl it back toward the entrance. Shoving it in his pocket wasn't an option because his opponent's NV would see the light through the fabric. He might as well paint a bull's-eye on his crotch—not an appealing visual.

Because of the light stick up ahead, Franco concluded the best way to advance down the gallery was a low crawl. He left his sniper rifle in the tool alcove, slung the M-4 over his shoulder, and pulled the pistol he'd taken from his mortally wounded man.

Feeling like a snake entering a gopher hole, he began slinking down the tunnel.

***

Nathan knew his way around rock climbing, but he'd never attempted it in total darkness. From this point on, he'd be caught in the clutches of a silent, black world. The dust on the walls presented a problem. Nathan would never be able to climb into the opening over his head without leaving handprints and scuff marks. The good news was, Franco wouldn't be able to see the disturbed areas without an artificial light source, and the instant Franco activated his IR illuminator—assuming his device had one—Nathan would have the upper hand. Brutally, the reverse was also true.

This showdown in the dark would become the ultimate test of wills.

Who would blink first and turn on the lights?

A step inside the secondary crosscut, he flashed back to when he'd activated his IR and formed an image in his mind. This connecting tunnel acted like an overly tall hatch on a naval ship. The ceiling was about ten feet high and extended upward at a shallow angle before intersecting the lighter-colored rock and rising much more steeply. From there, it went about thirty feet higher. The floor contained blasted rocks of all different sizes, but the miners had leveled it somewhat with smaller rocks and gravel.

Nathan didn't need to climb very high; he just needed to wedge himself about five feet above the tunnel's floor. Rock climbers called it a chimney climb, and it was one of the easier ascents they performed, assuming the gap didn't become too wide.

He felt for a foothold and found a sharp crag at knee height. Using his right arm, he reached across the narrow passage and braced himself. His clothes issued a barely audible whisper as he hoisted himself up eighteen inches. He extended his free foot to the opposite side and found an angled spot to bear his weight. He repeated the process three more times. With adequate light, he could've made this ascent in a few seconds, but blindly feeling for footholds and handholds had taken over a minute. He achieved a stable position by resting his bent knees on one side of the chimney and his back on the other side. He now wished he had his pack. These walls were far from smooth, and he felt every imperfection with perfect clarity.

If he had to stay like this too long, it was going to turn ugly.

***

Franco hadn't seen or heard anything in a long time. He didn't know how much time had elapsed since the tall man had entered the mine, maybe seven to ten minutes, but he *did* know a blood trail when he saw one. Rather than continue a low crawl down the main tunnel all the way to the light stick, he unslung his rifle, popped up, and ran the remaining ten yards, careful to tread only on the ties wherever possible. His footfalls made noise but not too much. He hurled the light stick as far as he could back toward the portal and quickly dropped prone. If any bullets were going to come his way, he expected them right now.

Nothing happened.

This gallery remained utterly silent other than the occasional sound of dripping water.

Could his quarry already be unconscious from blood loss? Franco had seen a lot of blood, but even superficial wounds could bleed freely. And he hadn't seen strong enough evidence to believe the guy had taken anything but superficial wounds. Blood was smeared along the left rail, but it was likely from bullet fragments, not a direct hit. Either way, his prey had to be under a tremendous amount of stress.

Without the light stick's blinding source in front of him, he could see a glow coming from the right side of the T junction. The left looked dark.

Franco gained his feet.

Aiming his rifle from the shoulder, he silently eased deeper into the mountain.

***

Once Nathan found a stable position, he reached into his thigh pocket and removed the stun grenade. Feeling its form, he quickly identified the dual-safety-ring system. Keeping his hand firmly around the cylindrical device, he gave the circular ring a clockwise twist and pulled it free. Rather than let it drop to the floor, he pocketed the ring. He left the triangular ring in place for now. If he pulled the secondary ring, the grenade would detonate if he released the handle. Even with the triangular ring still in place, he felt like he had a handful of sleeping wasps. Once he tossed it, detonation would occur in approximately two seconds.

Nathan waited and listened. He couldn't hear water dripping anymore. He strained to hear even the slightest sound and got nothing.

This was frigging unbelievable.

If there was such a thing as buzzing silence, this was it.

Did absolute silence exist? Did molecules make noise at the subatomic level? He didn't think so but wasn't sure.

After two minutes of being wedged in the chimney, he began to feel fatigue in his back and legs. He slowed his breathing and tried to remain calm, but a sense of resentment washed through him. He resented hiding in here like this. He resented Raven's turn toward crime. He resented this hole in the mountain and everything it represented. Greed. Power. Money. What real value did any of that crap have?

In less time than he'd hoped, his back was killing him, and his legs burned beyond all hope of ever recovering. At any moment, a crippling cramp threatened to seize one or both of his quadriceps.

His sense of time became a pain gauge, complete with a black needle. Each second moved the needle closer to the red zone and . . . failure.

It really frosted him that Raven might win this battle. How could he let that happen?

He tried to use his heartbeat to count seconds, but the burning in his legs overruled his ability to keep track of numbers. All he saw was the slow creep of the pain needle toward the end of its arc.

He had to hang in there a little longer.

He'd been through worse . . .

No!

He shouldn't have thought that—gone there—but it was too late to pull back now.

He'd opened the door.

It happened suddenly. Like a boiling kettle beginning its shriek, Nathan's mind reached critical overload.

Within seconds his entire body trembled. He closed his eyes and clenched his teeth. *Shit! Not now . . .*

The last time he'd felt this coming on, Harv had been there to help him suppress it. If he didn't compose himself, he'd end up charging the entrance in a panic just to get out of here.

Things got worse when the dark entity living in his soul saw an opportunity to test its chains. Hate-filled memories surged across his brain like time-lapse videos of dying flowers. Life and death, love and hate, strength and weakness all collided. He felt as if his body were being stretched and compressed at the same time. Nausea took his stomach as a sense of weightlessness made him gasp. He banged his head against the wall to verify he was still wedged in reality. His brain registered the impact but little else. Somewhere in the depths of his being, he knew this downward spiral had to end or he would die. If he didn't trigger his mental safety catch, *the Other* would get a foothold and climb out of its cage.

He couldn't let that happen. Bowing his head, he reached for a virtual switch he hoped was still there . . .

And found it.

Click.

Blackness turned to color as he pictured himself inside a grove of autumn-colored trees. A gentle breeze swayed the branches, freeing their leaves. Each descending leaf drained a small piece of hatred and malevolence from his soul. The leaves fell by the hundreds, then by the thousands. They swirled around his body and tumbled away on the wind.

Through the falling leaves, he caught a glimpse of Holly's face and extended his mind toward it. Like running toward a train, Nathan used the visual to stay focused. He had to get aboard before it left the station. A split second before the doors closed, he slipped inside.

And had her.

Holly's face filled his vision, giving him warmth and hope. She was so incredibly beautiful. He missed her and knew he had to survive in order to see her again.

Mind over matter.

He opened his eyes and didn't know how long he'd been in a trance, only that he'd been acutely aware of his surroundings at the same time and he'd heard no sounds from Raven.

He said a thank-you to God for giving him the ability to fight off the hatred consuming his soul. He could now focus on winning the battle against Raven—not himself.

It was time to kick some ass.

With renewed confidence, he pulled the triangular ring.

CHAPTER 35

Franco peered around the corner into the right side of the drift and saw two light sticks. They lit the craggy cave in eerie, unmoving shadows. He was tempted to try another peace offering, but that would make him look weak. He'd given the intruder his last chance, and there was a fair possibility he was mortally wounded and would die without further help.

Keeping his rifle up, Franco looked the other direction into the dark side of the drift. His goggles couldn't detect anything recognizable.

Wait, there *was* something down there, maybe fifteen yards away. He stared for a long moment. If he went in there to investigate, he'd be backlit by the light emanating from the other side.

It felt like a trap, but with a fully automatic M-4, lots of ammo, and well-honed combat instincts, Franco felt certain he could spray the entire area before his prey got a bead on him.

In a somewhat risky move, he crouched and reached up to activate his IR illuminator for a split second. If lurking eyes were down there, their pupils would reflect the invisible infrared flash and light up like a Christmas tree. He'd seen the effect many times. Then he remembered the guy had a pair of goggles on. Still,

Franco decided it was an acceptable risk. He felt fairly confident he knew what the object was, but he needed to be certain.

He twisted the knob for a split second and during the brief flare of light, he saw several things at once.

An ore cart.

A backpack hanging from it.

And a trip wire made of fishing line.

Oh, that's clever, he thought. Just inside the drift, one side of a nylon fishing line was tied to the rail, and the other end was attached to an empty water bottle covered with bloody hand-prints. If he hadn't activated his IR, he wouldn't have seen the trip wire. He would've walked through it, yanking the plastic bottle free. Although harmless, it wasn't silent.

Finding the trip wire became a valuable discovery. If his opponent had eyes inside this drift, he wouldn't have needed the booby trap. Franco knew there were several openings into secondary drifts on the right side. The discovery of that vein had led to an exceptionally high yield of gold per ton. He couldn't remember how many openings there were, but they all lay to the right-hand side.

His treasure was now within reach.

Licking his lips, he stepped over the water-bottle booby trap and eased down the railroad ties toward the backpack hanging on the ore car.

***

Like a spider Nathan waited, focusing on the opening below. The sudden blast of light startled him. From his elevated vantage point inside the short passage, he saw the rear half of the ore car flash for a split second, then nothing. Franco had activated his IR to look down this side of the passage. Since there wasn't enough light coming from the light sticks on the opposite side to create a shadow, Nathan was 100 percent dependent on sound. He wanted to close his eyes, but he needed to know if Franco used his IR a second time. The tiny amount of light spilling in here from the two light sticks on the right-hand side of the crosscut wouldn't allow Raven to see more than dark nebulous shapes in here.

When the plastic water bottle remained silent, Nathan hoped Raven had discovered it.

He waited through another minute of absolute silence, knowing Raven might be investigating the lighted side. Nathan thought he'd found the right balance between making the water-bottle trip wire too obvious versus too hard to find. He didn't want Raven to trigger it; he wanted Raven to think he'd defeated it.

Completely blind, Nathan focused solely on sound and hoped his mind could overrule his aching body.

***

Moving deeper into the drift toward the ore car, Franco experienced a growing sense of calm. He knew he was backlit and vulnerable, but no bullets flew his way. Surely if the man he'd chased in here were looking down this passage from beyond the ore car, he would've fired by now.

In five more steps, he'd be within reach of the backpack and wished he had x-ray vision. He'd be pissed if the damned thing was empty. With each slow step he took, his belief grew stronger that his enemy had abandoned the fight and left the gold behind. A wise move.

He stopped about four paces short of his goal and held perfectly still. A field mouse couldn't move in here without being heard.

After ten seconds of utter silence he took another step.

And felt the resistance on his right thigh.

He froze, but it was too late.

His skin crawled as he heard a rock slide, then fall to the floor. In the absolute silence, the sound was like a car alarm.

He'd been had!

Franco leveled his M-4 above the ore car, pulled the trigger, and swept it back and forth, spraying the entire passage.

***

Nathan heard the rock plummet from the alcove and knew exactly where Raven was. Half a second later, his world erupted again as Raven emptied an entire magazine.

Some of the bullets whizzed into the opening below him.

If he'd been standing there, he would've been nailed.

When the deafening salvo ended, Nathan tossed the stun grenade, started a mental countdown, and heard the grenade bounce off the wall next to the ore car.

Two seconds.

Nathan reached up and flipped on his IR.

One second.

Nathan timed it perfectly.

He dropped down at the same instant the M84 detonated.

The concussive blast took his breath away as white light bleached every surface.

As if shimmering from a mirage, the air seemed to throb for an instant just before the deafening concussion slammed his ears.

Nathan didn't know how fast Raven would be able to reload his M-4, but no human being could withstand such a disruptive blast unscathed. The man had to be hammered into submission from the simultaneous assault on all his senses.

Sig in hand, Nathan rushed through the opening.

Raven appeared to be holding his stomach, bent over at the waist. His rifle hung uselessly from its sling.

Nathan painted his laser on Raven's bowed head. "Show me your hands!"

Raven didn't move.

"Do it now!"

Raven looked up a split second before Nathan saw the handgun.

Nathan fired.

The bullet punched Raven in the upper stomach. The man's gun hand sagged, but he tried to bring it back up.

Nathan fired again.

Raven's arm shuddered and the handgun fell. It clanked off the rail and came to rest on a wooden tie.

"It's over, Raven, don't make me shoot you again."

"How do you . . . know that name?"

"Have a seat right there and don't move."

Raven plopped down and rested his back against the tunnel wall. His demeanor was that of resigned defeat. Blood poured from his arm wound, soaking his sleeve. His midsection was also getting wet. Raven had to know his wounds would be fatal without immediate treatment.

Keeping his Sig against the side of Raven's head, Nathan reached down and cycled the M-4. Empty. He checked Raven for additional weapons, found a knife in an ankle sheath, and tossed it and the handgun down the tunnel.

"Who are you?"

"You don't recognize my voice?" Nathan pulled out a light stick and activated it. Carefully, he removed Raven's NV visor, then his own.

"Rojo? Is that you?"

"Yeah, it's me."

Raven smiled through the pain, his face a sickly pale hue in the green light. "I wondered if I'd ever see you again. I guess I have my answer."

Nathan put the light stick down. "Why'd you do it? Why work for someone like Macanas?"

"It's complicated."

"Give me the short version."

"I needed work."

"The truth, Raven."

"All right, I was bored."

Nathan considered that, and although he didn't want to admit it, he understood it perfectly. He nodded at Raven's wounded arm. "You took a bad shot."

"Brachial?"

Nathan nodded.

"Don't tie it off."

Nathan didn't respond.

"How long?"

Nathan squinted. "Ten minutes."

"Ten minutes," Raven said slowly. "Will you stay with me?"

Nathan sat cross-legged between the rails.

Raven seemed remarkably calm given his circumstances. After a moment, he actually smiled. "Tell me something . . . Have you always wanted to be a sniper?"

"No, not really. It just sorta happened."

Raven closed his eyes and didn't say anything.

Nathan knew he was waiting for more. "I wanted to be a stage actor, but my high school drama teacher told me I was too tall. My father didn't like the idea either. What about you?"

"I wanted to be an engineer on a train."

"I can't picture it."

"It's true, but it's also ironic."

"How so?"

Raven indicated with his head. "The train tracks."

Nathan waited.

"The rails, they don't let you stray."

"No, I suppose they don't."

"Is Mayo here?"

"Yes, he's down below with Estefan, dealing with your other men."

"They're dead then."

"Perhaps not."

"Is my cousin really going to die?"

"I just said that to rile you. He'll be okay."

"He's had a tough life."

"Haven't we all?"

Raven went silent and closed his eyes again.

Nathan asked, "Did you like being a shooter?"

"If I say yes, does it make me a monster?"

"No."

"Then what?"

"There's no simple answer to that."

"We're the same then?"

Nathan spoke with conviction. "I've been tormented by this subject for decades. Why should I feel bad about killing serial murderers and rapists, who included children in their sprees? I—we—ridded the world of the worst psychopaths imaginable. My mission down here wasn't political; it was purely humanitarian."

"Nicaragua will always owe you for that."

"I don't count favors I'm owed. As far as I'm concerned, no one owes me a thing."

"I like that attitude. Tell me something . . . did *you* like being a shooter?"

Nathan wouldn't lie to this man. He'd created Raven and owed him the truth. "Maybe I should've . . . disliked it more than I did."

Raven coughed and tried to smile. "We did our jobs. You were always a man of deep conscience, something I've known . . . is missing in me."

"You didn't kill Estefan's wife."

"No women. No kids."

"Well, then you just confirmed it's there. You've just never embraced it. What's your real name?"

"Roberto Miravel. What about you?"

"Nathan McBride."

"I knew you had some Irish blood, but I'd never hold it against you."

Nathan smiled, and they didn't speak for a few seconds. "Is there anyone you want me to contact?"

"No, not really. What are you doing to stay busy these days?"

"I'm partners with Mayo in a private-security company."

"I'm betting you've pursued more . . ." Raven coughed. "More exciting ventures on the side, no?"

"A few here and there. Maybe it's in our blood. We're like moths."

"Thank you for being honest with me. I need to tell you something about Macanas."

"What about him?"

"You won't like hearing it."

Nathan felt his skin tighten. "I'm listening."

"He's the one who betrayed you to Montez."

Nathan grabbed Raven by the shirt and yanked him closer. Raven grunted in pain. "You know about that?"

"Yes."

"You're lying, Raven."

"I'm not lying. Macanas and Montez knew each other."

"That's horseshit. Why should I believe you?"

"You said it yourself . . . ten minutes."

Nathan didn't say anything; he didn't trust himself.

"Money."

"Money," Nathan repeated.

"Macanas stole Montez's money. The money your CIA paid Montez to let you go."

Nathan was stunned. "How can you possibly know about that?"

"Macanas was my recruiter. Viper's too. All of the kilos." Raven closed his eyes again. "He had ties with your government during Iran-Contra. Lots of money changed hands, but Macanas never got any of it. He was bitter—thought your government owed him."

"Are you saying Macanas and Montez worked together to capture me and then collect the ransom money?"

"Yes."

"I was there for *three weeks*." Nathan felt as though blood were going to burst from every pore in his body.

"I didn't know about it, or I would've tried to save you. I swear it. Macanas was really drunk one night and told me. All Montez was supposed to do was hold you, not torture you. Montez never found out Macanas double-crossed him."

"Let's say I believe you, which I'm not sure I do. Why didn't Macanas just kill Montez after stealing his money? Why leave a loose end like that?"

"I don't know."

Nathan's mind raced. Why hadn't Cantrell told him about Macanas? She had to know about this. He hated believing Cantrell withheld this and then asked him to come down here. No way. She'd never do that. Something was missing. Something that got Cantrell off the hook.

"There's more, but you must never tell Viper . . . Estefan."

Nathan waited.

"Your word . . ."

"All right, you have my word."

"Before the war, Pastor Tobias was in Macanas's pocket when he worked for the government."

"When who worked for the government? Macanas or Tobias?"

"Tobias. He negotiated the leases for most of the mines in Atlántico Norte. He'd been taking bribe money for years, giving Macanas inside information about land identified for gold mining."

"Here, in Jinotega or in Atlántico Norte?"

"Both, but mostly here . . . Macanas has been acquiring land up here for years. He's set to make millions from leasing it to large commercial operators next year."

Raven's breathing began to slow, and his body shuddered.

"Are you cold?"

Raven nodded.

"This doesn't sit right with me."

"I didn't think it would."

"No, I mean you. You're dying in the dark while Macanas lives on in luxury."

"Since when has life . . . ever been fair?"

"Point taken."

Raven's voice grew weaker. "Everything you need to bury Macanas is in the lumber mill's office. In the wall next to the shower. You'll see . . . fresh paint. I thought I might need it someday. It's yours now."

"You were a good soldier, Raven."

"I cared about my work."

"It showed."

"I don't . . . feel very good."

Raven reached out with his good hand, and Nathan grasped it. A few seconds later, his former student—his Frankenstein's monster, a man he'd mistakenly hated—lost consciousness.

That's when Nathan noticed that a sense of time had slowly returned to his world. At some point, the needle of his pain clock had reversed direction and returned to the green. Maybe he'd sit here for a while. It seemed wrong to walk away from Raven. He didn't think Harv would head up to their SP for at least ten more minutes, but he wasn't sure. It felt good to just sit here and do nothing. He closed his eyes and listened to Raven's breathing, knowing it wouldn't last much longer.

Thinking about his former student caused sadness. The man slumped against the wall had made some bad choices. He'd left the railroad tracks and ventured into lawless territory. Raven said he'd lacked a moral compass, but Nathan knew otherwise. A truly bad seed would've killed Estefan's wife without a second thought. Was there an honor code in cartels? Did they have standards they wouldn't betray? Nathan didn't know the answer, but he wasn't above the question. He'd bent the rules himself and ventured into his own landscape of lawless territory. Many times. The train tracks didn't always take you where you had to go. Did the ends justify the means? When can laws be defensibly broken? Sometimes? Never? Always? He knew life couldn't be defined by a book of rules. It simply wasn't possible. Sooner or later, everyone broke one of society's bones.

Nathan didn't know how long he'd been in here, but it seemed like hours. He wished he could doze off and sleep for several days, but alas, this wasn't over yet. He reached over and gently removed the gold bar from Raven's pocket along with one other critical item he'd need later. He was about to get up when Harv's voice boomed into the tunnel.

"Nathan! Are you in there?"

"I'm here," he yelled.

"Are you okay?"

"Yes." He listened to Harv's running footfalls grow louder and louder. "In here, on the left."

Nathan watched Harv peer around the corner before entering the tunnel. Harv reached up and turned off his IR.

"Nate."

"Harv."

His friend looked at Raven and took a knee. "I can't believe you came in here."

"Tell me about it. Weren't you supposed to head up to our SP?"

"It hasn't been thirty minutes."

"I shot two men outside the mine. Are they dead?"

"Yes."

"What do you think of my green campfire?"

"The light stick? Are you okay? There's blood all over your hands. Your leg too."

"It's just a fragment."

"How big a fragment?"

"I don't know."

Harv pulled his Predator. "It's still leaking pretty good, better let me have a look." Harv sliced the fabric above the wound. "Yep, it's a hole. I'm going to apply a pressure bandage just to be on the safe side. From all the brass I saw, your ears must be toast."

"It was loud, all right." He let Harv go to work on his wound with the med kit. "I'd like to sit here a while longer. How'd you do with Raven's other men down in town? They dead?"

Harv sat next to him. "One of them. The other's gonna limp for several months. Estefan's watching them. I got your message."

"The footprint?"

His friend nodded.

"It's really good to see you, Harv."

"Did you take a knock on the head? You don't sound so good."

"It's incredible. The complete absence of sound. Close your eyes and listen to it for a minute."

They sat there for thirty seconds, unmoving and utterly quiet. The only sound was Raven's irregular breathing.

"Wow," Harv said. "Did it mess with you?"

"Yeah, I felt it. In force."

"Your safety catch work okay?"

"Just barely . . . I miss Holly. I wish she wasn't so far away."

"Why don't you check her schedule and go out to DC. I know she'd love to see you." Harv smiled. "I'll bet you can even get a free ride."

Nathan nodded, then waited a few moments, listening to Raven breathe. Then he told Harv what Raven had said about Macanas and Montez, as well as Tobias.

"Incredible. Do you believe it?"

"Yeah, I do." Nathan looked at the puddle of blood next to Raven.

Harv shook his head. "And Cantrell sent us here, directly into an operation run by the man who helped put you in Montez's hands?"

"She didn't know."

"Know what? That Montez and Macanas had a history?"

Nathan shrugged. "Any of it. I doubt she even knew Macanas was our old Echo recruiter. All it would take is a change of ID, plastic surgery. You know the drill, Harv. If someone wants to disappear with a new ID, they do it. It's easier with money and connections, both of which Macanas has."

"I guess."

"What I'm saying is, I don't believe she would knowingly do this to us."

"I admire your faith in her, and I agree. There's no way she'd do it intentionally. It's too cold-blooded."

"Are you just saying that, or do you really believe it?"

"I believe it."

"Well, there's hope for you yet."

Having finished bandaging Nathan's thigh, Harv asked, "Now what?"

"We go home."

"We have to arrange for our extraction."

Nathan reached into his pocket and held out the keys to Macanas's helicopter.

"I love you, Nate."

"I know . . . Just a few more minutes, okay?"

With Harv at his side, Nathan sat there, in the lime glow of a light stick, in the middle of a Nicaraguan mountain, and watched a man die.

EPILOGUE: THIRTY-SIX HOURS LATER

Under a crisp afternoon sky, Nathan felt a little awkward. He had nothing against Congressional Country Club. It was a beautiful place, but it wasn't *his* kind of place. He liked greasy-spoon diners, where the coffee tasted like yesterday's brew and the food needed improvement. Places where people didn't look too closely at their fellow customers. In truth, Nathan preferred to avoid public places altogether. Too often, people stared. Harv, on the other hand, loved luxury and fine dining. Driving into the country club grounds, he'd said, "Now *this* is what I'm talking about."

After dropping their rental car off with the valet, they found Bill Stafford waiting inside the foyer along with several sharply dressed men with bulges under their coats. Stafford acted friendly enough, but he made no effort to engage in small talk. He stayed in pure business mode, acutely aware of everyone and everything within his visual range. They followed him into the restaurant's lounge where a few tables accommodated small groups of men. Nathan didn't recognize any of them, and he wondered how many legislators actually came here. He didn't think his father, the senior senator from New Mexico, showed up with any regularity.

Entering the lounge, Nathan saw two operations officers, one seated at the bar, the other near a fireplace, both in strategically located perches. He thought he recognized them as the same officers who'd met Harv and him at Dulles.

Seated next to a window overlooking the golf course was the only woman in the room. Roughly the same age as Nathan, Rebecca Cantrell wore black slacks and a blue sweater and her brunette hair was secured in a bun. Nathan and Harv wore newly purchased clothes—slacks and golf shirts. Their Nicaraguan civilian attire wouldn't have allowed them admittance.

She stood when they approached.

"Rebecca, you're looking lovely as always."

"Thank you, Nathan. Hello, Harvey."

"Director Cantrell," Harv said.

Bill Stafford helped Rebecca with her chair and left the table.

"I thought you were working graveyard," Nathan said.

"We collared our bad guy. I'm still adjusting to the change in hours." Rebecca glanced at her watch. "Since we don't have much paper on your op down there, fill me in from when we last talked."

Nathan thanked her again for sending in the recons to support their insertion. He also thanked her for permitting them some downtime before being debriefed. After landing at NAS Norfolk, both of them had been utterly exhausted. They'd slept for nearly twelve hours.

It took about five minutes for Nathan to go over the chronology. Rebecca asked a few questions but otherwise listened with genuine interest. Knowing the director's time was limited and valuable, Nathan kept his update brief and on point.

"Keying in on Antonia clearly paid dividends," Cantrell said.

"We got lucky. Things could've turned out quite differently."

"Still, you did a good job containing the situation."

The three of them fell silent for a moment.

"The *McClusky*'s skipper wasn't particularly happy about a civilian bird landing on his boat," said Cantrell, "but he said you made a competent landing. I'm paraphrasing here, but he also said you two looked like you'd been dragged down a dirt road without missing any potholes."

"That's probably an accurate assessment. Thank you for keeping her offshore."

"No problem. She's been used for drug interdiction, so it was a good fit. I'd just assumed the *McClusky* would be sending a helicopter *for* you, not receiving one *from* you."

"At the time, it seemed like our best option." Nathan looked at his friend. "Harv did all of the flying, even the landing. I handled the radio work."

She looked at Harv with a raised brow.

Harv said, "It wasn't as bad as I thought it would be. The helipad looks tiny at a distance, but it's actually pretty big. The worst part was flying one hundred miles out to sea without much of a fuel reserve. I gotta tell you, seeing the *McClusky* emerge out of the darkness was a damned beautiful sight."

"I can imagine."

Harv smiled. "Let's just say I have a renewed respect for naval helo drivers."

After landing on the frigate, they'd cleaned themselves up and eaten several pounds of chow. The Black Hawk ride over to Gitmo had seemed endless. From Gitmo, they'd hitched a ride on a Herky bird up to Virginia, practicing the old adage, "Sleep when you can."

"About the gold you brought back with you," said the director, "it's entirely your call what to do with it. Did you have something in mind?"

"Estefan has a good idea," said Nathan. "His wife wants to fund a program to care for people in Santavilla who're suffering from mercury poisoning. It should make a difference for quite a few villagers, and it's also a way for Estefan to honor his father's memory."

Rebecca nodded. "I like it."

"If we can get the program up and running, Antonia's going to be a part of it. She's planning to work as a volunteer and then pursue a nursing career. I told Estefan that Harv and I would pay for her schooling if she's truly serious about it."

"That's quite generous of you and forgiving. I'll make sure the full value of the gold is transferred when the program's ready. Just say the word."

"Thanks, Rebecca."

"How are they doing?"

"His wife isn't expected to have any complications, but they're keeping her a few more days just to be on the safe side. Estefan's going to rebuild his house with the insurance money. I let him keep one of the gold bars. At first he didn't want to take it, but I told him he'd earned it." Nathan smiled. "It didn't take a strong argument to persuade him."

"You delivered an expensive helicopter."

"What helicopter?"

"Exactly."

He shook his head.

"What?"

He looked out the window. "Just thinking about that mine."

Rebecca didn't say anything for a few seconds. "So how'd you do down there?"

He knew what she meant. "Better than I expected. To be honest, I didn't have a lot of time for introspection."

"Probably for the best," Harv added.

"About Macanas . . ."

"About Macanas." She pulled a tablet from her briefcase. "Needless to say, this is for your eyes only. We were able to confirm everything Raven told you except for the dirt on Estefan's father."

She slid the device across the table. The sound was muted, but the screen showed a green night-vision video, obviously taken from an orbiting aircraft.

"Macanas's home?" Nathan asked. The hilltop mansion looked big enough to be a small hotel resort, complete with two pools, a tennis court, and several freestanding buildings—probably his staff's residences.

"Keep watching."

Nothing looked out of the ordinary until a dozen figures emerged from various locations along the perimeter wall and ran toward the house. A few seconds later, all the ground-floor windows flashed simultaneously.

"SEALs?"

"Marines."

"Outstanding," Nathan said.

The video skipped. "That's a six-minute jump."

The same number of men emerged from the house, scaled the perimeter wall, and disappeared into the trees.

"This is good footage," said Harv. "A drone?"

Rebecca nodded as she took back the tablet. "A small one. It has the radar signature of a seagull. That footage is from ten thousand feet."

"Incredible," Harv said.

Nathan leaned back in his chair. "I'm assuming Mr. Macanas is no longer a . . . concern."

"Yes, that's a fair assumption. The NNP recovered close to $150 million worth of illegally obtained antiquities from his property: Mayan, Incan, Aztec . . . The man didn't discriminate. Many of the artifacts were solid gold."

"What happens to them?" Harv asked.

"This hasn't been confirmed, but Torres plans to donate them to museums, some of which are in Colombia and Venezuela."

"So Raven's evidence . . ." Nathan began.

"Is helping Colombian and Venezuelan authorities close the books on a pair of high-profile crimes. Consequently, relations between the US and Nicaragua are a little stronger than they were a week ago. It seems you and Harv have earned a few more brownie points in high places."

"We're not keeping score. Harv and I went down there to help a friend. Something's puzzling me, though."

"What's that?"

"How did you get permission to conduct the raid on Macanas's property?"

"We traded for it."

"Raven's evidence again?"

She nodded. "Since Colombia and Venezuela are resolving the murders, the economic summit is moving forward as planned. I'm assuming you didn't see my texts to get out of there."

"I checked for a signal after we were airborne and saw them. Thanks for the heads-up. I'm sorry we didn't see it in time."

"I appreciate your continued trust, Nathan."

"Like I told Harv, had you known who Macanas was, you would've told us. I don't doubt that for a second."

"Yes, I would have." She looked at her watch again.

"Look, if you're pressed for time . . ."

"I'm expecting someone."

"Who's that?"

"Right on time," Rebecca said, looking over Nathan's shoulder.

Nathan turned.

Holly!

"Harv, you arranged this."

"Guilty as charged."

Nathan got up and hurried over. Holly practically disappeared inside his grasp. He couldn't believe how good it felt to be hugged like this. "You saved my life," he whispered.

She looked puzzled.

"I'll tell you about it later."

"I'm just glad you're okay," Holly said. "You *are* okay, aren't you? No new holes or broken bones?"

"Nope, I'm good."

Holly wore a business outfit similar to Rebecca's, but slightly more muted in color. She and Rebecca had about the same build and hair color, but Holly was a few inches shorter. Holly's eyes were hazel, not brown, and her face reflected Slavic genes from a few generations ago.

"You look great, Holly. You really do."

"Thank you."

Both Harv and Rebecca stood as they approached the table.

"It's nice to see you again, Holly," Rebecca said.

Nathan recalled they'd met briefly in San Diego during the Montez situation. Holly gave Harv a tight hug and shook hands with Rebecca.

"Well," Rebecca said. "Look at the time. I'm afraid I've got to be going."

"Speaking of," Harv said. "My tee time has arrived."

"This is beyond staged," Nathan said. "It's a full-blown conspiracy."

Rebecca put a hand on Nathan's shoulder and thanked him again. Together, she and Harv left the lounge with the other operations officers in tow.

"Harvey asked me not to return your calls. He wanted to surprise you."

"I'd just assumed you were busy, but I should've known he'd do something like this. He's an amazing friend."

She gave him a long, dreamy look and smiled slightly. "Nathan?"

"Yes?" Nathan took a drink of water.

"Take me down to the driving range."

He nearly spit the water on the table. "What?"

"You know, where they hit golf balls?"

"Oh, that. Yeah ... Sure, I mean ..."

She grinned.

"You really want to do that? Right now?"

"Do you have something else in mind?"

"Well, no . . . It's just that you've never expressed any interest in learning to golf."

"Will you teach me?"

"I'm a horrible golfer, but I'll try. I know the mechanics, I just can't perform them." He gave her a long look of his own. "Are you messing with me?"

"No, I really want to learn. Helicopters too."

"Now that's something I can do. Do you want to get a rating or just know how to do it?"

"I want to be a pilot, like you."

"Well, aren't you full of surprises today."

"I've really missed you, Nathan. I need to get some pleasure back in my life. My new job is . . . stressful. Don't get me wrong. I'm very good at it and everything. But I feel like I've almost forgotten how to live. I never take vacation time anymore."

"Remember what I said about this when we first met?"

"How could I forget? I've been thinking about it a lot. Don't get me wrong—I love my work, but I don't want to be married to it."

They enjoyed a comfortable silence for a few seconds.

"You really serious about the driving range?"

"Absolutely. You'll have to teach me how to hold the club."

"I, ah . . . should be able to help you with that."

"Then let's go."

Walking out of the lounge, Holly leaned in and whispered, "Would you like to see my condo later?"

"You know, there are some things a guy just has to put up with."

She punched his arm and, thankfully, missed the bruised spot.

ACKNOWLEDGMENTS

Special thanks are owed to the entire Thomas & Mercer team. There are too many to list here, but my editor, Alan Turkus, is a joy to work with, and he makes the journey from story concept to finished product a treasured experience. Thanks are also owed to Jacque Ben-Zekry for coordinating the 2013 On The Lam conference. Jacque, we all had a great time. And a special thank-you goes to Jeff Belle, VP of Amazon Publishing. His vision for the future of publishing is second to none, and I'm honored to be included in Thomas & Mercer's family of authors.

My freelance editor, Ed Stackler, plays a huge role in my career. His insights into Nathan's character are downright scary. I think he knows Nathan better than I do. There's a lot of Ed Stackler in these stories. I'd be lost without him.

And of course, a special thank-you to Jake Elwell. Jake stuck with me during the early years, and for that, I'll always be grateful. Literary agents like Jake are rare, and I'm fortunate to have him in my camp.

Thank you to Tom Davin, who was a trained recon marine captain with First Battalion, First Marines (1/1). His help with the mountaintop scene is greatly appreciated. Tom is now the CEO of

5.11 Tactical, and I'm proud to consider him a friend. And yes, I wear 5.11 Tactical clothing!

Another person needs to be acknowledged here: Turalu Brady Murdock, attorney and title coordinator for Title Coordination Services (TCS) in Managua, Nicaragua. When I had questions about Nicaragua, she came through. Thank you for your trusted help, Tuey.

My wife, Carla, is an amazing and patient person. Being a writer is a solitary endeavor, but I never feel alone. She's always there for me when things aren't going well. I believe people are defined by the way they act when life is tough, not the reverse. Carla passes the test of character with flying colors.

I'd also like to offer my thanks to God for allowing me to live a blessed life. I don't take it for granted.

ABOUT THE AUTHOR

Andrew Peterson is a San Diego native who holds a degree in architecture from the University of Oklahoma. An avid marksman who has won numerous sharpshooting competitions, he has donated more than two thousand books to American troops serving overseas and wounded soldiers recovering in military hospitals. The bestselling author of *First to Kill*, *Forced to Kill*, and *Option to Kill*—the first three thrillers in the Nathan McBride series—Peterson lives in Monterey County, California, with his wife, Carla, and their three dogs.

Visit Andrew's website at www.andrewpeterson.com, and follow him on Twitter at @APetersonNovels, and on Facebook at www.facebook.com/Andrew.Peterson.Author.